T5-CVF-893

Roselt

Father Was A Caveman

The First Book in The Echoes in My Mind Series

June Harman Betts

Bloomington, IN  Milton Keynes, UK

authorHOUSE®

AuthorHouse™
1663 Liberty Drive, Suite 200
Bloomington, IN 47403
www.authorhouse.com
Phone: 1-800-839-8640

AuthorHouse™ UK Ltd.
500 Avebury Boulevard
Central Milton Keynes, MK9 2BE
www.authorhouse.co.uk
Phone: 08001974150

This book is a work of fiction. People, places, events, and situations are the product of the author's imagination. Any resemblance to actual persons, living or dead, or historical events, is purely coincidental.

© 2007 June Harman Betts. All rights reserved.

No part of this book may be reproduced, stored in a retrieval system, or transmitted by any means without the written permission of the author.

First published by AuthorHouse 5/21/2007

ISBN: 978-1-4259-8854-8 (sc)

Library of Congress Control Number: 2007901281

Printed in the United States of America
Bloomington, Indiana

This book is printed on acid-free paper.

Books by June Harman Betts

Echoes In My Mind

Toward Tomorrow

The Vagabond Years (soon to be released)

June Harman Betts is a talented writer whose life story is entertaining enough for many books! She brings you into her stories as if you were whisked into the mid part of the last century, experiencing that part of history and the characters' lives first hand.

June is a writer, honored volunteer, businesswoman, wife, mother and grandmother. She is someone who turns lemons into lemonade, and is a role model for anyone lucky enough to have her influence in their lives. You as a reader have a special opportunity to learn and be entertained through her writing.

Deborah Brown Sturgill

ACKNOWLEDGEMENTS

I want to thank Janice Large, my editor, for the many hours she has put into reading and rereading the book, and for her helpful suggestions and overall assistance; Ric Betz for the interior illustrations, and Mike and Eric Large for their technical assistance.

IN THE BEGINNING

CHAPTER ONE

IT'S A WHAT?

The smoke burned his eyes and the dim light made it difficult for Burrel to make out her dark flashing eyes and saucy smile as she leaned across the table and asked, "What do you think of my favorite place to go to have some fun?"

He glanced around at the surrounding tables and the well dressed men and women sipping coffee from dainty tea cups. "I've never been in a Tea Room before, but I always thought they were only open in the daytime, and that no self-respecting man would be caught dead in one," he replied.

Her laughing response was, "I'm not sure how self-respecting these men are, or even how respectable they are, but you will see why they come to this particular Tea Room." He was puzzled by her strong emphasis on the words, "Tea Room."

His thoughts were interrupted by the arrival of the waiter who announced, "Your coffee, Sir. I hope you enjoy it. If you want a refill, Della knows what to order."

Burrel looked down at the pale liquid in his cup and sputtered, "He must have mixed up our order. I didn't ask for tea!"

She coaxed him to try it before he decided whether or not he liked it. His large hands dwarfed the delicate tea cup when he brought it to his lips and sipped. He gasped as the burning liquid slid down his throat. "Good Lord Almighty!" he gasped. "That's whiskey!"

"Of course, it's whiskey," she laughed. "You didn't really think it was coffee or tea, did you?" A flush spread across his face at her teasing laughter as realization hit. She had brought him to a speakeasy! He felt like the country bumpkin that she probably thought he was.

He had never met a woman quite like her. She was the epitome of a modern day flapper with her dark hair cut in a smooth bob, her lips painted a fiery red, and the hem of her skirt barely skimming the top of her rouged knees.

He was saved from further conversation when the band struck up a rousing tune. "Do you do the Charleston?" she asked.

"No just the two-step and square dance," he haltingly admitted.

A man about four inches shorter than Burrel's six foot leaned down and asked Della if she would like to dance. He looked to Burrel for his approval. "That's up to the lady," Burrel responded.

"Well, twenty-three Scudoo!" the man exclaimed as he grabbed Della's hand and hurried her onto the dance floor. "Let's shake a leg!"

"So that is the Charleston," Burrel mused as he watched the dancers fling their arms and legs in the wild gyrations of the newest dance craze. As he kept his gaze on Della and the dapper young stranger, he felt an unexpected twinge of jealousy. "I'd better have her teach me this dance if I don't want to share her with some of these pretty boys," he thought.

When Della returned to the table, she sank into her chair, took a large gulp from her coffee cup, and reached into her beaded bag for a cigarette. Lighting it for her, he hid his surprise at seeing a woman smoke. Looking around the room, though, he realized that half the cloud of smoke in the room came from women's cigarettes, and he had a strong suspicion that like his date, they weren't drinking coffee or tea.

"They will play a two step in a little while. Shall we give it a try?" she asked.

He had barely nodded when the band began to play a slow dance, and they merged with the crowd on the dance floor. When she rested her head against his shoulder as they moved to the music, he was glad she had tricked him into coming to this speakeasy. Her dark beauty and the illegal consumption of alcohol, during prohibition, had combined to make this an exciting evening. He definitely wanted to see her again and find out what was behind that flirtatious smile.

～

The next morning when Burrel walked into the kitchen, his brother Mace and sister-in-law Mabel were sitting at the table drinking coffee from thick mugs. Burrel moved to the stove and poured the steaming liquid into the mug he'd adopted as his own when he had moved in with them three months earlier. Sliding into a chair across from his brother, he remarked, "At least I know this is coffee."

"Why shouldn't it be coffee?" Mabel asked. "It has been coffee every morning of the five years Mace and I have been married."

Smiling ruefully, Burrel related his experiences from the night before. When he'd finished talking, Mace glared at his younger brother before he unleashed his well-known temper as he shouted the words, "She took you to a speakeasy? What were you thinking? Those places are against the law! Didn't you know the place could have been raided, and I'd have had to drive all the way to Columbus to bail you out?"

"You probably would have had to bail Della out too," Mabel quipped.

"I might have let her stay in, just to teach her a lesson!" he retorted. "I never should have introduced you to that woman!" he fervently added. "I've heard a few things about her since you two started dating that you should know about."

Unfazed by his brother's outburst, Burrel calmly finished his coffee before he responded, "If you are talking about the baby she had when she was fourteen and her broken marriage when she was twenty-three, she's told me all about it." He refilled his coffee cup and took a big gulp before he continued. "She was only fourteen when a neighbor boy got her pregnant. Then when she told him about the baby, he just laughed and told her that was her problem, and that she shouldn't have let him do it if she didn't want a baby."

"Poor little girl." Mabel sympathized. "She was only a baby herself. That must have been a horrible experience for her."

"Having the baby wasn't the worst of it. She said that all the neighbors treated her like a piece of trash and wouldn't even talk to her."

"I bet they talked about her though," Mabel interjected.

"Yes, I guess the gossip was really bad, but with the help of her family, she managed to weather it."

"What happened to the baby?" Mabel asked.

"Since she was so young, her parents took over and have raised her daughter as one of their own," he replied.

The young couple listened intently as he went on to tell them how Della had gotten married when she was eighteen to get away from home and escape the gossip. "She said the marriage was good until she got pregnant for their little boy, then her husband started rehashing everything about her first pregnancy. Like the neighbors had, he treated her like a wicked woman. That was the beginning of the end of the marriage. She stuck it out for a few more months before moving out. Her husband kept the little boy."

"I admit she had a rough time, but I don't want you to get too serious about her until you know her a lot better," Mace cautioned.

"Okay, Big Brother," Burrel laughingly replied. "We've only had a few dates. It's not as if we're talking about marriage…yet."

Mace's eyebrows shot up in alarm when he heard the emphasis on the word yet, but relaxed when he realized his brother was putting him on.

On the Saturday night of their next date, when they strolled around the courthouse square, men and women alike cast envious glances their way. They were an attractive couple; her dark beauty and slender figure were the perfect contrast for his broad shouldered frame, dark blond hair, and blue eyes.

Despite his brother's misgivings, Burrel was beginning to think this woman was going to play an important role in his future, and he didn't have to wait long to discover what that role would be.

~

The day that changed both their worlds started as an ordinary one, but before it was over, the course of their lives took an unexpected turn. Anticipating no more than a pleasant outing, he'd arrived at her apartment before noon to drive the twelve miles to her parents' farm home in Rocky Fork for dinner.

Route 79 north of Newark was a country road built for buckboards and farm wagons with few improvements made to adapt to the automobile. Though it was a challenge to dodge the potholes, they were in a festive mood and enjoyed the ride. As they went around a particularly sharp curve, Burrel commented, "These roads are like a trip home for me. Add some mountains in the distance and this would be just like where I grew up in Germany Valley." Della could tell his mind was on those distant West Virginia mountains when he added, "You can put me in a town or big city, but no matter where I live, I'll always be a country boy at heart."

Her father Harvey greeted them warmly when Burrel drove into the farmyard. Then Della led him into the house where her mother Rhoda was busy in the kitchen putting the finishing touches on the meal. Her wrinkled face lit up with pleasure at the sight of her daughter and this new beau.

Burrel was drawn to Della's parents instantly, but never in his wildest dreams would he have known how important they were to become in his life.

After a few pleasantries, Rhoda removed her apron, hung it on a peg near the door, and ushered them into the dining room where the table was lavishly spread with some of the best tasting food Burrel had eaten since he last sat at his own mother's table.

Burrel was surprised to see a girl of thirteen already in the room. When Della introduced the girl as her daughter Velma, he was startled at the lack of affection between them. Though they hadn't seen each other for weeks, Della didn't hug or kiss her daughter, and Velma didn't seem to expect it. It was obvious to him that Rhoda had replaced Della in Velma's mind. Since Rhoda had mothered her since birth, this was understandable, but Della's cold reaction to the girl left him strangely disturbed. "What kind of mother would she make to our children if we were to get married?" he wondered.

When they'd finished eating, they went into the parlor where they continued their dinnertime conversation. After a while, Harvey asked Burrel if he liked fiddle playing. When Burrel replied that he loved it, the older man got out his fiddle and started sawing away at "She'll Be coming Round the Mountain."

As his audience tapped their feet to the lively tune, Harvey said, "Don't be shy. Come on and sing."

Burrel laughed and said, "This is my kind of music," before he added his bass voice to Della's alto, and Rhoda's soprano.

After playing a few more songs including Burrel's favorite hymn "When the Roll Is Called Up Yonder," Harvey put his fiddle away. While Burrel complimented him on his playing, Rhoda and Della hurried out of the room to return a few minutes later with a pitcher of lemonade and five glasses.

"Where'd you ever learn to play like that?" Burrel asked.

"I learned from my grandpa," Harvey replied. "He said when the family came here with a wagon train full of people from Pennsylvania to settle in Ohio, some of the men folks played fiddle around the campfire. One of the old men taught it to my grandpa, and what he didn't learn from him, he picked up on his own."

"Grandpa said that at night sometimes he thought he heard Indians in the hills and actually saw smoke signals in the distance once. Since he was just a boy, his Ma told him, he was just being fancy in his mind," Harvey concluded.

Rhoda pitched in with, "Well, my family was on that same wagon train, and they did see Indians. Mom told me about an aunt of hers who had beautiful long black hair that was her pride and joy. She was washing her hair in the creek one day when she saw Indians. Fortunately some of the men were nearby and heard her scream. When they ran to see what was happening, they saw three Indians on horseback at the top of a knoll intently watching the young woman. The Indians rode away when the men arrived, but no one could ever convince her that they weren't after that scalp of beautiful black hair." Rhoda grinned and added, "I guess from then on, not wanting to tempt fate, she kept her hair covered except at night in the wagon."

Burrel said, "I'd say she was probably right. My folks were pioneers too. They settled in this beautiful valley that they named after their homeland of Germany. Since the Seneca Indians roamed the valley and mountains around it, my ancestors built a fort where they lived and the settlers around came when there was any danger from the Indians."

"You sound like, you miss that valley," Harvey commented. "Why did you leave it?"

"I was raised on a farm, but farming wasn't what I wanted to do with my life. Since jobs were scarce at home, I just packed everything in my Ford and followed my brother Mace and sister-in-law across the mountains to settle in Newark. Mace got me a job where he works," Burrel responded.

"Do you plan to stay in these parts?" Harvey asked.

Burrel had noticed Della's sigh of boredom as Burrel and her parents had talked, but she seemed pretty interested to hear his response to that question. She relaxed visibly when he told her father that he planned to stay awhile and get some money saved. "My dream is to someday return home to West Virginia."

He had never shared this part of his dream with anyone before except his Pap, but the older couple seemed so interested in what he was saying that he found himself adding, "Several years ago, when my grandfather was out hunting on his land, he stumbled across a large hole in the ground. Thinking it might be a sinkhole, he went home and got his lantern and crawled down into it. When he got to the bottom, he found this huge stone room full of the most beautiful formations. He didn't go any further that day, as other than the light from his lantern, the room was in total darkness. When my brothers and I got old enough, we took lanterns and flashlights and explored the rest of it. It was at least a mile long, filled with the most beautiful stalactites and stalagmites. When we got to the end, we saw light coming from a hole at the top of a steep slope. We were able to crawl to the top and get out that way."

Burrel concluded by saying that his dream and that of his family was to be able to open this cavern to the public. "My family is trying to get the money together to be able to do that. I am a spelunker at heart, and I want to save enough money to add to the pot, and someday with me and my brothers working together, we should be able to accomplish it. It will be a lot of work, but it will be worth it."

"What would you do once it is open?" Della asked. He noticed that she wasn't very pleased with his answer that he'd stay on as the manager.

When he'd finished talking Harvey remarked, "That is quite an ambition. I hope you will be able to do it someday."

Della gave her father a withering look.

"I don't think Della likes the idea of you returning to West Virginia," Harvey said.

Burrel replied that it would be awhile before the family had enough money to even think about putting their plan into action. After Harvey nodded in understanding, Burrel sat back and gazed around the room. While admiring the rustic furnishings and noting the similarity to his West Virginia home, his gaze settled on a photograph of a young blonde haired, blue-eyed woman. There was a certain sweetness, innocence, and purity about the face; and something about those wide set blue eyes that fascinated him. As if transfixed, he stared at the picture. To him, she was the most beautiful girl he had ever seen. He had a feeling that fate in the form of the dark eyed beauty, sitting beside him, had led him to this moment. The instant he saw her picture, he knew his destiny was sealed. He had found the woman he wanted to marry.

Although he was sure everyone in the room could hear the pounding of his heart, he tried to keep his voice casual when he asked, "Who is the girl in the picture?"

"That's our daughter, Priscilla," Rhoda replied. "She's with her friends, the Wilson girls. They've gone to a church meeting, and she won't be home until after church tonight."

Seizing his opportunity to meet this young woman, he said, "I haven't been to church for awhile. Is it too late for us to go?" Della was startled at his sudden interest in attending services. She declined to go, reminding him they couldn't stay out that late, as they both had jobs to go to the next morning.

His disappointment was obvious to both Rhoda and Harvey, causing their admiration of this fine young man to soar. Deeply religious, they had been among the founders of the Rocky Fork Church of God. While they didn't approve of Della's present life style, they had always hoped she'd meet a good church going man. Until this moment, they had despaired that she ever would.

As they said their goodbyes, Harvey enthusiastically shook Burrel's hand and said, "It was so good to meet you. Now, don't be a stranger. We have prayer meeting on Wednesday night, and church services Sunday morning and night. You're welcome any time. When you come, you will hear some old fashioned preaching, maybe some fiddle playing, and definitely a dose of good old gospel music."

Turning to Della he added, "Why don't you bring him next Sunday for services and come over afterwards for one of your mother's fried chicken dinners?" Not understanding Burrel's sudden interest in religion, Della, nevertheless, agreed to come back with him the following week. Aware of her puzzlement, he felt a pang of guilt at his duplicity, but only momentarily as his mind flashed back to the picture of Priscilla.

~

The next morning, when he told Mace and Mabel how he felt when he first saw the picture, Mace couldn't believe what he was hearing. Without hesitation, he voiced his disapproval. "You think you fell in love with this girl without even meeting her? You're even thinking about marrying her? Are you out of your mind? You don't even know her. For all you know, she might be mean spirited, have a horrible temper or...."

Burrel interrupted his brother before he could come up with even more faults this girl might have. In his calm quiet voice, he said, "Very deep in my very being, I know that she is the woman for me. Now I just have to convince her of that."

"With all the girls back home you've had chasing you since you were in the eighth grade, I never thought I'd see you unsure about getting any woman to fall in love with you," Mabel said. He hoped she was right, and that Priscilla would grow to love him.

The next week seemed to be one of the longest in his life. His impatience didn't make the time go any faster, though, but after what seemed an eternity, Sunday finally arrived. Della, looking especially fetching in a new dress, was ready when he knocked at her door. Barely glancing her way, he hurried her to the car. With his foot heavy on the accelerator, the car seemed to fly over the potholes, causing her to exclaim in alarm, "The church will still be there when we arrive, but if you don't slow down, we won't get there in one piece!"

Despite her fears, they did make it to the church safely. When they walked down the church aisle, several faces turned to look at them, but Priscilla's wasn't one of them. Just when he thought he would have to wait another week to meet her, she came in with her friends.

She was tall, several inches taller than Della. Her blonde hair, held in place by a blue ribbon, was waist length. When she turned and smiled at her sister, he noticed her eyes were even bluer than they'd appeared in the picture.

She wasn't fashionably dressed, like Della, but wore a blue middy blouse and a skirt four or five inches below the knees. The term "old-fashioned girl" seemed to describe her, and he liked what he saw.

After the service, Rhoda reminded Burrel and Della that they were to come home with them for dinner. While the little group stood in the church yard of the small white clapboard church, Priscilla and her friends joined them. When her mother introduced them, she offered her hand in greeting, smiled warmly, and with her head tilted to look directly into his eyes she said, "Burrel, it is a pleasure meeting you. I've heard so much about you from Mom, Dad, and Velma that I feel I already know you. We're all glad you're coming to dinner."

Then as he continued to hold onto her hand, she reminded him that she might need it back if she were to help her mother cook the dinner.

A flush spread across his face as he reluctantly released her hand. Then for the first time in his life, Burrel found that he was tongue-tied around a woman, but while she laughed gently he managed to stutter, "Oh, I'm sorry." Regaining his composure, he fervently added, "I'm sure it's not as much as I have been looking forward to meeting you."

"I wouldn't have thought you even knew I existed," she retorted.

Without conscious thought, he replied, "I saw your picture, and I knew that I wanted to meet you."

A slow smile spread across her face as she looked into his eyes and without being coy or flirtatious, she simply said, "I'm flattered." Then with a toss of her long hair, she left to join her parents and Velma for the short ride home.

The dinner was a success, and the music was even better than the night before. While Harvey played the fiddle, Priscilla played the piano and added her sweet, clear voice to theirs. After a few more hymns, she and her father played "When The Roll Is Called Up Yonder", and she turned and smiled at him. He felt encouraged. The ground work had been laid, now he had to figure out a way to do some serious courting.

On his and Della's way back to town, Burrel was hardly aware of her presence as he thought about the warm, friendly way this family had received him and how much he enjoyed going to church with them and visiting in their home. He was convinced that he had made some headway in getting acquainted with Priscilla, and as he watched the headlights blaze a trail through the darkness, he silently vowed that he would be successful in winning this young woman's love. Deep in his heart, he knew, he'd find a way.

When he parked his car in his brother's driveway, he grinned in anticipation when he thought of how much fun he was going to have when he got to tell him how wrong he'd been about this young woman.

~

He found an excuse to visit the farm, when Harvey said he had some fences to repair. Burrel volunteered to help. For a heart-stopping moment, he thought Della wanted to go along, but his casual remark that he was going to be out in the field all day caused her to change her mind.

On the Saturday after meeting Priscilla, he arrived in his work clothes with enough energy to repair every fence in Rocky Fork. Priscilla's brothers, Charlie and Alvy, were there when he arrived. So were Rhoda and Priscilla, with a large pot of freshly brewed coffee and a bushel basket filled with donuts they'd made that morning. Unable to contain his amazement, Burrel exclaimed, "I've never seen so many donuts at one time!"

Priscilla laughed at his reaction and told him, "It is a family tradition. When the men get together to work Mom, Velma and I make at least a bushel of donuts and sometimes even more." In response to his smile of approval, she quipped, "That's nothing! We already baked five pies and two cakes for the weekend, before we started on the donuts."

Velma shyly added, "Priscilla and I have been cooking and baking since we were ten years old. We make our own clothes too." Burrel grinned appreciatively when the young girl whirled around the room to show off her newest calico creation. Before he had a chance to see if Priscilla was going to model her dress in the same way, her father stood up and announced that it was time to get started if they wanted to finish before dark.

While they were working that day, Burrel learned from her brother Charlie that Priscilla had graduated from the one room schoolhouse in the spring, and now attended the business school in Newark. During the week, she and Rhoda stayed in a boarding house in town and came home over the weekends. While they were gone Harvey, Alvy, and Velma kept things going on the farm.

Alvy, Priscilla's senior by five years, was amazingly perceptive. Before the fence posts were in place that day, he'd figured that Burrel had switched his attention from Della to Priscilla. Mulling this over, he decided not to say anything to his parents, yet. He liked Burrel and wanted them to get to know him better before they discovered his interest in their youngest daughter. Before they quit for the day, though, Alvy cautioned Burrel to be careful. "When Della finds out that it's her younger sister you want, she is going to be one mad woman. After her experience with men, she's going to think you're like all the rest."

"It's not like we're engaged or even talking about a future together," Burrel responded. "She is an attractive woman and a lot of fun to be with. I'll admit, I was thinking she might be in my future, but there was never anything serious between us."

"That's not the way she sees it. I overheard her tell Mom after church Sunday that you might be giving her a ring soon," Alvy confided.

"A ring!" Burrel exploded. "Where would she get a fool idea like that? I have never even mentioned the word love to her, let alone marriage!"

"Just be careful where you tread. You know that hell has no fury like a woman scorned," Alvy quoted.

"Yeah, I know," he gloomily retorted.

Burrel mulled Alvy's comments over in his mind while they continued with the fence posts. Then like a bolt from the blue, he realized what was behind that flirtatious smile that had fascinated him. Like he had with Priscilla, Della had made up her mind that he was the one she wanted to marry. "Oh, Lord," he thought. "What have I gotten myself into?"

He barely noticed the rough road on his way back to Newark as he thought about all the things Alvy had told him. He was glad when he drove into the driveway of Mace and Mabel's house to see his brother sitting on the porch. As he wearily sank into the empty chair beside him, Mabel came out carrying a pitcher of lemonade and a plate of freshly baked cookies.

"Donuts in the morning and cookies in the evening! I'd better watch or you women are going to fatten me up," Burrel teased.

"By the looks of you, I'd say you put in a hard enough days work to rate donuts and cookies," Mabel quipped.

Burrel was deep in thought as they munched contentedly, but once they'd finished, he told them about his day, and what Alvy had said about Della.

"I warned you that she was getting serious!" Mace vehemently proclaimed. "I was afraid she was going to be trouble."

"Hursh, Mace," Mabel chided. "Burrel has gotten himself in quite a mess. He can't tell Della how he feels about her younger sister since

Priscilla has no idea he is interested in her, but he can't string Della along either."

Mace shot back with, "Well, it sounds to me like an impossible problem to solve."

Mabel smiled and said, "Maybe impossible for us to solve, but Burrel, have you considered asking God to give you direction?"

Burrel answered, "Oh, Mabel, you sound like my dear mother. She has such a strong faith in God." He headed up to bed and thought about how his mother had taught him to pray as a child. Then before falling asleep, he did something he hadn't done for a long time. He silently sent up a prayer, "God, please give me a sign to let me know if Alice is the one who should become my wife." He slept soundly that night.

~

The next Sunday at the dinner table, Rhoda mentioned the upcoming Box Supper at the church. "Have you ever been to one?" she asked.

"They're popular back home," Burrel replied. "We usually have ours at the schoolhouse. The single girls in the neighborhood each pack a box supper for two. Then the boys bid on their favorite. Is that how it's done here?"

Rhoda nodded and quipped, "Be sure to come. This will give you a chance to taste some of Della's cooking."

"I've been told that my apple pies are almost as good as Mom's," Della asserted. While that was a tempting endorsement, he hoped that when Saturday night came, it would be her younger sister he would be sharing dinner with.

Things started to look promising when on their trip back to Newark, Della told him that she was going to spend Friday night at her parents' home so she'd have plenty of time to prepare their box supper. When he shared this news with his brother and sister-in-law later that evening, Mace said, "Maybe if you're a little late, Della's will already be auctioned off."

Burrel retorted, "Priscilla will also have to be late, or hers might be snapped up before I get there."

The day of the church social, Burrel was all spruced up and ready to drive to Rocky Fork hoping to be one of the first men to arrive. As he said goodbye to Mabel, the bottle of milk she held slipped out of her hand and shattered and splattered all over the floor. Burrel stopped to help her clean up the mess, and in the process cut his hand. Mabel rushed to get a bandage, and when all was cleaned up, he saw blood on his shirt. All this hurrying and he still wasn't out the door yet. After changing into a clean shirt, he rushed out the door and saw his elderly neighbor's trash blowing in the yard. Mr. Westbrook was trying to gather the papers, but they were getting away from him. Burrel stopped, took a deep breath, and quickly helped Mr. Westbrook clean up the trash. As he drove hurriedly to the church, he passed a woman with a flat tire, standing forlornly by her car. Turning his car around, he stopped and assisted her. After changing the tire, he continued toward the church thinking, "This box supper auction will be over before I even get there."

As he pulled into the church yard, he could see many couples already eating their supper. Only two girls stood in the auction area still holding their boxes. As he got out of his car and rushed toward the girls, he saw that Priscilla wasn't among the girls still standing.

Then he saw Priscilla carrying her basket and rushing to join the last two girls. His heart leapt, as he realized that he still had a chance to bid on her supper. As he walked briskly toward Priscilla, he saw Della sharing her supper with a handsome, young man he didn't recognize. Della's box supper had already gone to the highest bidder before he arrived. As Della flirted with the other man, Burrel felt relief, no jealousy, and free to bid on her sister's supper. Although Della glared at him throughout the bidding, he kept bidding until the last hopeful suitor walked away in defeat.

After he claimed the gaily decorated box, he and Priscilla joined the other young couples in the churchyard where white clad tables had been set up. Fortunately for him, they were all occupied. Feigning disappointment, he said, "Looks like we will have to find some place else to sit." Then pointing to a maple tree several feet from the others, he asked, "How does this look to you?"

"It looks fine," she said as she sat down, spread out a beautifully embroidered table cloth and began to remove the fried chicken, potato salad, fresh fruit, homemade rolls, and apple pie from the box. Then as he started to reach for a chicken leg, she bowed her head and offered a short prayer to bless this food. To her surprise, he completed the prayer by saying, "And bless the lovely girl who prepared it."

She blushed at his words, but only said, "Now, try the chicken."

"It is too bad that you were too late to get to eat with Della. She fixed a really nice supper, and I think she is upset that you were late." Then with an exasperated sigh, she added, "I can't believe that I was late too. So many things happened. First Velma got a comb tangled in her hair. She asked Della to help her, but Della said that she was too busy preparing her box supper, so I carefully detangled the stubborn comb from Velma's hair. Then as we started to leave, Velma discovered that her box supper which she had left on the front porch had been eaten by our neighbor's dog. When Velma asked Della to put together a new box, Della said, "Sorry, I need to get to the church early because I arranged to have my meal auctioned off first so Burrel and I will have plenty of time together. I am sure Priscilla can help you."

"So I helped Velma put together a nice little box using some of the food I had in mine since there was plenty to share. Then as we left the yard, the wind had blown some of Mom's laundry. I imagined what those sheets would look like if I left them on the ground and the neighbor's dog ran through them. So I quickly got that taken care of. This may sound strange, but so many obstacles came up, that I felt like God didn't want me to be on time for the church social."

"That might have been fate. Have you thought that things always happen for a reason?" he asked.

Startled she exclaimed, "What possible reason could their have been for us both to be late?"

He spread his arms in a wide gesture, "What better reason could there be, but you and I here together?"

As she stared wide-eyed at him, he was afraid he had gone too far, too soon, and frightened her off, but when she continued to sit and listen, he decided to go on, "When I saw your picture, I knew I had to meet you and get to know you better."

"What about Della?" she asked. "I thought you were her beau."

"We dated, and we had fun. She is an interesting woman, but there was never anything serious between us. I don't want to hurt Della, but I have to get to know you better." A little voice inside him warned not to tell her yet that he had made up his mind before he met her that she was the girl for him.

His heart sank when she said, "I am flattered, but I would never date one of Della's beaus."

"But I am not her beau!" he exclaimed.

"Well, she thinks you are!" she vehemently responded. "Mom and Dad do too. You're the first man she has brought home to meet the family since her divorce. Besides, I'm only sixteen and you're what? Twenty-four? Mom and Dad would never approve of me going out with someone that much older."

Discouraged, but not ready to admit defeat, he changed the subject and asked about her school.

Glad to be able to talk about something else, she told him, "Mom and I stay in town in a rooming house during the week when I have classes. We have our meals in the boarding house too. Mom misses having her own kitchen." She sighed deeply before continuing, "I like school, but I will be glad when I get out so I can get a job and a little apartment of my own in town. That way, Mom can stay on the farm with Dad."

As she spoke, he knew he had to disentangle himself from Della. He didn't relish the prospect, but this charming creature next to him would be worth whatever he had to face.

That night, he lay in bed thinking about how all the accidents of the day had led him and Priscilla to be together. Were they being directed by the hand of God, or were they directing their own fate, or was it a combination?

He thought about how we all have free will in this world, and how he and Priscilla had each been late because they had taken the time to handle each problem. Della had chosen today not to help her daughter with her problems. Instead, she decided to follow her own agenda and arrive at the church early. If she had been helpful during the problems, she would have been the late one.

Had today been a sign from God or the result of Burrel, Della, and Priscilla's decisions. Whichever, Burrel had his answer. Priscilla was the one for him.

~

The next day when he tried to break off the relationship, Della screamed, "You what?" Though he tried to be gentle, once the words, "I've met someone else," were out of his mouth, she erupted in a rage.

"You're lying," she snapped. "You've been spending most of your spare time with me or my family. Just when did you have a chance to meet another woman?"

"I'm not even sure that she will date me, so until I am, I'm not saying," he firmly stated. "I just wanted to be out in the open with you."

"Out in the open!" she shrieked. "You call that being out in the open! I thought you were different, but you are just like all the others."

He didn't know what he had expected, but certainly not this reaction. As she reached for a large glass ashtray, the mysterious smile that had intrigued him was gone and the eyes weren't flashing with laughter. Fortunately for him, her eyes betrayed her intent. Before she could let the ashtray fly, he managed to escape into the hall. A mere second after the door closed behind him, he heard the shattering glass as the well aimed missile struck. He felt the hairs on the back of his scalp rise as he hurried to the car and quickly drove away. If he had been a little slower, it would have hit his head. As he left her apartment behind him, he mulled over her reaction and thanked God he'd found out in time. He wondered how many flying objects he would have had to dodge if they had gotten married.

Mace laughed when Burrel told him what had happened. Before he could say a word, though, Burrel said, "You don't have to say it, I know, you told me so!"

Then Mace, Mabel and Burrel cooked up a plan to give Burrel a chance to be alone with Priscilla. "I'll call Rhoda this week and invite them over for dinner. Mace and I will keep Rhoda busy helping in the kitchen and that will leave you and Priscilla alone in the parlor. Since Rhoda is missing her own kitchen, when she thinks I need help with some recipes, she'll probably be glad to come teach me to cook," Mabel said.

"Pretending you don't know how to cook is going to take some good acting," Burrel whooped. "I appreciate it though as it will at least give me a chance to try to win Priscilla over."

As they had hoped, Rhoda was anxious to help poor Mabel improve her cooking skills. When they arrived she simply said, "Give me an apron, and we'll get started. Now the rest of you scoot, so Mabel and I can get this meal on the table."

Mace scooted out into the yard and found a few weeds to pull. When Priscilla offered to help, Mace waved them away.

Burrel urged, "Priscilla, you've been in class all day, and I've been working. Let's take advantage of the sunshine and go for a walk."

They laughed and headed down the tree lined streets at a leisurely stroll. When they were out of Mace's earshot, she said, "Della is fuming. What did you do?"

"I told her I was interested in another woman," he replied.

"You didn't," she gasped. "Was it because of me?"

"Knowing how I feel about you, you wouldn't want me to lead her on, would you?" he asked.

"I don't know what to think," she replied. "This is all so unexpected. I always thought of you as a nice man Della was dating....certainly not as a boyfriend for myself."

"Whatever happens, Della is out of the picture," he firmly pronounced.

"Maybe for you, but she's still my sister," she said. "I would never do anything to hurt her."

"All I'm asking is that you give me a chance to get to know you better. Maybe we could go to a picture show some evening," he suggested.

She shook her head vehemently and told him that her parents didn't approve and wouldn't allow it.

Amazed, he exclaimed, "You've never been to a movie!"

When the telltale flush began to creep across her face, he threw back his head and laughed. "You have, haven't you?"

She chuckled softly when she sheepishly admitted that she and her friends the Wilson girls had gone to see a movie starring Rudolph Valentino, but that they had never told their parents. He teasingly said, "So you like Valentino, the great lover,"

"Most of the women in the country like him. What's wrong with that?" she challenged.

He just grinned and replied, "Not a thing. It just shows that you have a romantic nature." Then with his finger to his lips, he added, "Don't worry. Your secret is safe with me."

They were talking and laughing when they returned to the house. Burrel wasn't sure what had brought about the change, but she seemed more relaxed, and he hoped, more receptive.

Mace poked his head out the door and motioned them to come in. "The women have dinner on the table, and Rhoda is asking about you two."

As they gathered around the table, Mace and Mabel exchanged knowing smiles as Burrel managed to out maneuver Rhoda for the chair next to Priscilla. The older woman gave him a puzzled glance, but soon turned her attention to the conversation and the compliments on the meal.

During a lull in the talking, Mabel explained that she was having trouble cooking chicken and dumplings. Priscilla happened to glance over at Mabel in time to see her cross her fingers before she rested her hands in her lap and boldly lied, "My dumplings aren't light like they should be." Immediately interested, Rhoda offered to come back anytime and show her how to prepare them.

A little smile played across Priscilla's face as she realized what these three were doing. It was flattering to have a man as strong and handsome as Burrel pursue her. "Who knows," she thought. "Maybe I am old enough to get married. And he isn't really too old for me. After all, a lot of men are older than their wives." Her cheeks flushed at the thought of being married to this man. Burrel noticed the smile and the pink cheeks and wondered what had brought that on. He would have been encouraged if he could have read the thoughts that were running through her mind.

~

As the cool days of fall gave way to the snows of winter, and the soft gentle days of spring, the dinners continued. Then one evening, Mace patted his tummy and remarked to Burrel, "With all these meals Rhoda and Mabel are cooking, I'm going to have to buy a bigger pants size if you don't get this courting over with."

Overhearing the conversation, Mabel said, "I think it is time to pop the question, Burrel."

Startled he asked what made her think that. His face lit up like a kid with a handful of pennies in a candy store when she told him that Priscilla had confided in her that she thought she was falling in love with him.

Armed with this new information, the next day, he invited her to meet him downtown during her lunch break from school. After lunch, they walked around the square and looked in store windows. After glancing in several windows, he steered her to a jewelry store. As they looked in the window, he casually remarked, "You'll be graduating soon, do you see anything that you would like for a graduation present?"

Though his thoughts were on the engagement rings, he went on to suggest a watch or locket, but he noticed that she was longingly looking at the rings. After what Mabel had said and her apparent interest in the rings, Burrel was definitely encouraged. After he walked her back to school, he quickly returned to the store, and by the time he left, the ring she had fancied was resting in his inside coat pocket.

The next night, Mace and Mabel kept Rhoda occupied while Priscilla and Burrel sat talking in the parlor. He had never been nervous around a girl before, but aware of the ring in his pocket and what he wanted to ask her, he suddenly felt anxious and tongue-tied.

When he sat on the sofa beside her, his heart was pounding so hard he thought she would hear it. What if Mabel had been mistaken, and Priscilla didn't want to marry him? What if she said no? Before he could lose his nerve, he took her hand in his and blurted out, "I have wanted to marry you since before we even met. I hope you feel the same about me." Then reaching into his pocket, he held out the ring box, and said, "I love you and want you to be my wife."

Her eyes were glistening with tears of joy when she softly breathed the words he wanted to hear. "I've loved you for a long time." Then she held out her hand and he slipped the delicate filigreed white gold ring on her finger. In her eyes, the tiny diamond shone as brightly as the Hope Diamond.

As they talked quietly about their plans, a look of fright crossed her face. Burrel asked, "What is it, Honey? You haven't changed your mind, have you?"

"No, never! This is for always. I was just thinking about how Della is going to react when she hears."

He reassured her, "Della will be alright once she knows that we love each other and are going to get married. Don't worry."

In time to come, he was to discover just how worried he should have been.

CHAPTER TWO

THE YOUNG MAN TAKES A WIFE

The wedding date was set for June 16, following Priscilla's graduation from business school.

After hearing the news, Rhoda's sister, Priscilla's Aunt Em Coon, invited the engaged couple to a lawn party. She lived on a farm adjoining Harvey and Rhoda's, on what is now the road to Falling Rock Boy Scout Camp. Burrel's first impression when he drove into the farmyard was that he must have mistakenly wandered into some kind of fair or festival. The farmyard was jammed with cars, and people were milling around. Tables covered with white cloths were set up under big shade trees. Women were bustling around, setting out plates and bowls of food while children were running and playing. One little boy, much to his mother's distress, was climbing to the top of a big maple tree, and two little girls were sitting under another shade tree, playing with their dolls.

Burrel felt the scene had turned to slow motion when they got out of the car. All eyes seemed to stare at them. Then everyone began to talk at once. "Priscilla, introduce us to your young man."

"Priscilla, show me your ring."

"Priscilla, wait until you see the cake Laura baked."

Then she introduced him to everyone. He'd already met her brothers Alvy and Charlie, but he hadn't met the rest of the family. Della was there with a new beau, David Keller. Acting mysteriously, she congratulated them and hinted there might be an important announcement in her future. As the engaged couple walked away, the look Della bestowed on Burrel's departing figure had all the venom of a rattlesnake's strike as she silently vowed, "It may take a long time, but someday you'll pay for this, Burrel Harman!" Burrel didn't know it, but he had made an enemy for life.

Looking around at all the people, he despaired of ever being able to sort them out, but the thought occurred to him, he was going to have the rest of his life to do it. These were Priscilla's people, and he knew they would be his for a long time to come.

Plates piled high with food, they gathered around the table. The country style food and gallons of lemonade tasted as good as it looked. Smiling at his bride-to-be, he murmured, "I'm really looking forward to all the meals you'll be cooking for us when we're living in our little house on Lawrence Street." She smiled, in response, but he didn't miss the faint blush that crept across her face. He had noticed this happening anytime he mentioned them living together and found it both pleasing and charming.

In the afternoon, some of the men played horseshoes while others fished in the pond. Once the men were out of the way, the women surprised Priscilla with a shower of gifts for their new home. Then when the men returned, they brought out the ice cream freezer and took turns cranking until the taster pronounced it perfect. While he and Priscilla sat side-by-side enjoying the ice cream and each other's nearness, Burrel thought, "It wasn't only the ice cream that was perfect. Life couldn't get much better than this." Little did he know what she had in store for him.

~

The wedding date was rapidly approaching. Between planning the wedding and Priscilla finishing her classes, the couple had little time they could spend together. Burrel had missed her and was especially looking forward to the two of them having dinner at Mace and Mabel's house.

Priscilla had told him she had a surprise for him. To say it was a surprise was an understatement! He asked Mace about it while they were waiting for the women to arrive. Mace just said, "You'll see." A few minutes after Mace uttered this cryptic statement, two strange women entered the room. They had identical hair bobs and were wearing fashionably short flapper dresses.

Burrel started to stand to greet them, but almost collapsed in his chair when he realized he was looking at Priscilla and Mabel. This couldn't be, not his old-fashioned girl! He took a longer look at the shiny, wavy hair, brushed softly over her forehead and at the loose skirt swirling softly around her knees as she came toward him.

His gaze didn't move from her knees while the beginning of a tiny smile flickered at the corner of his mouth. He'd never seen this part of her anatomy before. Her knees weren't bony or knobby, like some women's he'd seen, but pretty and smooth. As she moved toward him, her slim legs were accentuated by the flair of her skirt. Until this moment he hadn't realized what nice long legs she had.

Like the first time he saw her, he liked what he saw. Oblivious of anyone else in the room, he walked over to her, pulled her into his arms and said, "You are a beautiful woman." Priscilla breathed a sigh of relief. Her parents hadn't taken the change quite as well.

～

On their wedding day as she walked down the aisle toward him, he couldn't move his gaze from her. Even though he knew Mace and Mabel and Priscilla's family and friends were there, as they repeated their vows, for him, she was the only one in the room. This was, beyond any doubt, the happiest day of his life.

When Priscilla threw her bouquet, several of her friends tried to catch it, but it landed in Della's outstretched arms. This proved to be prophetic, as she and David Keller were married a few weeks later.

After the reception, the newlyweds left for a honeymoon trip to Burrel's home in Key, West Virginia. This was a long arduous trip in 1927, over treacherous, twisted, narrow roads. Priscilla, used to the gently rolling hills of Ohio, had never seen anything like the wild beauty of this state.

The mountain roads were frightening, some appearing to be little more than cow paths. If she had any doubt of the inherent danger, it disappeared when they drove around one S shaped curve and saw a broken guardrail. Getting out of the car, they looked down at a trail of broken shrubs and small trees to a crumbled car at the bottom of the mountain. It was evident, the vehicle was empty and the unknown occupants, whether alive or dead, had been removed.

Clearly frightened, Priscilla wasn't sure she wanted to continue this trip. Burrel reassured her, explaining that he had been driving these roads since he was sixteen. He knew the danger and would drive even more carefully now that she was with him. She believed him and felt safe.

Shortly after they left the accident site, he drove into a small town where they found a nice restaurant and a tourist court where they spent their wedding night. During their honeymoon, their first child was conceived. They chose to believe it happened in that tourist court, their first night together.

~

The next day, they continued their trip through one small town after another before they arrived at his farm home. The farm was located in a lush valley, surrounded by fields, woods and hills, with a gentle stream flowing by the roadside. The house itself was a weathered two-story farmhouse, with three wooden rocking chairs on the long front porch. The yard, ablaze with hollyhocks, was surrounded by a white picket fence. A wooden walkway led from the house to the Key Post Office next door where Burrel's father Ulysses was Postmaster.

Priscilla felt shy at the imminent prospect of meeting Burrel's family, but she received such a warm welcome from his mother Arletta, that the feeling quickly disappeared. It was obvious Arletta had missed her youngest son and was happy to meet his bride. He had spent too much time away from home, first when he worked in the wheat fields in North Dakota and now living in Ohio. She had hoped he would return to West Virginia to stay, but it was not her way to tell her children how to live their lives.

Gussie, Burrel's older sister, was there with her three children, Merlin a boy of eight, Avanelle a girl of six, and the baby Clyde. While Arletta was talking to Burrel and Priscilla, Gussie said, "I think I'll just set out a bite."

No sooner were the words out of her mouth than she and her daughter Avanelle started to bring food from the cupboards and from pots simmering on the stove. Watching this flurry of activity, Priscilla was astounded as dish after dish appeared on the table. Gussie's "bite" turned out to be a feast fit for a king.

While they ate, Arletta explained that Burrel's father was on his mail route. Since many of the houses were too isolated to be reached by car, he rode his horse "Ole Don". He and Gussie's husband Verde, who was working in the fields, would be home in time for supper.

Burrel could hardly wait to see both men. He had always loved his Pap Ulysses, and Verde had always been more than a brother-in-law. They had been close friends and traveling companions when they worked in the wheat fields of North Dakota the summer before Verde and Gussie were married.

After lunch, Arletta showed Priscilla through the house. The walls in each room were covered with wide pine boards that had been polished to a soft glow. A pot bellied stove dominated the living room.

When they got to the large bedroom at the top of the stairs, Arletta told her, "This is our bedroom where Burrel and my other six children were born. All of them, except Mace and Burrel, live close." Priscilla smiled shyly and responded that she was anxious to meet all of Burrel's family.

Returning her new daughter-in-law's smile, Arletta said, "I have something I made for Burrel and his bride." While speaking, she had moved to a large chest and removed a beautiful quilt. Handing it to Priscilla, she said, "While I was making this, I didn't know who you would be, but I knew if Burrel loved you, you would be someone special."

Priscilla was so pleased and touched by the gift and Arletta's words that big tears welled up in her eyes and rolled down her cheeks. Arletta, who understood the reason for the tears, wanted to give her time to get her emotions under control, so she continued to talk about some of Burrel's escapades while he was a little boy growing up in this house. As Priscilla pictured her big new husband as a mischievous tow headed little boy, her tears gave way to smiles.

She liked her new mother-in-law who bore a striking resemblance to her own mother. Both were tall, rawboned women with high cheekbones accentuated by wearing their hair severely pulled away from the face and fastened in a bun at the nape of the neck. The hardships they had endured as farm wives in the late nineteenth and early twentieth century had etched deep lines in each woman's face.

Priscilla turned startled eyes toward Arletta, as the sound of a booming male voice seemed to reverberate through the entire house. Arletta just smiled and said, "Sounds like Verde is home. Let's go downstairs so you can meet him."

When they returned to the kitchen, Burrel was talking to a man whose imposing physique matched the voice. Priscilla thought, though he must be as big as a bear, his smile and eyes were gentle. He and Burrel were so glad to see each other that they were pounding each other on the back and both talking at once.

Their racket made it impossible for anyone to hear Ulysses and Ole Don's return until they were just outside the gate. Burrel went to the door in time to see his father tie Ole Don to the post. Grabbing Priscilla by the hand, he led her to meet him as he was walking toward the kitchen door.

Ulysses welcomed them warmly. To him, Burrel and his bride looked so much alike they could have been mistaken for brother and sister. Looking into Priscilla's wide blue eyes, he thought, that though she was trying to look mature, with her bobbed hair and fashionable clothes, she was little more than a child. In that moment, in his heart, she became and remained, until his dying day, his daughter.

Priscilla was observing this man, her new father-in-law. He wasn't as tall as Burrel; his build was slight. In contrast to Burrel's blonde hair, his was dark, but his eyes were as blue as his son's. Under a slightly hooked nose, he wore the bushiest mustache she had ever seen. As her gaze surveyed his face, she could tell he liked her. The feeling definitely was mutual.

By the time Verde and Merlin had taken Ole Don to the barn, unsaddled and brushed and fed him, Gussie and Arletta had "set out another bite." The entire family gathered around the harvest table for a time of visiting while enjoying the good food.

Priscilla was quiet, listening, observing and learning about Burrel and his people. The conversation was lively. Their accent and some of their expressions were strange to her. They seemed to draw out their words, making a couple syllables out of one. When Arletta offered some pie, it sounded like pie-ah. When they were ready to be seated at the table, she had been told she could, "Sit right cheer, next to Burrel."

Priscilla, with her almost photographic memory, was absorbing all the new sights and sounds. As Burrel was to learn, sometimes to his regret, she seldom forgot anything.

That night as they lie together in his boyhood room, they could hear the rain softly falling on the tin roof. This seductive sound combined with this being the first time he had slept with a woman in his parents' home made him feel delightfully sinful. Holding her close, but knowing she didn't share his sentiments about sin, he decided it might be wise to keep these thoughts to himself.

~

Following a country style breakfast of sausage, gravy, eggs and biscuits, they left the next morning to spend the day alone. First, they drove through the fertile valley surrounding his home, stopping at one particularly lush spot where there was a deep green pool surrounded by willow trees. Their branches hung low, lazily swaying across the surface of the water. Taking her hand, he dipped it in the water saying, "Can you believe it is so cold in June?"

Abruptly, she pulled her hand back exclaiming, "Oh, it is like ice!" He laughed at the expression on her face as he explained, "I don't know why, but it is like this year round. I love to come here. It is always so cool and quiet."

"This is one of the most beautiful places I've ever seen," she responded. "I'd like to come back here sometime." Putting an arm around her waist as they walked back to the car, he assured her they would.

Burrel turned left on the main highway, taking them to Seneca Rocks. Priscilla gasped in pure delight when she saw them. She didn't know what she'd expected, certainly not this sheer cliff raising one thousand feet from the valley below. While she was admiring them he explained, "Mountain climbers come from miles around to scale them. I've tried it myself, but you have to have the right kind of equipment to make it to the top."

The thought of her new husband climbing these rocks frightened her. He'd told her about some of his experiences exploring caves and even going down into sinkholes. She was secretly relieved that Ohio didn't offer him as many dangerous opportunities.

Leaving Seneca Rocks, they drove a few miles into Harman Hills.

Getting out of the car, he led her across a meadow, stopping under a big shade tree beside a gently flowing stream. "I think this is a perfect spot for the picnic Mom fixed for us," he said. After expressing her wholehearted agreement, she helped him spread out the food his mother had packed for them.

Arletta had outdone herself. Everything tasted delicious, but their delight in each other's company far surpassed their enjoyment of the food.

After they ate, relaxing with his back resting against the trunk of the tree with Priscilla leaning against his chest, he told her how his ancestors Isaac and Christina Harman had crossed the mountain on horseback and settled in this area in the late 1700s. "The log house Isaac built for Christina and their 11 children is just around the bend," he explained. "Number 11 was my great-grandfather, the second Isaac. I guess I wouldn't be here, if they'd practiced birth control." He grinned when he noticed a flush flood her cheeks, but he continued with his story.

When he finished his story, they sat, quietly thinking about Christina and Isaac and their life here so many years ago. The mood was broken when Burrel looked at his watch and suddenly exclaimed, "I can't believe it is so late. We need to be going back." They hurriedly gathered the remains of the picnic and drove back to the farm in time for another of Arletta and Gussie's fabulous meals.

The next few days passed quickly with the newlyweds exploring the area and Priscilla meeting her new husband's brothers and sisters. The time seemed to fly until they only had one day left before returning to Ohio. Arletta and Gussie had invited Burrel's brother and sisters for a picnic so they could meet the new bride.

Priscilla was as overwhelmed at this gathering as Burrel had been at Aunt Em's. Cars started pulling into the farmyard before noon. Men, women, and children spilled out, carrying baskets filled with food.

At first, the women thought Priscilla was fancy with her bobbed hair and short skirt. After talking to her for a while, though, they realized that even with her funny accent, she was a warm friendly girl. While they were looking her over and forming their opinions of her, she was doing the same with them.

Calcie, Burrel's oldest sister was there with her husband Gordon and their five children. She was a tall pretty woman, warm, friendly, and kind. Her personality reminded Priscilla of Arletta. Gordon was also tall and one of the most handsome men Priscilla had ever seen, with his brown wavy hair, classic features, and white flashing smile. He and Calcie seemed to enjoy each other and take their large brood in stride.

His oldest brother Olie, his wife Josie, and their two little girls were pleasant, but both adults seemed more aloof. It was obvious they preferred their own company to that of the family.

Nellie, the youngest sister, and her husband were the only couple there without children. Burrel had told her how Nellie had three normal pregnancies, each time giving birth to a healthy baby, only to have it sicken and die. The local doctor could offer no explanation for the deaths.

It was obvious to Priscilla that the loss had taken its toll. Even though she was a pretty woman, with her blonde hair, blue eyes, and high cheekbones and dimpled chin, she looked frail, sad and older than her twenty-two years. Her husband, Curt, was slight and dark with small ferret-like features.

This party was almost a case of Deje Vous, from the tables covered with white cloths, and mounds of food, to the men playing horseshoes while the women showered Priscilla with gifts. As she opened one gift after another, she was hoping they'd have room in the car for all of them. The next day, with creative packing, they managed to make room.

As they drove away with promises to come back when they had another vacation, they had no idea that when they next returned it would be for one of the saddest occasions of their lives.

The newlyweds enjoyed the trip back to Newark, but were anxious to start their life in their new home. As they came closer to the Ohio River, Priscilla noticed the mountains seemed to recede, to be replaced by gently rolling hills. Crossing the river into Ohio, she thought that although she had enjoyed West Virginia she was glad they would be living in Newark.

CHAPTER THREE

THE NEWLYWEDS

After spending their first night in their new home behind 226 Lawrence Street, Burrel returned to work while Priscilla busied herself taking care of their little house. She enjoyed all the conveniences of living in town, electric lights, their new icebox, running water and especially the gas range. It was much easier to cook and bake when you didn't have to chop wood and build a fire in the cook stove.

The rest of the summer found them and Mace and Mabel inseparable, whether they were picnicking at Baughman Park, picking berries at the farm, going to church, or taking in a movie. The latter was a new experience for Priscilla. Because of her religious beliefs, Rhoda had frowned on her children reading novels or seeing movies. She thought they were too worldly and might corrupt a budding mind. Among the foursomes' achievement that summer was getting Priscilla to go to a movie. An even greater triumph was having Rhoda accompany them.

The movie "Up in Mabel's Room" had been advertised for weeks. They couldn't resist the title and teasing Mabel about what might be going on up in her room. When the movie came to town, the situation had changed for the foursome. Burrel was working the night shift and Mabel had been called home to West Virginia because of a family emergency. Since their curiosity had been piqued by the previews, Priscilla and Mace were still determined to go.

Priscilla broached the subject at lunch, "Up in Mabel's Room" is on at the movies tonight. Mace is going. Mabel wants him to see it so he can tell her about it when she gets back. He said I could go with him, if I wanted to. What do you think?"

Burrel, knowing how much she wanted to go and feeling guilty that his schedule was keeping him from taking her, responded instantly, "Sure. Why not? I don't want you to miss it."

Rhoda, who had been spending the nights with Priscilla while Burrel worked this shift, overheard the conversation and rushed into the room saying, "No Priscilla, you can't! You're a married woman. You can't go out with another man."

Burrel laughed, "This is my brother. She's not going on a date."

Still upset, Rhoda responded, "I know, but it won't look right. I don't want people talking about my daughter."

Priscilla had made up her mind, and nothing was going to stop her from seeing this movie. Burrel and Rhoda both knew her well enough to know, once she made up her mind, nothing they said would make her change it.

Burrel quickly came up with a solution. "Rhoda, you're just going to have to go along as a chaperone. I have the ten cents admission. It will be my treat."

Much to their surprise, she agreed. That night she determinedly strode into the theater, and anyone seeing her would have thought she was going to face a firing squad. When Mace started to sit down, he almost sat in her lap as she had firmly placed herself between them. Much to their delight and her surprise, she joined in the audience's laughter at the antics of the heroine. Later she told Harvey, "If that's an example of the movies, it wasn't sinful at all."

In this year of 1927, the country was still in a state of prosperity. Jobs were plentiful and prices had remained steady. A loaf of bread cost nine cents, a gallon of gas twelve and a new automobile sold for five hundred dollars. Prohibition was still in effect and speakeasies were flourishing.

This year was to be an eventful one for Burrel and Priscilla. On September 14th, Priscilla's 17th birthday, they announced they were expecting a baby in March. They faced the new year with excitement and anticipation. Before it came to a close, though, they would soar to the height of joy and plunge to the depth of despair.

CHAPTER FOUR

THE FIRST BORN

Winter had attacked wholeheartedly. The snow started before Thanksgiving and it showed no sign of letting up. The winterscape was beautiful with the ground and trees blanketed by mounds of glistening snow and icicles suspended like long sparkling spears from the eaves.

At first they found this to be fun as they played like children making a snowman and engaging in snowball fights. They even tried their hand at making ice cream from the snow. As more fell, the roads became impassable, keeping them away from her parents. Priscilla, with the time of her delivery drawing near, was becoming increasingly homesick for them. Though he was aware of her feelings, Burrell was reluctant to chance the trip as they might become stranded in the snow. He didn't want this to happen with Priscilla in her condition.

On February 29 they woke to a change in the weather. Priscilla was so excited when she looked out and could actually see bare patches of ground peeking through the snow. Waking Burrel, she said, "Look out here! The snow is melting and the roads are clear. Let's take advantage of it and go out to see Mom and Dad."

As Burrel looked at the eager expression on the face of his eight months pregnant wife, his heart sank. He hated to deny her anything, but the idea frightened him. "I don't know if that is such a good idea. You're getting close to your time," he replied.

Clearly disappointed at his reaction, but determined to go, she responded, "Don't be a fuddy-duddy! Doctor Smith said I'm strong as a horse. What could possibly happen?"

Knowing how important this was to her, he was finding it difficult to refuse. Seeing him begin to waver, she cajoled, "Come on, Honey, let's make a day of it. I'll bet Mom will be so glad to see us, she'll make some donuts."

Burrel capitulated, saying, "All right, you win. Let's go."

They quickly got ready for the trip, wearing their warmest clothing. Since automobile heaters weren't models of efficiency in 1928, Burrel tucked a blanket around her. Starting in a festive mood, this soon changed as they got underway.

The road to her parents' home, never a smooth highway, had become almost impassable after the harshness of the winter months. Though Burrel was a good driver, it was impossible to dodge the potholes. "I don't like this," he exclaimed. "I think we'd better turn around and go home."

Unable to stand the thought of not seeing her mom and dad now that they were so close, Priscilla replied, "It's okay. Let's go on. We've gone so far now, we're closer to their place than ours." Reluctantly, Burrel agreed and continued to the farm.

When Rhoda opened the door and saw them, she was delighted but surprised. As Priscilla had predicted, her mother did make the donuts as well as a big dinner for them.

~

During the trip, Priscilla had noticed a nagging pain in her back. Afraid Burrel would turn around and go back, she hadn't mentioned it. As the morning passed, the pain became even stronger at times seeming to engulf her entire midsection. "This couldn't be labor pains, could it?" she thought. "Oh, it couldn't be." Like whistling in the dark, she was trying to convince herself that just being jarred when they hit the potholes would be enough to make anyone sore, wouldn't it?

In the afternoon, the pain became more insistent. Though she didn't want to admit it, there was no doubt in her mind that she was in labor. All thought of being a liberated adult took flight, as with tears glistening in her eyes, she turned to her mother and cried out, "Mom, I think the baby is coming."

All eyes turned to her, followed by a jumble of voices asking questions. Seeing that Priscilla was clearly upset, Rhoda took charge, assuring her everything would be all right. She'd had her own babies at home. Since there was no way any of them would consider trying to take Priscilla in labor back to town, they called the doctor and asked her to come to the house.

When the doctor heard that Priscilla was at her parents' house, she didn't take the news kindly. An hour later, when she stomped into the house, none of them escaped her wrath. She lit into Burrel the moment he opened the door. "How could you do such a stupid thing? I gave you credit for more sense than this. Those roads are enough to make anyone go into labor."

Turning to Rhoda and Harvey she stormed, "Why would anyone with a grain of sense travel these roads? If I'm never on them again, it will be too soon."

Rhoda, who'd dealt with this bad tempered doctor before, quickly decided this tirade had gone on long enough and interrupted with, "We understand you're upset, but our concern is for Priscilla. It may have been a mistake for them to come out here, but they did. Now let's take care of getting this baby into the world."

Looking at Rhoda's determined face, Doctor Smith decided to get on with the business at hand. "Where is my patient?" she asked.

Rhoda took her to the back bedroom where Priscilla was pacing the floor. The doctor lashed out at the suffering woman the minute she entered the room, "Well, Priscilla, it looks to me like your stupid escapade brought this baby early!"

Before she could scold her anymore, Rhoda interjected, "I think we need to forget all that. My daughter needs your attention."

Burrel and Harvey timidly entered the room, only to be told this wasn't a place for men. "If you really want to help, you can make some coffee," Doctor Smith said.

"Coffee? Should Priscilla be drinking coffee at a time like this?" Burrel asked. Bestowing a withering look upon him, she informed him, "No, she shouldn't, but I drink a couple pots a day. Just keep it coming."

She didn't hear Burrel mutter as he walked down the hall, "That's probably why she's such a grouch." Harvey wholeheartedly agreed.

While the labor went on all day and into the night, Rhoda was with her daughter, holding her hand and murmuring words of encouragement. Burrel wanted to be there, supporting her, but the doctor scooted him out, saying, "I told you before, this is no place for a man. Go boil some more water and while you're at it, bring me some more coffee."

"What in the world are they doing with all that water?" Burrel asked his father-in-law. Harvey laughed, as he replied, "Don't you know, that's just their way of keeping us busy and out of the way." None of this made any sense to either man, but they weren't going to risk this cantankerous doctor's wrath by making an issue of it.

They heard a baby's cry followed by a tired but beaming new grandmother at the bedroom door announcing that Cecil Burrel Harman had made his entrance into the world at 1:43 A.M. March 1, 1928. He'd barely missed having a leap year birthday.

After the women had cleaned and dressed the baby, the happy father and grandfather were allowed to see him. He was so tiny, Burrel was afraid to hold him, but Rhoda wasn't having any of that. "Hold him!" she ordered. Then more gently, she added, as she placed the baby in his waiting arms. "He's not going to break. Just be sure to put your hand under his head to support it."

As Burrel looked down into the face of his firstborn, his heart filled with love and pride. Before closing her eyes for a well-deserved rest, Priscilla looked at her husband and little son, and the look she gave him was one of pure joy. Burrel didn't think he could love her more, but with this amazing gift she had given him, his feeling for her was beyond belief.

Before leaving, Doctor Smith made Burrel promise he wouldn't take Priscilla home for at least two weeks. She also informed Rhoda that Priscilla was not to be allowed out of bed for ten days.

When they heard this bad-tempered woman careen out of the farmyard, Priscilla said with a grin, "She may be a good doctor, but her bedside manner leaves a lot to be desired." No one disagreed.

Priscilla enjoyed the pampering she received during the next couple weeks. Rhoda, true to her word, kept Priscilla confined to bed for the full ten days. The new father, who had been driving back and forth to work, was glad when he was able to collect his little family and return to their own home.

∼

During the next few weeks, a steady stream of friends and relatives paraded through to see the newest addition. Priscilla was enjoying the visits and the attention she and the baby were receiving. Each day when Burrel returned from work, she regaled him with tales of the day's visitors.

One evening when he walked into the kitchen, he was greeted by a very angry wife. Her eyes were blazing; her cheeks flushed. He wasn't sure just what he should say or do, as he had never seen her like this before.

As it happened, he didn't have to do anything but listen. "That woman!" Priscilla said. "You won't believe what that woman said!" Burrel started to ask what woman, but all he got out was "What?" Before Priscilla interrupted him to say, "I can't believe she had the nerve to say what she did, in my own house, at that!"

"Who? What?" Burrel hurriedly said, before Priscilla again interrupted with, "If my mother hadn't taught me to be polite to my elders, I would have tossed her out of here!"

"Tossed who out of here? You are going to have to tell me what is going on. What happened?" he asked. When she didn't respond he patted the cushion beside him and said, "Come over here and sit by me. Now tell me what happened." His calm demeanor and gentle smile were having a soothing effect on her.

"All right," she said, sitting beside him. "I'm talking about Aunt May. She and Lidy were here today. When I went in to check on Cecil, she didn't think I could hear her, but I did. She was telling Lidy she didn't believe, for a moment, that story about Cecil being premature. She even laughed and said, "You know what they say, first babies can come anytime. After that they take nine months." Priscilla took a deep breath before she added, "Lidy set her straight, right away, by telling her that if she wasn't careful, people would think she had a dirty mind." Burrel wasn't surprised. Her Aunt May was the kind of woman who never had a thought without expressing it. He was sure she wasn't the only one talking about them. He understood how Priscilla felt. It had always been important to her what other people thought about her. It was to him, too. He could remember his father telling him that a good name was one of the most important things a man could have. On the other hand, his parents had said, that if you know you have done the right thing, don't pay any attention to anything people say or think, just hold your head up high and go about your business.

Putting his arm around her, he told her about his parents' philosophy, "I think this is the time for us to apply what I've been taught, and what I firmly believe. If we hold our heads up and ignore the gossips, they'll stop. It won't be any fun for them if we don't react. We have too much going for us to let a dirty minded old woman ruin it for us."

"I know you're right. I'll try to do what you suggest, but I don't think I'll ever forget what she said," she replied. True to her word, she never did.

As it turned out, Burrel was right. When it became evident the young couple was immune to the gossip, people found something else to talk about.

CHAPTER FIVE

THEIR FIRST CRISIS

That summer wasn't as carefree as the previous one, but both couples enjoyed it, maybe even more. After 4 years of hoping for a baby, Mabel had given birth in July to their first child Inez Gay, a pretty blonde, blue-eyed baby girl. Most days the babies slept in their bassinets as the women worked and visited. The two women were pleased to have joined the ranks of motherhood together. Mabel sometimes joked that she was glad that pregnancy was contagious in the Harman family.

This idyllic time in their lives came to an abrupt end one fall day, in the second year of their marriage. The day had started as any other, with Burrel leaving for work, and Priscilla working around the house and caring for little Cecil. She was startled when she heard the front door open and someone walking into the living room. "Who is it?" she called out. "It's me," Mace responded as he walked through the doorway into the kitchen where Priscilla sat holding the baby. The time of day, and one look at his face told her this was not a social call.

"What's wrong? What are you doing here this time of day? Has something happened to Burrel?" Priscilla anxiously asked. His voice barely concealed his own anxiety as he responded, "Burrel got sick at work this morning, and I had to take him to Doctor Smith. He's at her office now. She wanted him to stay there for a couple hours so she could keep her eye on him for a while. She asked me to bring you in, so she could talk to you."

Clearly frightened now, Priscilla asked, "How sick is he? What is it? What did Doctor Smith say?" Trying to remain calm, he replied, "I really don't know any more than I told you. I think we had better go, so you can talk to her yourself."

Even though Priscilla was upset, she knew she had to be strong for Burrel and Cecil. She said a silent prayer as she wrapped Cecil in a blanket, grabbed a few diapers, and hurried to the car with Mace. When they arrived at the doctor's office, a nurse ushered them into a room where Burrel lie on a cot writhing in pain. As Priscilla started to walk toward him, Doctor Smith entered the room. She always looked forbidding, but today there was a different expression on her face. One she couldn't read.

"I'm not sure what is wrong with him at this point. He is deathly sick with the symptoms of the flu, but he doesn't have a fever. I've given him some medicine, and he'll be sleeping soon. I want to keep him here for the rest of the day. You can stay with him if you like."

Then as if becoming aware of Cecil, she added, "If you have someone to watch the baby for you while you're here, it would be a good idea."

Mace told them he would take Cecil to his house, so Mabel could take care of him. After he left, feeling frightened and alone, she sat by Burrel's bed, holding his hand and praying. Between patients, Doctor Smith would come into the room and check on him. He slept most of the afternoon. Waking, he felt Priscilla's presence and was comforted by it. He wasn't sure what was wrong with him, but he knew he was a very sick man.

When Doctor Smith returned, and saw that he was awake, she sat and talked to them. "Burrel, do you still work at the same place?" Speaking for him, Priscilla answered in the affirmative. "I'm not sure yet, but I think you have a case of poisoning from the compounds you work with. I have seen a couple cases like this before. I'm not going to pull any punches. It is very serious and, and you will be off your feet for a while."

"How long?" he asked. Doctor Smith replied, "At this point I can't say for sure. You will need complete bed rest for a couple weeks. I'll be over every day to check on you. At the end of the second week, I'll be able to tell you more. You may have to stay in bed longer. It just depends on how you're doing by then. I can tell you that the better you obey my instructions, the sooner you'll be up and around."

"You won't have to worry about that," Priscilla emphatically replied. "I will see to it that he obeys your directions. Just tell me what to do."

The doctor wrote out her instructions, gave Priscilla some medication to give him, and told her she could take him home. True to her word, Doctor Smith stopped in every day to check on her patient. For the first week, he showed no improvement. Expecting more, she confronted them with, "I told you, you have to follow my orders if you expect to get better." Addressing Priscilla, she asked, "Have you been giving him his medicine?"

Not waiting for a reply, she turned to Burrel and demanded to know if he had been staying in bed. "I can assure you, I'm not going to waste my time on people who don't do what they're supposed to do!" she added.

Priscilla sprang to Burrel's defense. "Doctor Smith, I want you to know, we have done exactly what you told us to do! Burrel has been a perfect patient. He's taking his medicine, and he's stayed in bed. I won't have you blaming him!"

Priscilla's cheeks were flushed, her eyes flashing with anger. She had all she was going to take from this bad-tempered doctor. Burrel looked from one woman to the other, wondering who would win this battle of wills.

Doctor Smith wasn't accustomed to her patients or their families responding in kind. She knew she had met her match in this family, first Rhoda and now Priscilla. "All right," she said, "Let's forget this nonsense and see what we can do for my patient." She changed his medications and gave Priscilla more instructions, but one look at the fire in Priscilla's eyes told her it wouldn't be wise to say anything more.

～

Recovery was a slow process and since sick leave was an unknown concept in 1928, his illness wasn't their only problem. Having no income, their savings were quickly depleted. Fortunately, for them, they had a strong loving family. Everyone pitched in to see they had everything they needed. Mace even bought Priscilla a new dress when he bought one for Mabel. When they tried to express their appreciation, they were told that was what families were for. Priscilla's strong faith in God, her love for her husband and child, and the love and support of both their families sustained her through this difficult time.

During one of the doctor's visits, she told them that once Burrel had recovered, he shouldn't go back to work at the same place. If he did, he could expect the same life threatening reaction. Devastated, they spent many hours trying to decide what to do. Priscilla suggested that she get a job in an office until he could find one. He knew it was an option, but after all she had gone through with his illness, he wanted to take care of her himself.

At the end of five weeks the doctor told him he could resume limited activities, but cautioned him that he was to avoid hard physical labor for a couple more months. Then he should be as good as new. The latter was good to hear, but the labor restriction was going to make it even more difficult for him to find a job.

CHAPTER SIX
A FINAL FAREWELL

As had happened so many times in their marriage, Priscilla's parents came to the rescue. Harvey had bought a small combination country store and gas station in St. Louisville. Doing double duty, running the store and taking care of the farm was proving to be a frustrating experience. He'd tried to hire clerks, but none of them could handle it on their own.

When Priscilla told him that Doctor Smith had said it would be dangerous for Burrel to return to his old job, Harvey asked if he might be interested in running the store. He'd already discussed this with Rhoda, who, having found she couldn't handle the farm without Harvey's help felt it might be the answer. A problem she was beginning to have with arthritis was making it difficult for her to take on the extra farm duties his absence demanded.

Sunday after church when Burrel, Priscilla, and Cecil were at their house for dinner, they gingerly broached the subject. Prepared for resistance, they were pleasantly surprised when Burrel responded, "That sounds like something I'd like to do. If you want me to, I can start right away."

Since he enjoyed working with people, this job was more to his liking. From the beginning Priscilla became his partner, putting her bookkeeping skills to work. This turned out well for her, as she could work at home.

Though small, the store was a gathering place for locals. Stopping in to warm themselves by the pot-bellied stove, they'd remain to lunch on crackers from the open barrels, and thick slabs of cheese from the wheel Burrel kept on the marble countertop.

Their life wasn't all work. They still enjoyed time with Mace and Mabel and Priscilla's family. One evening, Burrel came home from work and said, "Your dad came in today and said he would take care of the store this evening, so we could go out if we wanted to. What would you like to do?"

Without a second thought, she replied, "Let's go to the picture show!" He was happy to hear the excitement in her voice. She had been working so hard, and it was taking so little to make her happy. He felt guilty he hadn't thought of it before.

"Should we ask Mace and Mabel?" he asked. "What do you think? We can probably stop at the confectionery on Mount Vernon Road on the way home," he added.

"That sounds good," she replied. The words didn't quite match her worried expression. Immediately concerned he asked, "What's bothering you, Honey?"

"Do you think we could take Cecil? I don't know whether or not he would sleep through it," She responded, still looking worried.

Happy this problem could so easily be alleviated he replied. "I already thought of that and called Velma before I left the store. She's going to come over and spend the night."

He was rewarded by the big smile she bestowed upon him. Burrel was overjoyed to see it. Even though she appeared to be happy, he worried sometimes that she had too many responsibilities for her eighteen years. If all it took was a ten-cent movie and five cent dish of ice cream to bring that big smile to her face, he was going to see that they went out more often.

Mace and Mabel went with them. Both couples enjoyed the picture show. They, along with the rest of the audience, roared with laughter when a cartoon mouse, named Mickey, came on the screen. This was the first animated feature ever produced with synchronized sound. Mickey Mouse, the object of all this laughter, was conceived by an unknown cartoonist named Walt Disney. No one in that audience could foresee that their descendants would be wearing Mickey Mouse ears and clothes adorned with his face or singing M-I-C-K-E-Y M-O-U-S-E. To them, this was not a historic event, just a very pleasant evening.

Everyone left the theater in a happy relaxed mood. True to Burrel's word, they stopped for ice cream at McNamee's Confectionery on the way home. A pretty black haired young woman waited on them. They noticed a picture of a dark haired boy of about three on the counter as they were placing their order. "Nice looking little boy," Burrel said. "Is he yours?"

The young woman looked at the picture fondly, as she replied that he was her son Richard.

"He really is a nice looking boy," Priscilla told the proud mother.

As they left, Burrel said, "Did you notice her name on her badge?"

"No. I don't think so. Why?" she responded.

"I've never seen the name before. It was Rowena," he said.

"Rowena? That is a pretty name. That was the name of a character in the book, Ivanhoe," Priscilla said as they got into the car for the ride home.

If they had been clairvoyant, they would have known, the little boy in the picture would someday be their son-in-law and father of three of their grandchildren.

~

The topic at the store that fall had been the presidential election. Burrel, a staunch Republican, had voted for Herbert Hoover. That was to be one of the few times in his life he was to vote for a presidential winner.

Some of his customers predicted dire things for the country with Hoover's election, but the majority expected continued prosperity. After all, he was a businessman. Who could be better to run the country in these good times?

~

A year had passed since they'd celebrated Thanksgiving together. As they gathered this Thanksgiving, they gave thanks for Burrel's re-covered health, for the babies, and the fact that they were all together. Burrel couldn't resist adding his thanks that there was a Republican in the White House.

Winter had again struck with a vengeance, making Burrel and Priscilla glad they had moved close to his work. It was fun watching the baby when he saw his first snow. Every time they went outside, he'd get so excited, trying to get his hands on it that Priscilla could hardly keep him from flying out of her arms.

One morning as they were leaving for church, and Cecil was squirming to reach for the snow, Burrel said, "Don't fight it. Since he is so determined, let's see what he thinks when he gets his own way!"

Holding him closer, she exclaimed, "No! It will freeze his little hands."

"Come on, Priscilla. Don't be a spoilsport! That's the only way he is going to learn what snow is like," he responded. "If you won't do it, give him to me."

Admitting defeat, Priscilla reluctantly placed Cecil in his outstretched arms. Burrel quickly stooped down, scooped up a handful of snow and filled the baby's hands with it. At first, this brought a puckered face and the threat of tears. Then Cecil put his hands in his mouth and tasted it. This was fun. He wanted more. The proud parents watched and laughed.

Priscilla gathered a handful of snow, throwing it at Burrel she laughingly said, "Who did you just call a spoilsport?"

Burrel had to retaliate, leading to an all out snow fight. They were having so much fun; they were late for church, arriving after the first hymn. When they walked in, Rhoda raised a questioning eyebrow, but when she saw the smiles on their faces, she knew she had nothing to worry about.

Then they turned their attention to their first Christmas with Cecil, and planned to make it a special one. The closet was bulging with toys, and Burrel had cut a tree from the woods in back of their house. Cecil's eyes danced and he almost jumped out of Priscilla's arms when he saw the tree sparkling with bright colored bulbs and glittering tinsel. First the snow and now this amazing tree; this was truly a magical time for him.

Burrel laughed at his son's antics as he said, "If he gets this excited when he sees the tree, how do you think he'll act when we take him to see Santa Claus tomorrow?"

Trying to hold on to the squirming infant, Priscilla replied, "I don't know, but I am sure you're going to have to hold him when we get there. If he gets any more excited than this, I won't be able to."

They were like kids themselves, looking forward to the visit with St. Nick. Before he left for work, Burrel said, "We can make a day of it tomorrow. Mace and Mabel are going with us so Inez can get her first look at Santa. We could go out for lunch afterwards. What do you think?"

"That'll be fun," Priscilla said, as she kissed him goodbye.

CHAPTER SEVEN

A BEGINNING AND AN ENDING

The much-anticipated outing never took place. Instead, the next day found Priscilla and Burrel, Mace and Mabel and the babies in their car traveling over snow covered roads to the men's home in West Virginia. A call had come from Gussie saying their mother had a heart attack. She said Doctor Harman told her to inform them if they wanted to see their mother again, they'd better come right away.

This was the worst trip any of them had ever experienced. With every mile they traveled, while they prayed she would still be alive when they got there, they also had to worry about their own safety. The roads, always a hazard, were like a nightmare come true with the poor visibility, snow, and unexpected patches of ice.

When they arrived, the farmyard was filled with cars. For as far as they could see the ground was covered with snow glistening in the soft glow of the moonlight and the lamplight that spilled from every window. Everything was so beautiful; it was almost impossible to imagine the tragedy being played out behind those lighted windows.

Burrel was almost afraid to open the door, not knowing whether they had made it in time. As they walked into the kitchen, though, they didn't need to ask if she were still alive as they were greeted by the sounds of raspy breathing.

Everyone was relieved to see them. They had been worried about them driving through the mountains in this weather. "Where is she?" Burrel asked. "I want to see her now."

"She's in their room. We wanted to put her in the downstairs bedroom, but she wanted to stay in her own room. She's really bad. She keeps asking for all of you. The doctor has told her she needs to rest and try to be as quiet as possible, but she keeps saying she wants to see the babies," Gussie said. "You'd better go up now."

Priscilla and Mabel told the men to go up first. If they thought it was all right, they would bring Cecil and Inez up so she could see them.

As they tiptoed into the room at the top of the stairs, Arletta looked up, smiling weakly, she said, "I'm so glad you're here. I so wanted to see you again."

Neither man could keep the tears from his eyes as he looked down at his mother. She had always been a tower of strength for them. It was almost more than they could bear to see her so weak, straining for each breath.

As Burrel leaned down to kiss her she spoke, but her voice was so faint he had to put his ear next to her mouth to hear her say, "I want to see the babies."

"You will," Burrel responded. "The girls are downstairs, waiting anxiously to bring them up to see you."

"I'll go tell them," Mace said as he left the room. When he walked into the kitchen, Mabel asked anxiously, "How is she? Is she up to seeing us?"

"She's pretty weak, but she really wants to see Cecil and Inez. I think we'd better go up now."

Both women hesitantly entered the sick room. Tears sprang to Priscilla's eyes when she saw her mother-in-law. The contrast to the last time she had been in this room, when Arletta had presented her with the quilt, was devastating.

Arletta's eyes moistened when she saw the new mothers with their babies. "Put them here on the bed beside me," she said. "I've been waiting to see them."

"One at a time," Burrel said as he took Cecil from Priscilla's arms and placed him on the bed beside her. "He is so beautiful. He looks just like Burrel did when he was that age," she said as she stroked his little arm.

Cecil smiled, showing off his dimples. "He has dimples like you have and look at those beautiful blue eyes. I love you, little boy," she whispered.

Priscilla, afraid this was going to be too much for Arletta, said as she held out her arms for Cecil, "I think it is getting to be his bedtime. I'll bring him back in the morning."

As she left the room, Mace was saying, "Mom, maybe you'd better wait until tomorrow to see Inez. You need your rest."

It was obvious she was exhausted, but she said, "I've waited too long to see her. I don't want to wait any longer."

As Mabel placed Inez on the bed beside her, Arletta looked at the baby with love in her eyes. "Another beautiful baby. I am so glad I got to see you, little girl. You'll never know, how much I love you, too," she said so softly, her words were barely audible to those in the room.

Mabel left with Inez, but Burrel and Mace stayed with their mother until Calcie and Nellie came in. Calcie said, "Gussie just set out a bite. You two better go downstairs and eat something. Priscilla and Mabel said you'd hardly taken time to eat since you left home. We'll stay with Mom until you get back."

Ulysses was at the kitchen table with Mabel and Priscilla. Mace and Burrel were shocked when they saw him. The agony he was feeling was etched in every pore of his being. He looked up when they entered the room and said, "I'm so glad you got here. We were worried about you. Your mother kept saying she wanted to see the babies."

Both men embraced their father. They felt overwhelmed by exhaustion from the trip, from the emotion of their mother's suffering, and now by the gaunt appearance of their father. Neither felt like eating, but Gussie insisted they needed to keep up their strength. They tried to comfort their father, but it was difficult, as their suffering was almost as great as his.

Only the children slept that night. Ulysses and the sons and daughters kept a vigil by her bedside. Priscilla and Mabel spent the long night praying. As dawn arrived, Arletta was straining for every breath she took. "I'm smothering," she kept saying. "I need some air."

Not having the luxury of oxygen in rural America in 1928, the family did the only thing they could think of. They wrapped her in a heavy quilt, opened a window in the bedroom, and carried her to the window so she could breathe the clean fresh air. She looked up into Mace and

Burrel's faces and smiled in gratitude.

While this drama was being played out upstairs, Priscilla and Mabel were downstairs keeping the children occupied. They were suddenly aware that, other than the normal sounds from the children, the house was quiet. As they exchanged knowing glances, Mabel said, "I'm afraid it's over."

Both women were quiet, wanting to go to their husbands, but knowing the children couldn't be left alone, they waited.

The next few days didn't allow the family time to deal with its grief. As soon as word was out about Arletta's death, the farmyard was filled with cars bringing friends and neighbors to offer their condolences.

The women who had been cooking and baking, as was the custom with country people of that time, in that area, arrived with baskets laden with food for the family.

Arletta's body was laid out at home for the traditional three days, and then moved to the church in Riverton for funeral services. Every seat in the church was filled. As the minister extolled the virtues of this much loved and admired farmwoman, her husband and children had their own private thoughts and memories to console them. Even though they didn't know it at the time, those thoughts and memories and her influence on their lives would be with them for years to come.

As the group huddled together, on the hilltop, at the Harman Cemetery, the cold wind whipped at them as the casket was lowered into the ground. Priscilla looked around at all the markers inscribed with Harman names. She saw the names of Ulysses's mother and father and others she knew must be Burrel's ancestors.

She realized they weren't far from where she and Burrel had their picnic when she had been so enthralled with his story about Isaac and Christina. She wondered if they would ever be that happy again.

She was brought back to the present by the minister's words, "On this day of our Lord, December 21, 1928, we entrust our sister Arletta Harman to thy eternal care. Amen."

Priscilla put her arm around Burrel as she felt his body shake with silent sobs. Cecil, who was in her other arm, reached up and patted him on the cheek. This didn't dispel his grief, but he did feel comforted.

He took Cecil from Priscilla and put his free arm around her as they left the cemetery. From somewhere behind them, they heard someone say, "She was too young to die. She was only fifty-nine." "Oh, yes, she was too young to die!" Burrel silently agreed.

The next day, as the little group prepared to take their leave for the trip home, both men hated to leave Ulysses. He looked pitiful, so alone and lost. Until this moment they hadn't realized how much of their father's strength came from their mother.

Seeing their distress, Verde said, "I know you hate to leave him, but you have your jobs to get back to. We'll look after him. Calcie, Olie, and Nellie will be around, too. We'll keep in touch." They knew this was true, and they consoled themselves with his words, but there was a hollow spot in their hearts when they left. Always before, when they drove away, they had known their mother would be there for them when they returned. A wise woman, she had held her children close by letting them go.

The sun was shining on the snow-covered ground, but the roads were clear. The trip home was not the hazardous one they had experienced a few days before. While under no stretch of the imagination could it be called a pleasure trip, there was a light moment when the women were changing the cloth diapers in the back seat. The pungent odor wafted its way to the men in front, causing Burrel to fervently exclaim, "Girls, if you will just throw those diapers out the window, I'll buy you more when we get home!"

They all laughed as Priscilla and Mabel opened the windows and gladly let them fly. They landed beside a lone cow, standing on the other side of the fence by the side of the road. Looking down at the dirty diapers at her feet, she continued, unperturbed, to chew her cud as they drove away. They all laughed when Burrel said, "I'll bet she'll be saying phew, instead of moo, for the next few days."

That night as they lie in bed, Burrel asked, "Do you believe there is a heaven?" Priscilla sat up and vehemently replied, "Oh, yes, I do! I don't just believe. I know! Right now, your mother is with Jesus. She is at peace. She is happy, because our Lord has told her the family will be with her someday. It will be a long time for us, but for her it will be like the twinkling of an eye."

"I want, more than anything, to believe that's true," he responded. She held him close, as she assured him, it was. As he drifted into sleep with her words of faith echoing in his ears, he felt at peace. He held the thoughts she had planted close to his heart. Her faith sustained him.

Returning to work was good therapy, as was Priscilla and the baby's presence when he returned home each day. As so many people, before and since, have learned, life does go on. Even though they thought the pain would never go away, gradually it lessened and the memories began to take over.

~

Winter gave way to summer with flowers replacing the snow in the woods behind their house. One evening, while they were sitting on the porch, drinking lemonade, and watching Cecil toddle after fireflies, Burrel commented, "I think this is going to be the best garden we have ever planted. I'd say we're going to have a good crop. Your flowers look good too. What do you think?"

"I think you are right. Mabel and I were talking today about all the canning we were going to be doing. I guess their garden is as good as ours," she replied.

Looking around at the garden and their child laughing as another firefly eluded his out stretched hands, Burrel smiled contentedly as he said, "I think we picked a good place for growing things. Look at how big Cecil has gotten!"

Gazing fondly at her two men, Priscilla softly replied, "This house is just perfect for a growing family. We could use the little room at the top of the stairs for a nursery."

Burrel studied her face for a second before asking, "Is this your way of telling me you want another baby?"

"No, this is my way of telling you we are going to have a baby. It should be here sometime after the first of the year."

It only took a second for him to absorb the news. When he did, he put his arm around her and pulled her close. "This is wonderful, Honey, but are you alright? How do you feel? I haven't noticed any morning sickness like you had with Cecil."

"I'm fine, so far, no morning sickness, knock on wood," she said, tapping him lightly on the forehead. "Cecil will be almost two when she is born," she added.

"She?" he asked. "Do you have some advanced information? Lidy hasn't been consulting that fortuneteller again has she?"

He looked so concerned that she hastened to reassure him. "You know I'm not like Lidy. I don't believe in fortunetellers. It's just that I want this one to be a girl."

He told her that would make him happy too, before he asked if she had seen the doctor yet.

"Not yet," she responded. "I've been dreading going to see her."

Burrel chuckled as he remembered Doctor Smith's reaction to their misguided trip to the farm when Cecil had unexpectedly made his early appearance. "I can understand how you feel. She certainly can be a holy terror! You can tell her we won't be taking any automobile trips in December or January."

Priscilla had been reluctant to go to the doctor, because she dreaded the lecture she was sure she would receive. His putting it in words made her realize she'd been worrying unnecessarily. She'd take Burrel's advice and bring it up before the doctor had a chance to light into her. After all, she reasoned, "The best defense was a good offense."

Neither suspected, as they looked forward to this birth, that they were making promises they wouldn't keep. Their life was about to make a dramatic change, and the automobile trip they would take before this baby was born would be a much longer one than to the farm at Rocky Fork.

~

Priscilla's happiness over the thought of the new baby was overshadowed by the worry over her mother's health. The arthritis that Rhoda had been experiencing had become so painful, that she was almost incapacitated. Though Doctor Smith had been treating her, she wasn't getting any better. Although the doctor didn't want to admit it, she had done all she possibly could for her.

Every day, Priscilla made the trip to the farm to help her mother. After taking care of the chores, she'd rub ointment on her mother's pain racked back. Then the two of them would spend the rest of the time praying together or sitting and quietly talking.

Burrel was concerned that she was overdoing. One evening he cautiously broached the subject by saying, "How have you been feeling? You seem tired lately. Do you think you might be overdoing it, a bit?"

She angrily responded, "How can you even suggest that I'm spending too much time with Mom! She needs me! Everyone else is too busy to help. If I don't do it, who will?"

"I know," he said, "but I don't want you to get too tired. You know it isn't good for you, in your condition. I'm going to talk to your sister Laurie and Aunt Lidy and see if they can help out. You know they'd want you to take care of yourself with the baby coming."

There were sparks in her eyes when she replied, "They don't know about the baby, and I don't want you telling them! If it got back to Mom, she wouldn't want me to do as much as I am doing for her. Don't you understand, I couldn't stand not being with her now?"

"I do understand, Honey," he said. " I'll go out with you, when I have some time off. You know how much I love your mother. She and your dad have always treated me like a son. I'd do anything for them, but I want you to promise me you'll get some rest. Okay?"

"Okay, I promise," she responded. "This seems like a good time to start. Let's turn off the lights and go to sleep." That was a line from a popular song of the day. They were both humming it as they slipped into bed.

True to his word, Burrel enlisted the help of other members of the family and Priscilla was able to take it a little easier.

~

One day when they were at the farm, Rhoda told them about a man she'd heard of, who claimed he could cure arthritis. The man was not a doctor, but he had perfected a treatment he guaranteed would help even the most severe cases. Even though they were skeptical, they were ready to try anything that would bring her relief from the pain.

They contacted him and he started the treatments immediately. First he had her fast for three days, then for the next week she was only allowed to eat oranges and drink water. His theory was that this would purge the body of impurities, including the arthritis.

At the end of that period, he allowed her to eat normally for three days, then the treatment was repeated. He said sometimes this was necessary for severe cases like Rhoda's.

They all wanted to believe in him and his treatment, but by the end of the second week they knew he was a charlatan and that they had been deceived and cheated out of their money. Worst of all, though, was having their hopes for a speedy cure destroyed.

From all appearances Rhoda was worse. She now had severe stomach pains and diarrhea and was so weak she could hardly get out of bed.

Really worried now, Harvey called Doctor Smith. Still unhappy with traveling on country roads, the doctor arrived prepared to tell them in no uncertain terms how she felt about it. Once she saw how ill her patient was, though, the angry words died in her throat.

Harvey told her about the treatment Rhoda had been taking, and that the family felt it had brought on this new problem. It was obvious, the doctor didn't approve, but the very fact that she didn't scold them made each person in the room aware of the seriousness of Rhoda's illness.

After she had examined Rhoda and talked to them about her symptoms, she motioned for Harvey to come out in the hall. Burrel stayed in the room with Rhoda while Priscilla and Harvey followed the doctor.

"I don't want to alarm you, but Rhoda is a very sick woman. I think I know what it is, but I need more time to be sure. I'll be back tomorrow. In the meantime, try to get her to eat something. Some hot broth would be good for her. She might be able to keep it down. She's going to need someone to take care of her though. She's too weak right now to be up and around."

"We'll see that someone is here to take care of her," Priscilla assured the doctor.

Doctor Smith pursed her lips, gave her a long searching look, before briskly stating, "You better take care of yourself, Missy."

Priscilla quickly changed the subject before the doctor had a chance to say anymore, but Harvey was too worried about Rhoda to pay any attention to the women's conversation.

～

The family rallied around, taking turns staying with Rhoda. The only one who didn't help was Della who informed the rest of the family that they were expecting a baby, and were afraid the strain of Della helping take care of her mother might be too much for her.

This led to a discussion at the dinner table that evening as Burrel timorously broached the subject, "Were you surprised to hear about David and Della?"

"Surprised? No. I can't say I was surprised. I think that is just an excuse to avoid helping out. Della has never thought of anyone except herself! I'd be more inclined to think she doesn't want to help," Priscilla angrily replied.

Although, Priscilla had remained determined she was not going to tell her mother about her pregnancy or let it keep her from doing her share, Burrel was shocked by her reaction. "What makes you think that? You act as if you don't believe she's even pregnant. That's not what you're saying, is it?"

Priscilla didn't hesitate a moment, before responding, "That's exactly what I'm saying."

Burrel, a trusting person always attributing his own sense of honor to others, found Priscilla's statement difficult to comprehend. Trying to make sense out of what he was hearing, he continued to probe, "Priscilla, I know you're upset, but you can't believe she would make up such a thing to avoid helping? Why? What makes you think such a thing?"

Priscilla's cheeks were flushed and her eyes blazing as she furiously replied, "Because she was on her period just last week! Lidy and I both knew it. There is no way she could be pregnant. She makes me so mad! I can't believe she is so selfish! After all the things she has put Mom and Dad through!" As so often happened when she was angry, Priscilla burst into tears.

Burrel put his arms around her to console her. "You know, Honey, people have to live with themselves. You've never done anything to be ashamed of. Can you imagine having to live with a lie like that?"

"I know." she sobbed. "I'm so worried about Mom. The doctor still hasn't told Dad what she thinks is wrong with her. That really scares me. You know how blunt Doctor Smith is, but now she's being so kind and gentle with Mom and with all of us. That's just not like her. I'm afraid Mom's not going to get well, and the doctor doesn't want to tell us."

He understood, as she was voicing the same concerns he'd been having lately. Rhoda had become such an important person in his life, the thought of losing her was almost as painful as losing his own

Father Was A Caveman

mother had been.

As they got ready for bed, he watched as Priscilla knelt by the bed and fervently prayed, first that God would heal her mother and secondly, if that were not possibly that he would grant her relief from the pain. Burrel looked on, in wonder, envying her faith.

~

It soon became obvious, they were going to need all the faith and strength they could muster. The doctor, who hadn't wanted to believe her own diagnosis, had finally told the family that Rhoda was in the final stages of colon cancer.

There was nothing she could do for her, except try to make her as comfortable as possible. She had come to care for this courageous farmwoman and her family and was almost as devastated by what she had to tell them, as they had been upon hearing it.

Cancer was even more feared in 1929, than it is now. Even though it was a major killer, few people talked about it and if they did, it was in hushed voices. It was as if the mention of the dreaded word might in some way bring it to one of their loved ones.

In horror, Priscilla watched the ravages of the illness continue to weaken her mother. At her young age, the fear she felt for this disease was so overwhelming it stayed with her for the rest of her life.

September arrived and with it peace for Rhoda, as she quietly exchanged this earthly life for the one she had spent her adult life preparing to enter. Her entire family felt she was with her Heavenly Father, but though the thought offered comfort, the pain of losing her mother was almost more than Priscilla could bear.

Closing the store, Burrel and Priscilla went to the farm to be with Harvey. No one had prepared Priscilla for the shock of seeing her mother laid out in her coffin and when she walked into the parlor and saw her, she almost collapsed. Only Burrel's strong arm around her waist kept her on her feet.

Years later when she talked about it, she said she remembered crying out and automatically wrapping her arms around her belly as if to protect her unborn child. When the baby was born, it had a faint birthmark on its side, and no one could ever convince Priscilla that this mark was not caused by her trauma.

Rhoda was buried on September 14, 1929, Priscilla's nineteenth birthday, in the Church of Christ's churchyard at the Rocky Fork Cemetery on Route 79.

This was one day Priscilla would never forget, and it would be years before she could celebrate her birthday without picturing that sad day when all of Rhoda's loved ones gathered together in that churchyard to say their final farewell.

~

Afterwards, she busied herself taking care of Cecil and Burrel, and finally she turned her attention to her unborn child. Having broken the news to both Lidy and Laura, they were helping her sew and crochet tiny clothes for the baby's layette.

When Laura imparted Priscilla's news to Della, she mentioned that she was glad her sisters were having babies at the same time. Laura was astounded at Della's response, "David and I were afraid it might happen. Mom's death brought on a miscarriage." Although Priscilla wasn't surprised to hear it, Burrel still had a difficult time believing Della could be so deceitful. It was to be years before Priscilla could forgive her sister. Although she eventually did, like many other things in her life, she never forgot.

A few days later, after she put Cecil to bed, and she and Burrel were relaxing in the living room, Priscilla started talking about her mother, not about her death but about her life. Although Burrel hadn't heard much about psychiatry, he knew talking would help Priscilla with the healing process. As he sipped his coffee, he gave her his full attention.

"You know, Mom was always strong and independent, especially when she was young. Dad wasn't her first husband. She was married before to a man named Elban. He was Fred's father. After Fred was born, Mr. Elban decided he was going to show Mom who was boss. Just in case she hadn't gotten the message, he started knocking her around. Mom told him she wasn't going to live that way, and if he did it again, she would divorce him. He didn't believe her, as divorce was almost unheard of forty years ago when Fred was a baby. The next time he got mad, he started hitting Mom and Fred again."

"She hadn't been kidding when she'd told him she wasn't going to put up with it. She waited until he went out to the barn, then she bundled Fred in heavy blankets and walked, carrying him from their house in St. Louisville to her parents' farm in Rocky Fork. I'm not sure how far it was, but it must have been several miles."

"Her dad was so angry when he saw her battered face that later when her husband showed up to take her home, he chased him off the property with a buggy whip. Mom said that he told him if he ever showed up again he'd use it on him. That was the last anyone ever saw or heard from, or about, Fred Elban. Mom divorced him. Then when she and Dad were married, he took Fred and raised him as one of his own."

She sat back and closed her eyes, as if lost in memories of her mother as a fiery young woman. Burrel, who had been absorbed in her story, took this opportunity to say, "Your dad and Fred have always been so close. I think your dad thinks of him as his own son."

"No doubt about it," Priscilla responded. "All my life, Mom has always been so calm and God fearing, it's hard for me to believe, but I guess she used to have a terrible temper. She told me once even the cows were glad when she became a Christian. I guess they bore the brunt of her temper more than once when she was bringing them into the barn."

This was difficult for Burrel to imagine, but he decided not to say anything that might interrupt her chain of thought. "Mom said the day she became a Christian changed her entire life. You know our church preaches that we all belong to the fellowship of saints, and that we should all work to become saints on earth. It wasn't always easy when I was growing up to live up to Mom's expectations."

Burrel could see it would be hard to have your own mother expect you to be a saint on earth. Thinking how thankful he was that his mother had been more understanding of his young foibles, he waited for her to continue.

"You know, something else that isn't easy, is having parents in their late forties when you're born. It isn't fair, because you don't have them with you as long. I always knew it and used to worry about it, but it's even worse than I thought it would be."

By now tears were rolling down her cheeks. Burrel pulled her close, as he tried to comfort her. "I know it's hard losing your mother when you're so young, although I don't think there is ever a time when it's easy." His eyes were moist, as he added, "I loved your mother, too. She was a wonderful woman. She couldn't have been kinder to me if she had been my own mother."

He smiled through his tears, as he reminisced, "I'll never forget the first time I met her. That was when I saw your picture and fell in love with you. Another thing I won't forget is the first time I came to help your dad, and you and your mom had made all those donuts. I don't believe that I'd ever seen so many in my entire life."

The memories were making both of them feel better. Priscilla actually laughed when she thought about the time her mother, though convinced going to the movies would send her straight to hell, had risked her soul's salvation to save her daughter's reputation.

"What's funny?" he asked.

Still smiling, she replied, "I was just picturing Mom, going to the movie house with us, the time Mace and I went to see "Up in Mabel's Room." When she walked through the lobby she looked about as enthusiastic as someone going to their own execution. You should have seen how fast she moved, though, when Mace started to sit next to me. She planted herself between us so quickly he almost sat on her lap. She told us both in no uncertain terms that she wasn't going to let anyone have a chance to gossip about us."

"I remember the three of you talking about that evening," Burrel said. "I do believe your mother enjoyed it as much as you did."

"I think she did, too," Priscilla replied. Then sighing deeply she said, "She was a wonderful mother. I'll miss her."

"I know," Burrel crooned softly.

As she continued to talk he could see that this evening had been a catharsis for her. The healing process was beginning. That night, for the first time since her mother died, Priscilla slept through the night.

~

Not wanting to stay on the farm without Rhoda, Harvey had listed it for sale and was planning to move into town. Depressed, he found it difficult to concentrate on anything around him. At this point, he hadn't said anything to Burrel and Priscilla about selling the store, but it was obvious to them it no longer held his interest. Burrel had liked being a storekeeper when it had been mutually advantageous, but now when he suspected Harvey was only holding on to it to provide him with a job, he felt decidedly uncomfortable. Accepting charity wasn't for him! As long as Harvey had needed him, he had been willing to stay, but now he felt Harvey would be relieved if he found another job.

In his pocket, he had been carrying a letter from his father that could be the answer to this dilemma. Ulysses had written and asked him to move to West Virginia to help open and manage the cavern Arletta's great-grandfather, Joel Teeter had found on their property in the late eighteenth century.

It had always been a dream of Ulysses and his youngest son to open it to the public, but Burrel's brothers and sisters had been reluctant to do so. If they were ever to make their dream come true, they would need the support of the rest of the family.

Like a miracle, when he desperately needed a job, he had received the letter. Having read and reread it so many times, the words were indelibly imprinted on his brain. "All they want," Pap had written, "is for someone to take charge. Your brother and sisters are talking about selling stock to raise the money to open it. We all feel we can make a success of it if you'll agree to come home and spearhead the operation."

Burrel was excited about the opportunity, but he had been so worried about Priscilla's reaction that it had taken him several days to get up enough courage to talk to her about it. Remembering how much she had enjoyed visiting West Virginia, he'd nevertheless realized she had been even happier when they'd returned to Ohio. He could feel the pounding of his heart as fear coursed through his body at the thought that she wouldn't want to live there.

When he finally got up enough nerve to broach the subject, he found his fear had been well founded. She immediately rejected the idea, saying she didn't want to leave her family now, especially her dad. Although he understood, he was crushed by her response. This was the job of a lifetime for him, and deep in his heart he knew he would never have this kind of opportunity again.

After several days of watching her young husband trying to cope with his disappointment, she relented. The decision wasn't reached lightly, but after much soul searching Priscilla told him she would go. She still didn't want to leave Ohio, but she loved her young husband, and she could see how much it meant to him to return to his roots.

A few days later, with Cecil seated between them they waved goodbye to Mace, Mabel and Inez who were standing on their porch. Trying to hold back the tears, Priscilla continued to wave until she could no longer see them. Then with a deep sigh she turned her attention to her husband and child as Burrel drove toward the mountains and their new home.

In years to come, when Burrel remembered that moment in time, he wondered if he could have prevented what happened to them later if he'd been more sensitive to his wife's feelings.

THE CAVE DWELLERS

CHAPTER EIGHT

TO GRANDPAP'S HOUSE THEY WENT

When the little family arrived at the farmhouse, Ulysses insisted they stay with him. When they expressed concern about how Gussie would react, Ulysses emphatically informed them that this was as much their home as hers.

Burrel quickly became immersed in his work. The physical aspects of opening the cavern were mind boggling and backbreaking. First its many passages had to be explored with the only light supplied by lanterns, flashlights, or the graphite lamp on his miner's style hat. The next step was to remove the many years' accumulations of dirt from around the formations and make walkways. Sometimes the stalactites and stalagmites were so fragile, this could only be done with his bare hands while other times he could use a pick and shovel. Day after day, he and Verde carried load after load of dirt out in a wheel barrel.

He would come home each evening completely exhausted, but excited by the progress he was making. Around the dinner table he and Verde would regale the family with their experiences. One night they told about having to crawl on their bellies into a particularly tight spot. "It was well worth it when we found a small room covered with formations. Verde named this chamber the potato cellar because the formations resembled new potatoes," Burrel said.

As Priscilla listened to the men talk about crawling on hands and knees on slippery, muddy rock, sometimes immersed in water up to their knees, she longed for the safety of Burrel's job at the store.

~

During the days she and Gussie spent at home with the children, she yearned for the home they left behind. She had soon discovered the difficulty of two women sharing one house. Many times, Gussie had made remarks about them being there. One day Priscilla was upstairs when she heard her say to someone on the phone, "I guess the next thing Pap will be doing is bringing in some stray dogs for me to take care of."

Hearing this, Priscilla was so angry, she forgot about being almost nine months pregnant as she dashed down the stairs and confronted Gussie. "How dare you say such a thing? I can tell you, I don't want to be here any more than you want me. When Burrel comes home tonight, we're getting out of here! I've never stayed anywhere I'm not wanted, and I don't intend to start now."

Gussie was astonished. She wasn't a mean woman, just frustrated with the changes in her life, but she knew she had to calm her down and keep her from leaving or Burrel, Ulysses, and Verde would be very upset with her. "Priscilla, you know I didn't mean anything by it. I'm just tired. You don't want to leave now. The baby will be here soon. You know I've been planning on taking care of you then."

Priscilla wasn't going to allow herself to be placated that easily. The anger hadn't left her voice when she replied, "You meant it, all right! Don't worry about where we'll stay. We'll find someplace, and I'll find someone to take care of me when the baby comes."

"Priscilla, I am sorry. Please don't say anything to Burrel. We can work this out. Don't go," she pleaded.

Priscilla had calmed down enough to see that Gussie was really sorry. She didn't want to say or do anything that would hurt or upset Ulysses. "All right, I won't say anything this time," Priscilla assured her, but she was thinking she wouldn't put up with it if it happened again.

Over the next couple weeks, both women felt they were living with an uneasy truce. Priscilla missed the privacy of her own home, as did Gussie. Though Gussie and her family had always lived with her parents, it was not the same as having another family living there.

One problem they had was the children fighting over toys. Clyde being a year older, inches taller, and several pounds heavier than Cecil usually won any battle they had. Each mother had tried to talk to her own child, but the situation wasn't getting any better.

~

The time they stayed at the farmhouse wasn't all bad. Priscilla especially enjoyed the conversation in the evenings when they all gathered around the big table for supper. Verde had a wonderful sense of humor and loved to tell jokes and stories. He could tell the most outrageous tall tales so convincingly that children and adults were left wondering whether it was truth or fiction.

One evening as they were finishing their supper, Burrel said, "Verde, I've never told Priscilla about the time we went bear hunting. Why don't you tell her about it?"

Everyone around the table grinned as Priscilla gasped, "Bear hunting! Are there bears around here?"

"Certainly," Verde replied. "There are big grizzlies." The children had heard this story many times and were giggling in anticipation.

Verde bestowed a smile upon them as he continued, "Well, Burrel and I had been hearing about this great big grizzly being seen up on the ridge, and we decided we were going to try to get us a bear. I thought Avanell might want to have a bearskin rug for her floor and Burrel reckoned that might be a good idea. Gussie filled a poke with vittles and we got our guns and took off."

"Well, we walked up to the ridge until we found an old abandoned cabin. This looked like a good place for us to camp while we looked for that bear. We built a fire and made some coffee and ate some of our grub before we started tracking it. We saw some signs he'd been there, but no bear."

"We bedded down for the night, but we had trouble sleeping since we were sure we could hear that bear outside the door. I don't think either of us got more than a couple hours sleep, what with getting up and making sure there was no way the bear could get to us while we were sleeping."

He paused and looked at his wide-eyed audience before continuing. "The next morning I decided I'd go down to the creek to get some water while Burrel fried us up some eggs and bacon. I no sooner got to the creek and started to fill the bucket, than I heard a rustling of dry leaves behind me. I turned around, and there was the biggest bear I'd ever seen."

"I sized up that bear and that bear sized up me. Well, you all know I'm a big fellow, but that bear would have made two of me! I figured I was a few feet ahead of him, and if I took off right then I could outrun him."

"I ran like greased lightning with that bear right behind me, straight for the cabin. Burrel looked up when the bear and I ran through the door. Before he could say anything, I ran straight through the front door and out the back. Before I slammed the back door I yelled, 'I brought this one for you, Burrel. Take care of it. I'm going out to get one for myself.'" Verde folded his arms across his ample belly, tilted back in his chair and chuckled.

Priscilla watched him and waited for him to continue. Then not able to stand the suspense any longer, she asked, "What happened?"

"I don't know," Verde replied. "I guess the bear must have et him."

Priscilla looked at him in amazement, and then laughed as hard as the rest of the family when she realized she'd been taken in by one of Verde's tall tales.

The bear story was Burrel's favorite. Over the years he loved to tell it to his own children and grandchildren.

~

Ulysses, who Priscilla, like the rest of the family, now called Pap, spent his free time with earphones to his ears listening to his crystal radio set. As they sat around the dinner table, many evenings he would share the news of the day with the rest of the family.

One evening he said, "The news I've been hearing is really disturbing. I don't think any of us thought too much about it when we heard about the stock market crash in New York back in October. I know I didn't, but I guess those people up there are not the only ones it's affecting. I heard today that big companies are going out of business, and thousands of people are losing their jobs. The newscaster even said men were out selling apples on the streets to try to support their families. The unemployed are marching into Washington and setting up camp towns they're calling Hoovervilles. I guess the only food these people have is what they can get standing in line at soup kitchens."

"It sounds pretty bad," Burrel said, "but I'm sure President Hoover will do something about it. Isn't that why we elected him?"

They all agreed, but as they looked at all the food on their table, they couldn't help feel thankful for what they had and sympathetic to those less fortunate. As they talked around the table, they had no inkling that the depression would soon change all their bright plans for the future.

As they needed additional funds to continue their work on the cavern, they decided to go public and sell shares. The majority of their stockholders were businessmen and bankers from neighboring communities. An exception to this was Walter Amos, a geologist, from Winchester, Virginia. He was of great help to Burrel in his exploration of the cavern.

He saw in Burrel a staunch spelunker, anxious and willing to learn all he could teach him. He became Burrel's mentor and his lifetime friend. They explored many caverns together, and he was instrumental in seeing that Burrel had a job as the depression deepened.

~

After Arletta's death, Ulysses had moved downstairs to the small bedroom at the back of the house, and Priscilla and Burrel were sleeping in Arletta and Ulysses's room at the top of the stairs. Since this was the warmest room in the house, Priscilla was glad it was theirs when she saw the snow blowing and heard the wind rattling the windowpanes.

The house, like many farmhouses of the day, was heated by a wood-burning stove with some help from the cooking stove. Instead of the stovepipe leading into the chimney, it was fed through their bedroom before exiting through the roof. As she snuggled down under the covers, she was grateful for this building quirk, as it guaranteed she didn't have to deal with the cold along with the discomfort of her pregnancy.

During the night, she woke with a nagging pain in her back. It was reminiscent of the beginning of her labor for Cecil, but it would come and go to the extent that she, at first, wasn't sure she was in labor. Uncomfortable as she was, she decided not to wake Burrel or disturb anyone in the house until she was more certain.

Before daybreak, though, the intensity of the pain changed and it was so bad, she could no longer ignore it. This child was making it evident it was ready to make its entrance into the world. She woke Burrel who, when he realized what was happening, roused Gussie. They started timing her contractions and soon decided they needed to call Doctor Harman. Priscilla was surprised to find that she missed Doctor Smith. Doctor Harman was somewhat of a chauvinist who, after examining her, told her it was up to her now. Gussie would be with her. She could let him know when it was time for him to deliver the child. Up until that time, this was women's work.

He left, going about his rounds, returning later in the day to check her progress and visit with the men until Gussie let him know she needed his help. At 8:45 PM, in the bedroom where Burrel had been born more than twenty-six years earlier, Priscilla gave birth to a baby girl.

When Gussie put the baby in Burrel's arms, he remembered how nervous he had been when Rhoda had handed Cecil to him almost two years ago. Priscilla voiced his thoughts when she said, "You don't seem afraid to hold this one. I thought Mom was going to have to force you to hold Cecil."

"I know," he replied. "I guess I've had experience now. This feels right. Did you notice how white her hair is? She's going to be a tow head, like I was."

Looking at Burrel holding his new daughter, Priscilla smiled tiredly before replying, "You can't take all the credit. I was a tow head, too."

"You got your little girl. Are you happy?" he asked.

"Happy and tired," she replied before drifting off to sleep.

He sat by the bed and watched her sleep, thinking about all the things that had happened to them since their first child was born. They had weathered some bad times, but looking down at the face of his daughter, he was sure their future was going to be good.

Being in this room with his sleeping wife and newborn daughter, he felt a connection to all the generations of his mother's family who had been born within these four walls. He was sorry his mother would never know this child, but he felt her presence as if she were saying she was happy about this new grandchild.

The baby was named Mildred June. Priscilla had heard the name June in a song called "The Trail of the Lonesome Pine." She picked

Mildred simply because she liked it.

After Priscilla rested, all the members of the household came in to see the baby. Verde teased Burrel and Priscilla about their patriotic baby with the white hair, beet red skin and blue eyes. Priscilla probably wouldn't have been amused if it had come from anyone else, but she liked Verde and his sense of humor.

Burrel, putting Cecil on the bed so he could get acquainted with the new addition to the family, said, "You have a little sister. Can you say hello to Mildred?"

Not quite two, there was no way he could wrap his tongue around such a big word. He tried, and they all laughed at his efforts. Priscilla was sure she could work with him and get him to say it, but that didn't prove to be the case.

~

The next day, January twenty sixth, Burrel and Verde returned to work on the cavern. Priscilla had to stay in bed making it necessary for Gussie to bring her meals to her and to take care of Cecil. This was a frustrating experience for both women, but the doctor had been adamant that Priscilla was to stay in bed for ten days.

The weather was typical for West Virginia in January with the temperature close to zero and the ground covered with snow and more falling. Cecil and Clyde whined to play outside, but it was too cold.

Priscilla could hear them fighting and Gussie fussing at them. This bothered her, but she consoled herself that she would be able to be downstairs soon and could care for Cecil herself. This confinement was so different from her last one when her mother had pampered her. Gussie took care of her, but it was obvious to Priscilla that she was overworked and felt imposed upon.

She talked to Burrel about it that evening, but he didn't take her concern seriously. He knew his sister. She liked to gripe, but he was used to it and never paid much attention to it. He again told Priscilla that this was as much their home as Gussie's, and the best thing to do was just ignore it. Things would be better when she was back on her feet.

Although she knew it was going to be difficult, she assured him she'd try to take his advice. She did try, but the situation accelerated to the point that an explosion was inevitable.

It happened the day the baby was five days old. Priscilla had just fed her and was softly crooning to her when she heard a bloodcurdling shriek from downstairs. This was followed by Gussie yelling, "You little brat! What have you done?"

This was all Priscilla needed to hear. She had never heard Gussie call one of her own a brat, so obviously Cecil was the victim of her wrath. Placing the baby in the cradle, oblivious for the moment of the doctor's instructions to stay in bed, she crept down the stairs.

She was confronted by an astonishing scene. Clyde, with a stream of blood running down his forehead from a cut on his head, was still howling. Cecil, holding on to his ride-on kiddie car with one hand and a little metal car with the other, was crying and between sobs yelling, "Mine! Mine!" Gussie was trying to stop the flow of Clyde's blood while scolding Cecil for being a bad boy.

"What's going on?" Priscilla asked.

Gussie was astonished to see Priscilla standing there, but she was too angry to be concerned about her disobeying the doctor's orders. "I'll tell you what happened! Your son hit Clyde over the head with that metal car! He could have killed him."

Cecil, still holding on to his kiddie car, came running to his mother and between sobs told her he'd been riding it when Clyde took it away from him. When he couldn't get him to give it back, he'd picked up the little car and hit him.

"See, the little brat admits he hit him! You and Burrel should teach him to share his toys! If he wasn't so selfish this wouldn't have happened!" Gussie screamed.

Priscilla furiously replied, "Share! Share! He hasn't gotten to play with any of his toys since we got here. Clyde is such a big bully, every time Cecil is playing with something he takes it away from him!"

"I would think Clyde could play with whatever he wanted in his own home! Who else is Pap going to drag in here? I don't know why you didn't stay in Ohio where you belong!" Gussie shouted.

"Believe me," Priscilla responded, "if I'd had a choice I'd still be there! Maybe I can't go back to Ohio, but I can and will get out of this house. The minute Burrel gets home, we're leaving."

Gussie was having second thoughts. She knew this was her father's house, and that he wanted Burrel and his family to stay here. She hadn't meant to say as much as she had, but she and Priscilla had both been like tigers protecting their cubs. Everyone in the family was used to her temper, knowing she could be angry one minute and completely over it the next. This wasn't the case with Priscilla. She didn't lose her temper easily and when she did, she meant what she said. Although Gussie was trying to get her to go back to bed and forget about leaving, Priscilla had made up her mind and there was no changing it. Taking Cecil upstairs with her, she was packed and ready to leave when Burrel and Verde got home that evening.

∽

They came in the door, laughing and talking, but their good mood was quickly shattered when Gussie told them what had happened. Burrel was hopeful he could persuade Priscilla to stay. After all, where would they go? The closest hotels were twenty miles away, either in Franklin or Petersburg. He wasn't relishing taking his family out on those roads in this weather. No matter what he said, Priscilla was still upset and determined not to spend another night in a house where she wasn't wanted.

Pap and Verde didn't want her to leave like this. They each tried to talk to her, to no avail. When they realized she wasn't going to change her mind, Pap suggested Burrel call Olie and Josie. Possibly, they could stay with them for a few days. This would give him time to find a place of their own. The call was made, and to Burrel's relief, Olie and Josie said they'd be happy to have them.

When the men came back into the house after loading the bags into the car, the two boys were sitting on the floor playing with the very car Cecil had used to clobber Clyde with earlier. Looking at them, Burrel said to Verde, "I wish our wives could patch up their differences as easily as these boys have."

"Give them time," Verde replied. "Give them time." He was really sorry this had happened and hated to see them go like this.

Before leaving, Priscilla told Pap she really loved him and appreciated him wanting them to stay with him and expressed her regret that it hadn't worked out. She hadn't wanted to hurt him or Verde and hoped they could understand.

Both men told her, again, they wished she'd change her mind and stay. Tears were rolling down her cheeks when she said she was sorry, but she just couldn't.

The men stood in the yard, hardly aware of the cold as they watched the car until it went around the curve, out of sight. Then with slow steps they returned to the house. As Pap started for his room he heard Verde say, "Gussie, I think we'd better have a talk." Before Gussie responded, Pap closed his door. This was one talk he'd just as soon not hear.

~

They stayed with Olie and Josie for a few days while Burrel looked for a place for them to live. This was not an easy task, since unlike Newark; Riverton was very small and almost without rental property. In the absence of a newspaper with its want ads, Burrel tried the next best thing, the general store. The proprietor, Mr. Kisamore, not only knew everyone, but also seemed to know everything that was going on for miles around.

Much to Burrel's relief Mr. Kisamore said he was sure there was an empty four-room apartment a few houses down the road from the store. Burrel checked it out and as it was the only available one in the village he made arrangements to rent it before returning to Olie's.

Within the next few days they were settled into the apartment, and Burrel was able, once again, to concentrate on his work in the cavern. Since she treasured their privacy, Priscilla reveled in having a place of their own and vowed she would never again share a home with another family.

It was soon evident that no matter how hard he tried, Cecil was not going to be able to pronounce Mildred, so they decided to call the baby by her middle name, June. Once that was decided Burrel told Priscilla confidentially he liked it better. He thought his little girl seemed more like June than Mildred. Priscilla agreed, but she was a little hurt, as she had picked the name and had really liked it.

Their new home was on the second floor overlooking the river. Each morning Priscilla would stand at the window, watching Burrel drive across the bridge on his way to the cavern. This also provided a good vantage point to observe the changing seasons. She watched the snow and ice disappear as the trees burst forth in blossoms and bright new leaves. When she heard the first robins of the season being joined by a chorus of sparrows, cardinals, and blue birds, she became aware the long winter was over and spring had arrived.

CHAPTER NINE

THE VISIT

They were planning a trip to Ohio the first of July, and Priscilla had been marking off the days. She was anxious to see her family and Mace and Mabel and to show off the baby. Mabel was expecting a baby in June, and they were all hoping it would arrive on time so they would see it during their visit.

As it turned out the new arrival, Rosalie Clair Harman, was a few days old when they arrived. Mabel was still confined to bed, but she insisted they stay with them. Although they spent the nights with Mace and Mabel, they also visited Harvey and the rest of Priscilla's family.

On the fourth of July, Burrel and Priscilla took Cecil and June to Buckeye Lake, an amusement park on Route 79 south of Newark. Having a wonderful time, they had taken the children on some rides, were munching on one of Priscilla's favorite treats, corn dogs, and strolling around the park feeling young and carefree. All their attention had been directed to each other until they heard an announcement from the loud speakers posted above them. "If there is a Burrel Harman in the park, will he please report to the park office." As they exchanged worried glances, the mechanical sounding voice repeated the words.

Priscilla could feel her heart pounding as they hurried to the office. She was sure something must have happened to her father, and it had to be something pretty serious to warrant being tracked down at the park.

The manager had a message for them to call her brother Fred immediately. Priscilla was more worried than ever when she heard this. Burrel smiled reassuringly and murmured, "Don't worry, Honey. We just saw your dad and he was fine." With Priscilla looking on, Burrel put in a call to Fred. As soon as he heard his brother-in-law's voice he asked, "Is Harvey alright?"

Fred assured him he was fine. Burrel quickly relayed that information to Priscilla before asking, "What is it? What has happened?"

"It's your brother Mace. He was hit by a car about an hour ago. He was taken, by ambulance, to the hospital. He won't let them call Mabel, since she just had the baby. Instead he had them call me to ask that I get in touch with you. He wants you to break the news to Mabel."

"How bad is he hurt?" Burrel asked. "What happened?"

"The doctor said he'll be all right. He was walking to the grocery store on East Main Street. I guess he was crossing at the firehouse when he was hit and thrown against the car's windshield. When he fell, he hit his head on the interurban tracks. He must be okay, but I think you'd better go to the hospital and see for yourself before breaking the news to Mabel," Fred explained.

Before hanging up the phone, Burrel said, "We'll leave right now."

Less than an hour later, when they walked into the hospital room, they were shocked at Mace's appearance. His head was bandaged and his face covered with cuts and abrasions. Lying so still, he looked so helpless it was impossible for them to tell whether he was sleeping or unconscious. The nurse who was standing by the bedside motioned for them to follow her into the hall. In a hushed voice, she said, "He is going to be all right. He was unconscious when he was brought in, but he revived and is sleeping normally now. He has a gash on his head from hitting the tracks. That required stitches, but the ones on his face won't require any. He'll have some bruises on the rest of his body and be sore for a while, but nothing was broken."

"Thank God for that!" Burrel exclaimed. "How long will he have to be in the hospital?"

"You'll need to talk to the doctor about that," was her reply.

Just then they heard Mace's voice, "Burrel, is that you?" In response, Burrel walked into the room, leaned over the bed and asked, "How are you feeling?"

"I feel like I was hit over the head with a sledge hammer," was his response. He tried to smile, but his face felt as if little men wearing cleats on their shoes were marching across it.

Noticing the look of pain, Burrel spoke quickly before Mace had a chance to say anything else, "Don't try to talk. We have talked to the nurse and will talk to the doctor before we leave. I think we'd better go now, so we can let Mabel know what's happened. I'm sure she's worried about you." Giving his brother's hand a reassuring squeeze, he added, "We'll be back tomorrow."

The doctor, who was waiting when they came out of the room, introduced himself, then said, "Your brother is a lucky man. He'll be all right, but he looked so bad when he was found that the man who called the ambulance wasn't sure whether he was dead or alive. He was unconscious and his face and head were covered with blood from the head wound. Believe me, the ambulance drivers were relieved to hear him moan when they bent over him."

"How long will he have to stay in the hospital?" Burrel asked the doctor.

"I want to keep him for observation for a couple days. I don't anticipate any problems, but I like to be cautious in a case like this. From what I understand, his head hit the windshield before he landed on the track. Injuries like his can result in a loss of blood, and we need to be sure there's no concussion. If you come back tomorrow, I should be able to give you a definite dismissal time. I understand his wife just had a baby. Be sure and tell her I said Mace will be as good as new in a couple weeks. Tell her not to worry. He'll be fine."

Informing the doctor he'd be back the next day, and that he would be sure to give Mabel his message, they left the hospital.

Back at Mace and Mabel's house, Mabel was extremely worried. She hadn't been too concerned at first, as she had thought Mace must have encountered a friend and started talking and completely lost track of time. After a couple hours, though, she had begun to worry and think of all the horrible things that could have happened to him. She told her sister Bonnie, "If he doesn't come home in the next few minutes, I'm going to have you call the police and the hospital to find out if he's been in an accident."

The words had barely escaped her lips when she saw Burrel and Priscilla in the doorway. Why would they have returned so early from their outing? Every nerve in her body was screaming that something was wrong. Mace! Something had happened to Mace! "What is it?" she cried. "What's happened to Mace?"

Burrel and Priscilla both went over and stood by her bed while they explained what had happened, and gave her the doctor's message. Burrel's voice was soft and calm, and his words were so reassuring, that her fears were eased.

~

After all that had happened that day, they were all tired and turned in early that night. That wasn't to be the end of the excitement though. It seemed they had hardly fallen asleep when they heard Mabel screaming, "The house is on fire! The house is on fire!"

Burrel jumped out of bed and ran down the hall to Mabel's room. In his haste he forgot that he was only wearing his undershirt. Mabel's room was so full of smoke she couldn't see him, let alone be aware of what he was, or wasn't, wearing. Yelling for Priscilla and Bonnie to take the kids out, he said to Mabel, "It'll be okay. I'll get you out of here."

The window was open and the slight breeze coming through fanned the smoke and caressed his bare bottom. "Uh oh!" he exclaimed as he grabbed a sheet and wrapped it around him before scooping Mabel into his arms and carrying her outside.

By then the fire truck, its lights flashing and sirens blaring had arrived. The firemen rushed in and quickly returned with one of them carrying a smoldering diaper. "Who put this over the light bulb?" he demanded.

"Was that what caused all the smoke?" Burrel asked.

"Yes, it certainly was. Don't you know how dangerous it is to put any kind of cloth over a burning light bulb? It could have been much worse if someone hadn't smelled the smoke and woke the family."

Bonnie sheepishly admitted she was the one who had done it. She'd draped the diaper over the lamp, so the light wouldn't shine in Mabel's eyes. She was so young, pretty, and obviously contrite, that the fireman didn't have the heart to scold her. In fact, as he looked at the women in their nightclothes and Burrel wrapped in a sheet, he couldn't hide his amusement as he climbed aboard the fire engine for the trip back to the firehouse.

As they watched the engine disappear from view, they first felt relief that the fire had not been serious. Then, looking around, they became aware of the picture they presented, Burrel in his toga, Inez and Cecil clinging to the hems of their mother's gowns and Bonnie holding the two crying infants. Looking at them, Mabel exclaimed, "We'd better get inside before any more of the neighbors see us. I think the Harmans have caused enough excitement for one day, don't you?" No one disagreed, as they sheepishly filed back into the house and returned to their beds.

As Burrel was drifting off to sleep, Priscilla asked, "Why were you wearing a sheet?"

"Go to sleep," Burrel responded. "We can talk about it tomorrow."

~

The next morning Burrel and Priscilla returned to the hospital to see Mace. Today was a totally different scenario. As they were walking down the hall, they could hear Mace telling the nurses, in no uncertain, terms that he was going home. When they entered the room, they couldn't believe what they were seeing or hearing. He looked like a wild man, with his head wrapped in a bandage and his face blood red from the mercurochrome they had used to paint his many cuts and abrasions. He was still berating the nurses about being forced to stay, when he became aware of their presence.

"Tell them I need to go home!" he told Burrel.

"Mace, calm down. You look like you were in a fight with a wildcat, and the wildcat won. You need to take it easy, and let the nurses take care of you. I don't think you'd better go home looking like that. You'd scare Mabel out of her wits. Okay?" Burrel replied.

Mace seemed to relax, much to the nurse's relief, he responded, "Okay." then added, " I really do have a headache."

They hadn't heard the doctor come in until he said, "That's why you need to stay at least another night. You know you can't even feed yourself. Just relax and you can go home tomorrow."

Mace looked like he was about ready to argue with the doctor, but Burrel gave him his look that said as clearly as words, "Hursh."

To everyone's surprise he did, but only momentarily.

As Burrel and Priscilla were ready to leave, George, one of Mace's neighbors stopped in to see him and began regaling him with the happenings of the night before. Although Burrel was trying to shush him, George was having too much fun spreading the news to be aware of Burrel's actions or Mace's reactions.

Sitting up in bed, oblivious of his aching head, Mace demanded to know if this really were true. Burrel tried to calm him but to no avail. "This is it!" Mace exclaimed. "I am going home and nobody is going to stop me!" As he was speaking, he got out of bed and began pulling on his pants.

Frantically, the nurse ran out of the room and returned with the doctor. Hearing them enter, Mace turned and said, "Don't try to stop me. I am going home!"

The doctor looked at Mace's determined face and turned in exasperation to the nurse and said, "Just send the damn fool home!" Then turning to Burrel, he said, "He's your problem now! If you can keep him quiet for a few days, he'll be fine. The nurse will give you some instructions before you leave." Having said this, without another look at his patient, he angrily strode from the room.

Before letting Mace go in the house, Priscilla prepared Mabel for his appearance and told her about the incident at the hospital. Mabel's face beamed as she said, "Well, I'm not surprised. You know how stubborn Mace is. He's not going to let much keep him away from me and the children." As it turned out, once he was home with his loved ones, he became a model patient and recovered swiftly and completely.

The days passed quickly, and Burrel and Priscilla's vacation was over too soon. Amid smiles, tears and promises from all that they would come and visit, the little family left for their trip home.

~

After all the excitement, it was good to be back in their little apartment and to resume their normal routine.

June had developed a bad habit of holding her breath when she didn't get her way. It would frighten Priscilla, but she had found that splashing a little water in the baby's face would shock her into crying. As she told Burrel, "She gets so mad at what I am doing to her that she forgets to hold her breath."

This went on for a few months until one day June held her breath until she almost lost consciousness. Frightened, Priscilla picked her up and with the baby's limp body in her arms, dashed to the kitchen for the water. When she ran through the doorway, June's head flopped against the frame. As soon as her head and the door made contact, her eyes sprang open. She gave her mother an accusing look and started screaming at the top of her lungs. That was the end of that bad habit.

When Priscilla related the incident later, she laughingly exclaimed, "Our daughter is a fast learner. I think she thought I slammed her head against the door on purpose and might do something even worse if she ever pulled that trick again." Her audience usually agreed with her.

CHAPTER TEN

THE NEW CAVE DWELLERS

Things were not going well with the cavern. With the deepening depression, it had become evident the family did not have the resources to open it. Some of the major stockholders, the bankers and lawyers, offered to take care of the rest of the financing. In exchange the family would have to agree to sell them the controlling interest. Seeing their dream of opening the cavern disappear and being inexperienced in business matters, they agreed to the proposal. They soon found the business incorporated and themselves minor stockholders with very little voice in the operations.

Burrel, who was worried this was going to effect his employment, discussed the matter with Walter Amos. Much to his relief, Mr. Amos, now the company representative, informed him the stockholders wanted him to continue with his work on the cavern and once it was ready to be open to the public, they wanted him to be the manager.

Much to Priscilla's delight, Mr. Amos also told Burrel that the company planned to build a house on the hill above the cavern for the manager and his family. Tired of living in an upstairs apartment, this appealed to her, almost as much as his offer to make her the official hostess. As a hostess she would provide meals and occasional lodging for him and other official visitors.

The salary with the house and other terms was acceptable to both of them. Before the evening was over, Burrel was officially hired as manager of the cavern, and a new phase of their lives had begun.

For the next few months, on Sundays, Priscilla would pack a picnic lunch, and they would take the children to the cavern grounds to observe the progress of the construction. They found it exciting watching their new home take shape as it changed from the basic framework into an attractive two-story frame house.

After being cooped up in a second floor apartment, the children loved all the freedom they had to run and play. The young parents enjoyed it almost as much as the children did. Putting June in her walker, Priscilla and Burrel would watch and laugh as their daughter's tiny legs tried to keep up with her older brother as he raced across the lawn chasing butterflies.

Their first night in their new home, they walked through the rooms, pleased with their interior decorating. The pale wallpaper and golden oak woodwork were the perfect backdrops for their wicker and chintz living room furniture. Priscilla's canary, in its cage, seemed to blend with the yellow of the dining room walls. The crisp white ruffled curtains, the embroidered table cloth, and the family's pictures on the wall provided the finishing touches to make this house uniquely their home.

The kitchen, also bright and cheerful with its oilcloth covered table and freshly painted matching white chairs, was dominated by the large wood-burning cook stove. It was similar to the one in her parents' home. Looking at it, Priscilla smiled ruefully before declaring, "Oh, well I guess you can't have everything."

"Do you mind very much?" Burrel asked. She only hesitated a moment, before ruefully replying, "No, actually, it seems like an old friend."

~

That winter Burrel, Verde, and Olie finished wiring the cavern. This was no small job, as stringing the wire involved crawling into some tight spots on the lower level and building scaffolding to enable them to strategically place lights to accent formations in some of the upper regions.

They were all relieved when this dangerous work was completed. Now all that remained to be done on the electrical work was to connect the generator. No one expected this to be dangerous, but as it turned out they were wrong.

The men had all been looking forward to the day when the generator would be operating, and they could finally see the cavern illuminated by electric lighting. When Burrel left for work the morning it was to arrive he had been excited. When he returned that evening Priscilla expected to see triumph on his face. Instead he was plainly upset.

When she heard the kitchen door open, she looked up from the potatoes she was mashing for dinner. As soon as she saw the expression on his face she knew that something had happened. Alarmed she asked, "What's wrong?"

His voice was low and full of concern when he replied, "Olie was hurt a few minutes ago. He was working on the generator when a cable snapped. It flew back and hit him across the face."

"Good heavens!" Priscilla cried, "How bad is it?" "Now don't get excited," Burrel said. "I think he's alright, but I wouldn't be surprised if he has a broken nose. When that cable snapped, his nose took the brunt of it. He has a cut across it, and it's pretty badly swollen. Verde took him into Riverton to see Doctor Harman. We'll know how bad it is when they get back."

This was like one of her nightmares coming true. She, Josie, and Gussie had all lived in fear that one of the men might get hurt. She knew they'd all breathed a sigh of relief when the dangerous work inside the cavern had been completed, but no one had considered working on the generator to be hazardous.

Olie did have a broken nose. The doctor said it would be pretty sore for a few days, but he wouldn't have any lasting effect from it. His diagnosis about Olie's nose being sore for several days was correct, but he was wrong when he said there'd be no lasting effect. When the injury healed he was left with a bump on the bridge of his nose that gave it a slightly hooked effect. He remained, as he'd always been, a very nice looking man. Only now he looked a little more like his father.

The next day the three men successfully tackled the job of connecting the generator. When they finished they walked through the cavern switching on all the lights. As the light spread it illuminated areas that their flashlights and lanterns had left in shadow. In a voice filled with reverence Burrel exclaimed, "This is more beautiful than I thought it was going to be."

"All the hard work was worth it," Verde said. The other two men nodded in agreement.

~

Now that the inside was ready it was time to turn their attention to the outside. As spring arrived, the area began to bustle with activity. Priscilla and the children sat on the porch and watched as workmen built the office in front of the cavern entrance and a bandstand between the office and their front yard. Picnic tables and benches were brought in and placed throughout the grounds. Although the children weren't sure what was going on, they found the hustle and bustle exciting.

The big day finally arrived, finding the entire family up early, dressed in their Sunday best and ready to greet the dignitaries who were there for the opening. Priscilla, who had been cooking and baking for the last couple days, had prepared a buffet for the owners and their guests.

People came from miles around to tour the cavern. Many brought picnic lunches and gathered around the bandstand, listening to the band and other entertainment. The atmosphere was festive with music playing, banners flying, and children laughing while holding onto brightly colored balloons. Burrel was in his element working with the people. He loved showing them through the cavern, pointing out different formations he and Verde had named and using the spiel he, Verde, and Priscilla had written for the guides. Its mixture of truth, legend and fantasy was reminiscent of Verde's tall tales. It always elicited laughter.

As the owners watched the people exit the cavern with their faces wreathed in smiles, they felt assured this venture was going to be a success.

All Burrel's family were there. The men were mingling with the crowd and helping Burrel anywhere he needed them. The bigger children were running and playing while the smaller ones stayed at the house with their mothers who were busily helping Priscilla with the food.

When they had time for a break, Priscilla sat on the porch with Pap, observing the activity below them. He sighed deeply, as he said, "I thought this day would never come. This is something I've wanted to have happen since I was a young man. Things didn't turn out the way we wanted, but I'm still glad it's finally open to the public."

She reached over and patting his hand said, "I'm happy, too. Tired, but happy."

They sat companionably in silence, until Pap observed, "I noticed you and Gussie seemed to be getting along fine today. I'm glad. I really felt bad when you left the way you did. Are things all right between you two now?"

"Yes, everything is fine. We just can't live under the same roof, I guess. It's true that no house is big enough for two women. I am sorry if I hurt you when I left. I hope you understand."

He smiled gently as he replied, "I do understand." Their conversation was interrupted by Burrel's sisters Calcie, Nellie, and Gussie who had decided to join them. They had brought lemonade, glasses, and a plate of sandwiches with them. As she placed the tray on the table by Priscilla's chair, Calcie said, "I don't think any of us have taken time to eat today. We thought everyone might want to have a bite while we listen to the music."

Agreeing, they helped themselves to the refreshments while watching the entertainment from their ringside seats. The women exchanged smiles when they noticed Pap tapping his feet to the beat of the music.

At the end of the day when the music stopped and all the people had gone home, Burrel was tired but exhilarated from the success of the day. While he and Priscilla sat at the kitchen table sipping lemonade, he remarked, "Never in my wildest dreams did I expect this day to be so successful." As the words continued to spill from his mouth, Priscilla gazed at him, lovingly, thinking how much at that moment her husband reminded her of a happy child. "Did you see all the people?" he asked. "Everyone seemed to think the cavern was great! You should have heard them laugh when I told them the names of some of the formations."

Priscilla replied, "I could tell from here it was going well. The stockholders seemed to like the food. Walter Amos said he didn't know how I managed to do all of it on that stove."

"He told me that, too. I informed him, you're a fabulous cook! He said I'm a lucky man." Becoming pensive, he mused, "You know, I am a lucky man having you, the children, this job, this house. We've had some rough times, but things surely are looking good now." Having said that, he pulled her to him and no longer sounding like a little boy, said, "Don't you think it's time to go to bed?"

Tilting her head and looking into his eyes, she softly replied, "Yes. I think so, too." He took her hand in his and led her up the stairs into their room. Silently closing the door, he turned and took her in his arms. As he held her close, he thought, "This is a perfect ending, for a perfect day!"

~

That day was the beginning of many successful ones. Business was booming with every weekend like a carnival. News of the beauty of the cavern was spreading by word of mouth and some strategically placed advertising. Like going to the movies, a trip to Seneca Caverns was inexpensive and brought people a respite from the depressing news of the economy.

One evening, after an especially exciting day at the cavern, Burrel walked into the living room and saw Alice writing in her notebook with a smile on her face. Knowing she expressed her feelings by writing poetry, he asked, "You must be writing about something that makes you happy. Will you read it to me?"

"With pleasure," she answered, as she dramatically read the title, "Seneca Caverns."

She had his complete attention as he listened to her read each heartfelt verse:

"At the foot of majestic North Mountain
With the towering spruce nearby
Like a glittering gem in the hillside
The beautiful Seneca Caverns lie.

For long years they slumbered in silence
Unseen by any eye
Until the red man sought it as a refuge
When the white man began to draw nigh.

When the red man at last was driven
Far away from his native home
The white man explored its wonders
And through its halls began to roam.

In its mighty ballroom so lovely
Princess Snowbird became a bride
As ancient legend tells us
With the brave Rock Oak by her side.

Now people from every country
Visit its stately halls
And gaze in awe and rapture
At formations on ceiling and walls.

We are proud of West Virginia
We are proud of its scenery so grand
We are proud of Seneca Caverns
May they all forever stand."

As she read her poem, the smile on his face grew with each verse. By the time she finished, he was overwhelmed with happiness to know that she had come to love the caverns, legends, and mountains of his home state.

He rushed across the room, and gave her a big hug, lifting her off her feet, proclaiming, "Priscilla, I love your poem and I love you. Thank you for writing it."

Soon she would see even more grand scenery of this beautiful state than she had ever imagined.

CHAPTER ELEVEN

TAKING FLIGHT

During the nineteen thirties a phenomenon known as barnstorming was sweeping the country. Daredevil aviators were touring rural areas performing stunt flying and participating in air races. Priscilla had read about them, but had never seen one.

On this particular Saturday, Burrel was taking a group through the cavern and Priscilla was sitting on the porch, visiting with his sisters while the children played in the yard. Suddenly, over the din of the children's voices, they became aware of the roar of a motor. As they listened, they could tell it wasn't coming from the road, but from the sky.

Looking up, the children starting jumping up and down and shouting, "Look, it's an airplane!" A plane was so rare, the roaring engine always made people look skyward. The children's shouts brought the women off the porch to watch the plane fly over.

Flying low, it was circling the field next to the house. The children became even more excited as it came in lower and lower. As they watched, its wheels touched the ground, and it slowly taxied down the field and came to a stop. The aviator, as pilots were called then, seemed to unfold himself from the cockpit and started walking toward the little group.

Tall and lanky, he was wearing a leather jacket and loose fitting trousers, a white scarf tied casually around his neck, and a leather aviator hat with the flaps fastened under his chin. His eyes were hidden behind tinted goggles.

Awestruck, the children stared wide-eyed as he approached. They watched as he removed his hat and ran his hands through his red curls. His eyes twinkled as he smiled, "I just came from an air show in Moorefield. I was on my way to the next one when I saw your field and all the children playing. I couldn't resist landing to see if anyone wanted to go for a ride."

A chorus of, "Mommy, Mommy please, can I?" arose from the excited children. All the mothers, except Priscilla, hushed them with an emphatic, "No!"

Astonished eyes turned to Priscilla when she said, "Yes, Cecil. You and I are going for an airplane ride." Appalled, they tried to talk her out of it, telling her she needed to ask Burrel. "Ask Burrel!" she responded. "I'm not a child who has to ask permission! Cecil and I want to ride in an airplane, and I don't know when we'll get another chance. Why don't the rest of you try it? It'll be fun." Although some of them were tempted, their fear of the unknown held them back.

The pilot told her that though it was in the eighties on the ground, they would need to wear a jacket and hat. It could get pretty cold up there in an open cockpit. Priscilla looked in on June, who was sleeping, got herself and Cecil ready and, with him in tow, headed for the plane. As they settled into the seat behind the pilot, their audience on the ground looked glum, the children because they couldn't go and the women concerned that Priscilla was taking Cecil to a certain death.

After they taxied down the field and became airborne, the pilot flew over the house and tipped his wings to the group below. From Cecil and Priscilla's vantage point, everyone looked small, even Burrel and his tour group who were coming onto the field from the cavern exit. They looked up and waved.

The pilot asked Priscilla where she wanted to go. She told him she'd like to fly over Seneca Rocks. He'd given her the thumbs up sign, the aviator's universal signal of agreement. On the way to the rocks, Priscilla showed Cecil Pap's farm, the one room schoolhouse, the green willow dipped pool, the river and other farms in the area. As the plane flew over, the landscape was dotted with people coming out of their houses and barns to look up and wave.

The aviator, who had been flying low, gradually ascended until they were flying through the clouds. Laughing, he watched Cecil trying to wave away the mist. He then descended, leveled off, and turned to his passengers and pointed downward. They were flying over Seneca Rocks. He gave them the thumbs up sign and circled the rocks.

Priscilla hadn't dreamed, that day on their honeymoon in 1927 when Burrel had first shown her the rocks that she would ever soar above them. They were even more beautiful than she could have imagined. Gazing down at their jagged peaks and crevices, she could understand everyone's fascination with them. As they circled them one more time, she and Cecil happily returned the thumbs up sign.

When they returned home, they were met by a grim faced Burrel, who after he'd heard the forecast of doom from his sisters, had been worried for their safety. He was ready to tell Priscilla in no uncertain terms what he thought of her irresponsibility. Cecil's joyful cry of, "Dad, Dad, we went up in the airplane! It was so much fun!" and the happy look on Priscilla's face caused the words to die in his throat and his anger to dissolve.

They all chatted with the aviator for a few minutes before he had to leave for his next air show. After they watched him lift off, Burrel hoisted Cecil on his shoulders and arm in arm, he and Priscilla walked back to the house where the women and children were waiting.

She and Cecil had a rapt audience as they excitedly told what it was like to fly and how different everything looked from the air. The children were delighted when Cecil talked about flying through the clouds. Adults and children alike were enthralled with their accounts of Seneca Rocks from the air, none more so than Burrel who had climbed them.

For months Cecil talked about the flight and played he was an aviator. That year when his parents took him to see Santa Claus he told him he wanted a toy airplane for Christmas. Priscilla saved her money from selling eggs and made his wish come true. If they'd been able to look into the future, they'd have seen the adult Cecil as an air traffic controller guiding jet airplanes to a safe landing.

CHAPTER TWELVE

GHOST OR MISER?

Winter at the cavern was quiet. The doors were closed at the end of September and didn't reopen until the first of May. This didn't mean Priscilla and Burrel were idle though. They busied themselves with taking care of the chickens, cow, and pig they had bought. Priscilla made all the clothes for the children and herself. Burrel met with Walter Amos several times during the off season, sometimes traveling to Winchester, Virginia while other times Mr. Amos would come to their house. The two men spent hours pouring over the books and making plans for the next season.

Burrel had bought a radio, bringing Priscilla hours of pleasure with the daytime soap operas. They both enjoyed the country music, since they had met many of the entertainers when they had appeared at the cavern. Several times during the winter, they found themselves snowed in, and the radio became their link with the outside world. In the evening the entire family gathered in the living room. The adults, pulling their chairs close to the radio, listened to Lowell Thomas bringing them the news of the day, and to their favorite shows, Amos and Andy, Lum and Abner, and Fibber Magee and Molly. Cecil and June usually sat on the floor playing with their toys, sometimes listening and laughing along with their parents at the antics of the radio performers.

~

When the roads were passable, they would go see Pap or Burrel's brother and sisters. This was a treat for the children as, no matter where they went, there were cousins to play with. They especially loved to visit at their Aunt Calcie's because there were six children in the house. Garth, Bea, Maxine, and Gerald were all at the age where they were neither adults nor children. Sometimes they would play with the younger ones, but mostly, they pursued their own interests while Cecil and June played with Harman and Bonnie who were closer to their age.

Bonnie, always one of June's favorite cousins, was a warm, friendly girl with brown hair and laughing brown eyes. Harman was a good-looking boy with dark curly hair and a bright friendly smile like his father's. June and Bonnie and Cecil and Harman were not only cousins, but good friends who would play together for hours while the adults visited.

The house where Calcie and Gordon lived was full of large rooms and nooks and crannies where the children would indulge themselves in hours of make-believe. June wouldn't have enjoyed the make believe if she'd known then the nightmare this house had in store for her.

On bright sunny days it was pleasant, but on days when the sun hid behind clouds it had an eerie look and feel to it. This was partly because of the old man the family lived with, Ulysses's brother Lucus, Burrel and Calcie's Uncle Luke. The children had heard their parents talk about him and knew he was a miser, but no matter how hard they tried to listen, they couldn't find out what a miser was supposed to be. Sometimes the adults sounded amused when they mentioned Uncle Luke. Other times they'd say it was a sad case.

As they watched him, they decided that being a miser certainly couldn't be funny, as he never told jokes or funny stories like their Uncle Verde or smiled and laughed like other grownups they knew. They decided a miser must be a ghost, because only a ghost could move through the rooms without making a sound and seem to disappear into his surroundings the way Uncle Luke did.

Cecil and June would watch, wide-eyed as the family sat at the dinner table with this tall gaunt shadow of a man. Amazed at his lack of table manners, they figured table manners must not apply to ghosts, as no one said anything to him when he reached across the table and ate from the serving bowls. They knew that if they'd done that, they'd have been in big trouble.

On the way home as June slept in the back seat, Cecil asked, "Dad, what is a miser?"

"A miser?" Burrel asked. "Where did you hear that word?"

"I heard you and Mom talking about Uncle Luke being a miser. We thought a miser was a ghost."

Priscilla turned to Burrel and laughingly said, "I guess we need to realize little pitchers have big ears."

Cecil heard the chuckle in his dad's voice, as he said, "Son, Uncle Luke isn't a ghost. He's just a man, like I am. He's your grandpap's brother."

"I know, Dad, but what is a miser?" Cecil continued.

"We're home now," Priscilla said, turning Cecil's attention from his questions about Uncle Luke. "It's time for you and June to go to bed. We'll talk about it later."

It was years before June and Cecil were able to solve the puzzle of Uncle Luke. They were able to piece together some of it from conversations they overheard and the rest from what their father told them when they were older.

~

It seems that from the time Luke Harman was a little boy, he loved money. He loved the sight, the feel, the color, and the smell of money. This love wasn't for what it would buy him. He loved it for itself.

As he grew to be a man, possessing money became an obsession with him. He had worked hard and bought a large farm as his means of getting money. The farm was soon stocked with cows, sheep, pigs, and chickens. In his fields he planted wheat, alfalfa, and corn. The farm produced a good income for him, but he couldn't bring himself to spend any of it, except as a means of accumulating more money.

After he bought the farm, he started courting a beautiful neighbor girl. Falling in love with her, he planned to ask her to marry him, but every time he started to propose, the words seemed to stick in his throat. One night, after this again happened, he walked home with his mind in turmoil. He loved this girl, didn't he? He wanted to spend the rest of his life with her, didn't he? What was holding him back? Why couldn't he ask her to marry him?

When he got home, he pulled his rocking chair up by the kitchen stove. As he sat rocking, engulfed by the warmth of the stove, he gave the situation some serious thought. If he married her, he would have to support her. How much would that cost him? She always wore pretty dresses and had ribbons in her hair, and her tantalizing scent must come from an expensive bottle. If they got married, she'd still want to buy pretty dresses, and gewgaws for her hair and maybe even perfume. His eyes widened in horror when he realized she'd be buying all those things with his money!

He'd never bought anything for a woman and had no idea what the prices might be. As he continued to rock back and forth considering his dilemma, tiny beads of sweat formed on his brow as he muttered under his breath, "I'd better be finding out what this is going to cost me."

With this thought in mind he moved from his rocking chair, picked up the Sears and Roebuck catalogue and flipped through it until he came to the section filled with women's clothing. As he slowly turned the pages, his eyes took on a glazed look as he looked at the prices.

With the catalogue open on his lap he spent the night sitting by the stove in his rocking chair weighing his love for the young neighbor against his love for his money. As the cold light of dawn crept into the room, he slowly closed the book, stood up and walked to the barn to take care of the animals. His decision had been made. His love of money had won!

From then on, he would entice family members to live with him; the women to take care of the house, the garden and the small animals while the men would help him work the farm. In exchange for this he would provide their room and board, a dollar a day and the promise that everything would be theirs when he died.

Calcie and Gordon's family had been one of several who had tried this arrangement, but like all the ones who came after them, they couldn't tolerate his personal habits and miserly ways so they left after a short period of time. Years later, when Luke Harman died, the money was not to be found. The stories were that he had buried it somewhere on the farm. The family who was living with him when he died inherited the farm, but they have always been silent about what happened to the money.

There have been rumors of lights shining in the woods and fields surrounding the house in the dead of night, and evidence of freshly turned dirt, as if someone had been digging for hidden treasure. No one really knows whether the money lies rotting in the ground somewhere on the farm, or whether it was turned over to his nephew before he died. There are even those who think, as much as he loved it, he might have found a way to take it with him.

CHAPTER THIRTEEN

A TOUCH OF MAGIC

In this year of 1932, there were too many things going on in Burrel and Priscilla's world to give much thought to Uncle Luke. Priscilla was expecting their third child in September. Burrel was busy with the activities at the cavern. Since they had discovered, it took more than the lure of the cavern to entice people to spend their depression dollars, he and Walter Amos had booked several entertainment acts for the summer, including a small carnival.

One morning Cecil and June woke to the sound of happy music winging its way into their rooms. It wasn't the familiar country music their parents played on the radio, but very special music, made for the child in all of us. They jumped from their beds and ran downstairs and into the kitchen where Priscilla was standing by the stove stirring their oatmeal.

"Mom, Mom what is it?" they exclaimed, almost in unison. Priscilla turned, her face wreathed in smiles, and said, "Let's go see!"

They followed her, almost tripping over each other in their excitement. When they reached the front porch, they stopped and stared in amazement. There, practically in their own front yard, was a merry-go-round, its bright colored horses whirling around and around and up and down. The horses' heads were thrown back, and their mouths were wide open as if they were caught up in the excitement of the music.

June stood still, mesmerized by this magical apparition that had sprung up in her yard while she slept. Cecil, being older, tried to hide his own excitement as he turned to June and said, "It's a merry-go-round. I rode on one last summer at Buckeye Lake."

June looked at her brother, and sighed, "You rode it?" Then turning to her mother and with her voice still filled with wonder, asked, "Mom, can we? Can we ride the horses?"

Priscilla picked her up, hugged her and said, "Of course you can. We're going to have our breakfast now. Then we'll all go down and take a ride."

This was too much for Cecil. He couldn't play the uninterested older brother any longer. "Wow! We're all going to ride. You, too, Mom?"

"Yes, me too." Priscilla replied. "If we coax him, I bet we can get your dad to ride with us."

Cecil dashed upstairs and came down wearing his toy holsters and six shooters slung low on his hips. If he were going to ride a wild horse, he needed to be prepared for any bad guys they might encounter. A cowpoke never knew when he might need to protect his women folk.

The music had stopped and the horses were standing still when the little group made their way to the bottom of the hill. June looked at her mother with tears starting to well up in her eyes. Before they could spill down her cheeks, Priscilla reassured her. "Don't worry, Honey. They'll start up again. The men were checking out the merry-go-round to be sure everything was in working order. They'll turn it on again so we can get on. Your dad talked to them about us riding before anyone else gets here."

Just then Burrel arrived with the operator. "Ready to go for a gallop?" he asked.

Without answering, Cecil scrambled aboard and raced for a fierce looking steed he immediately claimed as his own. June held back, suddenly feeling shy.

"Come on," Burrel said, picking her up and placing her on a gentler looking creature. Priscilla sat, sidesaddle, on a horse along side of Cecil while Burrel stood beside June's horse. Then the operator threw the switch, the music started, lights flashed, and the horses began their merry trek round and round the ring.

Cecil was lost in his world of cowboys and bad men. June looked up into her father's eyes, her blue eyes sparkling, and her blond hair flying. Riding on the merry-go-round was wonderful, but having her dad standing there, as if to protect her, made it perfect.

Looking at his wife's face, as full of excitement as the children's, Burrel again thought, "I'm really a lucky man with Priscilla and the children and this job at the cavern." Sometimes he was so happy, it frightened him.

As the week went by the children went for several more rides before the carrousel was dismantled and taken away, but none matched the excitement and wonder of the first.

Before the last two horses were hoisted onto the truck, Priscilla took a picture of June and Cecil sitting on their favorite steeds. Later when they looked at the pictures, the serious faces of a blonde little girl and blonde little boy looked back at them. Though they had been sad, saying their last goodbye to their friends, the memories stayed with them for a long time to come.

CHAPTER FOURTEEN

COUNTING THEIR BLESSINGS

In the evenings during late summer and early fall, Burrel and Priscilla along with millions of other Americans listened to the radio for news of the upcoming election. A political dynamo named Franklin Delano Roosevelt had appeared on the scene. He was running for president against President Hoover, promising a "new deal" for everyone. He quoted statistics showing that one-fourth the country's wage earners were unemployed. Families on relief received less than 75 cents a week for food, and farmers were desperate because of low crop prices. His strong voice with its upper New York accent inspired confidence, as he promised to enact programs that would bring relief to everyone. Burrel, loyal to President Hoover and skeptical that any one man could solve the country's ills, felt it was unfair to blame Hoover for all the nation's problems.

Also occupying the news was the investigation of the kidnapping and murder of the infant son of the country's much loved and respected aviation hero, Charles Lindbergh. "Lucky Lindy" as he was called by the American people, had fueled the country's interest in aviation by being the first person to fly non-stop from New York to Paris. He had received a hero's welcome in Paris, then again when he returned to New York.

The Harman family had followed with much interest his courtship and marriage to Anne Morrow, the birth of their son Charles Augustus Lindbergh Junior, and now in sadness and horror the news of the kidnapping and murder.

In March while the baby was sleeping, an unknown person had placed a ladder against the second story nursery window, crept so quietly into the room, that neither the parents nor the nursemaid heard a sound as the baby was taken from his crib and from their lives forever.

This real life drama had been played out on the radio, newsreels, and newspapers for months in 1932, as the news came of the ransom demand and payment. Then to everyone's horror, the baby's lifeless body was found only yards from where he had been kidnapped.

As Burrel and Priscilla and millions of American parents followed the reports of the investigation, they held their own children close and for once could find a reason to be glad that they were neither rich nor famous.

It would be nearly 4 years later in April of 1936 before the final chapter was written and the case closed with the conviction and execution of Bruno Richard Hauptmann for the kidnapping and murder. Damning evidence had been found that linked him to the ladder that had been left behind at the scene and to the ransom note.

No one, ever again, thought of Charles Lindbergh as "Lucky Lindy."

While the events taking place in the country aroused the interest of the people, an important event was taking place in Burrel and Priscilla's life. One week after Priscilla's twenty-second birthday, she gave birth to her third child, a boy, in the bedroom she and Burrel shared at the house by the cavern. Though this birth and confinement lacked the drama of their trip to the farm and Cecil's early birth or the hasty departure from Pap's during a snowstorm with newborn baby June, it still had its dramatic moments.

When Doctor Harman placed her new son in her arms, Priscilla was overwhelmed with love for this red faced crying infant. Burrel, hearing the lusty cry, tentatively opened the door and peeked into the room. Seeing him, Doctor Harman heartily called out, "Come in, come in. You have a son!"

Burrel glanced at the doctor, but he only had eyes for Priscilla and the baby. She looked tired, but her eyes were full of joy as she nestled this little one close to her breast. "Isn't he beautiful?" Priscilla asked, as she looked first at the baby, then at Burrel.

"You are both beautiful," he replied. "What do you think of him as a late birthday present?"

"This is the best birthday present I've ever had," she sighed. "Do you want to hold him?" she asked.

Burrel reached down and gathered his new son in his arms. Smiling, he held him the way Rhoda had shown him four years ago when she had placed Cecil in his reluctant arms. As if she sensed what he was thinking, she said, "Wouldn't Mom love him?"

"Wouldn't she?" he replied. Then after a silence he continued, "I was just thinking about my mom. She would have loved him, too."

Looking at the sleeping baby and catching Priscilla trying to hide a yawn, Burrel whispered, "I am going to put the baby here beside you, so you can both get some sleep. I'll be back later with June and Cecil." By the time he had tiptoed across the room and softly closed the door, Priscilla had joined the baby in much deserved slumber.

~

Standing by the wall phone in the dining room, he cranked out two long and two short rings to call his sister-in-law, Josie, to let her know the baby was here. She had been keeping Cecil and June while Priscilla was in labor. She told him they were sleeping, but that she would bring them home the next morning.

True to her word, bright and early the next morning she brought the two excited children home. Burrel's oldest sister, Calcie, who was taking care of Priscilla and the baby, was almost bowled over by blond whirlwinds that burst through the front door and were making their way to their mother's room before she caught them.

"Whoa!" she said as she held a squirming child in each arm. "Where do you think you are going?" she laughingly asked.

"We're going to see our new brother," Cecil yelled.

"Yeah, we're going to see our new brother," June echoed.

Calcie sat in Priscilla's rocking chair and pulled both children onto her ample lap while she explained, "Your mother is tired and may be sleeping. I'll go see. If she is awake, you can both go up and see her. For now, though, you have to wait right here."

It was a mystery to them why having a baby would make their mother tired. After all, everyone knew that the doctor brought the baby in his little black bag.

They knew this to be true because the day before the doctor had arrived carrying "the bag", their dad had hustled them off to visit their cousins, Irene, Idis, and Ruthalene. "You'll have a little brother or sister when you get home. Now run along and play with your cousins." Sometimes grownups can act pretty mysterious.

In a few minutes, their Aunt Calcie returned, her face bathed in smiles as she said, "Your mom is awake and so is your brother. They're both anxious to see you. Let me comb your hair before you go upstairs," she said as she tried to comb a squirming Cecil's cowlick.

Just then, Burrel came in the kitchen door carrying a pail of milk he had just gotten from Bessie, their cow. Turning to Calcie he asked if they'd seen the baby yet. When she said they hadn't, he said, "Give me a minute while I wash up. I want to be there when they see the little fellow."

In a few minutes, with Burrel leading the way, the little family quietly entered the bedroom. Both children looked in awe at their mother lying in bed, holding the new baby.

"He's so little," Cecil said. He'd thought he'd have a little brother to play with. It was going to be a long time before this one would be able to play cowboys and Indians.

"He is little!" June whispered, thinking how wonderful it was going to be, having a little baby in the house she could hold and love.

Priscilla looked at Burrel and smiled at her older children's reaction to their baby brother. She had been worried they might be jealous, but they didn't appear to be.

"What's his name?" Cecil asked.

"His name?" Priscilla and Burrel responded in unison. They had talked about names, but hadn't definitely decided on one. Priscilla wanted to name him Richard after a favorite uncle of hers and Burrel favored Marion. Before their visit was over the baby was named Richard Marion Harman. Cecil didn't have any trouble pronouncing this name as he had Mildred, but he was glad when he heard the baby was going to be called Dickie.

The family soon settled into its normal routine. June acted like a mother hen as she hovered over the baby, getting in her mother's way with her constant, "Mom can I help? Mom, let me do it." Cecil was another matter. He was impatiently waiting for this "littlest Harman," as he'd heard his dad call the baby, get big enough to play.

CHAPTER FIFTEEN
THE VISITOR

November 8, 1932, Election Day, finally arrived. Priscilla and Burrel bundled the children in their winter clothes and drove the three miles to Riverton where they hopefully cast their votes for Herbert Hoover. Before going home, they stopped at Kissamore's General Store where they bought supplies and ice cream cones for June and Cecil. There were three flavors to choose from; vanilla, chocolate and strawberry. What a big decision to make! Both children took their time deciding. Cecil wasn't always predictable, sometimes he'd choose one flavor and other times another, but with June it was almost always strawberry.

Once Mr. Kissamore placed the cone in their eager hands, they would see which one could make their cone last the longest. Since ice cream was a rare treat, they savored every lick or bite.

As Priscilla and Burrel listened to the radio it became evident early in the evening that Herbert Hoover was not going to be reelected. Later reports confirmed it. A seven million vote landslide had elected Franklin Delano Roosevelt.

Over the breakfast table the next morning, Burrel muttered, "I just hope he does what he said he would." Priscilla looked at his disappointed face and gave him a reassuring pat on the shoulder before returning her attention to the bacon and eggs she was cooking.

Knowing how serious Burrel was about politics, it seemed prudent not to respond. She hoped this new president "FDR," as the radio announcer called him, might be good for the country. "Time will tell," she thought, as she placed a steaming plate of bacon and eggs before him.

Conditions worsened between the time FDR was elected and when he took office on March 4, 1933. Thousands of banks failed as depositors, afraid of losing their savings, withdrew all their money causing a run on the banks.

In his inaugural address, words of encouragement rang out as he pronounced, "The only thing we have to fear is fear itself." The American people weren't too sure of this, as one of FDR's first acts was to call a special session of Congress to enact emergency banking procedures. One of these was to close all the banks to prevent further collapses and to establish the Federal Deposit Insurance Corporations to protect depositors' money.

This action was too little and too late for Burrel and Priscilla and thousands of other depositors who had money in the failed banks. Over a period of years they were paid back pennies on the dollar. Although they hadn't had a large amount of money in the bank, it did represent all their savings. The loss was monumental to them. It was to be a long time before people, who lived through the depression, learned to trust banks. Some never did.

～

This, and other news of the depression, was overshadowed by a letter from Harvey saying he would like to take them up on their long-standing invitation to visit. He missed his youngest daughter and her husband, hadn't seen his newest grandchild, and was looking forward to getting reacquainted with Cecil and June.

As the little family piled into the car for the trip to the train station, it was hard for Burrel to tell who was the most excited, Priscilla or the children.

It was so unusual for the children to see a train, that combined with the thrill of hearing the whistle and watching it chug into the station, they were jumping up and down with excitement by the time their grandfather stepped onto the platform.

"Is this all for me?" Harvey asked as Priscilla and the children rushed to greet him. Holding Dickie, Burrel stood back, waiting, giving Priscilla and the children a chance to welcome Harvey before he stepped forward, extending his hand in greeting. Shaking hands and enthusiastically slapping each other on the back, they engaged in the age-old male greeting ritual, expressing their pleasure at again being together.

Leaving the station, Burrel drove to a small cafe where they had lunch before going home. Properly impressed by the new addition to the family, the proud grandfather expressed what Priscilla and Burrel had been thinking, "I wish your mother could be here." Tears sprang into Priscilla's eyes as she heard the raw sound of pain and loneliness in her father's voice. Seeing the tears, he reached across the table, patted her hand and smiled reassuringly. For an instant, Priscilla again felt herself to be Daddy's little girl. She felt better.

The visit was a joyous occasion, with the first few days spent catching up on what had been happening in their lives. This was Harvey's first trip to West Virginia and the first time he had ever been in a cavern.

All Burrel's family came to meet him. He liked everyone, especially Ulysses with whom he had a great deal in common, most importantly their love for this young family. They spent many hours together spinning yarns about Burrel and Priscilla as youngsters.

The children loved listening to these stories, much more than their parents did. Sometimes, either their mother or father would try to shush the tale-bearing grandfather, to no avail. Whichever grandfather was telling the story would only chuckle and say, "It doesn't hurt for your kids to know you weren't always grownup, or perfect, for that matter." The chagrined parent would have to grin and bear it.

～

Many conversations took place around the dinner table. Most of them concerned politics and this young "whippersnapper" in the White House.

"I'm not sure whether Roosevelt is running the country or making alphabet soup," Burrel declared one evening as they were lingering over their coffee and a piece of Priscilla's homemade apple pie. "He's got the WPA, the TVA, the NRA, the CCC and the AAA. I don't know how many more he's coming up with."

Pap, who was an avid listener to his crystal radio set, shook his head as he responded, "I don't know what to think about what he's doing. That CCC is good for the young men who can't find jobs. Johnny, down the road from us, has joined. His dad says he really likes it. They wear uniforms and live in barracks. It sounds a lot like being in the army."

Priscilla chimed in, "The work they're doing, planting trees and working on the roads, needs to be done."

"It's good because otherwise these boys wouldn't have anything to do." Harvey agreed. "Even though I sold the store, I still stop in now and then to talk to some of the fellows. When Roosevelt first started talking about the AAA, farmers who came in thought he was crazy. Whoever heard of being paid not to grow something? It must work, though. Priscilla's Aunt Em's husband, John, has agreed not to plant on several of his acres. The government has already sent him a check."

Ulysses added, "Some of the folks around here are already involved. Verde and I are looking into it for the farm. I heard Lowell Thomas on the radio last night. He said by cutting back on production, it will make us more competitive with other countries and increase the prices farmers can get for their crops."

The children's ears had perked up at the mention of the President making alphabet soup, but after listening awhile, and hearing no more about it, they lost interest. Asking to be excused, they slipped from their places at the table and busied themselves with their own world of make-believe.

This wouldn't be the last time they would hear the adults around them discuss the changes FDR was making and the impact they were having on the country. Many times they were to hear their dad say, as he was saying now, "There is no way one man can cure all the ills of the country." No one knew, that night, in the house above the cavern, how right Burrel's statement was. Nor did they know that the little boy playing in the other room would be a teenager before the great depression was finally over, or that it would take a world war to end it.

~

As the dark clouds of winter were replaced by the sunny skies of spring, Priscilla delighted in being able to share with her father the emerging beauty around them. The apple trees were in bloom with fragrant blossoms. The forest in back of the cavern exit was dotted with spring flowers peeking from under the carpet of leaves covering the ground.

Priscilla, Harvey, Cecil, and June would stroll around the grounds absorbing the smell, sights and sounds of spring. June loved to walk beside her grandfather, with her small hand completely enveloped in his, as they ambled through the field next to the house.

This field was June's favorite outdoor spot in the entire world. This was where she and Cecil rode their sleds in the winter, rode their scooters and tricycles the rest of the year, and where they'd play a wicked game of tag when their cousins came to visit. Herself, as a little girl, walking in this field she loved, her small hand engulfed in her grandfather's was all she was to remember of this last spring she was to spend with this very important person in her life.

CHAPTER SIXTEEN

JOSIAH

A few days before Harvey returned to Newark, the family was enjoying a quiet evening at home. Priscilla with Dickie on her lap sat next to Burrel on the porch swing. They were flanked, on each side by Harvey and Ulysses, sitting in sturdy rockers as they watched June stretch her tiny legs skyward, moving, back and forth, higher and higher on the long rope swing Burrel had hung from the branches of the tall pine tree in the front yard. "I believe that girl is trying to touch the clouds," Burrel remarked.

"As determined as she is, she'll probably make it if she sets her mind to it," Priscilla responded with a sigh.

"As I remember, you were pretty determined yourself," Harvey remarked.

"So was Burrel," Ulysses added, "I'll never forget how upset his mother was when he first started exploring caves, but there was no stopping him."

Priscilla and Burrel exchanged glances as if to say, "At least the children didn't hear them this time." It could be difficult enough being parents, without having your juvenile shortcomings pointed out to your children.

These thoughts were interrupted by Clyde and Cecil's cries of "Giddy up, giddy up!" as astride their stick horses they galloped into view.

"Whoa!" they shouted in unison, as abandoning their make believe mounts, they scrambled up the steps onto the porch. Even at their breakneck speed they'd noticed the adults were drinking lemonade and eating some of the cookies Cecil's mom had baked that afternoon.

As they started to fill their hands and mouths with the delicious morsels, Priscilla said, "Not until you wash your hands. While you're in the kitchen, bring out some more glasses for your lemonade and while you're at it, bring one for June, too. She looks like she's about through swinging for now."

Harvey's eyes moved about, as if filing away mental pictures of this scene. First he watched Priscilla refasten a strand of hair loosened by the gentle breeze, then Burrel getting up to hook the porch gate so he could put Dickie down to crawl around. As his eyes followed the movement, June joined them on the porch, and sat down on the porch floor where she watched over the baby like a mother hen.

While, like a movie camera, Harvey's eyes continued to scan the panoramic view of the peaceful valley stretched out below them, the adults continued to talk companionably as they watched the children. June taking a bite, then offering one to Dickie, the boys each trying to see who could cram the most into his mouth. "One at a time, boys," Burrel chided as he moved the plate from their reach.

Harvey's mind's eye focused in on the view closer at hand, the bandstand, the office, the cavern entrance and the field where the children loved to play. His eyes came to rest on the gently moving swing, so recently abandoned by his granddaughter.

∼

"You don't realize how lucky you are," he murmured softly, as though talking more to himself than his audience.

"What did you say, Dad?" Priscilla asked.

"I was just thinking out loud, I guess." Harvey responded. "The older I get, the more I think about the past. I couldn't help compare your children's life here with you and Burrel, with what mine was like growing up after the war without a father."

What came to mind for people in the thirties when the word war was mentioned was the World War that had ended in 1918, when Priscilla was eight years old and Burrel fifteen. Harvey, being seventy-one himself certainly wasn't talking about that war.

All Burrel had to say was, "After the war?" to start Harvey talking about the one that had cost him his father.

"It was the Civil War," Harvey said. "You know, I don't know about it personally, but I have heard my mother, my aunt and some of the others who lived to come home talk about it so many times that I almost feel I was there."

"I was a baby, younger than Dickie, when my dad, Josiah Glancy, and his sister Sarah's boy, John Sullivan, were mustered into the army. This was in May of 1864. Abraham Lincoln was president. At that time, a lot of men in Licking County were caught up in a patriotic fever, wanting to save the Union and free the slaves. Dad and John were part of a group of one hundred men who joined up and left for what was to be a hundred day stint in the army."

"Mom always said they'd marched off with their eyes ablaze with enthusiasm, like war was a game they were going to play." Harvey sighed as he continued, "They just had no idea what they were getting into."

By now he had the rapt attention of his audience. They waited anxiously while he took a sip of lemonade before proceeding. "They couldn't have had much training, because within a week they left for Cumberland, Maryland with a regiment of eight hundred men. Then a short time later, some of the men were sent to protect Martinsburg, West Virginia and the rest to nearby North Mountain. Dad was in the group sent to North Mountain."

"On July third of that year, the town of Martinsburg was attacked. The officer in charge, who the history books say was a master at retreat, ordered the men to evacuate. This left the men at North Mountain on their own. When they were attacked by the rebels, they weren't aware that the rest of their troops had pulled out. Bravely, they fought for five hours, though they were outnumbered fifty to one. They neither had a chance to win or to escape, especially after the Confederate general ordered the bridge at Back Creek burned. This cut them off completely. All the surviving men were taken prisoner that day, including my dad and his nephew John."

He paused for a moment, as if overcome by the horror of what he was about to relate, then continued, "They were herded together like animals and taken to a prison camp at Andersonville, Georgia. Those who lived to tell about it said it was worse than hell on earth. From everything I've heard, hell would have been a picnic, in comparison. Remember, this was July. July in Ohio is hot enough, but nothing compared to the Georgia heat. Add to the heat the fact that they had thirty-three thousand men crowded into thirteen acres."

"Thirteen acres?" Pap exclaimed. "Why, that's only enough room for a few cows or a small flock of sheep!"

"You're right," Harvey responded. "There was hardly room for anyone to move around. I guess, a man would have to turn sideways to walk around at all."

"That wasn't the worst of it. The only water they had to drink was from a stream that ran through the pen, and the waste from the camps upstream polluted it. Their only food was corn meal with the corn and cob ground together. Once in awhile their capturers would throw in a few beans, but never any meat. This caused the worse cramps anyone can imagine."

His audience could hardly believe what they were hearing, but they nodded for him to continue.

"Can you imagine the shock this must have been to my dad and John? Here my dad was, a strong healthy thirty-four year old farmer and John was a farm boy of seventeen. They'd been used to the clean country air, fresh cool well water, and hearty country foods. Here, they were completely cut off from the outside world. They couldn't see or smell anything except the filth and stench inside the pen. Everywhere, they were surrounded by pitiful, starving men, many in the final stages of death."

"The whole pen was encircled by a log fence, twenty feet high with the logs sunk in the ground five feet deep. This was so the prisoners couldn't climb over them or tunnel under them. Some men had tried to scale the fence, but they had been caught and severely punished. The guards had then pounded stakes in the ground twenty feet in from the fence and warned the men that if they even touched one of those stakes they would be shot on the spot. Without a single shot being fired, one out of three prisoners who entered the prison died. In September 1864, over ninety men died each day. One of these was Dad's nephew John Sullivan." He sighed sadly before adding, "He was only seventeen years old."

"John Winder, the commissary general of prisoners bragged for all to hear, that with the death that month, of three thousand and eighty men, he had done more for the Confederacy than twenty regiments."

"Dad was so sick he could hardly walk when he was transferred that month to another prison in Charleston, South Carolina and the next month to Columbia, also in South Carolina. John McDonnel, a man who knew Dad before the war, saw him in that prison and was shocked at his emaciated appearance."

"He was so weak and coughing so hard he could hardly talk. Even though he was only thirty-four years old, Mr. McDonnel said he looked like a man of ninety. A camp doctor examined him and found one lung so bad it was almost gone."

"In this weak condition they made him sign a paper that he would never again bare arms against his enemies. He signed it and was sent home in time for Christmas of 1864. Mom and Doctor Caleb Linn did all they could for him. Mom said she tried to feed him the foods he loved, but his poor stomach couldn't tolerate them. The doctor said all they could do was love and comfort him."

"Mom always said she and the children did that for the pitiful time he had left. He died on January ninth, less than a month after his thirty-fifth birthday, seven months and a day after he had so enthusiastically set out to save the Union."

Harvey's eyes were moist when he added, "The doctor said he died of typhoid pneumonia, brought on by the horrible treatment he had received during the sixty days he was at Andersonville prison camp."

"My mom was left to raise five young children alone. The government awarded her a widow's pension of eight dollars a month. With this and the food we could raise on the farm, we survived, but there were times it was barely survival."

Priscilla could see the vestiges of the lonely little boy in her father's eyes as he again sighed deeply before going on, "Being poor wasn't the worse part. Growing up without a father was."

"My brothers and sisters were lucky, though. They were old enough to remember Dad. Laura was thirteen, Olivia eleven, Lawrence seven and Richard five. It has always made me feel bad that I was too young to know him at all."

~

When Harvey concluded his story, Priscilla, a sob in her voice and tears running down her cheeks, put her arms around her dad and held him close. "Oh, Dad, I knew your dad had died from what happened to him in the war, but I never really thought about how awful it was for him and for you."

It was obvious that Pap was visibly moved when he stood up, put his hand on Harvey's shoulder and said, "It's almost impossible for me to realize people could be so cruel to other human beings."

"How could they? How could anyone treat anyone that way?" Burrel demanded, looking angry enough to take on a few Confederates himself.

Nodding grimly, Harvey continued, "People both in the North and South were sickened when they heard about the horrible things that had happened to the men at Andersonville. As I understand it, though, of all the officers in charge, only the commandant of the prison's interior, Captain Henry Wirtz, was court-martialed, found guilty and hanged. We can just hope nothing like this will ever happen again," Harvey declared.

As he recounted the horrors of seventy years ago, he was unaware of the reign of terror waiting in the wings, a continent and less than a decade away. The holocaust was yet to come.

~

Harvey's story stayed in their minds and in their conversation for the next few days, but they had to turn their attention to his impending departure.

The few days passed quickly and much too soon it was time to take him to the station. This time, it was not as much fun as when he'd arrived. They had enjoyed having him around and hated to see him go.

To June's little ears, the rhythm of the wheels, as the train came toward them, seemed to be saying, "It's time to go. It's time to go." June and Priscilla had tears in their eyes as Harvey enfolded them in a bear hug before climbing aboard the train. Burrel and Cecil claimed the moisture in their eyes was from the smoke and cinders spewing from the engine as it left the station.

Standing on the platform, the little group watched until the train was out of sight, and they could no longer hear the lonely sound of the whistle. As Burrel observed the sad droop of Priscilla's shoulders, he said, "Don't worry, honey, we'll be going to Ohio to visit. We'll see him again soon."

"I know, but every time we say goodbye to him, I'm afraid it will be the last," she replied. "I'll be all right. It's just that sometimes I really miss my family."

"We'll visit them, and I'm sure they'll come to see us," Burrel reassured her, although he could feel his heart sink with each word she uttered. He had been sure she was happy here. Now he wondered.

CHAPTER SEVENTEEN

CLOUDS ON THE HORIZON

Before 1933 was over, the news coming from Lowell Thomas on the radio was about the repeal of Prohibition. Since 1920 when an amendment had been added to the Constitution prohibiting the sale or consumption of alcoholic beverages, the country had been equally divided in support or opposition to the amendment and now to its repeal, as were Burrel and Priscilla.

Burrel could see nothing wrong with having a drink and Priscilla was morally opposed to it. According to her religious beliefs, drinking alcoholic beverages was a mortal sin. Though surprised by the strength of her convictions, Burrel was not seriously concerned.

The first time he came home with alcohol on his breath, he discovered he should have been. He hadn't given Priscilla's beliefs a thought when on his way back from a weeklong spelunking trip, he and Walter Amos had stopped at a restaurant in Petersburg and each had a couple shots of whiskey with their meal.

Back at the cavern Priscilla, June, and Cecil had spent the day preparing for his homecoming. Priscilla had let the children stay up past their bedtime to welcome him home. With a pitcher of lemonade and a coconut cake waiting in the pantry, they were ready for his welcome home party. When they heard the car stop by the side of the house, the children ran to the door. Priscilla stood back, letting the children clamber over him, knowing she'd have the rest of the evening for them to be alone.

Any thought of a welcome was gone, though, when he leaned over and kissed her. "What is that smell?" she asked.

"Smell? What smell?" was Burrel's puzzled response.

"That smell. Your breath," Priscilla frostily replied. "You've been drinking. Haven't you?"

Burrel's mind was racing. On one hand, he'd known how she felt about drinking, but on the other hand, he hadn't expected this reaction.

"I'm sorry, Honey," he said, trying to placate her by putting his arm around her. "Walter and I stopped in Petersburg for dinner. We only had a couple drinks."

"I don't care how many drinks you had. Drinking is a sin. You know how I feel about it, but you went ahead and did it anyway," she responded, furiously pulling away from him.

June and Cecil were staring wide-eyed at their parents. This wasn't normal behavior in their house. Dickie, sitting in his high chair, started to cry. Aware of their audience, they exchanged a "not in front of the children" look before Priscilla picked up the baby and quieted his tears.

Although, she was coldly silent as she served the cake and lemonade, Burrel thought he'd be able to thaw her out later in their room, but he was sadly mistaken.

CHAPTER EIGHTEEN

THE ONE ROOM SCHOOLHOUSE

Nineteen hundred thirty-four, the year he started school, was a big year in Cecil's life. His face freshly scrubbed, his hair combed and his lunch box and book bag in his hand, he joined his cousins, Irene and Idis, for the long trek through the woods and fields to Germany Valley's one room schoolhouse.

The weathered frame building was nestled among the trees with a clearing to the side for the flag pole and play yard. The teacher, Miss Lily, was a pretty young woman. Her large wooden desk dominated the front of the room with the pot-bellied stove competing for space. Covering a large portion of the wall in back of the teacher's desk was a long blackboard, equipped with a fresh supply of erasers and white and pastel colored chalk. Rows of desks facing the front of the room were filled with fresh-faced boys and girls.

Miss Lily had the difficult job of instilling knowledge in these first through eighth graders. Cecil was the only one in the first grade and Clyde the only second grader. This wasn't to Miss Lily's liking, as she had to prepare lessons for each grade. Before the middle of the school year, she managed to rectify the situation by moving Cecil into the second grade. Fortunately he was a bright student, and the arrangement worked well for both of them.

The social life of the neighborhood revolved around the schoolhouse. There were box suppers like the one Burrel and Priscilla had attended in Ohio. Burrel beamed with pleasure when he related the story to the children of the box supper social and how he had outbid the other young men to win her meal and later her heart.

Other activities at the schoolhouse were spelling bees which would bring out proud parents from miles around, who would sit in the small, uncomfortable seats, beaming at their young geniuses as they carefully spelled out words the parents had never before heard.

Cecil, June, and Dickie, too young for these activities, were looking forward to the Christmas party! For weeks at the supper table, Cecil had been regaling them with tales about the preparations. Some of the kids were making chains out of popcorn, cranberries or construction paper loops while others were coloring and cutting out angels to hang on the tree.

As he talked about the tree that had been cut and placed in the corner, the red and green wreaths Miss Lily had hung in the windows, and the fresh smelling greenery she and the bigger students were looping around the room, June had only to close her eyes to find herself in the midst of all these activities. His words painted such vivid pictures, she and Dickie could hardly wait for the big night!

His eyes sparkled when he imparted his most important piece of news. "Santa Claus is coming! He's coming in his sleigh! Miss Lily said he's going to have a horse pull it so his reindeer can rest for Christmas."

Saving the best for last, he paused dramatically before adding, "And he's going to give each kid a bag of candy and an orange!"

"Even if we don't go to school yet?" June asked.

Cecil from his lofty position as a second grader looked down his nose at her as if to say, "Don't you know anything?" before replying, "Sure, Santa Claus wouldn't leave little kids out."

Though June thought it never would, the big day finally arrived! Even more exciting than she had expected, the schoolhouse was full of people of all ages. Grandpap, all the aunts and uncles and cousins were there along with all their friends and neighbors. The only one missing was Uncle Verde who didn't show up until after Santa Claus had come and gone.

Miss Lily's battered desk had been shoved under the blackboard against the wall. The long table next to it was soon covered with plates and bowls of food as each family unpacked its baskets of goodies. Someone, probably Miss Lily, had used colored chalk to draw a jolly looking Santa Claus on the blackboard, but what June found most fascinating was the wall mounted kerosene lamps with their golden lights glowing softly against the pewter reflectors behind them. They, along with the candles, provided the only illumination within the room.

The sound of horses hooves and the jingling of sleigh bells brought screams of, "Santa Claus, Santa Claus!" from every child in the room. As they watched in wide-eyed wonder, the door was flung open and Santa Claus burst into the room, brushing snow from his red suit. His deep voice boomed the words, "Have you all been good little girls and boys?"

He was answered by a chorus of, "Yes! Yes!"

"Since you've all been good, I won't have to give out any of these switches, will I?" Santa asked with a smile.

"No Santa, no!" they assured him.

"If that's the case, I guess I'll give out these bags of treats. Does that sound good to you?"

"Yes, yes!" was the roof raising response.

"Mommies," he instructed, "let's get them lined up, the little ones first."

Seeing that Dickie was the youngest, other than babes in arms, June saw to it he was first in line.

Noticing, Santa said to June, "He's a little one. Maybe you should stay with your little brother." June beamed from ear to ear as Santa put the first sack in Dickie's little hands and the second in hers. She couldn't believe she not only had her own bag of candy, but a sweet juicy orange. The latter was a big treat for children during the depression. The last one she'd had was the one Santa had brought her the year before.

After Santa Claus left, Priscilla played the piano while everyone sang Christmas carols. The high point of the evening was Cecil singing "Away In A Manger" as his mother accompanied him on the piano. To this day, June never hears that carol without remembering that special night when she was one month short of her fifth birthday.

When Santa Claus came to their house a couple nights later, he left the children just exactly what they had asked for. Cecil got the sled he wanted and a cowboy outfit, June a doll baby and set of china dishes, and Dickie a box of blocks and a toy truck. Their stockings were full of candy, Brazil nuts and wonder of wonders, an orange for each of them.

CHAPTER NINETEEN

THE LIFE CHANGING CALL

Five months later on the last day of school, Cecil sauntered through the door chanting, "No more lessons, no more books. No more teacher's dirty looks." His eyes were shining and his face flushed as he said, "Just think, Mom, I've only gone to school one year, and I'm going to be in the third grade."

Priscilla smiled fondly at her oldest child, then noticing his rosy cheeks asked, "Cecil, are you feeling alright? You look a little flushed." As she was speaking she cupped his face in her hands and looked in his eyes.

As she suspected, his face was hot and the sparkle in his eyes was not just from the excitement of the last day of school. He was running a fever.

"Oh, Mom, I'm okay," Cecil said, jumping up, ready to run outside and play.

"Hold on a minute," Priscilla said. "You're not going anywhere until I have a chance to look you over. I've heard some of the kids have been out with chicken pox. I just want to make sure you're not getting them."

Despite his protests that he was fine, Priscilla took off his shirt and looked him over. As she suspected, there were a few red spots on his chest and back. "I'm sorry, Son," she said. "I'm afraid you've got them. You'll have to take it easy for a few days. You can stay in the living room on the couch and listen to the radio. I won't make you go upstairs to bed."

Reluctantly he trudged out of the room, muttering, "It's not fair. A person should be able to play when school's out." Feeling sorry for her oldest son and knowing there was no way she could keep June and Dickie from being exposed, she didn't try to keep them apart.

Within two weeks Cecil was better, but the telltale marks were beginning to show up on June. So far, it appeared Dickie might escape getting them. Under the circumstances, Burrel hated to go, but he was scheduled to leave for a spelunking exploration at a couple of yet unopened caverns in Virginia. Before packing his gear in the car, he kissed the children goodbye, promising them he'd buy them some apple candy when he met Walter Amos in Winchester.

As Priscilla walked to the car with him, he explained as he stored his bag in the back seat, "We'll be exploring a couple caverns. Walter thinks both should be opened. That is, if he can get the backing. I'll be back on June fifteenth, so we can celebrate our anniversary. I wouldn't leave now, with the kids sick, but we're meeting some other guys there. It's now or never."

"Go on. Don't worry about us. We'll be all right. Cecil is over his, and it looks like June is going to have a mild case. If I need anything, I'll call on Josie and Olie. After all, they're almost within shouting distance," she assured him.

"They sure are," he said, looking toward the house beyond the entrance to the cavern grounds. "I'll miss you all," he murmured, before soundly kissing her goodbye.

Priscilla and the children waved until they could no longer see the car. As she watched the children smiling and talking as they went back into the house, she wondered, "What in the world does Burrel think would happen that I couldn't handle?"

She had no premonition of what was to come, but she was soon to find out.

~

The first call came on the fourteenth. She and the children had just finished breakfast when the phone rang. She was busy with the dishes when Cecil called out, "Mom, that's one long and two short rings. It's for us."

"Go ahead and answer it," she said as she dried her hands on the dishtowel. "Tell whoever it is, I'll be right there."

"It's Uncle Fred," he said, handing her the earpiece.

Her heart was pounding so hard, she was sure Fred would hear it. Something had to be wrong! Fred would never waste money on a long distance phone call unless there was a problem. She stood close to the phone and shouted into the wall mounted mouthpiece, "Fred, what is it? What's wrong?" Then without giving him time to respond, "Is something wrong with Dad?"

She felt as if her legs would buckle when he replied. "I'm afraid so. He woke up this morning with severe stomach pains. Mollie called and said he was in so much pain, she had to call the doctor."

"What did the doctor say it is?" Priscilla asked.

"He doesn't know," was Fred's response. "He ruled out appendicitis. He did say he was a pretty sick man. I'm sure he'll be alright, but I think you should come home for a few days."

"Come home? It's worse than you're telling me. Isn't it?" she inquired.

"I honestly don't know. I just thought you would want to know," he answered. "Can you come?"

"I can't come right now. Burrel isn't here. He went to Virginia and won't be back until tomorrow. I'll be ready so we can leave as soon as he gets here. Tell Dad we'll be there," she said.

"I'm going over to his house now and I'll tell him," he said. "I'm also going to try to talk to the doctor. I'll call you if I find out anything, or if there is a change,"

Before he could hang up, Priscilla moved her mouth even closer to the phone to be sure Fred could hear her as she said, "Tell Dad I love him."

The children had been watching her face and listening to her side of the conversation. "What's wrong with Granddad?" Cecil asked.

Priscilla looked at June's wide frightened eyes and Cecil valiantly trying to hide his fear. "I need to be brave for them," she thought just before she burst into tears.

"Granddad is sick," she gulped, trying unsuccessfully to contain her sobs. "We're going to go see him as soon as your dad gets home." Getting herself under control, she continued, "You'll have to help me get ready."

"But, Mom," June wailed, "What about my chicken pox?"

Priscilla looked at her in astonishment. She'd been so worried about her father, she hadn't given a thought to the chicken pox. Since they never left their children with a sitter, she certainly wouldn't consider it at a time like this. She reassured her daughter that chicken pox or not she was going with them.

Her thoughts were interrupted by the telephone with its one long and two short rings. It was Burrel's brother Olie. Josie's sister-in-law, had listened in on the party line, heard Priscilla and Fred's conversation and called Josie to tell her about it. He wanted to know if Priscilla wanted him to try to get hold of Burrel. He knew she would want to try to keep her line open in case Fred called.

Priscilla said she'd appreciate it if he'd give it a try. If he'd call Walter Amos's house, his wife might be able to get in touch with them. Olie made the call, but Mrs. Amos didn't know where they were. They'd left one cavern and were on their way to another. If she heard from Walter, she'd tell him to have Burrel call home right away.

Before the evening was over she'd had one more call from Fred and a frantic one from Della, informing her that Harvey was worse. She said she wasn't sure he was going to make it through until morning.

Priscilla slept little that night. Her dreams were full of her father and mother together on the farm, laughing and happy. Then her dream turned to nightmares as she could see him on his deathbed, writhing in pain. As the first rays of the sun crept through her windowpane, a bird, its feathers black as coal, landed on the sill. Her heart pounded as the bird gave her an ominous look, spread its massive wings, and flew away. Bolting upright in bed with her gown soaked in sweat, she stared at the now empty windowsill. Was this part of her dream or was it a sign her father was dying or already dead?

She buried her face in Burrel's pillow as she began to weep. Hearing her, the children crept into the room, climbed into her bed and cuddled close, trying to comfort her.

The familiar sound of one long and two short rings drifted up the stairs. As it reached their ears, they all jumped from the bed and raced down the steps. Priscilla stopped the children in their tracks, as she said, "I'll get it."

It was Burrel's welcome voice that answered her timorous, "Hello."

Relief flooded through her entire body as she cried, "Burrel, Burrel, I'm so glad it's you! Did you hear about Dad?"

"Yes, Mrs. Amos told me. Have you heard anymore since Olie talked to her?" he anxiously inquired.

She told him about the calls she'd had from Fred and Della, then asked, "When will you be home?"

"I'm on my way. I'm so sorry I couldn't be there with you," he answered.

"I am, too. Be careful driving home," she added, thinking about the mountains he'd have to cross.

"Don't worry about me," he replied. "I love you, Honey," he added before hanging up the phone.

Feeling the relief of knowing he would be here soon, she busied herself with preparations for the trip. She had packed their bags and a basket of food to eat on the way. As she started out the back door to feed the chickens, she became aware of the sound of an approaching automobile. "It's too soon for Burrel," she thought as her eyes followed the slow movement of the vehicle.

Without seeing Olie in the driver's seat she would have known it was he by the way he drove. Burrel had always said that if Olie had a race with a snail, the snail would win. She found herself smiling at the thought.

One look at Olie and Josie's faces caused the smile to vanish. She waited quietly, for a second, afraid to ask why they had come. Then with her voice full of apprehension, she managed to say, "What has happened?"

Olie hesitated before responding, "I'm sorry Priscilla. Fred didn't want to tell you over the phone, so he called and asked us to break the news in person."

Postponing the inevitable, she said, "Dad's worse, isn't he? That's it. He's worse?"

Undemonstrative though he always was, Olie was so overcome with pity for his young sister-in-law that he put a comforting arm around her, as he would one of his own daughters, as he said, "Priscilla, Fred said your father passed away this morning." Taking a white handkerchief from his pocket, he wiped the beads of perspiration from his brow before adding, "I don't know how to tell you how sorry we are. We all know your dad was a wonderful man."

Tears rolled down her cheeks as she heard Olie's words. Gently, he put his hand on her arm and guided her into the kitchen where she collapsed in the nearest chair. Handing her a steaming cup of coffee, Josie said, "Drink this, it will help." As Priscilla stared blankly into the cup, Josie added gently, "I'll stay with you until Burrel gets here."

As these words penetrated Priscilla's consciousness, she turned to Josie and replied, "I appreciate the offer, but I really need to be alone with the kids for awhile. Burrel called. He's on his way home. We'll be alright."

Olie and Josie were reluctant to leave, but Priscilla was adamant. Before starting his slow drive down the hill, Olie told Priscilla, "Call if you need us." She assured him she would.

Returning to the house, she was met by a trio of silent children who had overheard the adults' conversation and were waiting for their mother's reassurance. When she saw their somber faces, her heart went out to them. She knew she had to set aside her own grief, so she could deal with their fears.

"Let's go upstairs to my bedroom. I want to talk to you about your granddad," she said as she picked up Dickie and took June by the hand. Cecil trailed along behind them. As she sat on the bed with Dickie on her lap, June and Cecil climbed up and snuggled close to her, one on each side.

"Your granddad is in heaven now. He's happy, because he is with your grandmother. I told you how God loves all of us, and how some day we will all live in heaven with him. When we go to heaven, we'll see your granddad and grandmother and all the people who have already gone there."

Feeling the comfort of their presence and talking to them was helping her regain control of her emotions until Cecil asked, "If granddad is happy in heaven, why are you crying?"

"Because I'll miss him!" she said as she again burst into tears.

When Burrel returned a few minutes later, he found the four of them stretched out on the bed, crying and trying to comfort each other.

One look at the scene told him, the worst had happened. "Priscilla," he said gently. "I'm home."

As he started to walk toward the bed, the children ran to meet him. "Dad," Dickie said, in his piping, almost three year old voice, "Grand-dad is in heaven."

Disentangling himself from the clinging children, Burrel went to Priscilla, sat down on the bed, gathered her in his arms, and held her close, all the time murmuring words of comfort. He felt guilty, not being home when she needed him and couldn't understand how this could have happened so quickly.

Although his heart was full of grief for this man he had come to love, he knew he had to be strong for Priscilla and the children. Sometimes he lamented the strong silent role assigned to men. It would be a relief to vent your emotions as women did through the relief of tears.

CHAPTER TWENTY

NOT FOR LITTLE EARS

Since Priscilla had done such a good job with the preparations for the trip, they were soon in the car and on their way. After awhile, the boys grew tired of looking at mountains, trees, and an occasional farm-house and fell asleep. June, dozing, with pictures running through her mind of her grandfather holding her hand as they'd walked through the meadow, was half listening to her parents' quiet conversation.

She woke with a start when she heard her mother's voice say, "She killed him! I know she killed him!"

"What?" Burrel exclaimed. "What are you talking about?"

"That woman killed him. Dad wasn't sick. He's never had any trouble with his stomach before. What would cause such pains to come on so fast?"

"Are you thinking his wife poisoned him?" Burrel asked. "I can't believe a thing like that."

"Yes, I do. I think when he moved into her rooming house after Mom died, she went after him because he had the money from the farm. He was alone and lonely, and she took advantage of it to get him to marry her."

"I've never thought your dad seemed happy with her or that they loved each other, but that doesn't mean she killed him," Burrel responded.

June couldn't keep quiet any longer. She'd heard her mother mention "That woman" before, but this was the first time she'd ever heard anyone talk about her granddad having a wife. "Mom," she said, "I thought granddad's wife was in heaven. Who are you talking about?"

Her words were greeted by a stunned silence, then Burrel spoke so low June couldn't make out what he was saying, "I thought they were all asleep. We can't have her repeating what you just said. I'd better talk to her."

After Priscilla's nod of agreement, Burrel said, "June, come up here. You can ride in front with us for awhile."

"Uh oh," June thought, "Am I in trouble?" as she scampered over the seat. When her dad turned and bestowed a reassuring smile on her, she realized she wasn't.

"You said you thought your granddad's wife was in heaven. His first wife, your grandmother, is in heaven. He got married again to a woman named Mollie. She's your mother's stepmother."

"That woman is no relation to me!" Priscilla exclaimed.

Burrel pursed his lips, as if to warn her not to say any more, before he continued. "June, you know your mom is sad and upset right now. Sometimes people say things they don't really mean when they're feeling that way."

As he and Priscilla exchanged glances, despite her look saying, as clearly as words, "I do mean it," she remained silent.

"You know we've told you before that you are not to repeat anything you hear me and your mom talk about. Do you remember us telling you that?"

June looked from one parent to the other before saying in a small frightened voice. "I remember."

"I want you to promise you won't repeat anything you've heard in the car today. I know I can trust you to keep your word, if you promise," Burrel said softly. "Do you promise?"

June's voice was so low they had to strain to hear her over the sound of the motor, as she replied, "I promise."

Burrel rewarded her with a warm smile as he said, "You can stay up here with us while the boys are sleeping. Would you like that?"

"Oh, yes," she sighed, as she snuggled close to her mother. This was a treat. Usually, if anyone got to sit up front it was Dickie, since he was the baby.

∽

Despite her intention to stay awake in order to savor every moment of the rest of the trip, the hum of the motor and the sound of her parents' hushed voices soon lulled her to sleep. When she awoke it was morning, and she was in her cousin Rose's bed in her Uncle Mace and Aunt Mabel's house at 669 East Main Street in Newark.

Conscious of someone's eyes upon her, she sat up, rubbed her eyes, and turned to face her cousin Rose. Laughing, Rose said, "Well, good morning sleepy head. Are you going to sleep all day?"

"How did I get here?" June asked.

"Your dad carried you in. You were still asleep. I woke up when they put you in bed, but Mom told me I wasn't to wake you," Rose answered. Then noticing the bumps on June's face, she asked, "What's that on your face?"

"Oh, that!" June replied, "That's my chicken pox."

"Are they catching?" Rose asked.

"They sure are," June laughed. "I got them from Cecil. Mom said I'd probably give them to all the cousins while we were out here. She told me she wasn't going to leave me at home, chicken pox or not." Then remembering what her dad had said about not telling anyone what she heard her parents say, her hand flew to her mouth and her eyes widened as she whispered, "Maybe I shouldn't have told you that."

"Why not?" Rose asked.

"Dad told me not to tell anyone what I hear them talk about at home," she replied.

"Oh, that," Rose exclaimed, "Mom and Dad told me that, too, but that doesn't count with us. We're cousins." Looking at her cousin's laughing face, it occurred to her that Rose was more than a cousin. She was one of her best friends. It had probably been okay to tell her about the chicken pox. After all, they were there for anyone to see, but she had promised her dad not to tell anyone what she'd overheard in the car. As much as she loved and trusted Rose, she still couldn't tell her.

Just then they heard Rose's mother calling from the bottom of the steps, "Come on everybody. Breakfast is ready."

June found, when they got downstairs, that everyone was talking about her chicken pox. Aunt Mabel had even known about it before they got here. June was relieved when she heard her say to Burrel,

"When you called and told me you were coming and that June had the chicken pox, I figured the girls would be getting them soon anyway. I'm just surprised Inez didn't bring them home from school this year." "Besides," she said, turning to Priscilla, "You had to come, and you certainly couldn't leave her with anyone."

"I hope everyone else is as understanding," Priscilla replied.

CHAPTER TWENTY-ONE

TOGETHER AGAIN

For the next couple days, Burrel and Priscilla went to the funeral home for afternoon and evening visiting hours. The children stayed with Aunt Mabel and their cousins, Inez, Rose, and Annamae. Mabel and Mace now had three daughters, the youngest less than a year younger than Dickie. Mabel had laughingly reiterated, after this last birth, that she thought it must be catching, since every time Priscilla became pregnant, she did, too. She said that she certainly hoped Priscilla was ready to call it quits. Priscilla kept mum, but she still wanted to have another one, hopefully a girl.

A few days later Priscilla stood beside her husband and children, and watched as her father was placed in his final resting place beside her mother. The memory of herself, on her nineteenth birthday standing in this same spot, saying her final farewell to her mother, intruded upon her grief. She had thought then that it was more than she could bear, but at least she'd been able to be with her mother when she had needed her.

As if sensing her thoughts, Burrel held her close, letting her cry on his shoulder. As he murmured soothing words of comfort, he felt guilty for not being there when she'd received the call. He wondered if he'd ever be able to forgive himself.

He felt a momentary chill as the thought flickered through his mind that she might not be able to forgive him or to forget.

Hearing her sobs and feeling her need for his comforting arms, he dismissed the unwelcome idea. As her tears began to subside, he felt an overwhelming pity for his young wife. Here she was, not quite twenty-five years old, and she'd lost both her parents. He found it hard to believe the coincidence of having each of these tragedies happen on such important days in her life. Her mother had been buried on her birthday and her father had died on her wedding anniversary. He knew it was difficult for her to celebrate her birthday without thinking about her mother's death. Now it would be the same for their wedding anniversary.

Watching the first shovelful of the rich Rocky Fork soil fall on her father's casket, Priscilla turned her tear stained face to Burrel and softly murmured, "At least, they're together again."

That night, she poured out her emotions in her notebook writing these words:

FATHER

F is for the faith in God he gave me
A is for the days of Auld Lang Syne
T is for the time he labored for me
H is for his hands so dear and kind
E is for his eyes so blue and tender
R is for the right he loved so well

Put them all together they spell father
Whose memory in my heart shall ever dwell.

CHAPTER TWENTY-TWO

THE GATHERING OF THE CLAN

The next day they went to a family get together at Aunt Em and Uncle John's farm. This was a bittersweet experience for Priscilla, giving her the chance to visit with her brothers and sisters and their families, but at the same time emphasizing the absence of her mother and father.

Burrel couldn't help compare this gathering with the first time he'd been here when they'd celebrated Priscilla's engagement to him. So much was the same, the white clothed tables set up under the trees, women bustling about with bowls and platters of food, children running and playing.

In fact, as before, there was a boy climbing to the top of a big maple tree. As he cupped his hand above his eyes, to shade them from the glare of the sun, he followed the little boy's progress. "Some things never change," he thought.

These thoughts were interrupted by the sound of Priscilla's voice, "Cecil Harman, you get down from up there!"

Startled, he first looked at Priscilla's alarmed face, and then back to the boy perched on the highest branch at the top of the tree. "Good Lord," he thought, "It is Cecil!" He hadn't been able to tell before, because the boy's face had been hidden from view by the dense foliage.

In a couple strides he was at Priscilla's side. Putting an arm around her waist, he tried to reassure her, "Relax, he'll be alright. Look, he's already on his way down."

As they watched, Cecil quickly scampered down the tree to the bottom branch, then like a trapeze artist, swung to the ground. "I think he's part monkey," Burrel chuckled.

"Don't encourage him," Priscilla grumbled, "I think you're worse than he is." Turning to Cecil, she said, "Young man, I don't ever want to see you climbing that high again. Do you understand?"

"Yes, ma'am," Cecil responded, "You won't." Fortunately for Cecil, his innocent smile hid his less than innocent thought, "If I do it again, I'll make sure you don't see me!"

He was saved from his mother's wrath by the ringing of the dinner bell. She became so busy filling Dickie's plate and helping June with hers, that he and his escapade were soon forgotten.

~

After the meal was over and the food cleared away, people could be seen strolling about the grounds or sitting under shade trees, talking and drinking lemonade. June and Rose walked around, picking up bits of conversation as they passed one or another group. They heard June's cousin Lawrence Rine saying to her cousin Charles Glancy, "She won't let me have Granddad's fiddle. He always said I could have it when he was gone, but she just said it belonged to her now, and she was going to keep it."

"She told Dad the same thing about the pocket watch Granddad wanted me to have," Charlie retorted. Noticing the girls, he said, "Hi, did you girls enjoy the picnic?" They nodded, shyly, enjoying the attention of their teen-aged cousins.

"Don't go too far," Lawrence said, "We're going to make some ice cream a little later." Assuring him they wouldn't miss it, they moved on to the cluster of chairs where their mothers were sitting with Laura and Della. Priscilla looked up and said, "Don't go too far girls. We're going to have some ice cream."

Not wanting to take the chance of missing out on the treat, they picked a spot on the other side of the tree. From there they could hear their mothers calling them when the ice cream was ready. While waiting, they busied themselves making necklaces out of clover blossoms.

From where they were sitting, they could hear the women's voices, but weren't paying much attention until the words June had first heard in the car wafted their way to their ears, "I think she killed him."

Rose gave June a startled glance, but June motioned her to be quiet. She wasn't sure whether or not they should leave. Her dad had told her not to tell, but he hadn't said anything about listening. Before she could decide what to do, Aunt Laura again said, "I think she killed him. Dad had never had any problem with his stomach before. Everything happened too fast. The doctor said he died of peritonitis, but what caused it?"

"I agree with you," Aunt Della said. "I think she killed him. Did you know she didn't even call the doctor when she told Fred she had? She didn't call him until right before Dad died."

The girls couldn't see June's mother's face, but they could hear the shock in her voice when she exclaimed, "She didn't call the doctor! I can't believe it. Fred told me on the phone how much pain Dad was in, and that the doctor had been there. Didn't she get any help for him?"

"No. She didn't, even though she was telling everyone the doctor had been there," Aunt Laura responded.

"How do you know the doctor hadn't been there?" Priscilla asked.

"When the doctor got there he bawled us out for not calling him sooner," Aunt Laura replied. "Fred told him we thought he'd seen Dad the day before. You know Fred never gets mad, but he looked like he'd like to strangle Mollie."

As June quickly glanced at Rose, she saw her own shock and fear mirrored in her cousin's large brown eyes. "Poor Granddad," June mouthed.

"As soon as the doctor got there, he insisted Dad be taken to the hospital, but by that time it was too late," Della said. "I think he was suspicious, too. Why else would he have ordered an autopsy?"

"When are we going to get the results?" Priscilla asked.

"We should have it any time, now," Aunt Della responded.

The listening girls exchanged puzzled glances at the mention of an autopsy. "What's an autopsy?" Rose whispered.

June shook her head as she responded, "I don't know and if we ask, they'll know we were listening."

"Maybe I can ask Mom," Rose offered.

Before they could decide how to solve this puzzle, the sound of the dinner bell reached them. Forgetting all about trying to be quiet, Rose jumped up and yelled, "Ice cream! It's time for ice cream!"

"Uh oh!" Rose gasped, at the sound of her mother's voice, "Rose, is that you? What are you doing back there?"

Rose looked down at the ground as she meekly replied, "Nothing. We're just making clover necklaces."

As she joined Mabel, Priscilla demanded, "June, were you listening to us talk?"

June briefly considered denying it, but knowing her parents feelings about lying, she decided honesty would be the best policy. "We didn't mean to. We were afraid if we went too far, we might miss the ice cream."

Before Priscilla or Mabel could say any more, Laura interrupted, "Priscilla, I think you've got a girl here who likes homemade ice cream as much as you did when you were little. These girls have been waiting long enough. If we keep them here any longer, there won't be any left."

At the sound of Laura's words, both girls turned with stricken faces and cried, "Aw, Mom!"

"Scoot, go on. Go get some ice cream," Priscilla said. "We'll talk about it later."

The girls gratefully made their escape. Much to their relief, there was still plenty of ice cream. As June let the first bite melt on her tongue, she could hear a little voice in her head repeating, "We'll talk about it later." The cold spot spreading through her stomach wasn't entirely from the ice cream.

CHAPTER TWENTY-THREE

LITTLE GIRL LOST

The next day, June, Rose, Inez, and Cecil went to play with Maxine and Juanita Sponagle, who lived a couple houses down the street. What started out to be an innocent game of hopscotch soon turned into one of the most frightening experiences of June's young life.

From the moment they arrived at the girls' house, June knew it wasn't going to be a fun day for her. Juanita took one look at her face and asked, "Why do you have scabs on your face? Your face looks funny."

As Juanita continued to laugh and taunt her, June kept quiet, all the while thinking, "I hope my chicken pox is still catching and you get twice as many, and everyone laughs at you." Her only regret was that she wouldn't be here to see it. Maybe she could get Rose to tell her about it.

She wanted to go back to Rose's house, but she didn't want to give Juanita the satisfaction of knowing how much she had hurt her feelings. Her chance to escape came when Maxine came out of the house and announced, "I can't find any chalk," before turning to Inez and asking if they had any at her house.

Inez was pretty sure they did. "Who wants to go get it?" she asked, looking at June and Rose. Before Rose could object, June, seeing her opportunity to escape yelled, "I'll go!" As she left, she heard Juanita say, "Let's play Mother May I? I'll give the orders."

"I'll bet you will!" June muttered as she turned toward her cousins' house.

She looked at the first house. "That can't be it," she thought. It wasn't big enough. The next one had hedges like Uncle Mace's house, but they were too tall. As she walked on, she passed one house after the other. They all started to look alike, but none looked like the right house. The yard was too small on one, too large on another. Her heart started pounding as she realized she was lost.

She tried to picture the house in her mind's eye, but all she could remember was that it was big and white and had a row of hedges across the front. She had only passed one with hedges, but it hadn't looked like Uncle Mace's house. She decided to keep walking.

Soon, the sidewalk ended, but she didn't stop. As her reluctant feet carried her on, she thought about her mom and dad. What would they do if she never found her way back? Would Cecil and Dickie miss her? That old Juanita would probably be happy.

She found herself walking alongside a tall black spiked iron fence. Turning toward the sound of voices, she saw two women sitting in lawn chairs, surrounded by laughing, playing children. As her eyes went beyond them she could see a monstrous, red brick building. Her entire body turned cold, as she realized she was in front of the orphans' asylum.

As she stood, dumbstruck, one of the women advanced toward her and touching her on the shoulder asked, "Are you lost?"

Frightened, June drew back from her touch while exclaiming, "No, I'm just looking for my uncle's house."

"Who is your uncle? Where does he live?" the woman asked.

June started to cry, as she replied, "He lives in a big white house with a big hedge in front of it. I've been walking a long time, but I can't find it."

Reassuringly patting June on the arm, the woman said, "Come on in. You can play with the children while I find your uncle."

"No!" June shouted, "I won't go in there." She had seen a movie about a little girl who lived in an orphanage. Everyone had been mean to her. No way was anyone going to get her inside a place like that!

Startled, but soon realizing why this little girl was frightened, the woman stooped down to June's level, looking into her eyes, she gently uttered the most reassuring words the five year old girl could possibly have heard, "You don't have to go in. I'll go with you. We'll find your uncle's house. If you want to, you can hold my hand."

June was leery at first, but the woman's gentle smile and kind face soon reassured her. Shyly, June reached up and the woman took her out-stretched hand. Walking along beside this woman as they retraced her steps, she felt safe.

"I see some hedges up there," the woman said. "Do you think it's your uncle's house?"

June wasn't sure, but as they got closer she saw her dad and Uncle Mace in the driveway washing her dad's car. Running toward them, she yelled, "Dad, Dad!" and almost toppled him when she wrapped her arms around his legs.

"Good heavens. What's going on?" her astonished father asked. Then noticing that his daughter was not alone, he turned an inquiring look on the stranger.

"I think we had a lost child on our hands," she explained, going on to tell him about June showing up in front of the Children's Home and her part in helping her find her way home.

Burrel's heart sank at the thought of how frightened his little girl must have been. What made it even more frightening was that they hadn't even known she was missing, since the other children were still playing down the street, and they had assumed she was with them.

Having seen June with a strange woman, Priscilla and Mabel came out of the house to see what was happening. When she heard the story, Priscilla joined Burrel in expressing her thanks. They invited this Good Samaritan to stay for coffee and a piece of the piping hot apple pie Mabel had just taken from the oven, but she expressed regrets, saying she needed to get back to the children.

June was the center of attention for the rest of the afternoon, first with the adults, then the children. When she and Rose were getting ready to go to bed, she turned to Rose, and her face like a small storm cloud, demanded to know why they hadn't missed her. "I would have thought one of you would have noticed I was gone such a long time!" she exclaimed.

"We thought you were mad at Juanita and just didn't want to play anymore," was Rose's reply.

"Well, I was mad at her. She didn't have to be so mean," June retorted. "Is she always so nasty?"

"Afraid so. I don't like her either," Rose said. "The only reason we play with her is because we like Maxine, and their mother won't let Maxine play with us unless we play with Juanita."

"That's mean," June announced. "Her mother must be as mean as she is."

Rose laughed, "No she isn't. She's nice like Maxine."

"Huh!" and a shrug of her shoulders was June's only reply, before she changed the subject and told Rose how the woman tried to get her to go into the orphanage and how she had refused to go.

"You're smart," Rose said. "I wouldn't let anyone take me into that place either."

CHAPTER TWENTY-FOUR

THE CONVERSATION

Meanwhile, Burrel and Priscilla were sitting on the front porch with Mace and Mabel, discussing the events of the day. The girls were aware of the sound of their parents' voices coming in through the open window, but they were too absorbed in their own conversation to pay any attention until they heard Priscilla say, "I can't help think, she might have been trying to run away."

June and Burrel exclaimed in unison, "Run away!" Since sound rises, the girls heard Burrel, but no one on the porch heard June.

In true astonishment, Burrel continued, "Why would she want to run away?"

Priscilla sighed as she replied, "It was something I said to her at the picnic yesterday. She and Rose were listening when Mabel, Della, Laura, and I were talking about our suspicions about Dad's death. After we caught them, I told her she could go and get some ice cream, but I'd talk to her about it later. I thought she was worried about what I said, didn't you, Mabel?"

"Yes, I think she was upset, but I don't think she'd run away," Mabel replied.

"There's no way that girl ran away," Burrel emphatically declared. "She'd never do anything like that. You'd know she didn't, if you'd seen how glad she was to see me. She tackled me like a football player. I'll probably have bruises to show for it," he chuckled.

Listening, from their vantage point by the upstairs window, June turned to Rose and smiled. It felt good having her dad defend her. Like most little girls, she thought her dad was the most wonderful man in the world.

~

"What did Fred say the doctor told him about the results of the autopsy?" Mace asked.

June almost cried out when she heard that word again, but she clamped her hand over her mouth and remained quiet, listening more intently.

Priscilla hesitated before replying, "He said Dad died of peritonitis, caused by an intestinal obstruction."

"At least you know Mollie didn't have anything to do with it," Mace responded.

Priscilla was quiet for so long, the girls didn't think she was going to answer. Finally, with a voice full of tears, she said, "I don't know about that. Maybe she didn't actually kill him, but if she'd gotten a doctor when she said she did, he might still be alive." Then sobbing uncontrollably, she cried, "If I could only have been here, I might have been able to save him."

Tears were running down June's cheeks as she listened. It was so frightening to hear her strong mother cry.

Upstairs, Rose was trying to comfort June by telling her that everyone cried when their dad died.

At the same time downstairs, Burrel, Mace and Mabel were trying to console Priscilla. Burrel had put his arms around her to let her cry on his shoulder. Mace was saying, "You can't blame yourself. Your brothers and sisters were there. I'm sure they did everything they could. You couldn't have done any more than they did."

"I'll never forgive her, though," Priscilla muttered. Burrel wondered if he would be the one she wouldn't be able to forgive. He would have been more alarmed if he'd been aware of her conversation with Della earlier that afternoon.

Knowing they were leaving the next day, Della had stopped in to say goodbye. While she and Priscilla sat on the porch watching Dickie and Annamae play, Della had opened the conversation by saying, "I don't know how you can forgive that husband of yours for not being home when you needed him. He could at least have let you know where you could get hold of him. If he'd just done that you could have been here before Dad died."

Priscilla's voice was frigid as she turned flashing blue eyes on her sister and declared, "Don't you dare criticize my husband. Working with Mr. Amos is part of his job. He had no way of knowing Dad was going to get sick while he was gone."

"I thought his job was managing the cavern. What does that have to do with all these little side trips he's going on. That just gives him an excuse to leave you and the kids at home while he goes out and has a good time."

"Good time! Are you crazy? Since when is it fun to climb around in a cold damp cave?" Priscilla demanded.

Dark eyes blazing, Della replied, "He must think its fun or he wouldn't do it. I've never heard of Burrel Harman doing anything he didn't want to do."

Priscilla bit her tongue to keep from expressing what she was thinking, "That sounds like the talk of a jealous woman." They had never mentioned Burrel and Della's relationship before and this probably wasn't the time to bring it up.

"I think we've both said things we wouldn't have said if we hadn't been so upset about Dad," Priscilla said. "We won't be seeing each other for awhile. I don't want to go away on this note."

"I know," Della said, "but I can't help feel that Burrel let you down. I could cry when I think of what you went through trying to get in touch with him."

Priscilla sounded calmer than she felt when she firmly stated, "I don't blame Burrel. He would never deliberately let me down."

"Are you practicing for sainthood?" Della tauntingly asked. "I know if he were my husband, he wouldn't go away like that and not let me know where I could reach him if I needed him."

Priscilla tried for a light touch when she replied, "Well, I guess you're lucky he's not your husband."

Della wasn't amused. First she glared at Priscilla, then laughed mockingly as she said, "That's right. He is your husband. You wanted him, now you've got him. If you can forgive him, why should I care?"

"There's nothing to forgive," Priscilla responded, but Della had accomplished what she set out to do. The seed had been planted. Even though she tried to suppress it, a little voice deep inside her mind kept repeating, "He should have let me know. He should have let me know."

Totally unaware of the afternoon happenings and the effect on her, Burrel, Mace and Mabel continued to talk to Priscilla about her feelings about her father's wife. "I can understand how you feel. It's hard enough losing your father without having something like this happen," Mabel said. "Try to think how happy he is to be with your mother again."

"That's right," Burrel added. "Your dad was telling me how much he missed her. He said some day they would be reunited in heaven."

"He won't have to worry about being reunited with Mollie. She'll be burning in hell!" Priscilla stated scornfully.

June turned a shocked face to Rose as she whispered, "Mom said hell. She would have spanked me if I'd said it."

"Maybe it's okay to say it if you're talking about someone going there," Rose said.

No matter how interesting the downstairs conversation was, both girls found themselves yawning. It had been a long day. They were tired and soon drifted off to asleep.

~

When they awoke, it was to the smell of frying bacon drifting up the stairs. "Time to get up," Rose said. "Mom will be calling us for breakfast, any minute."

No sooner had the words left Rose's mouth when June heard Aunt Mabel call from downstairs, "Breakfast will be ready in a few minutes. Come to the table."

As they finished dressing, they could hear the sound of the rest of the family moving about on their way to the breakfast table. They raced down the stairs and sat down, just as Priscilla and Mabel placed heaping platters of bacon, eggs, and freshly baked biscuits on the table.

"Um, this looks good," Cecil said as he speared a piece of bacon.

"You wait until your Uncle Mace says grace!" Priscilla admonished.

Looking sheepish, Cecil replied, "Yes, Ma'am," as he joined the others in bowing their heads while his uncle said a brief blessing. Finishing, he smiled at his nephew before saying, "I'm like Cecil, I can't wait to sink my teeth into this good food. Let's eat."

As they were completing the meal, Priscilla's eyes were moving around the table, storing memories of this scene to last her until they would again be together. As her eyes moved past Dickie, she noticed his cheeks looked abnormally red, suspiciously like Cecil's and June's had such a short time ago. "Do you feel alright, Son?" she asked as she moved around the table and placed her cool hand on his hot forehead.

Trying to squirm away, Dickie replied, "Aw, Mom, I'm okay."

"No, you're not," Priscilla firmly stated. "You've got a fever." Then turning to Burrel, she sighed, "I'm afraid he has the chicken pox."

All eyes turned to Dickie as Mabel said, "He was bound to get them. I noticed his face was a little flushed, but I thought that was because he and Annamae had been running and playing."

Dickie didn't like all this attention, and he was relieved when his mother turned to June and demanded, "What are you and Rose whispering and giggling about?"

Trying to contain her laughter, June angelically replied, "We were wondering if we could go down to Juanita's, so I could say goodbye to her. We wanted to take Dickie with us."

Looking innocent, Rose added her plea, "Juanita really liked Dickie. She'd hate to miss saying goodbye."

Dickie looked startled at Rose's words. This was the first he knew Juanita liked him. Every time he and Annamae had gone near her, she'd called them pests and told them to get lost. He couldn't help think that big kids had a funny way of showing they liked you.

His thoughts were interrupted by his mom's and Aunt Mabel's shocked voices declaring almost in unison, "June, Rosalie! Dickie is contagious!"

The women went on to patiently explain to the girls what would happen if they took Dickie with them. Juanita and Maxine would both get the chicken pox. They wouldn't want that to happen, would they?

Chagrined that their plot had failed, they innocently replied that they certainly wouldn't. With their fingers crossed behind their backs, they were thinking, "At least, not Maxine."

Neither was very happy, though, when Mabel added, "Just because you can't take Dickie doesn't mean you can't go say goodbye. I'm sure Juanita will understand why Dickie couldn't come with you."

"Run along," Priscilla instructed, "but don't stay long. We have to get started home."

"Good try," Inez whispered as the girls reluctantly headed for Juanita's house.

As they glumly walked down the street, Rose determinedly stated, "Just wait until I get the dumb chicken pox. I'll come down and play with Juanita. Then when she gets them, I can make fun of her, just like she made fun of you!"

Both girls felt better, now that was settled. Their only regret was that Rose couldn't yet write, and June would have to wait until they saw each other again to find out what happened.

CHAPTER TWENTY-FIVE

HOME AGAIN

Again the two families said goodbye, with promises to write and visit each other soon. Burrel drove all day, stopping only so they could eat the lunch Mabel had prepared for them. By the time they arrived home, it was dark and June and Cecil were asleep. The heat in the car had brought Dickie's chicken pox out more. His skin was so peppered, it was difficult to find a clear spot, and he was too uncomfortable to sleep.

Rubbing calamine lotion over his hot little body, Priscilla said, "His case is so much worse than the others. I'll see if I can get him to fall asleep." As she sat in her rocking chair, she held him on her lap and rocking back and forth she softly crooned a lullaby until he finally fell asleep.

For the next few days Dickie was so miserable he couldn't stand the touch of the band of his trousers against his skin. Despite his protests that he was not a girl, his mom decided to put June's dresses on him. She convinced him they would be loose and soft and would cut down on some of the itching. He wouldn't agree though, until she promised that no one except the family would see him. His brother and sister were given strict orders not to tease him. Although Cecil was tempted, one look at his mother's face convinced him that it wouldn't be a wise move.

Full of sympathy, June couldn't do enough for him. Priscilla was alternately amused and vexed by all June's help. As she told Burrel as they sat relaxing on the porch after the children had gone to bed, "I don't know whether she is helping or hindering. Today, she tried to put one of the new dresses on him that I made for her to wear to school. She got upset when I wouldn't let her do it. She takes this mothering job pretty seriously."

Burrel was aware of how much attention June was giving to her little brother. Secretly, he was pleased and thought Priscilla should appreciate the help she was getting. "Every time I see them, June seems to be keeping him busy playing. She's been sharing all her toys or playing with his with him, like they're the same age. Just this evening she was helping him build something with his blocks. Don't you think all her attention is helping to take his mind off the itching and having to wear dresses?"

"I guess you're right. Even though she does get under my feet sometimes, she has been a big help. You know, I don't think he minded the dresses at all, once he found out how much better they felt than his pants. He's getting so much better, he's not going to have to wear them too much longer," she said, then sighing deeply, added, "This is one summer I'll be glad to say goodbye to."

"Of course you are," Burrel sympathized. Priscilla smiled, as he held out his hand and said, "Come on. Maybe we can go to Circleville to a movie once Dickie is better. Would you like that?"

Priscilla smiled, looking like a child anticipating Christmas as she murmured, "I'd really love that."

Holding out his hand for hers, "Come on, let's go to bed." Hand in his, they walked up the stairs, down the hall to their room where Burrel softly closed the door, and they were alone in their own private world.

～

After what seemed an eternity, Dickie was better, and Burrel kept his promise to take Priscilla and the children to a movie. There was no movie theater closer than Franklin or Petersburg, but the proprietor of the general store in Circleville had set up a screen and chairs in the room above his store where he showed the latest picture shows.

The movie that night didn't interest the children, but June's eyes lit up when the coming attractions flashed on the screen. A Shirley Temple movie, "The Littlest Rebel" was going to be on in a week.

June, like every other little girl in the country, loved everything about this little actress. They loved her movies, the way she sang and danced, the way she wore her hair, but most of all they loved the pretty clothes she wore.

The moment she danced across the screen, June turned to her dad and pleadingly asked if they could come back and see it. Burrel looked at her upturned face and turned an inquiring glance toward Priscilla. At her affirmative nod, he replied, "Sure, we'll come to see it."

Although most adults wouldn't admit it, they enjoyed a Shirley Temple movie almost as much as the children did. This curly top actress brought them a respite from the reality of the depression.

June could hardly wait for the big night to come. Priscilla had told Josie about it, and she, Olie, and the girls were also going. June and her cousin Ruthalene could talk of little else until the big night finally arrived.

The room was packed with parents and their children. They were showing a double feature, but most of the families were here to see The Littlest Rebel. The lights dimmed, and the movie started. Sounds of protest filled the darkness. June's heart sank. They were showing the other movie first!

This night she had looked forward to with so much excitement turned out to be one of the most disappointing nights of her young life. By the time the first movie was over, it was an hour past her bedtime, and she had fallen asleep. No matter how hard they tried, they couldn't wake her. She'd open her eyes and stare unseeingly at the screen before closing them and going back to sleep. When she awoke the next morning in her own room, she couldn't believe she had missed the entire movie. Her parents tried to comfort her, but she was almost inconsolable.

She moped around for a couple weeks until a letter came from her Aunt Mabel that cheered her. Priscilla read it to them at the dinner table. Mabel wrote that everyone was fine. The girls had all gotten the chicken pox. They were over theirs, but the little girl, Juanita, the one who was so fond of Dickie, had gotten them. According to her mother, she had a pretty bad case.

Priscilla was too absorbed in reading the letter to notice the knowing glances Cecil and June exchanged before they murmured, "Aw, that's too bad."

June, always a daydreamer, could picture Juanita, her smug face covered with pox and the kids around her laughing and chanting, "Juanita has funny marks on her face." She could hardly wait to see Rose and hear all about it.

"What are you smiling about?" Priscilla asked.

"Nothing. I was just thinking," June replied. Priscilla decided not to ask any more questions, but she did wonder what had brought about the smile.

CHAPTER TWENTY-SIX

SCHOOL DAYS

The long summer was finally over with the arrival of the first day of school. June, though only five years old, was starting in the first grade. Dressed in one of the dresses Priscilla had made, a big bow in her straight hair, she and Ruthalene joined the big kids on their trek to the schoolhouse. Priscilla and Dickie walked down the road with them and stood waving as they walked through the field, climbed the first split rail fence, and disappeared in the dense woods.

Arriving at the school, they were met by the teacher, Miss Nina Harman, who stood at the door ringing the bell and greeting them. Although, actually a tiny woman, she held herself so straight and tall, it made her appear much larger and imposing to the children. After ushering them in and directing them to their seats, she stood at the front of the room consulting the watch she wore pinned to her bodice. "It is precisely 8:30 a.m. Time for school to start," she firmly stated.

June watched, fascinated, as Miss Nina released the watch and it sprang back into place on her ample bosom. "Hmmm, she looks like a robin," June thought, but she decided it might be wise not to voice that opinion.

The older kids asked what had happened to Miss Lily, their teacher from the previous year. Miss Nina explained that Miss Lily had gone away and wouldn't be back this year. She didn't know any more than that, so it wouldn't do any good to quiz her anymore. She sounded evasive causing the children to exchange quizzical glances. This seemed very strange. There certainly seemed to be a mystery here.

June and Ruthalene weren't interested, but the older children were full of curiosity. Miss Lily hadn't said a word to them about going away. During recess, between the games of tag and Red Rover, the girls, especially, were buzzing about it.

Later, when Miss Lily came home, the adults in the community gossiped and speculated, but she ignored it. Holding her head high, she never answered anyone's questions. Shortly after her return, her parents took in a newborn baby telling everyone it belonged to a relative from out of state. It was duly noted by the local gossips that there was a strong resemblance to Miss Lily, and that she quickly took over the infant's care.

The school year was full of new experiences for June, who found everything about it fascinating. She loved the books and all the new things she was learning, the children in the school, the games they played in the school yard, reciting the pledge of allegiance as they raised the flag, the prayers the teacher recited to start each school day.

She even loved the chores the students performed. The older ones got to keep the fire going in the pot bellied stove and draw water from the well, while the younger children were allowed to gather kindling for the woodpile and pound the chalk dust from the blackboard erasers.

High at the top of things she enjoyed was the walk to and from school. No matter what kind of weather a day brought, they walked. It would never have occurred to their parents to drive them.

In the fall they were surrounded by the colorful foliage and in the spring the wild flowers. Then all through the winter, the ground was covered with snow. Bundled in snowsuits, hats, scarves, gloves, and galoshes, it was a miracle they could walk, let alone climb the fences between their homes and the school. Although the walk was extremely long, with their lively conversations, the shared laughter, and the songs they sang, the time passed quickly.

When they arrived at the schoolhouse, they would peel off their layers of clothing and warm themselves by the stove. If it was especially cold, Miss Nina would allow them to drink some of the hot chocolate their mothers had sent in their thermos bottles. During the first classes of the winter mornings, the smell of the wet wool snowsuits and the rubber galoshes, drying from the heat of the stove, could be overpowering. This was a small price to pay, though, to have warm dry clothes to wear during the long walk home.

~

Once both of the older children started school, time seemed to take wings. At the house, above the cavern, the radio continued to be their main contact with the outside world. Burrel still listened to Lowell Thomas for the news. The airways were full of talk from Washington about President Roosevelt and his unsuccessful efforts to end the depression.

More disturbing was the news coming from Europe about a man by the name of Adolph Hitler who had been elected chancellor of Germany, at the time Roosevelt had been elected president of this country.

The newscasters didn't know whether to take this comic looking former paperhanger seriously or not, with his Oliver Hardy style mustache, lock of limp black hair falling onto his forehead, and his high-pitched voice ranting about a master race.

It was difficult for the journalists, who were following his moves, to understand his apparent charisma, but every time he spoke thousands of cheering Germans flocked to hear him. The sound of "Heil Hitler" would fill the air as his followers raised their right hands toward him in a frenzied salute.

Americans had enough problems of their own. They didn't need to worry about what was happening on the other side of the ocean. Adolph Hitler had nothing to do with them, did he? No one could possibly imagine the havoc he was soon to unleash on an unsuspecting world.

When the news was over, it was more fun to turn the dial and listen to a new entertainer, a crooner named Bing Crosby. He had appeared in movies and was now making his debut on radio on the Kraft Radio Theater. His smooth relaxed style of singing and delightful sense of humor appealed to people of all ages, and the entire family soon became big fans.

CHAPTER TWENTY-SEVEN

THE MONSTER'S HEARTBEAT

During the summers when school was out, the children loved to visit their cousins. It was a long walk to Aunt Gussie's and Uncle Verde's, but they enjoyed it. Sometimes they would walk through the fields and other times by the road. Priscilla preferred they stay away from the road when they took Dickie with them, though he protested that he wasn't a baby anymore.

Monday was their favorite day to go, because that was the day they could hear "the monster's heartbeat." No sooner would they climb the first fence, then they would hear a rhythmic thump, thump, thump coming from the direction of their cousins' house. The closer they got to Aunt Gussie's, the louder it became. The sound seemed to encircle them, reverberating from the surrounding hills. It was so thunderous, they could actually feel the thumping under their feet. The first time they heard it, they were frightened, but now that they knew the source, they'd made a game of pretending it was a monster. Sometimes, their make believe creation had horns, other times it had a long tail and fire spurting from its nostrils, like the dragons their mom had read to them about.

The first time they'd run into their aunt's house babbling about a monster, she'd laughed as she led them to the back porch and showed them her pride and joy, a new washing machine.

The sound they'd heard was from the gasoline motor Uncle Verde had installed to operate the machine. Since there still was no electricity in the farmhouse, this was his way of providing her with an alternative to the washboard she'd always used.

They weren't sure whether or not to believe her, until she started the motor for another load and they heard the familiar thump, thump, thump, thump. At this close range, it was so loud it hurt their ears. Putting their hands over their ears, they stared in astonishment at the machine producing all the ruckus. Laughing at the expressions on their faces, Aunt Gussie led them into the kitchen where she fixed their favorite treat, whipped cream pie. She had already milked the cow, separated the cream from the milk and baked the pie shells. Now all she had to do was whip the cream and heap mounds of it into the waiting shells. No matter what fancy confections they were to enjoy in the future, nothing ever tasted quite as good as the fresh whipped cream pie their Aunt Gussie sat before them in that farm-house kitchen when they were still small children.

CHAPTER TWENTY-EIGHT

THE GUIDED TOUR

The next two years were busy ones for the family. In addition to the many activities at the cavern, they enjoyed visits of family members from Ohio.

Laura, Gene and their children arrived early in the summer, stayed a few days then returned home. They were followed shortly by Alvy, Bess and their children, then just before school started, Lidy arrived by train and stayed for an extended visit.

Priscilla and Burrel had a routine they followed for these first time visitors to West Virginia. First, they were given a private tour of the cavern, conducted by the host family. They were regaled with behind the scenes antidotes, reserved for very special guests.

Burrel told them how the cavern looked when he'd first entered it, about the mud and debris he and Verde had dug out and hauled away. He pointed out the lights they had installed thirty or forty feet above where they were standing and horrified them with tales of climbing over wet slippery rocks getting to some of the spots. Then he asked, "Would you like to see what the cavern looked like the first time I saw it?" To their affirmative answer he'd reply, "Alright, but you must all stand completely still, then I'll show you."

As they waited in anxious anticipation, he would turn off the lights, leaving them in the most complete darkness any of them had ever experienced. There would be cries of protest from his audience, bringing peals of laughter from the host family.

He always brought props with him and would start his demonstration by saying, "This was what Verde and I had to start with. Then we added this," he continued, as he turned on the large flashlight he always carried during the cavern tours.

This prompted sighs of relief, intermingled with nervous giggles from the children. At least one person would declare, "That's more like it!"

"The flashlight helped, but we needed to have our hands free so we could dig. That's why we added this," Burrel would say, as he lit the graphite lamp on his cap. "The lamp worked fine, but it only threw the light in front of us. When we added coal oil lanterns, we had plenty of light to work with," he said, lighting the lantern Cecil had been carrying.

The lights cast eerie shadows among the stalactites and stalagmites, causing children and adults alike to be relieved when he again turned on the lights.

While the men questioned Burrel, Priscilla told the women about how she and Josie had stored food in the cavern before they had refrigerators. Feeling the chill within these stone walls, they could well believe her.

June, Cecil, and Dickie, not to be outdone, whispered some of their escapades to their cousins. They were particularly proud of a trick they liked to play on the guides. As a tour group was being lined up, they would quietly watch until the group entered the door and started down the stairs to the first room of the cavern. Then the three of them would quietly follow at a safe distance, not making a sound until it was too late for the guide to make them go back.

"One time," June proudly stated, "We made it almost all the way through before he heard us!"

Listening, the Ohio cousins would cast fearful glances at the darkness behind them, wondering if someone might be sneaking in behind their group. Their shivers weren't only from the cold.

Priscilla and Cecil would be the center of attention the day they'd take their guests to Seneca Rocks, as Priscilla told about their flight over them. Since no one else in the family had been in an airplane, the tale of their adventure drew looks of wonder, envy, and an occasional admonishment of Priscilla for endangering herself and her child.

CHAPTER TWENTY-NINE

OH, JOHNNY

No visit was complete without a picnic at the cool, green willow draped pool, the one Burrel had introduced Priscilla to on their honeymoon. This had soon become not only one of Priscilla's favorite places, but the children's, as well.

When they visited the pool, a teen aged neighbor boy named, Johnny, would often join them. Their farm was adjacent to Ulysses and Arletta's, and Burrel had known Johnny's family all his life. Johnny's brother Ward had been one of Burrel's best friends since they had played together as little boys.

Burrel and Priscilla had become friends with this young teenager the summer he worked at the cavern. On summer nights he would visit them, sometimes listening spellbound while Priscilla and Burrel talked about life outside of Germany Valley. Other times, they would drink lemonade while they played a lively game of hearts. Never having been further from home than Franklin, he dreamed of what life must be like in other places. Fascinated by the visitors from Ohio, he pumped them for even more information on what life was like in what he had come to think of as the outside world.

In his quest for adventure, he had joined the Civilian Conservation Corps, commonly referred to as the CCCs. This program, for boys in their late teens, was one of those Burrel referred to as part of FDR's alphabet soup designed to put Americans to work.

Johnny's eyes sparkled when he talked about it. He and other

Pendleton County boys his age lived in barracks and ate in a cafeteria style community dining room. Working together, they planted trees along the roadway. The only time he had ever been away from home, the experience was whetting his appetite to see more of the world around him.

Besides, he was fast approaching the age where he would have to leave the corps. The day he joined the picnic they were having with Alvy and his family, Priscilla and Burrel noticed his exceptionally good humor. It was obvious he had news he wanted to share. His dark eyes were bright, and he couldn't keep his lips from turning upward in what Burrel called his ear-to-ear grin.

Having listened to him talk about his unhappiness with life on the farm and about his dream to see what the rest of the world was like, they both knew him well and could easily understand him. "Okay, out with it, Johnny. What are you so excited about?" Burrel asked.

Johnny continued to grin, as he announced. "I have decided to join the army."

"Join the army!" Priscilla and Burrel both exclaimed. This was peacetime. There was no draft and it was not common for young men they knew to enlist.

"Why do you want to do that?" Burrel asked.

Johnny explained, "You know how much I like the work we do and the way we live in the CCCs. Well, I am getting too old to stay in. I just can't face coming back and living on the farm. I have to do something different with my life."

Burrel could understand this boy's yearning. He had felt somewhat the same when he was his age. "What do you have to do? How do you go about joining?" he asked.

"I have to get Dad's permission," Johnny responded. For a second, Priscilla thought she saw a fleeting look of fear cross his face, but when he smiled, she was certain she had imagined it.

"I'm sure that won't be a problem," he continued. "Then I have to go to Franklin to enlist. I am so anxious, I think I will walk across the mountain if I can't get a way over there."

"Don't worry about that, Johnny. We'll be here a few more days and we'll take you, if you want us to," Alvy said.

"If Dad doesn't take me, I might take you up on it," he responded.

After Johnny helped them polish off the coconut cake Priscilla had baked, he left, saying he'd let them know whether or not he'd need a ride.

For Priscilla, this day had been perfect with her brother and his family with them, Johnny and his news, and being in her favorite place. What more could anyone want?

As she looked back at the willow branches blowing gently in the breeze, their tips brushing the cool green surface of the water, she had no way of knowing this would be the last time she would ever see this spot in such a peaceful light.

~

That night as the children were playing and the adults were sitting on the front porch, quietly talking, they could hear the phone ringing. "Is that your ring?" Alvy asked.

Everyone was quiet as they listened. "One long and two shorts. That's for us," Burrel said, as he got up from his place on the porch and made his way to answer its insistent ringing.

They could hear his soft voice repeating the words, "It can't be. It just can't be."

"This is bad news," Priscilla murmured. "I hope nothing has happened to Pap." Now that he was the only one of their parents living, she and Burrel both worried about him.

When Burrel rejoined them his face was white and drawn, and tears were gathering in his eyes.

Priscilla's heart was pounding as she asked, "What is it? Has something happened to Pap?"

She was totally unprepared for his answer, "It's not Pap. It's Johnny. He's dead." Burrel's voice was flat as if he, himself, could still not believe what Verde had just told him.

"Dead, how could he be dead? We just left him a couple hours ago," Priscilla exclaimed. "What happened? Was he in an accident?"

Alvy and Bess were looking as stunned as Burrel and Priscilla, as Alvy said, "You don't mean that nice young man we spent the afternoon with, do you?"

The tears were running down Burrel's checks. It was obvious how difficult it was for him to speak, as he replied, "That was Verde on the phone. He said Johnny shot himself. His dad wouldn't sign for him to join the army. Verde said that when his dad told him he wouldn't let him go, Johnny tried to talk him into it. When he found out he couldn't get him to change his mind, he went to his room without another word, waited until his dad went to the barn, then got his gun and told his mother he was going hunting. She didn't know what had happened and didn't think anything about it, but when his dad came back in and found that Johnny had left with a gun, he was frightened and went out to look for him. When he found him it was too late."

"Where did it happen?" Priscilla asked.

Burrel knew she was going to ask this question, but he, nevertheless, hesitated as he looked at her tear stained face and barely whispered his response, "At the willow pool. His dad found him beside the fence by the pool." The thought of this happening in the peaceful surroundings of the pool, where Priscilla and Burrel and their family had spent so many happy hours, made the horror almost unbearable.

They sat in stunned silence, each in their own private hell as they thought about Johnny and his dreams and his laughter, forever silenced. How could such a thing happen?

They were released from their morbid thoughts by the shouts and laughter of their playing children. "It's their bedtime," Priscilla said as she stood and called for them to come in and get ready for bed.

"Let's wait until morning to tell them," Burrel said, as still laughing, the children ran up the porch steps in response to Priscilla's call.

Priscilla and Bess nodded their agreement as they herded the children into the house and upstairs to the bedrooms. Tomorrow would be soon enough to wipe those happy smiles from their faces.

~

The day of the funeral, the casket was surrounded by beautiful bouquets of summer flowers. In the midst of them sat a vase of plain paper roses. People looked at them and wondered why anyone would bring paper flowers during this time of year when everyone had at least one kind of flower in bloom.

To Priscilla, this was her gift of love. She could remember Johnny's eager face as he and Burrel had sat across the table from her while she carefully crafted each individual rose and placed them, one by one, in the vase. She could hear his voice saying, "Those flowers are beautiful. If you ever decide to give them away, you can give them to me."

Later, as they stood together at the cemetery, Burrel glanced at Priscilla as he moved her flowers from the obscure spot where they had been relegated and placed them close to the casket. "Johnny would like that," he said. Watching solemnly, June thought of Johnny looking down at them and felt, surely he would. Then as she watched the mourners silently file from the cemetery, she knew this was an experience she would never forget.

On their way home, they had to pass the spot where it had happened. Someone had put up a crude wooden sign, marking this as the spot where Johnny had died. Seeing it, Priscilla cried out, "Oh, how could they?"

Sadly, Burrel responded, "You never know. It must help someone deal with their grief."

For the first time since she'd first seen the pool, Priscilla turned her face away as they drove past it.

CHAPTER THIRTY

FROM OHIO, THEY CAME

Soon Priscilla's sister-in-law came from Ohio to visit. Her companionship was good for Priscilla and helped her deal with what had happened. Then a few days after Lidy's arrival, as Priscilla and Lidy were sitting on the porch shelling peas and visiting, they saw a car pulling a trailer come around the bend in the road. They watched, expecting it to pull into the cavern parking area, but instead it continued up the road to their private drive.

"They must have missed the turn to the cavern," Priscilla said, "I guess I'd better direct them." As she started to get up from her chair, the car doors opened and a petite dark haired woman and short curly haired man stepped out.

"Della, David!" Priscilla cried. "Oh, my heavens! It's you!" Jumping up, and running to meet them, she was so excited, she was unaware of the peas spilling from the colander she'd had on her lap and rolling like tiny green marbles across the porch floor.

After the excitement of the greeting, Priscilla discovered that they had just gotten back from a trip to Florida and planned to stay for a while with them. "That is if you'll have us!" David said. "As you can see, we've brought our house with us."

Taking Priscilla by the hand, Della said, "Come see the trailer. It's just like a little house. You come, too," she said to Lidy. By now, they had been joined by the children, who trailed along behind them eager to see the inside of this strange vehicle.

As their visitors took them on a tour of their tiny dwelling, they were amazed to see a couch turned into a bed and the table and booths in the kitchen transformed into a second bedroom.

As they completed the tour, Priscilla studied David's face, and again wondered why she didn't like him, and never had. He had a happy-go-lucky quality about him that charmed children and adults alike. Like a modern day Pied Piper, he had a quality that drew the children to him, probably because he was like a big kid himself. As Priscilla watched him entertain the children, she decided she was going to try to like this man, for her sister's sake. Then mentally shaking herself, she remembered a cardinal rule of her parents' home and now of her own, "A guest in your home is to be treated courteously and with respect." This applied whether you liked the person or not.

Exiting from the cavern with a tour group, Burrel, as usual, glanced toward the house. He was surprised to see his family gathered around an unfamiliar car and trailer. He was too far away to identify their new visitors, but the sounds he heard appeared to be happy ones.

Much as he wanted to send his group on their way, so he could join his family, he contained his curiosity until he could properly escort them to their cars, bid them a fitting farewell, with a heartfelt invitation to not only return but to bring their friends and neighbors with them.

As he watched the last car drive away, Burrel opened the office door and called to his assistant, Estel Lambert, "Take over here. I'm going up to the house to see who our visitors are. I'll be back shortly."

"Go ahead. Everything will be fine here," Estel called after him as Burrel quickly walked toward the house.

As he got closer he could see it was Della and David. No wonder he hadn't recognized the trailer. This was not the one they'd had the last time they'd been here. It had been a homemade job while this was obviously fresh from the factory.

"I hope this visit doesn't turn out like the last one," he thought as he continued toward the group.

Dickie was the first to notice his father's approach, "Dad, Dad, Aunt Della and Uncle David are here!" he shouted as he ran toward him.

Hoisting him onto his shoulders, Burrel moved forward to meet their guests. As he was welcoming them and responding to Della and David's enthusiastic greeting, he felt a chill of apprehension. Despite her efforts to hide it, he knew how his wife's sister felt about him. Just as long as she didn't do anything to hurt Priscilla, he thought, he could handle her dislike.

As Priscilla had done earlier, he reminded himself of their house rule, she was their guest and she would be welcomed and treated with respect.

~

That night as he and Priscilla were getting ready for bed, he reminded her of their last visit. "I couldn't help remembering the last time they were here. You don't think we'll have a repeat of that, do you?"

"We could hardly have a repeat, could we? Lawrence isn't even with them. If they go during the night, they won't be leaving a child for us to take care of. Will they?"

"No, I guess not. Where is Lawrence now?" Burrel asked.

"He's with his grandfather, his father's father. Except for the time Della and David brought Lawrence and left him with us, he's lived either with his dad's brothers or father."

Since it was obvious Priscilla didn't want what had happened the last time to infringe on her happiness at having them here again, Burrel decided to drop the subject.

As he began to drift off to sleep, he heard the sound of a car motor. "Is it happening again? Are they leaving in the middle of the night, without telling us?" he wondered as he got up and looked out the window. From the light of the full moon, he could see the car and trailer were still parked between the house and garage. The car he'd heard must have been someone driving by or stopping at their neighbor, Ernest Scraggs's house.

Not able to get back to sleep, he lay silently in bed thinking about the last time they'd been here. That had been almost six years ago. Cecil had been under three years of age, and June was still a baby. They had only been in this house a few months. Like this time, Della and David had arrived unexpectedly. Only that time, they had brought with them Della's son from her marriage to Ross Rine. It was obvious, Lawrence, a nice looking boy with dark hair and eyes like his mother's, was happy being with his mother and stepfather.

This visit was the first stop on what was to be a trip through some of the southern states, with their ultimate goal being to spend a couple weeks in Florida.

At the dinner table they had talked about some of the things they were going to do. Lawrence's eyes sparkled when he talked about the prospect of picking oranges from the trees and going swimming in the ocean.

Talking about the trip, they had stayed up past their normal bedtime. That was probably why he and Priscilla had slept so soundly they hadn't heard the sound of the car driving away during the night.

The first they knew something was wrong was when Priscilla looked out the bedroom window the next morning at the bare space where the car and trailer had sat the night before. Unable, at first, to comprehend what had happened, it had hit her full force when she walked into the kitchen and saw Lawrence sitting there, alone and forlorn.

"Oh, my Lord!" Priscilla exclaimed. "What has happened? Where are your mother and David?"

Looking like a poor lost soul, Lawrence replied, "That David Keller must have made Mom leave me. He acts like he likes me, but I can tell he doesn't." Then trying to hide his tears, he added, "Mom would never have left me unless he made her do it."

"Of course she wouldn't," Priscilla had murmured, over and over, as she drew him close and quieted his tears.

Taking in the entire scene when he walked into the room, Burrel's heart went out to this little boy. "Don't worry, Lawrence. They'll be back. In the meantime, we'll see that you have a good time here. I could use a helper in the cavern. Would you like to go with me when I take people on tours?"

Using his shirtsleeve to wipe his eyes, he nodded his agreement, but he knew it wouldn't be the same as playing on the beach or swimming in the ocean. It would be a long time before the pain from this betrayal would be wiped from his young eyes, but it would stay forever in his memory.

Lying there, remembering, Burrel moved closer to Priscilla and breathed softly against her neck, "I'm so glad you're the sister I married." Although she stirred in her sleep, she didn't awaken.

"I have to get some sleep," he thought, as he rolled over and again closed his eyes. Just before drifting off to sleep, he remembered something else. Lawrence hadn't even had a pair of shoes when they'd left him. He and Priscilla had taken him into Franklin and bought him a pair. "I wonder if he didn't have any or if they were in the trailer when they drove away," was his last thought before finally falling asleep and his first thought the next morning when he awoke. "I guess that's something I'll never know," he thought as he got out of bed and started getting ready for the day ahead.

He had thought Della would be good company for Priscilla after Lidy went home and June and Cecil were back in school. He was in for a rude awakening one day when he returned home earlier than expected and heard raised voices coming from the kitchen. His foot had barely touched the first porch step when he heard Della venomously snarl, "I wish you would just look at yourself! That self-centered husband of yours has turned you into a drudge! You're a young woman who should be having fun, but what do you do?" As Burrel stood frozen in place wanting to call out, the words seemed to stick in his throat as her tirade continued to ring in his ears. "When we were growing up on the farm, and had to build a fire in a monster like this stove and cook three big meals a day, I made up my mind that wasn't going to be the life for me! I thought you felt the same way! But you had to have Burrel Harman, didn't you?" Her voice rose as she contemptuously asked, "Well, where has it gotten you? Is he worth everything you had to give up?"

The silent listener let out his breath as he heard his wife's reply. "You see this as drudgery, but I thank God every day for my husband, home, and children. Sure, I would rather have the conveniences I had in Newark, but my life is full and happy here. I didn't give up anything compared to what I got."

Della quickly responded, "When you come visit me in Mansfield, I'll show you what fun is. You know there is actually a nightlife where people, who wouldn't dream of living your boring life, dance, laugh and have fun. The men would really go for those big blue eyes of yours."

Burrel heard the shock and anger in his wife's voice when she retorted, "Della, if Mom were alive and could hear that kind of talk from you, she'd wash your mouth out with soap! I'm not going to listen to another word. You've made it clear you wouldn't want my kind of life, but I think you protest too much. I think you would change places with me in a minute if you could have my husband."

Despite Della's vehement denial, Burrel thought Priscilla's remark had hit home. For the first time he realized how dangerous this woman could be to his and his family's happiness. Although he knew Priscilla loved him, he also knew she was young to have so many responsibilities. As he quietly inched away from the back porch, he vowed to do anything in his power to make life a little easier for her. Monday he'd put out feelers for a hired girl to help with the housework and care of the children.

Feeling better with that decision made, he began to whistle to announce his presence before entering the kitchen. When the women looked his way, the only evidence of their quarrel was the telltale red blotches on his wife's cheeks, and the poisonous look Della cast his way.

A couple days later, Della informed them they were ready to go back home. Since he'd overheard Della remarks, he'd looked at her as a viper amongst them, but he was going to miss David. It had worked out well for him having David around, since he had been forced to release one of his employees, and David had been able to take his place.

Like the children, he enjoyed David's good humor. It felt like a breath of fresh air in the midst of the glum reports they heard on the radio about the depression and the war clouds gathering in Europe. With that and the problem with his employee, he needed to have something to laugh about.

CHAPTER THIRTY-ONE

A MATTER OF DISCIPLINE

He had released people before, but none had been as difficult as this time. The employee was his neighbor, Ernest Scraggs. Although they had never been close friends, they had gotten along reasonably well as neighbors.

He had cautioned Ernest numerous times about his irresponsibility, being late for work, some days not showing up at all, and other times leaving the office unattended if he felt he had something better to do.

Priscilla had always told Burrel he was too soft hearted for his own good, and in this case it had proved to be true. He had hated the thought of hurting Ernest or causing a problem with a neighbor, so he had put off taking any drastic action. Instead, he tried to gently counsel him.

As it turned out, this didn't work. Ernest kept taking advantage of Burrel's good nature, missing more and more work, constantly leaving Burrel short handed. The situation had finally come to a head on Labor Day, traditionally one of the busiest days at the cavern.

While Burrel and Estel were each taking a group through the cavern, Ernest was left to sell tickets and man the office until they returned. When Burrel came back with his group, he found people mulling around the grounds and in the office, but no sign of Ernest.

Even though the cash register had been left unattended, the money all seemed to be accounted for. It was impossible to tell though whether anything had been taken from the shelves of souvenirs or from the candy or pop case.

Burrel was stunned, angry, and determined. Ernest Scraggs would have to go! He was going to discharge him the moment he returned. Ernest knew he'd gone too far this time, so he waited several days before he returned to work, sauntering in as if nothing had happened. This worked out well for Burrel, as by now his anger had cooled, but not his determination to dismiss this man.

Ernest tried to wheedle his way back into his employer's good graces, but there was no changing Burrel's mind. When Ernest discovered his cajoling wasn't going to work, his tone and words became threatening. "You'll be sorry you ever did this, Burrel Harman!" he shouted over his shoulder as he angrily stalked away.

Burrel wasn't happy with the way things had not turned out, nor was he worried about Ernest's threats. As it turned out, he should have been.

~

During the months that Della and David stayed in the trailer next to Burrel and Priscilla's house, June finished the second grade and Cecil the fourth. Burrel hired a young woman to help Priscilla with chores. President Roosevelt was elected for his second term. The cavern closed for the winter and reopened in the spring. Gene Autry, the singing cowboy, recorded his first hit song, "Back In the Saddle Again." Gordon, Calcie, and their family moved to a farm near Brandywine, about twenty miles away, on the other side of the mountain.

That summer, Priscilla and Burrel had given June a baby pet lamb she called Blackie. She had been bottle-feeding him since he was a newborn. His round little body was covered by thick black wool making him look like a stuffed animal. Since June fed him and Dickie played with him while she was in school, he would follow them both around like a little puppy.

Since he looked and felt like a stuffed animal, Dickie tended to treat him like one. Unfortunately for the little lamb, this sometimes meant carrying him around by the tail.

One afternoon while Priscilla was in the house, he lugged the hapless lamb out on the porch and holding him by the tail, dangled him over the porch railing. At the sound of a loud Baa-a-a-a-a, and a thud,

Dickie found himself holding onto the tail as he looked, in astonishment at Blackie on the ground below.

Dickie managed to survive his mother's anger and Blackie his ordeal, but it was awhile before either could comfortably sit down.

Priscilla was the disciplinarian of the family. When she felt the children warranted it, she would give them a quick spanking. Each time it happened, she would say, "This hurts me as much as it does you." Then she would cry along with the child, all the while holding and cuddling her repentant offspring.

On the other hand, Burrel never spanked. He would give the misbehaving child what he called his "talking to"; which would go something like this, "You are such a wonderful child, always so good and honest. Your mother and I have always been so proud of you. I can't believe my child would do such a thing. I have always expected so much from you, and I've never been disappointed." Sighing deeply he'd quietly add, "Until now." Another sigh, and he'd conclude his talking to by telling the now repentant child, "It hurts me so much to have to talk to you like this."

After a few minutes in this vein, the disobedient child would be full of guilt and remorse. It didn't take long for all three to decide their misbehaving was too hard on their parents. They certainly didn't want to make their mother cry or be such a disappointment to their father. It was easier to behave.

Being children, though, there were times they either forgot or thought they could get away with it. For Cecil, that summer was one of those times.

One afternoon, Priscilla looked out and saw her nine year old son coming up the hill from the direction of the cavern. As he came closer she noticed he seemed to be having difficulty walking.

"Oh, no! Something has happened!" she thought, running toward him. "What's wrong, Cecil? Are you hurt?" she cried.

"I'm okay," he replied, trying to sidestep her.

"Hold still!" she demanded. "I need to take a good look at you."

Returning from taking his last group through the cavern and seeing Priscilla stooped down talking to Cecil, Burrel hurried to join them. As he drew near, he saw that Cecil was unsteady on his feet. Looking at his glazed eyes and listening to his slurred speech, he knew, immediately, what was wrong with his son.

Turning to Priscilla, he exclaimed, "This boy is drunk!"

"Drunk! He couldn't be drunk. Where would he get it?" Priscilla asked. "Cecil Harman, have you been drinking?" she demanded.

"No, Mom," he mumbled. "I haven't been drinking."

Burrel squatted down in front of him, took his face in his hands and said, "Let me smell your breath!"

Cecil squirmed, trying to escape the inevitable, but Burrel persisted. "Good Lord, Priscilla. It's gasoline. He's been sniffing gasoline."

Both parents questioned him, but in Cecil's intoxicated state, it was awhile before they found out he'd discovered the gas tank by the cavern, unscrewed the cap, stuck his nose in it and inhaled the fumes until he'd gotten dizzy.

His escapade earned him a "talking to" from his dad. He appeared properly contrite, leading Burrel to believe it would never happen again. Much to Cecil's regret, his father was proven wrong.

It was about a week later when Burrel found him on the ground near the gas tank. He had sniffed so much of the fumes, that he was groggy, barely able to hold up his head. Burrel's heart sank when he realized what had happened. He knew if he didn't put a stop to it, Cecil could do irreparable damage to himself.

For the first time in his life, he didn't give a child a "talking to." Cutting a switch from the nearest tree, he brought it down against Cecil's legs every step of the way home, saying, "You are never to sniff gasoline again! Do you hear me? Never! Never! Don't you know you could have killed yourself?"

Cecil was sober by the time they reached the house and this time he really meant it when he said he'd never do it again. He was cured.

CHAPTER THIRTY-TWO

THE MYSTERY BEGINS

A few nights later, a disturbing incident took place. The family had been in a festive mood with Priscilla and the children making sea foam candy while Burrel sat at the kitchen table watching and visiting. The children were chatting excitedly. This was not only their favorite candy, but their mom was letting them help make it. They'd turn the handle on the eggbeater while she poured the hot syrup into the soft mounds of stiffly beaten egg whites.

"It won't be long now," she said. "It will be ready to drop by spoonfuls as soon as it loses its sheen."

"Let me do it!" June pleaded. "No, I'm the oldest! I get to do it," Cecil said.

"Don't fight over it. You can both have a turn," Priscilla firmly replied, ending the argument.

Sniffing the mouth watering aroma that was filling the kitchen and observing their anxious looks of anticipation, Burrel picked up the platter and carried it outside. "I'll put it on the porch, so it will cool faster," he volunteered. He didn't want to admit it, but he was as anxious as the children to sample it.

Giving the children the pan, spoon, and beater to lick, Priscilla joined Burrel in the living room to listen to the news. They didn't hear much of it for answering the children's constant inquiry, "Is it cool yet? How much longer will it be? Is it almost ready?"

Finally, when the news was over, Priscilla brought the candy into the kitchen. She watched in anxious expectation for the look of pleasure she always saw on their faces when they bit into the first piece.

Tonight, the scene was entirely different. They were gagging and spitting the candy into the sink. "Ugh! This is awful! Phooey!" they were crying.

Burrel grabbed the plate and sniffed it. "It smells like kerosene. Someone has poured kerosene over it," he exclaimed.

"Kerosene! It can't be!" Priscilla responded. "Who would do a thing like that?"

"I don't know," he replied, but for a heart wrenching moment he wondered if he should have taken Ernest's threats more seriously.

After calming them, Priscilla ushered three disappointed children upstairs to bed. She and Burrel lay awake a long time, talking. It was almost unbelievable to them, that someone could have sneaked up on the porch while they had been in the house and done this terrible thing. Until now, they had always felt so safe in their home.

Finally, convincing themselves, it must have been someone's idea of a prank, they fell asleep.

CHAPTER THIRTY-THREE

THE BIRDS AND THE BEES

All thought of the incident took a back seat to Mace, Mabel, and the girls' visit. The cousins paired off, according to their ages; nine year olds Cecil and Inez, seven year olds June and Rose, and almost five year olds Dickie and Annamae.

Rose filled June in on the saga of Juanita and the chicken pox. Rose and Inez had played with them everyday, so it was inevitable that Juanita would be exposed. June listened with obvious glee when Rose explained, in detail, how peppered and miserable Juanita had been. Rose feigned innocence when June asked if anyone had teased Juanita, but the sparkle in her eyes said otherwise.

During that visit, Cecil and Inez decided it was time June and Rose were told the facts of life. They both still believed the doctor brought the baby in his black bag, but before the afternoon was over they had been told otherwise.

June's reaction was a complete rejection of what she'd heard. "Liars!" she yelled. "My mother wouldn't do such a thing!"

"Mine, neither!" Rose exclaimed. "Why do you make up such stuff?"

The more the older ones tried to convince them, the less they believed them. Finally, in total disgust, June said, "I'm going to ask Mom."

"Me too! I'm going to tell Mom what you said," Rose shouted.

Thinking they may have gone too far, Cecil and Inez tried to talk them out of it. Ignoring their pleas, the girls ran into the kitchen and demanded, "Do babies really come out of their mommies' tummies?"

"Who told you that?" Priscilla asked. She and Mabel were both red faced and flustered while they waited for an answer.

Cecil and Inez came in the kitchen, just in time for Rose to point an accusing finger and say, "They did! They told us."

Priscilla had hoped she wouldn't have to answer these questions quite so soon. She was both embarrassed with the subject and angry at Cecil and Inez for telling the girls. "What did you tell them?" she asked. Then, her blue eyes flashing, she demanded, "Who told you?"

"We both heard it from kids at school," Cecil replied. Then stumbling over their words, they explained what they had been told about how the baby got in there, and how the baby grew until it was time for it to come out.

While they were talking, Rose and June were nodding their heads in disagreement and murmuring an occasional "Yuk!" It only took one stern look from their mothers to put a stop to that.

It was obvious, this wasn't a subject either woman felt comfortable discussing. Watching their mother's red-faced embarrassment, the girls were beginning to be sorry they'd asked. Still flustered, Priscilla quietly told them this was the way God had planned for babies to get into the world. She explained, she hadn't said anything before because she hadn't thought they were old enough to be told. Then, going back to her dinner preparations, she said, "We'll have a talk about it later. Now go out and play."

Glad to escape, they were gone like a flash.

The events of the rest of the summer deferred "the talk". In fact, when it finally took place, it was a different place, a different time and the information was imparted by someone they didn't even know existed, that summer of 1937.

CHAPTER THIRTY-FOUR

BLACKIE

The next disturbing incident was more serious than the apparent prank of pouring kerosene over the candy. It was a few days after Mace, Mabel, and the girls had gone home, when June, wiping sleep from her eyes, sauntered into the kitchen ready to prepare Blackie's bottle for his morning feeding. Her cheerful greeting was met by a silence so overwhelming it frightened her.

Her mom was sitting at the table, tears running down her cheeks, while her dad sat quietly across from her. His blue eyes were the color of steel; his face was pale with a spot of red burning high on each cheek. She had never seen him look so angry. Standing stock still, June could hear her heart beat as she looked from her mom to her dad. What was wrong? Why was it so quiet?

Usually, this time of morning, the radio was playing, her parents were talking, and Blackie was standing outside the door loudly baaing for his breakfast. "Blackie! Where was Blackie?" June thought. He had never missed coming for his bottle since the first time he'd wobbled over to her on his unsteady baby legs.

"Where's Blackie?" she asked.

Coming around the table, Priscilla stooped down and looking into her daughter's eyes, softly said, "I'm sorry. Blackie is dead. Your dad found him by the back door when he went out to milk Bossie."

"Dead? Blackie can't be dead!" June sobbed.

"I'm sorry, Honey, but he is," Burrel softly told her as he pulled her onto his lap and tried to console her.

Later, after she had gone to her room, Burrel and Priscilla sat at the table talking about the morning events. "I can't believe anyone would do such a thing," Priscilla said. "How could anyone kill him? Everyone around here knows he was June's pet."

"I know, but there's no doubt in my mind, that's what happened. The poor little fellow must have been fed ground glass. I don't know anything else that would have caused him to bleed like he did. He'd vomited and had diarrhea and both were full of blood," Burrel explained.

"What do you think is going on?" Priscilla asked. "Whoever did this must have poured the kerosene over the candy, too. We were just fooling ourselves when we thought that was just a prank."

"This certainly isn't a prank," Burrel responded. "You know Ernest threatened me, but I didn't think anything about it."

"Ernest? Do you think it was Ernest?" she asked.

"I don't know what to think. I imagine he or Elsie, either one, would be capable of it. Don't you?" Burrel said.

"It's hard for me to believe it. Look at all the times I've helped Elsie when any of their children have been sick. She's always said she appreciated it," Priscilla replied.

"He was pretty mad when I had to let him go. You know how people are. It would be pretty easy for him to forget all you've done for them and just think about the other," Burrel stated.

"This is going to be hard on June," Priscilla said. "It's hard for a child to understand someone doing such a thing. I told you that Calcie has been wanting the kids to come and visit. Maybe this would be a good time for June to go. What do you think?"

"I think the way she loves to play with Bonnie and Ruby, it would be a very good idea."

"I'll go ahead and write to Calcie and see when she wants us to bring her over."

Arrangements were made for June to go for a visit in a couple weeks, then for Cecil to stay the following week.

~

Since she didn't get to see them as often now that they lived in

Brandywine, June was excited about the prospect of spending an entire week with her cousins.

The house they now lived in was open, bright and airy, just the opposite of the dark, dreary, cold one, where they'd lived with Uncle Luke. A plain weathered farmhouse, it was encircled by wooden walkways. One led to the well where an oak bucket, hanging from a rope, was used to draw water. June loved to watch the older cousins lower it into the well, turn the crank, and bring it to the surface full of cool fresh water.

During her visit, as her dad had predicted, she had a wonderful time playing with Bonnie and Ruby. Aunt Calcie and Uncle Gordon with their warm loving ways made her feel welcome. Her aunt let the three girls help her cut out and ice sugar cookies, and Uncle Gordon took them, one by one, on a horseback ride around the fields.

She was having a good time, but she had gotten homesick for her brothers and her mom and dad. The day they came to pick her up, she, Bonnie, and Ruby had been standing by the gate, listening and watching for the car to approach and were the first to see them arrive.

Watching them alight from the car, she thought her dad looked especially handsome in his white dress shirt and white trousers and her mother beautiful in her sky blue dress. She hardly had a chance to notice what her brothers were wearing, as they tumbled out of the car hardly pausing to say hello as they ran past her to play with their cousins.

After they all feasted on the lunch Calcie had prepared, the children went outside to play while the adults talked about the disturbing incidents that had been taking place. Although they all thought the killing of the pet lamb was probably the end of it, they still felt apprehensive.

CHAPTER THIRTY-FIVE

THE BUSHWHACKING

It was late afternoon before they left for home, leaving Cecil to enjoy a week with his cousins. By the time they stopped at a store in Franklin for supplies and at the hotel restaurant for a dish of ice cream, it was dark when they crossed North Mountain and both children were sleeping.

When they got home, Priscilla led the sleepy children upstairs to help them get ready for bed. Burrel said, "I'll go check on the chickens before I come in," as he headed toward the hen house.

Upstairs, Priscilla was having trouble getting June to wake up enough to change into her pajamas, when a sound, like a car's backfire, exploded the silence of the night. This was followed by a faint cry from Burrel, "Priscilla, help me. I'm shot."

"Oh, my God!" Priscilla screamed as she ran down the stairs.

Completely awake now, Dickie and June ran after her. When they arrived in the kitchen, the scene that greeted them was to be forever seared into their brains. Their father was leaning against the stove; blood from his many wounds seeping through his white shirt and trousers. Running to him, Priscilla put her strong, young arms around him and helped him into a chair before she ran screaming onto the porch, "Help! Help! Burrel's been shot!"

Seeing and hearing, Burrel was afraid for her. "Priscilla," he called, "Come in here. He might still be out there."

His voice was too weak for her to hear. Turning to June, his voice barely more than a whisper, he said, "Go to the door and tell your mother to come inside. He might still be out there! Now don't go outside. Just tell her from the door." June, afraid her father was going to die, and that something was going to happen to her mother, obeyed instantly.

As soon as Priscilla heard Burrel's message, she realized her danger and quickly came back into the house. She knew, though, that if she didn't get help, he was going to die. Grabbing clean towels, she tried to arrest the flow of blood, but it was coming from too many places for her to be successful. "The telephone! I have to call someone," she thought, but at that moment she couldn't remember the most familiar ring.

"I can't let him die," she silently screamed as she frantically cranked the telephone. The frenzied ringing awakened people on their line, and one by one they answered. They were greeted by Priscilla's cry of, "Burrel's been shot! Someone help me."

Nellie was the first one to hear these horrifying words. "Priscilla, is that you? What has happened?"

Priscilla's voice was filled with relief when she realized Burrel's sister was on the line. As soon as Nellie had been assured Burrel was still alive, she said her husband Curt would be there, and that she would call the rest of the family.

Curt and Verde arrived simultaneously. The minute Nellie had told Verde what had happened, he was out the door and on his way. Priscilla almost fainted with relief when she saw the two men walk through the door. Verde's soft voice and strong demeanor were reassuring. For the first time that night, she dared to hope everything was going to be all right.

The men were shocked when they took in the scene, Burrel sitting in his chair, his blood soaking through his white clothes, his face the color of the few white places still visible on his shirt and trousers. Nearby were the silent frightened children and Priscilla with her tear streaked face and blood-stained dress.

~

Within minutes, the men had Burrel in Verde's car, wrapped in a blanket, with Priscilla sitting close beside him, heading for the hospital in Harrisburg, Virginia. Dickie was taken to stay with his aunt Gussie and cousin Dale. June went to Olie and Josie's to be with her cousin Ruthalene. Riding in Curt's car on their way to stay with their cousins, they watched fearfully as the taillights of their Uncle Verde's car disappeared from their sight.

The thirty-five mile drive across the mountains to the hospital seemed endless, but they finally arrived. As Verde drove under the canopy, by the emergency entrance, they were met by doctors and nurses who had been alerted to expect them. The injured man was lifted from the car, placed on a gurney, and wheeled into the operating room, where the waiting doctor removed the buckshot pellets from his body. One could not be removed because it was lodged too close to the base of his brain and others were too close to his spine. These, he carried with him for the rest of his days.

Sitting in the waiting room, Priscilla and Verde were afraid they might have gotten him to the hospital too late, until they saw the smile on the doctor's face as he walked into the waiting room. He reassured them, "He's weak from the loss of blood, but in a few days he'll be back on his feet. You can both go in and see him, but he's not going to wake for awhile." His eyes turned to Priscilla's wan face, and his heart went out to her. Putting a reassuring arm on her shoulder he softly said, "You look exhausted, young lady. You need to get some rest."

Priscilla had been too focused on what was happening to Burrel to realize, until now, how tired she was. It would be good to lie down, but she wasn't going to leave Burrel until she could see for herself that he was going to be all right.

When she voiced this to the doctor, he told her they could set up a bed for her in Burrel's room. Once this was done, and Verde was sure they were both in good hands, he left, so he could call home. He knew no one would be sleeping until they heard from him.

By the time they returned from the hospital a couple weeks later, the officer's investigation was well underway. He had no trouble finding the spot along the path to the second henhouse where someone had hidden, waiting for Burrel to come by. It was obvious by the number of cigarette butts littering the ground behind the stump, that the person had been there a long time.

Usually Burrel's routine when they returned late at night was to first check the henhouse left of the garage, then walk down the path to the one a couple hundred yards back of the house. For some reason that night he had decided not to go to the second one. The officer said that decision, no doubt, had saved his life. If he had taken that path, he would have been within a couple feet of the bushwhacker and received the full brunt of the shotgun blast.

As it was, the attempted murderer, seeing his chance to kill Burrel slipping away when he started up the back steps, had fired from his position one hundred feet away. From that distance the shots had been spread out over a wider angle preventing him from taking the full force.

"You are one lucky man!" the officer said. "If you'd taken that other path, I'd be investigating your murder."

Burrel told him he'd been hit with such force, it spun him around and propelled him into the kitchen. One minute he was walking up the steps, and the next minute, he found himself leaning against the stove.

He was at a loss to explain why he hadn't followed his usual routine that night, but Priscilla was convinced that Somebody was watching over him.

~

The officer filled them in on the rest of the investigation. He had been talking to people in the community. One source had told him Ernest's two brothers-in-law had been heard boasting a couple weeks earlier that one would get on one side of the house while the second one got on the other and "they were going to get the son of a bitch tonight."

When he talked to them, they confessed they'd been drunk when they said it, but had never had any intention of going through with it. They'd told him Ernest had talked to them about "getting even" with Burrel, but they didn't think he had the guts to do it himself.

Priscilla's eyes were flashing when she demanded, "How much guts would it take to hide behind a stump on a man's own property and shoot him when he walked by?"

The officer agreed that whoever did it was indeed a coward. Before leaving he assured them he would leave no stone unturned until he had arrested the guilty party. Ernest was the prime suspect although there were some who pointed the finger at his wife, Elsie. The only alibi they had was that they were home in bed together. It was clear the officer didn't believe them, and he wasn't sure he believed her brothers.

"As soon as I know anything, I'll let you know," was his parting remark before getting into his cruiser and driving away. They watched as he stopped in front of Ernest's house and knocked on the door. It was cautiously opened, and he disappeared inside.

"He'll take care of it," Priscilla said, then added, "You'd better come inside and rest. You know what the doctor said about taking it easy for a few more days."

Since his body was telling him the doctor knew what he was talking about, he didn't argue. While he stretched out on the couch listening to the radio and watching the children play, he felt grateful to be here alive with the ones he loved.

He'd always scoffed when he'd heard others say you didn't die until your time came, but he was beginning to wonder. Could that be why he hadn't walked down that path to certain death? Could it be this wasn't his time? If it wasn't, did God have something he wanted him to do? He pondered this as he closed his eyes and drifted off to sleep. It was years later, before he had his answer.

~

When he'd gotten home the children had stayed close to him as if to assure themselves he was safe. As he lie on the couch, they silently watched his chest rise and fall as he slept, grateful he was alive.

The horror of that night had hung over their play while their father had been in the hospital. Dickie and June hadn't been able to erase from their minds the picture of their dad with his white clothes soaked with his blood. Sometimes the adults had noticed a look of horror, sadness, or fear creep across their faces in the midst of a game, at mealtime, or when they were getting ready for bed. Although they had tried to reassure them, they hadn't always been successful. Neither child could believe their father was safe until he got home, and they could see for themselves.

For Cecil, it was a different matter. Aunt Calcie had broken the news to him after his dad was out of danger. He, like his brother and sister, had worried until they were all together again.

The events of this summer marked the beginning of the end of life as they had known it. The children were not given the freedom they'd had to roam the woods and fields. Their walks to Aunt Gussie's, accompanied by the monster's heartbeat, were curtailed unless their mother could go with them. Burrel and Priscilla were cautious about being outside after dark. Any time it couldn't be avoided, they were watchful and wary.

When school started, different children were occupying their seats in Miss Lily's class at the one room schoolhouse. June and Cecil were attending school in Riverton where Burrel's brother, Olie, and his family had moved several months earlier. Olie had gotten a job as a school bus driver with his route taking him within a couple miles of the cavern. Burrel and Priscilla had gone to the school board and gotten permission for Olie to drive those extra miles to pick up June and Cecil and take them to school in Riverton.

Their new school was larger with a separate class for each grade. At first, they missed Miss Lily and their classmates at the one room schoolhouse, but it didn't take long for them to make new friends.

CHAPTER THIRTY-SIX

THE VICTIMS

At first Priscilla and Burrel had received progress reports from the officer at least every other week. He seemed confidant that he would be making an arrest at any time. Then there was total silence. They neither heard from him or had their calls returned. One morning after the children were off to school, Burrel said to Priscilla, "I don't know what's going on. The officer acts like he doesn't want to talk to us. Do you think I'm just imagining something, or is he acting strange?"

Priscilla had been thinking the same thing. "I've noticed it too. He acts more like we have committed a crime, instead of being victims. What do you think is going on?"

Looking perplexed, he replied, "I don't know, but I intend to find out. This Saturday let's take the kids and go over to see Calcie. On our way we can stop at the police station and talk to him in person. I don't like the way we have to live, always looking over our shoulders. I won't feel any of us are safe until he is behind bars!"

There was a marked difference in the treatment they received this time when they saw the officer. Distinctly cool, his manner furtive, he was reluctant to answer their questions. When he responded to an inquiry, he avoided looking either of them in the eye. Instead he looked at the floor, ceiling or somewhere over their shoulders.

Finally, in frustration, Burrel demanded, "What is going on here? When you were at our house, you said you were about ready to make an arrest. I just want to know why you haven't."

"Just a minute, Mr. Harman, I'm doing all I can do. I can't arrest anyone without evidence," the officer responded defensively, addressing a spot about two feet left of Burrel's ear. "Sometimes, in cases like this, we just can't find out who did it. You just need to be patient. I assure you, when I find out anything, you'll be the first to know."

"Are you telling me that you're going to let Ernest get away with it? You don't even sound as if you care whether you arrest someone or not," Burrel angrily replied.

Apparently speaking to the filing cabinet, the officer said, "There's no need for you to get upset." Switching his attention to a scratch on his desk, as if the answer might lie there, he mumbled, "I just wanted you to know that this might end up being one of our unsolved cases. It's not that we're not trying." His voice trailed off, barely audible as he muttered the last sentence.

Burrel studied him for a moment before saying, "You wouldn't be so quick to give up on trying to find the killer if you were the one who'd been shot, or if you had to worry about the safety of your family."

"Now, Mr. Harman, calm down," he cajoled before continuing, his voice full of sarcasm, "We're not looking for a killer, are we? You look alive to me."

Burrel very seldom lost his temper, but he was close to it as he sternly charged, "You're hiding something! I've always found if a man can't look me in the eye, he usually has something to hide. What is it?"

The officer's voice wasn't quite convincing when he hesitantly replied, "I don't have anything to hide," but his eyes still didn't quite meet Burrel's.

Burrel shook his head in disgust as he turned to Priscilla and the children and said, "Let's go. We're wasting our time here." As they started out the door, the officer's protesting voice followed them, "Mr. Harman, you don't have to act that way. I'll be in touch."

"I don't think we'll hold our breath," Burrel informed Priscilla as they headed for the car.

"That man acts like he's been paid off," Priscilla said when they had all settled into the car and were headed for Calcie's house.

"That would explain how he's changed his tune, wouldn't it?" Burrel said. They rode on for a few minutes in silence before Burrel added, "I can't believe the change in his attitude. I don't think we can expect any more action from him."

"I don't think so either," Priscilla replied. "I've heard about crooked lawmen before. I just didn't think he was one of them."

"I don't know what else could have made him change like that, do you?" Burrel said.

Priscilla responded that nothing else made sense to her.

They only visited a short time with Calcie and her family before going home. Mindful of what had happened the last time, they wanted to be home before dark.

~

The next few months saw rumors flying and the family engulfed in a rash of gossip. Nellie had overheard people talking in the general store and told Burrel about it. "People are saying the reason the investigation was called off is because you were fooling around with Elsie, and Ernest was only trying to protect his happy home."

Momentarily, Burrel was stunned into silence, and then he exploded, "Elsie Scraggs! People are saying I've been sleeping with that Elsie! Are they crazy? I've never even given her a second look."

The accusation was ludicrous, but he knew that wouldn't keep people from believing it. That wouldn't bother him too much as long as the people who mattered to him believed in him.

"You don't believe it, do you?" he asked Nellie.

"You and Elsie? Heaven forbid! Of course I don't believe it!" she exclaimed. Even though she had assured him she didn't believe it, she still looked troubled.

"What's the matter?" Burrel asked. "Is there something else you're not telling me?"

"No," she responded. "I was just wondering if Priscilla has heard yet, and what she'll think when she does."

He looked at his sister as if the idea that his wife would doubt him had never crossed his mind, but once the thought had been planted, it was hard not to wonder. Would she believe the gossip, or would she see this as further victimization? He fervently hoped it would be the latter.

Putting his arm around his sister's shoulder, he said, "Thanks, Sis, for telling me. I think I'd better go home and talk to Priscilla. I don't want her to hear this from someone else. She's been through enough."

Nellie told him how sorry she was to have to tell him such a thing, but she thought he needed to know. He assured her she had done the right thing, before he headed home to tell his wife what was being said.

One look at Priscilla's face told him that she'd already heard. She was sitting at the kitchen table, staring unseeingly into her coffee cup. Her face looked pale except for the two bright scarlet spots high on her cheekbones. When she looked at him, her eyes were bright. "Uh, Oh." he thought. "Those eyes look like the sparks are flying." He recognized the signs of anger. Was the anger directed at him or at the gossip?

He walked over to the stove, poured himself a cup of coffee then pulled up a chair and sat down beside her. "I just talked to Nellie. She told me what people are saying. You've heard, haven't you?"

She nodded. "Who told you, and what did they say?" he asked.

"I picked up the phone to call Nellie, and I overheard someone talking," she answered. "I sure gave them a piece of my mind! I told them just what I thought about people spreading gossip when they didn't know what they were talking about. They were so sorry, but I'm sure the only thing they were sorry about was being caught."

For the first time since he'd talked to Nellie, he smiled. "Good for you! I'm glad you set them straight." Again looking troubled, he said, "This isn't going to be the end of it. It's hard to tell what they'll be saying next."

"I just don't understand how all of a sudden we've become the villains. If the officer would just make an arrest there would be an end to these vicious rumors," she said.

"Don't count on it. He's not going to do anything!" Burrel fervently declared.

~

That night, as they were getting ready for bed, he watched her sitting at her dressing table brushing her hair. Gone was the short bob of the twenties. She now wore it with the sides softly waved and the ends tucked into a soft roll. No longer the young girl he'd married, she was now a lovely, mature woman.

The birth of each child had added a few pounds. In his eyes this made her appear even more womanly. A proud woman, she always looked her best and saw to it that their children did too. He couldn't help think about all the storms they had weathered together. He hoped they would be able to weather this one.

"Priscilla," he said. "How could anyone think I would look at Elsie when I have you? Just look at the two of you. You're always so clean and pretty. Elsie is a mess! Her hair is never combed. She always has a baby on one breast and a toddler on the other. The few times I've seen her smile, all I can see is the gap from her missing front teeth. How could anyone think I could turn to a woman like that when I have you?"

His words made her smile. The picture he had painted was an accurate one. Priscilla had always felt Elsie was too overwhelmed by having one child after another to care how she looked. It was true her children were so close that it was not unusual to see her nursing two at once.

In Priscilla's mind she knew the rumors weren't true, but somewhere deep inside her was a nagging doubt. There had been other women in his life before her, how could she be certain there wouldn't be others.

The next gossip they heard was that Elsie had shot Burrel, because they had been having an affair and Burrel had broken it off.

As they had done before, when gossip surrounded them after Cecil's birth, they went about their business, holding their heads high and taught the children to do the same. They had staunch supporters, though, in Burrel's family and some close friends whose steadfast backing made some of those spreading the rumors realize how ridiculous they were. As with all gossip, as time passed, it died, to be replaced by rumors about some other hapless victim.

CHAPTER THIRTY-SEVEN

STARING INTO THE BARREL

In the midst of this, Burrel had heard from his spelunker friends about a group of investors from Moorefield who wanted to open a cavern in the next county between Seneca Rocks and Petersburg. They needed someone to explore it and get it ready to be opened to the public.

It would involve the kind of work he had done at Seneca Caverns. This prospect was both exciting and overwhelming. He remembered all the hard work he and Verde had put into opening the other cavern and wasn't sure he wanted to go through it again.

Undecided, he and Priscilla spent several evenings discussing it. They hated the prospect of leaving everything they loved here. Besides having the house and a job Burrel liked, they were able to save money by having their own cow and chickens and space for a garden. If he took the job, they would have to leave all this. Reluctant to change their life, they decided that Burrel should at least talk to the investors before they made any decision.

He was full of enthusiasm when he got home since they had offered him a job with a man named Lige Allen to prepare the cavern to be opened to the public. Then if he wanted to continue, they wanted him to stay on as manager. It would be a package deal with Priscilla working in the office selling tickets and keeping the books. No house would be provided, but they would be paid an extra twenty-five dollars a month and would receive stock in the company.

It didn't take them long to decide to take the investors up on the first part of the offer. That would give him time to make up his mind whether he would stay at his job at Seneca Caverns or take the one as manager at the, as yet, unnamed new cavern.

The day Elsie helped make the decision for them dawned clear and bright, with the scent of early summer flowers in the air and a few clouds drifting lazily across the sky. The atmosphere at the house by the cavern was carefree and relaxed with everyone enjoying this beautiful day. Burrel was working at the new cavern. The boys had been playing cowboys and Indians while June helped her mother bake a cake and some cookies for the weekend.

When they'd taken the last batch of cookies from the oven, they came out on the porch and sat watching a squirrel fly from tree to tree. Priscilla called the boys to come join them for some warm cookies and to watch the squirrel's antics. As if aware of his audience, he became more and more daring, causing them to hold their breath as he swung from one branch to another. The sound of a motor and blare of a car horn startled him, causing him to scamper into the foliage and disappear from view.

Turning toward the road, Priscilla and the children returned the mailman's wave as he drove by. "I guess the mail's here," Priscilla remarked.

"Let us go get it," June pleaded. Their mailbox was located past the Scragg's house at the bottom of the hill. Priscilla agreed to let them go, but cautioned them not to walk in the road in front of Ernest and Elsie's house. After giving their promise that they'd stay on their own property, they started down the hill, full of good humor at the joy of such a lovely day.

Their happy mood was shattered by the shrill sound of a female voice. Looking upward to the second floor porch of the Scragg's house, they discovered its source. "You brats had better stay away from my property!" Elsie shrieked. Ready to reply that they weren't on her property, the words died in their throats when they looked up and saw her pointing a gun at them.

Cecil's eyes darted from where his sister and brother were standing, to the long barrel of the gun pointing unwaveringly at them. Yelling for them to hide behind a tree, he turned and ran to the house to get their mother.

At the first sound of his cry, "Mom, Mom, she's got a gun!" Priscilla was out of the house and on her way down the hill to protect her children. As she ran down the steps, she could see June and Dickie still standing where Cecil had left them while obscenities were spewing from Elsie's mouth. Priscilla thought she looked like a madwoman with her hair sticking out in wild clumps, her eyes blazing, and spittle mingling with the sweat running down her face.

The gun was no longer pointing at June and Dickie. It was now pointing directly at Priscilla. Like a tigress protecting her cubs, Priscilla wasn't thinking of her own safety, only of getting her children out of harm's way. Then she could try to reason with Elsie. In a firm steady voice she told her two youngest children, "Move slowly, but get behind that tree. I'll stand in front of you until you've hidden. You'll be all right, but you have to do it. Now!"

Her words seemed to unglue their feet from where, frozen with fear, they had been standing. June took Dickie's hand, and together they scampered to safety behind the nearest tree. Priscilla silently blessed the unknown person who had planted it, as she steadily turned, and showing more confidence than she felt, faced Elsie and the gun. She tried to keep her voice calm as she talked to Elsie. "Elsie, we've always been friends. You don't really want to hurt me or my children."

This brought wild laughter and more obscenities, but the gun didn't waver. It was still pointing at Priscilla.

"Elsie, don't you remember the time I sat up all night with you when little Ernest had the croup? Remember how I helped you keep the steam pot going? Do you remember how his croup broke and he was better the next morning? Weren't we friends then?" Priscilla said, still trying to keep her voice composed and non-threatening. She knew if she raised her voice in anger, it might cause Elsie to lose the tiny thread of sanity she had left.

"You think you're such a big shot, don't you?" Elsie screeched. "Coming here from Ohio, acting like you own the place, married to the boss. You and that stuck up husband of yours don't care whether people like us have a job or not. You wouldn't care if my children starved, would you?"

While she had been talking, her oldest daughter, Maudie, had quietly opened the door onto the porch and was silently moving across the floor behind her mother. Not wanting Elsie to become aware of Maudie's presence, Priscilla continued to talk, "Elsie, I know how much you love your children. I've always thought you were a good mother."

Before Elsie could reply, Maudie had crept up behind her and grabbed the gun from her hands. Priscilla and Maudie were both praying it wouldn't go off. Their prayers were answered. There was no explosion.

Without the gun, Elsie became docile and allowed her daughter to lead her into the house.

～

Now that the danger was apparently over, Priscilla felt ready to collapse, but she still had to hold on until she had all her children safely in the house.

A small voice came from behind the tree, "Mom, can we come out now?"

"Yes, June, you can come out now. Let's walk quickly to the house," Priscilla said. As she took their hands, she spoke soothingly, trying to allay their fear. "We're alright now. Let's go into the house and have some more of those cookies. Then if Uncle Verde can come and get us we'll go visit your grandpap, and you can play with your cousins. I'll even bet Aunt Gussie will make you a whipped cream pie."

By now they were in the house and despite the heat of the day, Priscilla had Cecil help her close and lock all the windows and doors and pull the blinds. They didn't open the door until Verde arrived. Leaving a note for Burrel, Priscilla took her children to the safety of their grandfather's house.

When Burrel returned that night and saw the closed house, he knew something was wrong. With his heart pounding, he unlocked the door, calling, "Priscilla, I'm home. June, Cecil, Dickie, where are you?" Then seeing the note propped up on the kitchen table, he read it and quickly headed for the car and Pap's house.

When he saw Priscilla in the kitchen helping Gussie with supper, he breathed a sigh of relief. Seeing that she was all right assured him the children were, too.

That evening as they gathered around the table at his father's house, he looked at the faces of his wife and children, and knew Elsie had

made the decision for them. If his wife and children weren't safe, he'd
have to take them someplace where they would be. He would take the
manager's job, and they would move to Petersburg.

That night he and Priscilla talked into the wee small hours of the
morning, and they agreed they would have to move as soon as possible.
He'd call Moorefield tomorrow and let them know he would take the
job.

"While you're in Petersburg you'd better look around for a house,"
Priscilla told him. Grimly, he nodded agreement.

CHAPTER THIRTY-EIGHT

A NEW HOME

A house was found and preparations were made for moving day. Leaving their home at the cavern was a sorrowful experience for all of them. There were so many memories here: Dickie's birth, the children starting school, playing cards with Johnny, sitting around the table talking to Walter Amos, walking through the field and woods, the children's game about the monster's heartbeat, the plane landing in the field and taking Priscilla and Cecil soaring over the rocks, the merry-go-round, opening day at the cavern, sitting on the porch listening to Priscilla's father talk about his father and his childhood, visiting with friends and family on this front porch, and looking down over the serenity of the valley during the changing seasons.

This was all overshadowed by the events of the last year. It was time to close the book on this chapter of their lives and move on. As long as they were all together, that was all that mattered. They were confident, this was going to be a good move for them, a new home, the new cavern, Burrel's new job, and a chance to meet people and make new friends. Since the children had never lived in town, they were beginning to find the prospect exciting. If they'd been able to look into the future, though, and see the path their lives would soon be taking, they might not have been as optimistic.

As they rode down the long drive for the last time, Priscilla looked back at what had been her home for so long and thought, "All the things that have happened here will, like echoes in my mind, be with me forever."

They all liked the house Burrel had found for them. It was a large yellow house on Main Street with spacious airy rooms. A wide porch surrounded the front and two sides, and a flower bordered white fence enclosed the tree-shaded yard. The porch soon became the children's favorite spot. Whether June and her friends were setting up a play house, playing with paper dolls, or she and Dickie were playing with his toy cars, or the boys shooting marbles, it was a wonderful place to play. Best of all for June it turned out to be a perfect place to learn to roller skate.

Street skating was the rage for the neighborhood children. It was not only fun, but also their main method of transportation. Buckling their skates onto their shoes, they'd travel from one end of town to the other.

They had quickly made friends with neighbor children, Cecil with Dick Oates, and Dickie with Dick's brother Jerald. June's first girlfriend was Helen Layton, but she had her eye on Dick Oates as a boyfriend. Since his parents owned the Pepsi Cola Bottling Company, he and Jerald were allowed to invite friends to visit the plant. Free Pepsi was always available to the neighborhood children.

Helen's father owned the local automobile agency. Burrel would tease June by saying that it was too bad Helen's father wasn't the one giving out free samples. While that would never happen, Mr. Layton did allow them to play in the show room, even letting them sit behind the wheel pretending they owned this sparkling new vehicle.

Helen, a pretty blonde blue-eyed girl, lived in a big brick house at the top of the hill on Main Street. Since she had come along after her brother was grown and married, her parents treated her as an only child and couldn't refuse her anything.

The first time June went to their house, she was astonished at the number of dolls Helen had. Her bed and dresser were covered with them, and they spilled over onto the floor to ceiling shelves her father had built for her. This collection was unusual in depression era America. June being eight years old had received eight dolls in her entire lifetime, one for each Christmas. They were well worn and much loved, not new looking and untouched like Helen's display.

She liked her new friend, although there were times Helen could be bossy. This sometimes resulted in a good-sized battle of their wills. The first time Priscilla witnessed one of their arguments, she'd been standing at the kitchen sink, washing dishes and casually observing them at play in the back yard. "I'm so glad June has made such a nice friend," she was thinking, when without warning their play had erupted into a loud shouting match.

Quickly wiping her wet hands on her apron, she'd dashed for the yard. Certain she was going to have to separate them before they inflicted physical damage on each other, she was amazed to see them heading for Helen's house, arms looped around each other's shoulder. She stood, hands on her hips, staring after their retreating figures, shaking her head, she murmured, "Well, I'll be...."

Later that evening, June appeared puzzled when her mother questioned her about the quarrel. "I don't know what you mean, Mom. She's my best friend." From then on Priscilla observed that although the girls' relationship was sometimes volatile, they had too much fun together to remain angry for very long.

Saturday was special for all the neighborhood children, since they got to go downtown to the picture show at The Alpine Theater. Priscilla would hand Cecil, June, and Dickie eleven cents each for the movie and to buy a lollipop next door at Sites Restaurant.

Priscilla cautioned June and Cecil to take care of their little brother. For June this was a pleasure. Though he was quite self sufficient, she was reluctant to give up her "mother hen" role. When they finally settled in their seats, it was to watch a double feature and an episode of a serial. It was a continuing melodrama, each week leaving the hero or heroine in a dangerous spot, usually tied to a railroad track with a train barreling toward the helpless victim, or a buzz saw whirling only inches from the skull.

To provide variety, at other times, he or she might be in a runaway car heading over a cliff. Whichever it was, the audience was left in suspense until the next week when the hero or heroine was miraculously saved at the last split second.

CHAPTER THIRTY-NINE

OPENING DAY

The entire family went to see the progress being made with the new cavern. It was exciting going in after the electricity had been installed. As Burrel threw the light switches, and they wound their way down the path, golden light illuminated every nook and cranny causing them to discover formations they hadn't seen when they had first viewed it by lantern light.

As opening day approached, the challenge of naming the cavern fell on Burrel and Priscilla. They'd experimented with different names but none had caught their fancy until one Sunday when they took the children picnicking at a rugged spot in the area known as Smoke Hole. Opening day was fast approaching and feeling the pressure of not yet deciding on a name was causing them to feel glum.

They'd eaten and were sitting in gloomy silence when Priscilla speaking in a hesitant voice, said, "Why don't we call it Smoke Hole Caverns, after this area? After all, the cavern is right in the middle of the Smoke Hole region."

They all liked the idea, and the cavern was officially named. This bit of history was lost over the next few years as the cavern was bought and sold to numerous owners. Each new owner related the history as they knew it adding or subtracting bits and pieces of folklore as the years passed.

One of the subtractions was the part Burrel and Priscilla had played in making this cavern a major tourist attraction. Years later when June toured the cavern as a visitor she was surprised to hear the guide credit Lige Allen with the total responsibility for opening the cavern. No mention was made of the work Burrel had put into this venture.

June corrected this erroneous information both with the guide and one of the co-owners. She was aware this might be an exercise in futility, and that it was possible this early explorer, her father, might never receive the recognition he deserved. Even if this would turn out to be the case it couldn't take away the memories of those early days and the enthusiasm the young family had felt at being a part of the exciting venture.

~

That year, of 1938, in the entertainment world Kate Smith introduced a new song called God Bless America, Orson Welles and The Mercury Radio Theater frightened Americans with War of The Worlds, a newscast style presentation of an invasion by little green men from Mars. Bette Davis won an Oscar for the movie Jezebel, and Spencer Tracy won for Boys Town. Of far more importance to the Harman family, Smoke Hole Caverns was opened to the public.

Before the big day arrived, Burrel, Cecil, and Dickie had traveled the roadways, distributing pamphlets and getting permission from farmers to have advertisements painted on their barns. Priscilla had written and mailed news releases to newspapers from one end of the state to the other.

Opening day attendance was a testimony to the success of their efforts. Priscilla sold the first ticket when the doors opened at noon. This was followed by a steady flow, until nightfall, of people anxious to see West Virginia's newest tourist attraction.

While June spent most of the day in the office with her mother, Cecil and Dickie were busy attaching bumper stickers to the cars for the grand sum of one penny for each one. They worked hard for their money, as they had to string thread-like wire through small holes on each end of the sign, and then secure it to the car's bumper. As they watched cars exiting the parking lot, Burrel smiled his approval, "Well, boys, I'd say this is pretty good advertising for us. Each of these cars will be like a traveling billboard. What do you think?"

Their faces were bathed in smiles at their dad's approval as they hurried off to affix "billboards" to the new arrivals.

Stepping through the door into the office, Burrel asked Priscilla and June, "How are you two doing?"

"I don't think they've stopped coming since I opened the door. I've enjoyed meeting and talking to the people, though. We've had some come through from as far away as Parkersburg," Priscilla said. "I do think June would like to get out of here. How about taking her with you the next time you show a group through?"

Looking at his daughter, Burrel was sorry he hadn't thought of it himself. Staying in the office couldn't be much fun for an eight year old. "How about it, June? Do you want to go with me?"

Before the words were out of his mouth, she'd slipped down from the stool and grabbed his hand. "Let's go!" she said as she started pulling him toward the door.

"Wait a minute," Burrel grinned. "We have to wait until these people get their tickets. Then we'll be on our way."

June waited patiently while her mother made change and handed over the tickets, then she proudly walked alongside her dad as he gathered the group together and headed for the entrance to the cavern.

~

As the group walked under the stone archway and through the wrought iron gates, they appeared to be entering a different world. Seconds before, they had stood in the glare of the bright hot sun, fanning themselves and complaining about the heat of the day. Now they found themselves in a cool dim chamber surrounded by stone walls and a ceiling vaulting thirty feet above them. A sound, like the gentle flow of water in a mountain stream, soon reached their ears.

Burrel turned on another light and started his spiel by telling them that this was an underground stream and its source hadn't yet been found. As they moved on, he showed them formations that looked like icicles. Some were suspended from the ceiling and others seemed to be spouting up from the floor. Others intertwined, grew together to form a column.

As all eyes turned toward Burrel, he explained that the ones hanging from the ceiling were called stalactites and the ones from the floor stalagmites. If anyone had trouble remembering which was which, just keep in mind that the stalactite "had to hold on tight, to keep from falling from the ceiling."

Before he could go on, someone from his audience pointed to the ceiling and said, "That water dripping from it makes it look like a melting icicle."

"That dripping water is what causes the stalactites to take shape. That same water dripping onto the stalagmites causes them to form. It took millions of years for all these formations to get to this size. They aren't much bigger now then they were in the days of the cave men," Burrel responded.

Everyone looked around as if picturing cave men in the dim recesses. "Are there any cave men here?" a freckle faced, red headed little boy asked. Burrel eyes twinkled as he looked down into the anxious face and replied, "Not unless you count me. My partner Lige Allen and I are what's called spelunkers. We explore caves before they're open to the public. That's what we did here." He went on to tell them what it was like when they first saw it and about the work they'd done to prepare for this day.

As June listened, she remembered the many times he'd come home, looking like he'd crawled out of a coal bin, his face and hands black from the dirt they'd dug and carried out to make this wide path and to unearth the formations they were now viewing. She could almost smell the lingering fumes from the graphite lamp he'd worn on his cap.

She couldn't help compare, in her minds eye, the way he'd looked then to the way he looked today, tall and handsome in his white shirt and gray flannel trousers, his blue eyes twinkling and his white smile flashing.

Her thoughts were interrupted by the sound of indrawn breath and sighs of, "Oh! Ah!" from the crowd. Her father had flipped off the lights, throwing the room into total darkness. Then he turned another on, casting lights of red, green, and blue onto a cascade of flowing, rippling stone. She had seen the formation before, but not with the special effects.

She stood, feeling as much in awe as the rest of the audience, while her dad changed the lights from one hue to another. She had heard her parents talk about the formation they were going to call aurora borealis or northern lights. She'd read about the real northern lights and thought

206 Juane Harman Betts

this was well named. It certainly had the audience's approval.

The group moved on, gingerly making their way across a bridge spanning a goldfish filled pool and came to a formation aptly named the pipe organ. It was so called because the series of long pipe-like formations was similar to organs they'd seen in church. To further illustrate the resemblance, Burrel gently tapped the pipes with a baton surrounding them with the mellow sounds of music.

This cavern, unlike Seneca Caverns, did not have a rear exit, making it necessary for them to retrace their steps to return to the entrance. Anyone who thought the tour was over, though, was in for a surprise, as Burrel still had other attractions to show them. First, he played his flashlight over dozens of ribbon thin rocks hanging suspended from above their heads. When he had their attention, he turned a switch, causing the light he and Lige had positioned behind them to accentuate the translucent shades of amber and mauve.

"Can you see how much it looks like strips of bacon? I think some-one must have left us some for breakfast," Burrel quipped. Grinning, he added, "Now all we need is an egg to go with it."

Swinging his light to the left of them, he said, "Well, I do believe someone has cooked one just for us."

"It does look like an egg," a man in the group called out, as all eyes turned to look at the formation shaped like an egg cooked sunny side up.

June had been waiting for her dad to point out the next one, so she could observe people's reaction. She wasn't disappointed when he pointed to the left and said, "And here we have a baby crawling away from us. Looks like it must have lost its diaper."

Everyone laughed, as they looked at the perfectly shaped stone buttocks. They were still laughing when they exited into the bright sunlight.

As she and her dad walked back to the office, she looked up into his face and grinned. "That was fun! Can I go again?"

"You'll have plenty of chances. We'll be coming out here so much, you'll probably get tired of it."

As she started to protest, he added, "Go tell the boys to come into the office. You each can either have some ice cream, candy, or pop." She ran over to where the boys were stooped down fastening a sign to the bumper of a black Ford. When they heard the message, they finished quickly and followed her back to the office.

They each took their time deciding what they wanted. In the end, June picked a chocolate covered square of vanilla ice cream, called an Eskimo Pie, Dickie selected five pieces of penny candy, and Cecil swaggered away swigging a Coca Cola.

The five Harmans went home that night, tired but happy. The opening had been a success, as was the rest of the summer.

CHAPTER FORTY

BECOMING TOWN PEOPLE

Now it was time to turn their attention to a new school year. For the first time Dickie was going to start while June would be entering the fourth grade and Cecil the sixth. Dressed in their new clothes, their faces freshly scrubbed, and every hair in place they walked to school with Helen, Dick, Jerald and Bobbie. Having their friends beside them made it easier to go into a new school, but they each experienced a twinge of shyness when all eyes turned toward them as the teachers introduced them as the new students.

Their shyness didn't last long and by the time the first day was over they had each made more friends. June had met Maxine Eye, who soon became Helen's rival as her best friend. Cecil and Dickie had gotten acquainted with several boys they played with at recess, but the Oates brothers remained their best friends as long as they lived in the house on Main Street.

The school was a two-story brick building for grades one through eight. As in Riverton, each class had its own teacher, but this school was much larger. There were at least twice as many students.

At the supper table that evening, the children were excitedly talking about the day's events. Words tumbled over each other as they each strived to be heard. Priscilla finally stepped in, insisting they take turns. "Ladies first," she said, turning to June.

Over the boys' groans of protest, June said, "You'll never believe who my teacher is." She paused dramatically to give her parents a chance to guess, but before they could say anything, Dickie piped up with, "I know. It's our landlord, Mr. Feaster."

June gave her little brother a scathing look before continuing, "I couldn't believe it when I walked in and saw him standing there."

Her mom said she was sure he'd be a good teacher and started to give Dickie his turn, but June wasn't through yet. "He's calling me Mildred, and the kids are calling me Midge."

"Are you kidding?" Cecil demanded. "Didn't you tell them your name is June?"

"No one asked, so I didn't say anything. Anyway, I thought it would be fun having a new name."

Priscilla gave Burrel a look that clearly said, "See, there's nothing wrong with the name," before she said to June, "That's fine, if that's what you want to do, but if you want me to talk to Mr. Feaster I'm sure we can change it to June."

She wouldn't hear of it, so for the time they lived in Petersburg she was called by three different names: Mildred by the teachers, June by her friends and family, and Midge by the other kids at school.

$\sim$

The boys finally got their chance to talk. Cecil was excited about the gymnasium where they were going to get to play basketball. Dickie told about the swings and teeter-totter they had on the playground. Along with the other six-year-old children, he was starting in what was called the primer. This was similar to present day kindergarten and would lead in a few months into the first grade.

Priscilla and Burrel exchanged smiles over the heads of their excited children. This move to town seemed to have turned out well. Although neither was sorry they'd come here, and things were going well at the cavern, it was more difficult for them financially since they now had to pay rent and utilities and to buy food they'd previously raised. Even though Burrel was making more money, it didn't make up for all the added expenditures.

Like many depression era housewives, Priscilla learned to stretch the budget by buying food in bulk. It was not unusual to see Burrel carry in a fifty or a hundred pound bag of flour or dried beans or a ten-pound tin of lard. Since Priscilla was such a good cook, and the children had been taught to eat what was set before them, they were happy with their meals and unaware of any difficulty.

The parents always waited until the children were in bed before discussing their financial problems.

~

Everyday June, Cecil, and Dickie rushed home from school so they could listen to two of their favorite shows: Jack Armstrong All American Boy with His Sister Jane, and Tom Mix with His Trusty Sidekick, The Wrangler. As the exciting adventures poured from the radio, the pictures were as vivid in their minds as if they were on a movie screen.

Their favorite was Jack Armstrong and His Sister Jane. Like many children around the country they had ordered secret code rings. By deciphering the secret codes they could help Jack and Jane in all their escapades. The characters were good role models who through their exploits made it clear that young people could do anything they set out to do.

The Adventures of Tom Mix was based on an earlier movie cowboy by that name, and his and the Wrangler's fight against the bad men in the old west. The episodes were always exciting and fun. To the children's delight, justice always triumphed.

Both shows were sponsored by breakfast cereal. Jack and Jane advertised Wheaties, the Breakfast of Champions, while Tom and the Wrangler advertised a hot cereal with a taste a little better than cooked sawdust. Although they all liked Wheaties better, in loyalty to their western heroes they gave the other one equal time.

Later, in the evening, after June and Cecil had washed and dried the dishes, they'd sit at the dining room table and work on their homework while their parents listened to the radio in the other room. Though they were not consciously listening, they couldn't help hear bits and pieces of the news about what was going on in Europe. Hitler had promoted himself to Military Chief and shortly afterwards Germany had taken over Austria.

This sounded frightening to the young listeners, but they knew President Roosevelt was still assuring the people in his radio "Fireside Chats" that no matter what happened in Europe, this country was not going to be involved. Even though Burrel still didn't like him, he had been president ever since the children had been old enough to remember, and they secretly admired and looked up to him as a hero.

~

Priscilla had quickly gotten herself and the children into the United Brethren Church. Attending church on a regular basis was a new experience for the children. Cecil had been too young when they'd left Ohio to remember going with his Mom and Dad. While they lived at Seneca Caverns, the closest church had been in Riverton. The distance had made it difficult to attend except for special occasions, such as Christmas programs or weddings and funerals.

Instead, Priscilla had taken on their religious training. They had been so young when she first started, that they hardly remembered being taught. What she instilled in them was deep in their hearts and souls and combined with what their father had taught them about honor, became a code by which they lived, not only as children, but when they became adults.

The church became very important in their lives, with Priscilla and the children attending church services and Sunday School. Priscilla also became active in the Ladies Aid Society, and in the summer the children went to Bible School.

It was a great disappointment to Priscilla that Burrel wouldn't accompany her to services or take part in any of the activities. His excuse was that he was too busy with his work, but she was certain that because of his smoking and drinking and refusal to go to church, he wasn't really a Christian, and she worried about his soul.

June had overheard her parents talk about it and couldn't believe anyone would think such a thing about her dad. To her, he was always kind and gentle. She knew her mother must have felt the same way since she'd overheard her say he was too good to people for his own good. Thinking about the apparent contradiction of these statements she shook her head wondering if she'd ever understand adults and their reasoning.

One evening, Priscilla composed a song expressing her deep concerns:

When My Lord Calls For You

(1)
There's coming a day when you must go away
When my Lord calls for you
He'll take you with Him if you've walked the narrow way
When my Lord calls for you

Chorus

When my Lord (blessed Lord) Calls for you (calls for you)
As He says in His word (blessed word) He will do
Will He say (will He say) Well done (well done)
When my Lord (blessed Lord) Calls for you (calls for you)

(2)
Will He find you ready waiting for Him then
When my Lord calls for you
Or will you be like the foolish virgins ten
When my Lord calls for you

(3)
So be ever ready waiting for the day
When my Lord calls for you
It may be noon-time or the darkest night
When my Lord calls for you.

~

June's new friend, Maxine Eye, lived on a farm between Petersburg and Smokehole Caverns. The two girls soon became frequent overnight visitors in each other's homes, and their parents became good friends. When June stayed with Maxine, Mr. Eye would place them on one of his horses and let them ride around the farm. At first, since June wasn't used to riding a horse, she and Maxine would ride double, but after awhile she was able to ride alone. When Maxine stayed with June, they'd skate around the neighborhood or play hopscotch or jump rope on the sidewalk in front of June's house with other neighborhood children.

One evening June watched Maxine twirl the rope as she jumped, her brown hair flying and dark eyes sparkling while she chanted, "June and Dick sitting on a fence, trying to make a dollar out of fifty cents. How many kisses did she get? One, two, three, four." While Maxine continued jumping and counting, June's eyes wandered to a large red stain on the pavement a few feet from their house. Not wanting to think about its source, she quickly averted her eyes, especially if Dick or Jerald were playing with them.

They'd heard the story shortly after they'd moved here, about Jerald being struck by a car on that very spot, and how close he'd come to dying. The way he kept up with the other kids, no one would have known that stain was his blood or that as a result of his injury he would wear a metal plate in his head for the rest of his life.

The stain remained for a long time and served as a grim reminder to neighborhood children to be careful in traffic.

~

Maxine and Dick Oates introduced June and Cecil to the old swimming hole. To get to it they had to walk up the hill on Main Street, through the colored section of town, past a gas station and a bar and grill. Turning onto another road they had to follow it until they reached a cornfield. When they came to the cornfield they would speed up their steps because they knew once they were through the tall rows of corn they would be at the river. On their way past the farmer's house they always stopped to ask permission. He didn't allow all town children to swim, but since he knew both Maxine and Dick's parents he always gave them permission.

The natural damming of the river had formed the swimming hole. Completely surrounded by large shade trees, the low hanging branches created a private oasis for them. A long rope dangled from one of the branches. Maxine and Dick would grab hold of it and whooping like wild creatures, propel themselves back and forth across the width of the pool before letting go with a whoop and landing with a splash in the water.

Cecil and June had never been swimming before, but under Dick and Maxine's tutelage they learned to swim and soon after were taking turns with their friends swinging on the rope and jumping into the water.

Their adventure didn't always end when they left the pool. On their way home as they went by the bar and grill, the music coming from the jukebox would start them singing as they walked along. Songs they all liked were "Three Little Fishes In An Itsy Bitsy Brook" or "A Tisket A Tasket."

Sometimes their singing was like whistling in the dark to keep from being intimidated by the colored children who would yell at them or make menacing gestures as they hurried through their neighborhood. In the thirties, blacks and whites were segregated and never had a chance to get to know or understand each other.

Another favorite playing spot was closer to home. It was an area where rumor had it Indians had roamed during past centuries. It was apparently true, as arrowheads made from flint could still be found there. This was a preferred spot for teachers to take the class on field trips and the neighborhood children to go on their own. Maxine, Helen, and June would join Cecil, Dick Oates, Dickie, and Jerald for a day exploring the field and the surrounding woods. Their mothers would pack lunch, and the Oates boys always brought Pepsi Cola for all of them.

In the evening, seven tired children would get home in time for supper. Their lunch bags would be full of flint, arrowheads, and other treasures. In the fall the hickory nuts and walnuts they gathered from under the trees would be mingled with their Indian riches. Priscilla would shell the nuts and add the nutmeats to the candy, cookies, and cakes she'd make. The children especially liked anything made with the hickory nuts. Though they were harder to shell and the nutmeats were tiny and difficult to remove, they were so delicious, that even Priscilla thought the results were worth all the work involved.

CHAPTER FORTY-ONE

THE END OF A DREAM

One day when the children returned from one of their jaunts, they found a neighbor woman waiting for them. She gently told them their mother had become ill that afternoon, and their father had taken her to the doctor. They couldn't remember her ever being sick, except the time their mom and Cecil both had their tonsils removed. Their memories of that time were of getting to eat ice cream along with the patients. They hoped this wouldn't be any more serious, but as it turned out it was.

When Burrel had gotten Priscilla to the doctor's office, the doctor informed Burrel she had a tubal pregnancy and that her situation was critical and would require immediate surgery. They again made the trip across the mountains to the hospital in Harrisonburg. Only this time it was Burrel who was frightened he might lose Priscilla. When they arrived, he held her hand while he walked along side the gurney as she was wheeled down the hall to the operating room. He reluctantly removed her hand from his as the doors swung open, then closed behind her.

Lying on the operating table, Priscilla was aware of looking into a brilliant white light above her. It gradually faded to a pinpoint then disappeared entirely as a mask was clamped over her face, and she inhaled the sweet smell of ether.

Sitting in the waiting room, aimlessly turning the pages of a Saturday Evening Post magazine, Burrel was startled when the doctor and his nurse entered the room. "Is Priscilla alright?" he fearfully inquired.

Lowering himself into the chair next to Burrel, the doctor explained she was doing fine, but he had discovered that her uterus was full of fibroid tumors. While the tubal pregnancy was what had prompted the emergency surgery, the fibroids had been causing other problems and would continue to do so unless they were removed.

Unnerved, Burrel listened as he further explained that he would have to perform a hysterectomy. He concluded by saying he would need Burrel's signature giving him permission to do so.

"I don't want to do this while she is out. I'd rather wait until she can make that decision herself," Burrel protested.

The doctor didn't like his reaction, but patiently explained as if talking to a child, "This is going to have to be done, whether it is now or next month or next year. Until she has them removed she is going to continue to have bleeding. This will eventually cause anemia." The doctor paused, placed a reassuring hand on Burrel's shoulder before continuing to speak, "Since it has to be done, wouldn't it be better to do it now, rather than expose her to another surgery?"

Burrel peered anxiously into the doctor's face before asking, "Are you sure there's no other choice?"

The doctor's voice was firm and sure when he responded, "There's no other choice."

Burrel reluctantly signed the form.

As the anesthetic gradually wore off, Priscilla became aware of a pain like none she'd ever experienced. As she felt waves of it engulf her entire midsection, she slowly opened her eyes and looked around the room.

Sitting in a chair next to the bed was Burrel with his head tilted back and his eyes closed. As she became more aware of her surroundings, she realized it was nighttime. She could see nothing but darkness when she tried to look outside the window. The lamp on the stand beside her bed cast the only light in the room.

As she moved slightly, a soft moan escaped causing Burrel to open his eyes and say, "Honey, you're awake. I just closed my eyes for a minute. I'm so glad you're all right. Do you need anything?"

"I'm thirsty. Did they leave a pitcher of water for me?" she asked.

"I'll get the nurse and let her know you're awake," he told her on his way out the door to the nurses' station.

When the white clad nurse returned, she wet Priscilla's lips with a damp cloth and gave her an injection for the pain. She explained to Burrel that it would not only make her comfortable, but help her sleep. He could stay with her until she fell asleep, but since it was past visiting hours, he'd need to leave then.

As he watched her close her eyes and drift off, he dreaded the thought of the news tomorrow was going to bring her.

~

Before coming back the next day, he made arrangements for the children to stay with their cousins: June with Ruthalene, and the boys with Clyde and Dale. This was not far out of his way, as he had to drive through Riverton on his way to Harrisonburg to the hospital.

He had informed the doctor he wanted to be there when Priscilla was told about the hysterectomy, but when he entered the room it was obvious from her red eyes and tear stained face that he hadn't waited.

There was no welcoming smile on Priscilla's face when he leaned over to kiss her, nor did she kiss him in return.

"The doctor told you?" he anxiously inquired as he pulled the chair closer to the bed.

Tears rolled down her cheeks as she nodded, "Yes, he told me. I've been lying here thinking, I'm only twenty-nine years old. I'm going to go into the change of life, and I'll never be able to have another child."

Even though he went over what the doctor had told him and tried to comfort her, she was grieving for the loss of the second daughter she had always wanted and would never have. He knew the doctor had offered him no choice, but his heart ached at her unhappiness and the part he'd been forced to play. Had he done the right thing? What choice had he had? Would Priscilla really have wanted him to wait until she could make the decision herself? This would have meant another surgery. The doctor had said this was their only option. Had he been wrong?

Before leaving, he made arrangements with the doctor to let the children come see her in a couple days. The news seemed to penetrate her unhappiness, and she smiled for the first time since he'd walked into her room.

Seeing her smile lifted his spirits, making him think they would weather this as they had all the other problems they'd encountered. He wouldn't have been so sure if he'd been able to read her thoughts after he left the room, or seen her turn her face to the wall as she softly wept for what was never to be, for the loss of her dream.

The children were excited about the visit, and Burrel had been afraid their enthusiasm might tire their mother. He needn't have worried, as the sight and sounds of the hospital and seeing her lying in a hospital bed was a sobering experience for them. The three children who trooped into the room were quiet and subdued not wanting to do anything that would keep their mother from getting well so she could hurry home to them.

Dickie stared in fascination as the nurse made a circle with her thumb and forefinger and slowly poured Priscilla's cereal back and forth through this makeshift funnel, until it was cool enough for her to eat. As Priscilla became aware of his attention, she softly teased, "I don't want any of you to think I'm going to do this with your cereal when I get home."

Everyone laughed at the mental picture and from then on the visitors were more relaxed. As they said their goodbyes, Burrel felt this visit had been good for her. Smiling and with a slight wave, she told them to be good and mind their aunts and uncles. She'd be home soon and life would be back to normal. As they drove home, he remembered her last statement and sincerely hoped she was right.

By the time he brought her home he had hired a girl named Ruth who had moved into their house to take care of Priscilla and help with the children. They all liked her and soon thought of her as a member of the family.

She was short in stature, of average size for her height from her waist to the tips of her toes. When you observed her walking away from you there was nothing unusual about her, but when seen head on it was a different matter.

She was endowed with a truly magnificent bosom. It seemed to start a little below her collarbone and extended to her waist. Her brassiere, seen drying on the clothesline, resembled a slingshot for watermelons. Seeing it hanging next to Priscilla's clearly demonstrated that not all females were created equal. After hearing a ribald comparison from a neighbor, Priscilla saw to it they never again hung side by side.

Having Ruth to help care for the children and to do the housework helped speed Priscilla's recovery. Glad to have her home, the children tended to stay close by, watching her sitting on the porch, reading, or gingerly walking around the yard, delighting in the flowers that had sprouted from the seeds she had planted such a short time before. In a few weeks she was able to start helping Burrel at the cavern. They were both happy they had Ruth to stay home with the children.

CHAPTER FORTY-TWO

BICYCLES, SPELUNKERS AND THE BARE TRUTH

A few evenings after Priscilla returned to work, June had been sitting on the porch, reading, while waiting for them to come home. Looking up from her book when she heard their car stop in front of the house, she was surprised to see they were not alone.

A tall, lanky, dark haired man and a short, chubby woman stepped out of the back seat. They were complete strangers to her. As they came closer, she saw that the man had a dark bushy mustache and wore thick horn rimmed glasses. The short woman, who also wore glasses, appeared plain until she smiled.

Her smile was both joyful and sweet, causing her eyes to sparkle and her entire face to glow. As she watched this transformation, June wondered why she had ever thought this woman was plain. Then watching them step onto the porch, she felt suddenly shy. She was relieved when the front door burst open and Cecil and Dickie dashed out.

"Here they all are," Burrel said to his guests. "This is our daughter June, and our sons Cecil and Dickie." He then introduced the guests as Tony and Pauline Eno from Arlington, Virginia.

Sitting around the table after they'd eaten the dinner Ruth had prepared, the children were fascinated as they listened to the guests talk about their experiences. They belonged to a spelunker's society in Washington, D.C. and had ridden their bicycles over two hundred miles, from the capital city to the cavern. Cecil asked if they'd had to cross any mountains to get here.

Mr. Eno laughed as he talked about the ones they'd gone over. It hadn't been bad going down the mountains, but unbelievable having to pedal up. They both loved to cycle and had gone on several short junkets, but this was the first long trip they'd ever taken.

Mr. Eno explained that when they'd looked at the route on the map, they'd had no idea what they were getting into. Casting a beseeching glance in her husband's direction, Mrs. Eno said she wasn't sure she wanted to ride bicycles home.

"We've never seen bicycles like these," Priscilla told the children. "They're English. You'll get to see them before they go home. Their tires are really thin. They don't have any fenders and the brakes are on the handle bars."

Neither Cecil, June nor Dickie had a bicycle, but they had seen ones the older neighborhood kids had. They didn't look anything like what their mother was describing. Their curiosity was aroused. They could hardly wait to see these strange sounding vehicles.

Later in the evening, after making arrangements to pick up their new friends the next morning, Burrel took the visitors downtown to the inn where they had reservations. Sitting in the car, watching them walk up the steps, Burrel shook his head at the thought of anyone riding a bike that far. As he backed out of the parking place and headed for the house on Main Street, he felt grateful that he was having this chance to get to know them.

～

The next day he took Tony and Pauline on the regular tour through the cavern, then later took Tony to explore the sections he and Lige were still clearing.

As they climbed to the top of the ladder and flashed their lights over the ceiling with its mass of stalactites and other formations, Tony exclaimed, "Wow! This is really something. I can't wait to tell the other club members about it! I'm sure they'll all want to come see it."

As they explored the rest of it, Tony said, "It's so rare to find a cavern that is both commercial and natural. I would imagine we're among the first to be in this section."

Burrel told him that he wouldn't be surprised. He figured he and Lige were the first ones to explore this spot, unless some Indians had somehow found it earlier. He had his doubts though, because of the problems they would have had getting to it.

He and Lige had come across this area when they were stringing wire for the lights. At first, they'd thought it was a stone alcove, but closer exploration had shone an opening leading to at least two other rooms.

Over the next few days Burrel and his visitor explored into even deeper recesses of the second room. Tony, an amateur photographer, brought his equipment and took pictures to take home to show fellow spelunkers.

Burrel and Priscilla took June, Cecil, and Dickie with them on one of their trips to the cavern. Tony and Pauline, childless themselves, showered them with attention. Tony took Dickie for piggyback rides around the grounds. Then they offered to let all three ride the bikes, but none of them knew how.

The bicycles were sleek and streamlined and although all three children coveted them, each one's price tag was more than a month's salary for their father. He knew that during these depression years, he was lucky to be able to put food on the table and provide a nice home for his family. Luxury items, like these bicycles, were not in the picture.

~

Tony and Pauline continued to surprise and amaze Burrel. During one of their conversations Tony casually mentioned that he and Pauline were nudists.

"Nudists! What do you mean nudists?" Burrel exclaimed.

"You know, nudists!" Tony replied. "We don't believe in wearing clothes. They're too confining."

Amazed, Burrel stared at him. "You don't believe in wearing clothes? You go around naked?" Burrel knew Tony and Pauline both worked for the government in Washington. He smiled as he pictured him setting off for work wearing only his hat and carrying a briefcase.

"What are you smiling about?" Tony asked.

"I'm just picturing you going to work in your birthday suit," Burrel chuckled.

"It's not like that. We only go around nude at home or when we go to the nudist camp," Tony said.

"They have camps where people go around without clothes? You mean men and women go to these places together?" Burrel asked.

Tony was amused by his friend's reaction, but not surprised. "Not only men and women, but children too. Whole families go. There are old people, young people, fat people, and skinny people. They all look wonderful and free. You'll never know what its like to be liberated, until you learn to go around without wearing any clothes," Tony said. "There's no reason to feel ashamed of the body God gave you."

"I'm not ashamed, but I can't imagine doing something like that," Burrel said. His curiosity getting the better of him, he asked, "What do you do at these camps?"

"We spend a lot of time outside, because we think the sunshine is good for you. They have tennis and volleyball courts, and a swimming pool. There's a craft house and activity room where people play cards or checkers. Some people just walk on the nature trails or go bird watching. Its pretty much like any other camp, except we don't wear clothes."

Scratching his head in puzzlement, Burrel continued to inquire, "Isn't it uncomfortable in the woods without clothes?"

Tony grinned as he said, "Well, we're not completely nude."

"I'm sure glad to hear that," Burrel replied.

"Sometimes we wear shoes and sun tan oil," Tony said, his voice full of amusement.

Taken off guard, Burrel first looked perplexed, then threw his head back in laughter. This new friend was certainly different from anyone he'd ever met, but that was all right. He wouldn't want to be like him, but he was fun to be around.

"I'll tell you what I'll do," Tony said. "When I get home, I'll send you a copy of a magazine I get. It's called Sunshine and Health, and it's all about nudism. The pictures will show you what life is really like in a nudist camp."

"If you send it, it'd better be in a plain brown wrapper," Burrel chuckled, picturing the mailman's face if such a publication arrived uncovered.

During the rest of the visit, Tony devoted his time to photographing the cavern and the surrounding scenery. The children were his willing models.

Too soon it was time for the guests to return to Virginia. Pauline had prevailed, so with the bikes stowed in the baggage compartment, they traveled home in style, by train.

The men had formed a friendship that lasted for years to come, and they were to see each other many times. But June and Cecil were able to say, in time to come, that they, quite literally, saw more of Tony Eno than either of their parents ever did.

CHAPTER FORTY-THREE

SEEDS OF DISCONTENT

The family had barely returned to its normal routine when another set of visitors arrived. It was Della and David, who again appeared towing their trailer. Burrel made arrangements for them to park it on the cavern grounds, and they were soon comfortably situated. For several months the dark blue trailer became as much a fixture as the blue painted office and the stream flowing from the mouth of the cavern.

Della and Priscilla spent a great deal of time together, both at the cavern and in town. In Della, Priscilla had a confidant who would listen for hours to her expressions of frustration and depression about her life in general, her anger at Burrel about giving permission for the surgery, the difficulty making ends meet on Burrel's salary, and her continued opposition to his drinking and smoking.

"He's such a dreamer," Priscilla confided. "He can't look beyond working at the cavern. He thinks if he stays, one day he'll be rich."

Still feeling resentment of her own toward Burrel and subconsciously toward Priscilla, Della wholeheartedly sympathized with her younger sister, even though she didn't agree with some of Priscilla's more puritanical beliefs. She was thinking if she had been married to Burrel, she wouldn't have minded if he took a drink. She would even have gone with him or allowed him to keep some beer in the refrigerator.

She also chose not to point out to Priscilla that most of the American people were having financial problems during these depression years, and that it was unrealistic to think that other people had it any easier.

Burrel and the children, oblivious to these conversations or Priscilla's growing frustration, continued with their lives as usual. To them, these were still happy times with the prospect of a promising future in Petersburg.

June's friendship with Maxine and Helen deepened. She looked upon the two girls as sisters, as they did her. Since all their siblings were brothers, their ties were even stronger.

In their nine-year-old minds and hearts, they vowed to be friends forever. Not one could picture anything that could tear them apart, certainly not Priscilla and Della's conversations or the news they heard on the radio or saw in the newsreel about what was happening to countries in Europe.

Germany had invaded Poland and Czechoslovakia. Great Britain and France had declared war on Germany. To reassure the American people, President Franklin Roosevelt had declared this country's neutrality.

On the home front, everyone was talking about a new movie, The Wizard Of Oz, and singing its hit song, Over The Rainbow. June, Cecil, Dickie, and their friends were no exceptions. They had each spent their eleven cents one Saturday afternoon to go see it. "Mom, it was wonderful," June cried as they got home. "There was a cowardly lion, a tin man, and a scarecrow without a heart. Judy Garland met them and they all went to see the wizard." She went on to tell about the wicked witch and the beautiful witch of the east and the little people called munchkins. "Mom, you should go see it."

Then she uttered the words she never thought she would ever say, "It was as good as a Shirley Temple movie."

June, like most girls her age, was still fascinated with Shirley Temple, and now that she lived in town, never missed one of her movies.

"It must have been good," Priscilla said. "Maybe your Aunt Della and I can go see a matinee sometime." Turning to the boys, she asked, "What did you think of it?"

"It was okay. Especially when they poured water over the wicked witch and she melted," Dickie stated.

"That's enough! If I keep listening to you kids I won't need to go see it," she laughingly responded.

It was nice hearing their mother laugh. She hadn't laughed very much since she'd had her operation.

~

After school started the months seemed to fly by. The Halloween decorations in the classroom gave way to turkeys and pilgrims as Thanksgiving came and went. Now the children's favorite holiday was drawing near.

All the stores were decorated with red and green wreaths, shining silver bells, tinsel, and Santa and his reindeer. Strains of Jolly Old Saint Nicholas, Jingle Bells, and Christmas carols could be heard in every store and from every radio. One Sunday the family went to a program at the Presbyterian Church where all the children were dressed as toys that came to life and danced around the room. Another night found them at their own church where the traditional Christmas story of Mary and Joseph and the baby Jesus was presented.

On Christmas Eve Helen stopped at their house and asked June to go with her to her dad's showroom. She had something she wanted to show her. When they got there June stood awestruck as she stared through the glass. There in the middle of the room sat a shiny new 1940 maroon car wrapped in pink cellophane and tied with the biggest brightest red bow she had ever seen. The lights overhead and those twinkling from the Christmas tree seemed to be reflected a thousand fold from every surface of the car and its packaging.

Helen's eyes were sparkling as she looked at the expression on her friend's face. "Isn't it something?" she asked. "Dad has been planning it for a long time."

As they stood and listened to passersby, they smiled at the comments they overheard. "Wouldn't that be something to find under your Christmas tree?" "Honey, if you get me that, you won't have to get me anything else."

Burrel, walking by on his way to buy Priscilla's gift, stopped and told Helen what a nice job her dad had done with the display. As he ambled on, he couldn't help think how much he'd like to be able to buy something that nice for Priscilla for Christmas. Maybe that would make her happier.

Lately he'd been feeling like such a failure. He knew Priscilla thought he was a dreamer, and maybe he was. He needed to think about finding another job, one that would pay more. He'd hate to leave the cavern, but he would if that would make her happy.

When June got home she found her mother pacing the floor. She was worried because Burrel wasn't home yet. "Helen and I saw him downtown. He said he was on his way to buy your present," June said, before going on to tell her how beautiful the car was in Helen's dad's showroom.

While they waited for him to come home, Priscilla talked to them about Christmas and the way they'd celebrated when she was a little girl, and about how they had made their own decorations. They hadn't had the modern shiny store bought glass ornaments, tinsel or colored lights that hung on this tree.

As she talked, she'd glance at her watch, then toward the door. She was becoming increasingly worried, and her obvious anxiety was dampening the children's celebration.

It wasn't like Burrel to be late, especially on a night like this. They still had toys to put together and set under the tree from Santa Claus, since Dickie was still a believer.

Every eye turned to the sound of footsteps on the porch. The door was flung open and Burrel walked in carrying a large brightly wrapped package and a few smaller ones. "Ho, ho, ho, Merry Christmas!" he shouted, as he placed them under the tree. The children's mood quickly changed to match his good humor, as he laughed and sang and teased them about Santa Claus. This quickly changed when their mother spoke.

"What's wrong with you?" she demanded. "Why are you acting like this?"

"It's Christmas Eve, and I'm full of Christmas cheer, and I bought my baby a pretty present," he said. As he spoke he picked up the big package and tried to hand it to her.

"You're full of Christmas cheer, alright!" Priscilla angrily exclaimed, as she got close enough to smell his breath. "You're smashed. How could you? On Christmas Eve at that!" As the children looked on she pushed the present away and turned her back on him.

"Come on Honey, open it," Burrel coaxed, but she would have nothing to do with it.

Not ready to give up, he unwrapped the package and again tried to put it in her hands. As she again rejected it, the box fell to the floor spilling a beautiful long, pink satin quilted robe from its cocoon of white tissue paper. June was overwhelmed by the beauty of the gift and frightened by her parents' behavior. If they had fought before, it had not been in front of her.

Looking at her white-faced children, Priscilla tried to smile as she said, "Santa Claus will be coming soon. You need to go to bed, so you can get up early and see what he's brought you."

Reluctantly, they trudged off to bed, but their dreams weren't the usual night before Christmas ones.

The next morning, when the children walked into the living room, their parents were sitting drinking coffee. As Priscilla and Burrel watched their off-spring open their presents, they acted as if the quarrel of the night before had never happened.

June felt better when she saw her mother was wearing the new robe. "You look so pretty, Mom," she breathed. "That is the most beautiful robe I've ever seen."

As her dad smiled his agreement, June relaxed, thinking everything was going to be all right. She wasn't even too disappointed when she'd opened all her presents and found that she hadn't gotten the satin Shirley Temple pajamas she'd had her heart set on. Maybe next year, she thought as she cuddled her new doll.

CHAPTER FORTY-FOUR
FAREWELL THIRTIES/ HELLO FORTIES

Nineteen-forty arrived, marking the beginning of a new decade. June and Dickie had spent their entire lives in the thirties while Cecil from his lofty position as the oldest child, though not quite twelve, could claim to have been around during three decades. For all three, though, marking this new one was something they would always remember.

The events of Christmas Eve appeared to be forgotten, as Burrel and Priscilla decided it was time to buy their own home. Having enjoyed being homeowners when they lived in Newark, they had been talking about buying one ever since they'd moved to Petersburg.

New homes were selling for close to four thousand dollars, but they were able to find an older one on Pine Street for twenty-four hundred. Since their payments were going to be less than they were now paying for rent, this would help solve some of their financial problems.

Painted brown, the house had six rooms and a bath downstairs and a large upstairs loft where the children slept when the relatives were visiting from Ohio. There was a small front and back porch, but nothing on the order of what they were used to at the house they had been renting on Main Street. They missed the spacious porch, but being homeowners more than compensated.

Their new home was closer to school, but further away from their friends. Dickie quickly got acquainted with a neighbor boy and they became inseparable. They could be seen every evening rolling hoops in their yards and up and down the street or sitting on the steps playing jacks or mumbly pegs.

~

June and Helen discovered a shortcut between their houses that took them through the cemetery. Aside from walking to and from each other's homes, they would spend hours reading the inscriptions on the markers and using their imaginations to create stories about how those who silently slept beneath these stones had lived and died.

They were no more frightened in the cemetery then they would have been in any part of town. If there were any ghosts around, they were friendly ones.

During this time, in this town, adults cared for and looked after all children, not just their own. In the children's minds, this had its disadvantages, as well as advantages. As the children all knew, whatever they did, good or bad, adults would see. They would correct them if they were doing something they shouldn't and compliment them if they were being especially good. Whichever, their parents were sure to hear about it.

In their treks through the cemetery, one marker they found made both girls feel sad. It was of a girl who had died in nineteen eighteen when she had been their age. June had gone to a funeral, when they still lived at the house at Seneca Caverns, for a little boy of five who had died from eating the contents of a bottle of aspirins. So she knew children did die, but she couldn't get this little girl out of her mind. What could have taken her life when she was so young?

She would lie awake nights thinking about the little girl, wondering what could have happened. Before falling asleep, her mind would shift from the mystery girl to thinking about children in war torn Europe who were being hurt or killed by German bombs. The pictures she saw in the newsreel at the Saturday matinee played across the screen of her mind as vividly as if she were one of those frightened children.

Every night when she said her prayers after asking God to bless her mom, dad, brothers, Helen and Maxine, she'd ask Him to please protect the children in Europe from the horrible war. These children were to be in her prayers until the war was finally over, years later when she was in her teens.

The mystery of the little girl was solved when Helen's mother told them there had been an influenza epidemic in nineteen eighteen that had killed thousands of people across the country. She was almost certain that was what had happened to the little girl.

~

Priscilla was busy with preparations for Easter Sunday. One of Burrel's sisters, her husband and their children were coming to town to spend it with them. June loved her aunt, but had always been afraid of her aunt's husband. He seldom smiled, always appeared angry and sly. She had heard her parents talk about what a miserable life Burrel's sister had with him. From what June had seen and overheard, she knew he didn't have the best disposition under normal conditions and could be downright mean when he was drinking. Her aunt did everything she could to keep alcohol away from him, but she wasn't always successful. Before the holiday was over, her failure was demonstrated clearly to the host family.

Since they had no foreboding of what was to come, everyone was in a festive mood as the guests arrived bright and early the day before Easter. The children had set up their makeshift sleeping bags on the floor of the loft, and the older children were regaling the younger ones with tales of the Easter Bunny.

Two large pots full of dozens of eggs were bubbling on the stove. Priscilla had promised Cecil, Dickie, June, and Sissie they could help color them later in the afternoon. Some were going into the Easter baskets and others would be used for the Easter egg hunt that was planned for the next day.

While the eggs were cooling, Priscilla, June, her aunt, and cousin walked downtown for some last minute shopping. The girls were looking forward to it as they'd been promised a Pepsi at Sites Restaurant when they were through.

As they strolled downtown they enjoyed the fresh spring weather, the soft breeze and the crocuses blooming where such a short time before there had been snow.

June showed Sissie the steep hill where she'd taken a nasty spill on her skates when she had spun out of control after she'd hit some new gravel that had spilled onto the sidewalk from a driveway. Sissie was properly impressed when June displayed the scars on her knees and elbows.

After they finished their shopping, the foursome walked by a tavern as the door opened giving them a clear view of the backs of several men sitting at the bar. June's aunt stopped in her tracks and stared at the reflection of her husband's face in the mirror as he drained his shot glass in one swallow and pushed it toward the man behind the bar saying, "Give me another."

Before the bartender had time to respond, June's angry aunt was through the door, raising her voice above the sound of the strains of the song, Beer Barrel Polka, as it blared from the jukebox. She demanded, in no uncertain terms, that her husband come home with her.

June and Priscilla stood on the sidewalk, fervently wishing it would open and swallow them. This was the most humiliating thing that had happened to them since they'd moved to Petersburg. They both hoped no one they knew saw what was going on, or knew they were related to this battling couple. Both voices were raised now, with her aunt determined to get him out of there, and her uncle stormily determined to stay and have the drink he'd just ordered.

The angry woman won, and she, her husband, and daughter started up the hill toward the house on Pine Street. Priscilla and June could not hear what was being said, but every movement and gesture from each of them showed that the argument was escalating.

~

June turned to her mother, wondering what they should do now. In response to the question in her eyes, Priscilla said, "I think it would be best if we have our Pepsi before we go home. That will give them some time to cool off and settle down." She always enjoyed the times she and her mother went downtown together and despite the scene they had just witnessed, this was no exception.

They didn't linger though, as Priscilla was worried about her sister-in-law. Many times she'd tried to tell her that since he got so mean when he was drinking, she shouldn't say anything to him when he was in that condition. Her advice had always fallen on deaf ears.

As they neared the house, Cecil came running up to them saying, "Don't go in there! They're killing each other!"

His words didn't stop his mother. After all, she was the woman who had stood face to face with a madwoman holding her children at gunpoint. She wasn't prepared though for the scene that greeted her when she walked into the kitchen. The water and eggs they'd left on the stove were scattered from one end of the kitchen to the other. The eggs had been smashed, first from being hurled from the stove, then from being stomped underfoot as her brother-in-law had slammed his wife against the wall.

The kids, having silently crept in behind Priscilla, were stunned by the scene and even more so by their mother's action. Pointing her finger at this apparent madman, Priscilla spoke in a strong unwavering voice as she said, "Stop that this minute! Take your hands off her and go outside and sit down until you cool off."

The angry young man was so surprised at having a woman talk to him in that manner, that he stopped in his tracks, momentarily letting his hands fall to his side. This gave his wife a chance to slip out of his reach.

Before he could react further, Burrel came through the back door and surveying the scene exclaimed, "What in blue blazes is going on here?"

Moving to the safety of his side, his sister tearfully told him what had happened. Although Burrel, like Priscilla, had tried to convince her not to confront her husband when he was in this condition, he felt too much compassion for her now to even consider lecturing her.

He managed to diffuse the situation by getting his brother-in-law outside. Then he spent some harrowing moments trying to sober him up with hot black coffee and sandwiches.

Meanwhile, the women sent the children out to play while they set about clearing up the mess. Priscilla was glad to see that when all water, eggs, and broken crockery had been cleared away that no damage had been done to the house.

As she dropped the last egg shell in the wastepaper basket, the thought ran through her mind that they'd waited too long for this home of their own to have it damaged by such childish behavior. One thing she knew was that it would be a long time, if ever, before this man would be invited back to their home.

The next morning the children found their Easter baskets complete with colored eggs, and the Easter egg hunt took place as planned even though it had meant an extra trip to the store for Burrel to buy more eggs, and the women staying up most of the night coloring them.

Before the day was half over, all the children, except Sissie had eaten most of the candy from their baskets. She took hers home and sat it on the buffet shelf next to the Easter candy she'd saved for the last five years. But she hadn't been without candy that Easter Sunday as the other children had shared theirs with her, relying on her promise to share hers later. In her case later never came, since as in years past her urge to add this year's candy to her collection was too strong.

~

As spring gave way to summer, and the children were out of school, like many small town children their lives continued to be happy and carefree. They spent their days swimming, skating, playing with their friends, going to the movies, and occasionally going to the cavern with their parents.

When they did go along the boys still made a penny for each bumper sticker they attached, and now that June was ten years old her mother would sometimes let her help in the office.

One thing none of the children liked at the cavern was the newest attraction, a glass cage full of rattlesnakes. Several times each day the handler would reach into the squirming mass and pull one out. While he held its jaw open with one strong hand so he wouldn't be bitten, he'd slowly milk the venom from their deadly fangs.

He would then hold these deadly reptiles up for all to see. Then to the background noise made by the warning sound of their rattlers, he'd wrap one snake after another around his body while his audience looked on from a safe distance.

Living in the country where rattlesnakes were common, Cecil, June, and Dickie had been taught to fear and avoid them. Even though they had been told these snakes were harmless, the fear was too deeply in-grained for them to enjoy this demonstration.

A hit song that summer of nineteen forty was Blueberry Hill. In years to come, June never heard it without remembering the trip the family took, that summer to pick huckleberries on Huckleberry Mountain.

As they pulled on extra sweaters to protect themselves from the howling wind and the chill at this high elevation, on Dolly Sods, they filled their pails and baskets with the sweet, juicy fruit. They sang about finding their thrill on Blueberry Hill. Only in their version, it became Huckleberry Mountain.

It didn't take long for them to pick enough berries for Priscilla to bake a couple pies and can some for the winter. Like so many things that happened that summer, the time together as a family and the fun they'd had that day on Huckleberry Mountain was precious to them.

CHAPTER FORTY-FIVE

THE CIRCLE WEAKENS

Against a background of the world seeming to swirl out of control, with Denmark and Norway captured by Germany, the allies evacuating Dunkirk, and German troops parading victoriously through the streets of Paris, Priscilla and Burrel's life and that of the children seemed to start on a downward spiral. Once started, it couldn't be stopped.

No one, in years to come, could say exactly when or why it began, but once it started it was like being on a runaway train heading for disaster.

Maybe it started when other people began to infringe upon their lives, influencing them to do and say things they might not otherwise have done.

Priscilla, through her sister Della, had met Olive and Virginia. Party girls, they were dedicated to having a good time. They delighted in teasing Priscilla about being a stick in the mud, staying home with her children, and being the dowdy housewife.

When they discovered her ongoing resentment toward Burrel about his drinking and smoking, they laughed and said, "What's sauce for the goose is sauce for the gander. Only in this case it's, what's sauce for the gander should be sauce for the goose. You could show him a thing or two if you took up his habits."

At first Priscilla thought they were out of their minds since in her opinion decent women didn't do such things. After going out with them a few times though, and seeing the fun they were having, it didn't seem like such a bad idea. They were just having a good time. They certainly weren't hurting anybody.

In weeks to come, Virginia and Olive became frequent visitors to their house, laughing and telling jokes June and Dickie didn't quite understand. Cecil did understand and quietly disapproved, especially when he heard his mother laugh along with them. She would have washed his mouth out with soap if he'd told such a joke.

Maybe Priscilla wouldn't have become friends with these women if Burrel hadn't gone away to work, or if she had gone with him. Reluctantly, he had left his job at the cavern to work in Baltimore after Verde had told him the shipyards there were hiring electricians and starting them off at twenty dollars a day. Almost as much as he was making in a week at the cavern, this was an opportunity he couldn't pass up. In his mind this was the answer to all their money problems.

He and Priscilla had discussed it and decided it was the right thing to do. Burrel could start the job, and once he was sure it was secure they could sell the house. Then Priscilla and the children could join him.

He tried to come home every weekend, but sometimes he had to work overtime. Even though FDR was still saying we weren't going to war, it appeared the country was gearing up for it in factories and as Burrel observed, in the shipyards. For the first time in over a decade the economy was looking better, and Burrel was confident there were going to be better times ahead.

~

Before the children's eyes, their mother seemed to grow younger. She let her hair grow, allowing it to cascade in soft curls around her shoulders. Her dresses were no longer matronly, but youthful looking and fashionable. The real shocker for them was when they saw Virginia offer her a cigarette, and she not only accepted it, but also leaned forward while Virginia lit it.

As they watched her draw the smoke in and blow it out, not really inhaling, they looked on in amazement. Knowing how much she hated their dad's smoking, they couldn't have been more shocked if they'd caught her playing with one of the hated rattlesnakes.

At first she had started smoking and drinking to show Burrel and to keep from seeming like such a fuddy-duddy to her new friends, but before long she found she was enjoying it.

Although she was changing, Priscilla was still making plans for them to join Burrel in Baltimore. One weekend she had a hired girl come in to stay with the children while she boarded a bus for Washington to spend a few days with him and to check out the area around Baltimore. They wanted to get some ideas of where they would like to live.

She had never taken a trip alone before and had been nervous at the thought of arriving in a big city. But when she looked out the window and saw Tony and Pauline's smiling faces, she relaxed and knew she was going to have a good time. This was especially so when Tony started teasing her about her new hat, telling her he'd never seen a woman wear a blue velvet pancake on her head before. His eyes sparkled behind his thick glasses when he added, "On you, it looks good!"

After helping get her luggage from the bus, they took her to their house in Arlington to stay until Burrel got off work. Tony explained that it wasn't far from here to Baltimore, and Burrel should be here anytime.

They spent the first night with the Enos where they found the friendship was as strong as ever. Tony told Priscilla he was shocked when he heard Burrel was leaving his job at the cavern, since he knew how much it meant to him, but he could understand their need to earn more money.

The next morning they checked into the hotel room Burrel had rented and, like a couple of kids, went sightseeing driving through Washington, looking at the monuments, the capital building, and the White House.

Priscilla thoroughly enjoyed the day and the next when they went to Baltimore. She was fascinated by the rows of houses where housewives on their hands and knees were vigorously scouring the white stone steps with scrub brushes and soapy water. Burrel explained that Dutch and Germans settled this section of town, and they were famous for the cleanliness of their white steps.

Before the day was over they knew Baltimore was a nice place to visit, but not a place they'd want to live. Instead, they looked at several small towns nearby, and decided they particularly liked Laurel as a place to raise their children. It would be a thirty to forty minute drive for

Burrel, but he didn't mind the extra time involved if it would mean the children could live in a safer place.

~

When the weekend was over and Burrel returned to work, Priscilla stayed in the hotel, or close by, until he returned in the evening. One afternoon while sitting in the coffee shop, watching people come and go in the lobby, she noticed a middle aged man who had just checked in being joined by a brassy looking young woman.

As she watched them disappear behind the closed elevator doors, she thought there was something vaguely familiar about her. Since she didn't know anyone except Tony and Pauline, she couldn't imagine where she could possibly have met her. "Oh, well," she thought, "I probably just saw her on the street or in a restaurant."

She didn't give the woman another thought until that evening when she and Burrel stepped out of the elevator and collided with her as she was getting on. Priscilla glanced at the man with her and was surprised to see he was not the one she'd been with earlier.

As she thought about it, she realized why this woman looked familiar. "Well, now," she thought, "I've seen her over and over again, each time with a different man." Having figured out what was going on, she was amused as she sat in the lobby the next day and watched the brassy blonde and three or four other young women and their numerous male friends parade in and out of the elevators. Her amusement turned to alarm when she was approached by a well dressed man, of indeterminate age, who made a proposal that sent her flying to her room, her face on fire and her heart pounding. He had mistaken her for "one of those women."

She locked and double locked the door and didn't leave the room again until Burrel returned.

~

That night over dinner when she told Tony and Pauline what had happened, Tony threw back his head and laughed so hard tears streamed down his cheeks. As he removed his glasses and wiped his eyes, he said, "Burrel, do you know what kind of a place you took this woman to?"

Looking sheepish, Burrel said, "I didn't, but I do now. It looked like a perfectly respectable hotel to me."

"You two are like babes in the woods," Tony said. "But don't feel too bad. That hotel used to be a perfectly respectable place until the call girls and their Johns showed up. You're not the first tourist to be shocked when they found out what was going on."

"You can stay with us for the rest of your visit," Tony told them. "Priscilla will be much safer here."

That night when they had settled into the Eno's guest room, Burrel said, "I'm really sorry. I would never have taken you there if I'd known what kind of place it was." Then sighing, he added, "Do you think we are ready for the big city?"

"Maybe not, but if we get a house in Laurel, we won't have to worry about it," she replied. Then she laughed as she said, "This has been quite an experience. I never in my wildest dreams thought I'd ever be mistaken for a prostitute. Virginia and Olive will get a big kick out of it when I tell them."

The mention of their names brought a frown to Burrel's face. He didn't like or approve of her new friends and wasn't happy she was spending so much time with them.

"I wish you and the kids could move here right away," he said. "It's going to be lonely when you go back."

"I know," she said. "But we can't just pull up stakes and leave. We have to get some money set aside for moving expenses and to help us get settled. It won't be too much longer."

As Burrel lay awake staring at the ceiling and thinking about their conversation, he thought she'd fallen asleep until he heard her trying to stifle a giggle.

"What's so funny?" he asked.

"I was just thinking, I'm really glad Tony and Pauline have kept their clothes on."

"You thought about that, too, did you?" he chuckled as he relaxed, letting go of the worries of the last few minutes.

Hearing the laughter from the room next to theirs, Tony and Pauline looked at each other and smiled, blissfully unaware that their tendency for going about, as Burrel would say, "As naked as a jaybird" was the cause of it.

When Burrel saw her off at the bus station he said, "I really wish you wouldn't spend so much time with Virginia and Olive."

On the way home, she thought about what he'd said, but could see no reason she should have to sit at home while the children were at school, and Burrel was working away from home. Besides, they were fun to be around. She had worked hard since she'd married Burrel when she was sixteen. Now it was time for her to enjoy herself, she thought, defiantly. She couldn't see how it was hurting anyone.

The children, happy to have her home, were excited when she told them about her visit to the big city. Washington, D.C. was a place they'd read about. The prospect of actually living near enough to go see it was helping them overcome their reluctance to leave their friends in Petersburg.

~

A few weeks after returning from her trip, she and her friends were in a neighborhood tavern when a man in his late thirties came over to their table and spoke to Virginia and Olive. Although he was addressing them, his eyes never left Priscilla.

"Bill, this is our friend Priscilla Harman. Priscilla, this is Bill Helser," Olive said. From then on, Bill joined them everyday either at the tavern or at the house on Pine Street. He was of average height with brown thinning hair and the beginning of a pouch. Behind his glasses his blue eyes followed Priscilla's every movement, making her aware he found her attractive. Although flattered by his interest, she only thought of him as one of the gang who was always laughing and telling jokes.

Although he was married and the father of three children, he had earned the reputation as a ladies' man. He soon let Priscilla know the marriage was not a happy one. When he was nineteen he had wed a schoolteacher several years his senior. "She treats me like one of her students!" he grumbled. As a young man he had inherited an entire city block of business properties including a hotel in the next county. When the depression came, lacking business experience and unwilling to listen to her advice, he had made some bad decisions, and they had lost everything.

His wife had minced no words in letting him know their financial loss was his doing and that she had lost all respect for him. The laughter left his eyes when he complained about being reduced to his current job of delivering bread and other baked goods door to door.

When he found out Priscilla's husband was out of town, Bill was quick to say, "He'd better watch out. A pretty woman like you, someone is liable to steal you."

Priscilla blushed, but didn't take him seriously.

When he was introduced to the children, it was as Olive's boyfriend. The two of them, along with Virginia, always seemed to be there when Cecil, June, and Dickie returned from school. After awhile, he and Priscilla would be there alone, at which time they were quick to say Olive had just left or would soon be there.

Cecil was the first to have kids at school tease him about the bread truck so often being parked in front of their house. As can happen with children, the teasing became cruel. June was teased, too, but being younger and trusting, she didn't pay much attention to it.

One late evening, while Bill was visiting, someone got into his truck and tore wrappers off the baked goods, throwing bread, cakes, and cookies all over the ground. The birds and neighborhood cats and dogs had a feast. The culprit was never found, although everyone who heard about it said it seemed like a prank or the act of a child. June always had a suspicion that Cecil may have found a way to vent his anger, but if so, he never admitted it.

In small town America in 1940 before television became a main source of entertainment, many people amused themselves by gossiping about their neighbors. The bread man's frequent visits to the Harman household while Burrel was out of town became a hot topic.... The explanation that he was there to visit Olive didn't seem to stop the talk.

If Burrel had read the poem Priscilla had recently penned, he would have had some warning:

You ask why I treat you as if you were merely a friend
What you have done that I'm so indifferent and cold
I'll only answer and say that you once killed my love
I won't be with you when we are withered and old.

I don't want you to offer me diamonds or mansions so fine
I only want clothes to cover my shivering frame.
I once longed to forever be yours
But now I wish that I had never heard of your name.

Don't you remember how I used to beg for your love
And how oft you'd turn your back on me?
Then when at last my love died and I wanted free
Why don't you leave me and we will both happy be?

Maybe some glad day in Heaven again we shall meet
Maybe our love can once more be made complete
Won't you remember that I once loved you true
And it is your fault that now we forever are through.

But her notebook was discretely hidden away, as were her accusing
and conflicting feelings.

~

The gossip reached Burrel on one of his weekend visits home when
an acquaintance couldn't wait to be a Good Samaritan and tell him
about it. This well-meaning person concluded her comments by saying,
"Of course, I don't believe it myself, but I thought you should know
what was being said."

That night when Priscilla and Burrel were at a club in Moorefield,
he overheard someone else whispering about it. By the time they arrived
home, he was fuming and the fact that they'd each had a few drinks
didn't help the situation.

Later that night the children were awakened by the sound of loud
voices coming from their parents' room. Slipping into the hall, they
were alarmed by the fierceness and violence of the argument and the
fight that ensued. Their easy-going father, who could hardly stand to
spank any of his children, had seemingly snapped and appeared to be
completely out of control.

Priscilla had never seen him like this and was clearly frightened.
Her cry of, "The children, the children are watching," snapped him
back to reality.

Seeing them standing in the doorway, Burrel tried to reassure them.
"Go to bed now. Everything's going to be alright."

They looked to their mother for reassurance. She nodded her agreement.

It is doubtful any of the five members of the Harman household slept much that night. As June lie in her bed, staring at the ceiling, she thought she heard someone sobbing in her parents' room, and to her ears it didn't sound like her mother.

Burrel had to return to Baltimore the next day, even though he didn't want to leave Priscilla under the circumstances. She'd said she forgave him, but he wasn't sure. He felt, given time, he could make it up to her. If only she didn't have Virginia, Olive, and now Bill in her life.

The children watched, but their mother seemed to be doing fine. The only thing that happened that disturbed June was overhearing her mother making fun of the note their dad had sent her with his gift of two long satin and lace night gowns.

Olive and Virginia were there when Priscilla opened the gifts and read the card, "To my blue-eyed baby. I'm sorry."

Priscilla laughed bitterly when she said, "He just thinks I'm his blue-eyed baby."

Olive and Virginia joined in the laughter as if they found Priscilla's statement to be hilarious. Not for the first time, June thought, "I wish those two would stay away from here." Like her father, she didn't like them, and as it turned out, she never would.

~

They celebrated June's birthday with her favorite coconut cake and eleven candles. It was a wonderful birthday, because her dad was home, and they were discussing moving to Maryland to live with him.

He'd been trying to talk their mother into going sooner, but she remained adamant she didn't want to take them out of school until the end of the school year. Cecil was finishing the eighth grade, June the sixth, and Dickie the third, and as she told Burrel, these were crucial grades.

THE CIRCLE BROKEN

CHAPTER FORTY-SIX

SHATTERED LIVES

They were all surprised when a short while after their father returned to Baltimore, their mother informed them she'd come around to his way of thinking. She would join him, staying long enough to find a place for them to live. Since this might take her a couple weeks, she had made arrangements for them to stay with their aunts. So as not to get behind in their classes, they were going to school with their cousins. June and Dickie were to stay with one of the aunts, and Cecil at Grandpap's with Aunt Gussie.

With tears in her eyes, June said goodbye to Helen and Maxine. None of the three suspected this was to be their final farewell. June assured them she'd have her parents bring her to visit when they came back to see their cousins. She was sure that would be often.

When they piled into the car with their mom, Olive, Virginia, and Bill for the trip to their aunts, they looked back at their home and waved to friends they saw skating, playing hopscotch, or shooting marbles in front of their houses.

They were sad to be leaving, but excited at the prospect of their new home, being together as a family again, and the adventure that awaited them.

The atmosphere in the car was festive as they made their way to their aunt's house. Priscilla was a little quiet, but the other adults' lighthearted chatter made up for it.

Their aunt and uncle were now living in the house of shadows with

Burrel's Uncle Luke, the one who years ago June and Cecil had suspected of being a ghost. June was to come to know him as a self-centered,
silent, old man, living on the fringes of other people's lives.

When they were saying goodbye, Priscilla decided Dickie, only
eight years old, was too young to be left with his aunt. So when they got
back into the car to take Cecil to Grandpap's, Dickie was with them.

Before leaving, Priscilla hugged June and told her she'd write and
let her know when they found a place.... Then they'd come back for her.
"Mind your aunt, and when I return I'll bring you the Shirley Temple
pajamas you've been wanting."

June watched them drive away, already missing her mother and
brothers. It would have been better if at least she and Cecil could have
been together. "Oh, well," she thought. "It won't be for long."

From the distance as she watched the car disappear from sight, she
thought she heard the sound of laughter. Puzzled, she wondered what
her mother's friends found amusing.

The next day Cecil went with Clyde to the Germany Valley School
where he had started seven years earlier. He was welcomed back by Miss
Lily, the teacher who had advanced him into the second grade those
many years ago. Coincidentally, when June walked into the one room
schoolhouse she was to attend with her cousin, at the front of the room
stood Miss Nina, who had been her first grade teacher.

Her aunt had already talked to Miss Nina and told her June would
be with her for a couple weeks until her parents found a house near
Baltimore. Miss Nina seemed genuinely glad to see her former student,
as June was to see her. This happiness didn't extend to being back in
a one-room schoolhouse. Trying to make the best of it, she again reminded herself, "At least it's not going to be for long."

She sat at her desk, looking out the window at the bare trees and
snow covered ground, staring into space, imagining the kind of house
they'd live in and the trips they were going to take into Washington.
Miss Nina's voice penetrated her musing, "I can see, June, one thing
hasn't changed. You're still a daydreamer."

Looking up into the face of her teacher, she could feel a warm flush
coloring her face red as she realized all the other students were looking
at her. "Sorry," she mumbled, "I was just thinking."

Miss Nina smiled reassuringly and, much to June's relief, moved on to another class, leaving her embarrassed student to busy herself with work she and the other sixth graders had been assigned.

~

The following weekend all June's bright dreams were shattered when she woke during the night to hear voices coming from downstairs. It was late and the family, being farmers, had retired hours earlier.

Lying in bed trying to listen, she couldn't imagine who could possibly be visiting at this time of night. As she lie quietly trying not to awaken her cousin, she realized one voice was her dad's and the other was her aunt's. She couldn't hear her mother's voice, but her first thought was, "They've found a house and come for us!" As she jumped out of bed and started to run downstairs, she was stopped in her tracks when she heard her father say, "She's gone, Sis. I can't believe it. She's left me and the children."

The banked fire in the stove had died down and the air in the house was frigid. As June stood on the stairs, she was unaware of the cold penetrating her bare feet or creeping through the thin nightgown she was wearing. She was only aware of her father and aunt in the parlor and the pain in the pit of her stomach as her father's words echoed over and over through her mind.

"This must be a nightmare! I'll wake up in bed with my cousin hogging the covers and forget all about having a bad dream," she thought, but as if glued to the spot, she continued to stand and listen.

Burrel's sister was speaking quietly, her voice soothing as if talking to a child. Then the silent listener heard something she'd never heard before. Her father was crying, deep sobs seeming to come from the very depth of his being.

Alarmed, she quietly slipped upstairs and into bed. Not wanting to awaken Sissie, she lie still, reliving everything she'd heard since she crept out of bed such a short time before.

She knew she couldn't let them know she'd overheard their conversation or heard her father cry. She was crying herself, but in nineteen forty it was acceptable for children and women, but not for men to cry. Everyone expected them to be strong and always hide their feelings.

She silently vowed that she would never let her dad know she had stood outside the doorway and been a witness to his emotional pain.

That was a promise she was to keep. In fact, as she stared into the night waiting for the morning to come, she felt a fierce sense of protectiveness toward her father, a feeling she never outgrew.

~

The next morning after breakfast, Burrel took his daughter for a ride. Pulling the car over to the side of the road, he stopped and gently told her that her mother had left them. He didn't know where she was, but he figured she had probably gone to Ohio.

"This isn't going to be easy for any of us," he said. "We'll just have to try to be strong. I'm going to do all I can to get her to come back to us, but if she doesn't, you kids are going to have to decide which of us you want to live with."

"What a terrible thing to have to even think about. How could you choose one parent over the other," she thought. The reality of what was happening was almost overwhelming, but she decided she wasn't going to cry. Her dad had enough on his mind without going away thinking she was a crybaby. She and Cecil, who Burrel told later that morning, both grew up a lot that day. Their childhood, as they knew it, was over. They no longer thought they were the center of their parents' universe. Instead they were forced to see themselves as separate entities, unimportant to their mother.

Anger, grief, a sense of loss, abandonment, and betrayal were all feelings they had to deal with that moment and for a long while to come. Their father tried to help them on the weekends he was able to be with them, but the winter of nineteen forty-one brought some fierce snow storms and created dangerous driving conditions in the mountains, making it impossible for him to come as often as he would have liked.

~

He didn't tell Cecil or June what he'd found the night before, when he got home from his job in Baltimore. Instead of the usual lights shining through the windows, the sound of children's voices, and the radio playing, a dark, silent house met him.

Entering the front door, the air was icy and damp, seeping through the heavy clothing he was wearing. There was a sound of running water from somewhere in the house and the feel of something slippery under his feet.

When he flicked the switch, and light filled the room, he was stunned by what he saw. There was water everywhere, gushing from burst pipes in the kitchen and bath. The coal-heating stove was cold, and from the condition of the pipes, had been for a while.

Going to the basement to turn off the water, he was not surprised to find more burst pipes. "First things first," he thought as he turned the water off at the main valve.

As he threaded his way through the flooded cellar, his mind was racing, "Where are Priscilla and the children? What has happened? Has there been an accident? Is someone sick?"

Walking through the upstairs rooms, surveying the damage, he soon had his answer. In the dining room, propped against a shelf on the buffet was a white envelope. As he picked it up, he saw one word, his name, written in Priscilla's familiar hand.

Tearing it open, he read that she could no longer live with him. She had left June at Uncle Luke's, and Cecil at Grandpap's and taken Dickie with her. She wasn't coming back, so it wouldn't do any good to try to find her.

He talked to several neighbors. They told him the house had been dark for several days since shortly after he had been home the last time. One neighbor informed him that the kids at school had been told the family was moving to Baltimore.

For a second, his hopes soared, then plummeted when his fingers touched the envelope in his pocket. No need kidding himself. She was gone. Even though he wanted to rush off and start looking for her, he was first going to have to deal with the house, trying to salvage what he could. Then he'd have to go talk to his sisters and June and Cecil.

After building a fire in the stove, he set about getting rid of all the water and surveying the damage. He felt certain the furniture would be all right. He made arrangements with a neighbor boy to keep a fire going for a few days to give the floor, walls, and furniture a chance to dry out.

Before he left the house, he found a forgotten paper, in the desk drawer, on which Priscilla had written a poem declaring her love for him but also for another.

Would You Care

Lift your eyes to mine my darling
Let me see the love light there
For you know I love you darling
And to me there's none so fair
Yet sometimes I often wonder
Would you care if I dared
Tell you that my love had vanished
Tell me darling would you care?

Would you care if I should leave you
Would you care if we should part
Would you care if someone told you
That another had won my heart
Would you care if you should find me
Closely held in someone's arms
Would your heart ache just a little
Tell me darling would you care?

Just suppose I should forsake you
Break my vows and leave you alone
Just suppose I should reject you
Take another for my own
Just suppose that duty called me
Would you care if I should die
Would your heart ache just a little
Tell me sweetheart would you care?

As he read the words, his heart wrenched as he wondered, "Can this really be happening? How could she not know how much I cared?"

More bad news greeted him as he opened the overflowing mailbox. It was full of bills, stamped overdue, final notice. Most alarming were the ones for the mortgage and the car. He was told the house was going to be foreclosed and the car repossessed if payment wasn't made immediately.

These things had been heavy on his mind as he had driven to his sister's house and sat in her parlor telling her what had happened. This was also why he hadn't been aware of his daughter standing on the stairs, silently listening.

CHAPTER FORTY-SEVEN

PRISCILLA'S NEW LIFE

When Priscilla had boarded the bus for Mansfield, Ohio with Virginia, Olive, and Dickie, careful arrangements had been made for their future. In exchange for Priscilla financing their trip, the two women were going along to help take care of Dickie while she worked, and Della had promised she would help her get started in a new life.

The long bus ride to Ohio was an unusual experience for young Dickie, who missed the familiar presence of his brother and sister. Virginia and Olive were, as usual, in a gala mood. Interested in everything around him, Dickie was most impressed by the bright lights he glimpsed through the bus window as they rambled through one small town after another. He was especially captivated when the bus passed through a large city where they stopped to change buses. Being a small town boy, he had never seen anything quite like it. Bright lights were shining from overhead, and neon signs surrounded him, flashing and dancing like a million stars. When they arrived in Mansfield, the bus drove by a bakery that was completely surrounded by neon. Pressing his face against the window he watched the lights glowing until they disappeared from sight.

Priscilla found out shortly after their arrival that Virginia and Olive had used her as a ticket out of Petersburg. Honoring their promise to help with Dickie was the furthest thing from their minds. As Priscilla commented later, "They took off like scalded cats when we got to Mansfield, leaving us to fend for ourselves." Later, when she saw them around town, it was obvious they'd continued their playgirl ways.

While Della was delighted that her sister had finally given Burrel his comeuppance, she had her own life to live, and didn't have any place in it for a single mother and little boy. Until Priscilla was able to afford a place for herself and Dickie, they stayed with Velma, Clarence and their two boys, little Burrel and David.

The only work she could find was as a waitress at Mac's Diner. The pay was ten dollars a week and tips. If she was lucky, in any given week, she might bring home fifteen dollars. Dickie started in the third grade and got his first job, selling magazines, to help make ends meet.

~

The second story apartment they'd rented was across the street from the police station. From their living room, they had a front row seat of the comings and goings outside the station house. Most of the time, all they'd see were people being brought in for fighting or drunkenness. One afternoon, Dickie, who had been looking out the window, cried out, "Mom, look out the window! It's Dad and Uncle Mace. They're going into the police station."

Peering out, she had no problem recognizing her husband and brother-in-law, even from the slight glimpse she had of their backs as the doors of the station house closed behind them. "Stay back. Don't let them see you," she cautioned Dickie.

As they stood shielded from view by the sheer curtains, they watched the two men walk out of the station and dejectedly climb back into the car and drive away.

This was to be the end of Burrel's search. He'd first gone to Newark where he'd talked to Priscilla's family. He'd felt battered and bruised as if he'd run into a brick wall. All these people he had thought of for years as his own family, had closed their doors and minds against him, making it clear it would be up to Priscilla to contact him if she wanted to be found. The most crushing blow was Fred and Lidy's complete rejection of him.

Priscilla's sister Laurie and her husband Gene were the only ones who showed any sympathy for his and the children's plight. Unfortunately they knew nothing of her whereabouts. Their guess was that she would probably have gone to Mansfield, since that was where her cousin Velma and sister Della lived. "I would think," Laura informed him, "They're most likely at Della and David's."

Shortly afterwards, June and Cecil each received a letter from their mother telling them she loved them, but since she and their father weren't happy together, it would be better if she left him. "I'm fine," she wrote, "So is Dickie. I'm sure you're enjoying being with your cousins." The return address was a post office box in Mansfield.

June's letter had been opened, as were all subsequent letters she received. Her aunt said it had arrived that way. As a child, June felt helpless to do anything about this invasion of her privacy, the same way she felt about so many other things that were going on in her life.

She replied to her mother by pleading with her to come home, telling her that if it was something she'd done, all she had to do was to just tell her what it was, and she'd never do it again.

Years later her mother told her that when she'd received that letter she'd almost given in and come home, but she'd seen too many other women leave their husbands and come running back to them. She'd vowed that if she ever left, it would be for good. Even hearing this, as an adult, June had experienced a rush of bitterness at the thought of her mother's stubbornness.

CHAPTER FORTY-EIGHT

LIFE IN THE HOUSE OF SHADOWS

During those long winter months while she stayed with her aunt and family, June felt as if she had somehow been plucked from everything she'd known and loved and been plopped down in the middle of hell. Living in the house with the two men she had most feared in her young life was like a nightmare come true.

Sitting at the dinner table, she would see her aunt flinch as Uncle Luke reached across and stuck his fork into the serving bowls.

Even though she lived there several months she never felt she got to know this shadow of a man. One thing was clearly evident to her, he did as he pleased, and no one dared to say anything to him about it. A perfect example was his atrocious table manners.

He wasn't mean or cruel, just silent and seemingly oblivious of everyone around him. In all the time she lived in that house, she didn't remember him ever speaking to her. She did recall hearing that Uncle Luke was wealthy. If so, it wasn't evident from the clothes he wore or anything about him unless it was his farm equipment or sleek, well fed animals.

To make it worse, every time her aunt's husband turned his face toward June, she could see his resentment of her presence in the household, and this resentment was often vehemently expressed.

Sitting next to her at the dinner table was her cousin Sissie. Having been the only surviving child for so many years, she had been pampered and spoiled and was accustomed to getting her own way. All the cousins were aware of her petulance and selfish ways. June certainly more so then the others by the time she was able to escape from that dismal house.

Like bright spots of sunshine, Sissie's four-year-old brother and two year old sister sat, one on either side of their mother, their young voices and bright smiles helping to dispel the gloom.

~

June liked to help her aunt by entertaining the two little ones, either by reading or playing with them. Their company helped ease her homesickness for her own brothers. The girl would patiently sit on her lap, the smile in her large blue eyes matching the one on her lips as June ran the brush through her soft blonde curls.

In typical little boy fashion, the little boy loved running and playing unless June was reading to them. Then the three of them would let their imaginations run rampant, and it would transport them from the big chair in the corner of the living room where they sat snuggled together, to the land of make-believe where he was slaying dragons, and the little girl became the beautiful blonde princess.

Her aunt's kindness and the younger children's presence helped make up for her uncle and Sissie's mean behavior toward her. From the time Sissie had found out June's mother wasn't coming back, she had made June's home life miserable.

No matter what June had, her cousin wanted it, and her father would see to it she got it. If June was playing with a toy, Sissie had to have it. The same thing was true regarding books she was reading and food she was eating. Whichever cookie or slice of cake her aunt gave June, it was the one her cousin had to have.

Things always got worse at night. The two girls shared a double bed and no matter what side of the bed June got into, that's where Sissie wanted to sleep. She'd whine and complain, causing her dad to come into the room and demand that June get on the other side.

Then, as if June couldn't hear, he'd turn to his daughter and say, "I don't know what the world is coming to. Your mother's folks drop kids off here like they're dropping off a sack of potatoes."

Then, still sneering, he'd turn to June and say, "Get over on the other side. Sissie wants to sleep on this side."

His eyes would soften as he'd look at his daughter's pouting face, "Come on Sis, move over here. You can sleep wherever you want to." As the two girls changed places, he'd mutter, "I guess the next thing that brother of your mother will ask us to take care of will be some stray dogs or cats."

No matter what June said, especially her protest of, "But I was on the side you told me to sleep on last night," didn't help. If anything, it seemed to make matters worse as he'd snap, "I don't care about last night. This is tonight, and Sissie wants to sleep on this side."

June soon learned it didn't help to talk to her aunt, since he didn't respect his wife and didn't pay any attention to anything she said. Help was to come from a surprising source.

~

One night Sissie had started her whining, and her dad was berating June when something inside June snapped. She jumped out of bed and stood looking up into his dark surly face and screamed, "I'm getting out of here! I'm not going to stay here one more minute and be treated this way!"

Angrily she tore about the room, pulling on layers of heavy clothing. "I'm going to Grandpap's house. He'd never let anyone treat me this way."

"It's ten miles to your grandfather's house, and there's snow on the ground, up to your knees. You're not going anywhere," he scornfully replied.

Too angry to listen, June shouted, "I don't care. I'm getting out of here. No one wants me here, and I'm leaving!"

Her uncle had just thought he had one whirlwind on his hands until the door flew open and a second one, his younger sister Maggie, burst through. "What is going on in here?" she demanded.

He had almost forgotten his sister and her friend, June's cousin Avanelle, were spending the night. The sheepish look on his face made it obvious he hadn't expected anyone outside of his own household to be aware of his verbal abuse of this child.

June didn't give him time to answer before she told Maggie what had been going on, and that she wasn't going to take it anymore. "I'm going to Grandpap's now, and he," she concluded, pointing to her uncle, "isn't going to stop me!"

Maggie had heard enough. Turning on her brother she told him in no uncertain words what she thought of him for treating this child in this manner. "I'm ashamed of you!" she said. "I can imagine how bad it's been if she's ready to leave here in the middle of the night.... In a snow storm!"

Standing there in her long white nightgown with her dark hair tumbled about her shoulders and sparks flashing from her black eyes, she must have looked like the wrath of God to her brother and his daughter, but to June she was like a guardian angel.

"What would Mom and Dad think if they knew how you were treating this helpless child? What would Burrel say? How about the rest of the Harmans? I can tell you I'm not going to allow you to talk that way to her.... Ever again!"

He stood backed up against the wall. His skinny legs encased in long underwear looked like they were about to collapse and leave him like a crumbled doll on the floor at his sister's feet.

June watched in stunned disbelief as this scenario unfolded. She could hardly believe her good fortune. This young woman, almost a stranger to her, was coming to her rescue.

"Come on," Maggie said, taking June by the hand and leading her into the next room. "You're going to sleep with Avanelle and me tonight." Then smiling, she added, "You can sleep on whichever side you want, and no one is going to make you move."

Before June fell asleep nestled between the two girls, Maggie whispered, "Don't worry. You're not going to have to put up with it anymore. I'll see to that." Feeling safe and protected for the first time since she'd learned her mother wasn't coming back, June felt as if the weight of the world had been lifted from her shoulders.

As Maggie and Avanelle left the next day, Maggie said to her brother, "I'll be back to see how everything is going." Then as if to emphasize what she had just said, she turned to June and gave her a hug and in a voice loud enough for all to hear, told her, "If you need anything, you know where to get hold of me."

June hardly dared to hope things would be better, but much to her surprise, they were. Her uncle hardly spoke to her at all, and when he did, it was no longer in the same rude hurtful manner.

While things improved within the household, outside was a different matter. Given the size of the community and the lack of entertainment or recreational facilities, Burrel, Priscilla, and the children left behind provided many hours of enjoyment for the local gossips.

Everywhere June went it seemed as if they, like small vicious dogs, were nipping at her ankles. She would try to shake them off by ignoring them. One favorite ploy of the adults was to ask when her mother was coming after them.

Even though their words were hurtful, she would straighten her spine, pulling herself to her full height and look them straight in the eye as if daring them to say anything more. She was aware these people knew the answer to their question was "never" and that they were only amusing themselves by asking.

The children at school were more considerate. They had been told by Miss Nina that June was there temporarily, that she would be moving to Baltimore soon. If their parents had told them differently, they never mentioned it. They seemed to feel that if June wanted to pretend nothing had changed since she'd gotten here, it was all right with them.

~

She and Louise, a little redhead in her class, soon became fast friends. Louise lived in a farmhouse on top of a big hill across the road from Uncle Luke's. Mornings she and her sister would zoom down the hill to walk to school with June and Sissie. Sometimes they'd come running with the wind whipping their hair around their faces. Other times when the snow was deep, they'd whiz to the bottom on their sleds.

The winter of 1941 was fierce with one snowstorm after another erasing the sleds' tracks one day, only to see them replaced the next.

Going to school in town for the last two and one half years had spoiled June. She'd almost forgotten the rigors of walking through snow-covered fields to a one-room schoolhouse.

All the girls wore long mud colored stockings over long underwear to protect their legs during their lengthy walk to and from school. Accustomed to wearing ankle or knee socks, she at first couldn't bring herself to don the ugly stockings. But after the first long trek through the snow left her legs red, raw, and aching, she decided there were times to be fashionable, but this wasn't one of them.

She felt like crying the first time she slipped her legs into the thick ugly stockings. Later when she and Sissie started for school and were greeted by a blast of arctic air, she was thankful for them.

One particularly stormy morning as they watched Louise and her sister descending the hill at a breath taking speed, they thought they heard jingling bells in the distance. As they listened, the sound came closer and was joined by a clop clippity clop.

Someone jokingly remarked, "Sounds like Santa and his sleigh." It wasn't Santa who came around the bend, but a farmer from down the road, seated in a horse drawn sleigh. The horse was sleek and brown, bedecked in a black harness and reins covered with bright glistening silver bells.

As the farmer hollered, "Whoa!" the horse stopped in front of the delighted children.

"Climb in," the Good Samaritan jovially said, "There's always room for more."

As the horse stood snorting and shaking his head up and down, they clamored aboard the sleigh and snuggled under the blanket with their friends. They felt as if they had stepped back into time.

After making sure they were settled in, the farmer called out, "Giddy up!" and the horse with one more shake of his head and a whinny that seemed to say, "That's more like it," resumed his clippity clopping toward the schoolhouse.

To the background sound of the horses' hooves, the almost silent gliding of the sleigh's runners, and the tinkling of the bells, the children laughed and sang all the way to school.

Meeting them at the door, Miss Nina was caught up in their festive mood and, for the first few minutes of class, let them continue their joyful singing.

This special day, her friendship with Louise, and caring for the little black lamb her aunt let her bottle feed were the pleasant memories June carried with her when that long winter was over, and she was able to move on to another chapter in her life.

~

As they walked to school the children began to notice wild flowers peeking through the remnants of snow, the buds appearing on the trees, and the air that had bitterly nipped at their faces beginning to softly caress their cheeks. At last the hated stockings were replaced by anklets or knee socks. Spring was here!

Another Easter arrived, this one without the drama of last year. June could hardly believe that she was living in the home of the couple who had battled in her parents' kitchen last Easter. So much had changed in the past year. She tried not to dwell on that or happier Easters as she, Sissie and the younger children helped color the Easter eggs and bake a cake. June's aunt let them use food coloring to tint each of the three cake layers the colors they'd used on the Easter eggs. When they were finished, she scooped mounds of white fluffy icing from the bowl and swirled it over its top and sides.

Looking at the bouquet of spring flowers the children had picked, the smile on her aunt's face, the two little ones licking the spoon and bowl, the brightly colored eggs nestled beside the luscious looking cake, and the warm sunshine streaming through the freshly washed windows, June felt as if the room had been transformed from its usually gloomy state into a warm happy place. Thinking about it, she realized the dismal atmosphere didn't come from the house, but from some of its occupants. This realization was reinforced a few minutes later when the men walked in wearing their customary frowns, and a dark cloud seemed to settle over the room.

Even their cantankerous manner couldn't dampen June's excitement. Her dad was coming for the weekend and taking her to her grandpap's to spend Easter vacation. She would get to be with Cecil, play with her cousin Hilda, and see Grandpap, but best of all, escape from here.

She and her dad didn't leave until Easter morning, and by then June had again fallen for her cousin's, "Let's eat yours first, then we'll eat mine when you get back."

When she arrived at Grandpap's, her candy all gone, Hilda was amazed Sissie had again managed to sucker her. All the cousins had fallen for it at one time or another, but as Hilda said, "All those dried up Easter eggs and candy setting on the buffet show she never has shared any of hers."

June told Hilda she wouldn't let her talk her into it next year. As it turned out, she didn't have to worry about it, as that was the last Easter she was ever to spend with Sissie.

Burrel left early that afternoon, as he had to be back to work the next morning. Before leaving he told June and Cecil that when school was out he was going to take them to Washington. Tony and Pauline Eno wanted them to spend a couple weeks with them. "I won't be able to spend much time with you during the week, but I'll be there over the weekends," he assured them.

This was good news for both children. Although things had improved for June since Maggie had befriended her, she still wasn't happy where she was living.

It was different for Cecil. He was happy where he was, even though he and Clyde still argued as they had when they were small children. The passing of time hadn't changed that or cooled Aunt Gussie's temper. Both boys often felt the sharp edge of her tongue, but it didn't seem to curb their fighting or keep them out of mischief.

One particular episode took place after Aunt Gussie had made sauerkraut to which she had added apples. As the cabbage had wintered in the thick crocks, all the fermented juices had seeped into the apples making them quite tasty, a little intoxicating, and completely irresistible to the boys.

Many a time, after they'd lifted the heavy lid and speared a few slices of the mouth-watering fruit into their mouths, Aunt Gussie would ask, "Who's been eating all the apples from my kraut? Clyde, Cecil have you been into it?"

Rolling their eyes heavenward, the most innocent look would steal across their faces as they'd each say, "Who me?" She never quite believed them, nor did she ever catch them.

~

Getting to school was much easier for Cecil, Clyde, and Hilda than for June and Sissie. They only had to walk about a quarter mile beyond Grandpap's house to the one room Germany Valley schoolhouse. The road, with no fields to walk through or fences to climb, could reach it.

Grandpap was still Postmaster at the Key post office, but no longer had a mail route of his own. Six mornings a week he would sit at the kitchen table and sort the mail that the two mailmen would then pick up and deliver on their rural routes. Some close neighbors would stop in the post office every morning to visit and pick up their mail.

Many times while June was visiting over Easter vacation, after Grandpap finished his work he would put her in front of him on Ole Don and they'd ride around the farm. "I know what has happened is hard on you," he said on one of their rides. "The people around here aren't making it any easier by the way they love to tear everyone apart. I always told your dad, when he was growing up, to be proud and hold his head high no matter what happened. It isn't always easy, but it's better than letting people get you down."

June listened, thinking how her parents had tried to instill in her these same views. Although she didn't know it at the time, in a few years she'd be saying the same to her own children.

"I don't want you to be too hard on your mother. You never know what goes on in another person's heart." His eyes softened when he continued, "Your mother was little more than a child the first time your dad brought her back here when they were on their honeymoon. Maybe she just took on too much too soon, never really giving herself time to grow up."

As he talked, June could feel tears spilling down her cheeks. She was moved because he was the first person who had spoken kindly about her mother since it became common knowledge she had left them.

"I love your mother," he said. "She has always been a favorite of mine." "Now tell me, how are you getting along with your cousins?"

She hadn't meant to tell him, but all her unhappiness spilled out as she told him what had been happening, the dislike on her uncle's face every time he looked at her, Sissie's selfishness, and how her uncle had treated her until his sister Maggie came to her defense.

Grandpap chuckled softly at the thought of Maggie standing up to her brother, before he asked, "How about your aunt? I'm sure she is kind to you."

"Oh, yes. She's always nice and I love the two little ones, but the others...," she said letting her voice trail off.

"I know, I know," he murmured, soothingly. Then shaking his head, he added, "I think I'll have a talk with Burrel."

That was not to be the last ride they'd take around the farm. Subsequent ones found him talking about the past. He told her about having been a schoolteacher in one-room schoolhouses, including Germany Valley School and the one she was attending. "The students didn't think I knew it, but they called me "Old U" behind my back. Of course to my face they called me Mr. Ulysses. I guess they thought I was pretty strict, but I had to be. Some of those boys in the eighth grade were bigger than I was. If I didn't get control right away, I wouldn't have been able to teach them anything. I think teaching young people is one of the most important jobs a person can have. I guess I've always loved books and learning and I've tried to pass that love on to all my students."

"I love books, too," June said, "I must have gotten it from you."

"You couldn't have helped loving books. Your mom loved to read and your dad does, too. I guess you get it from both sides of the family," he responded.

"I've taught most of the people around here, including your daddy," he said.

"I remember Dad said you were his teacher. He said the only time he ever got in trouble in school was with you," June said.

She could hear the smile in his voice when he said, "I didn't know whether he'd told you kids or not. I wasn't going to mention it if he hadn't."

They dismounted and let ole Don graze in the meadow while they sat under a tree, and he told her about her dad as a little boy.

He seemed to be looking at June, but in his mind's eye he was seeing Germany Valley schoolhouse and himself at the front of the room those many years ago with his young charges squirming in their seats while he tried to instill some knowledge in their reluctant minds.

He could hear himself telling them for the last time to quit talking and pay attention to their lessons. Some of the rowdier boys had continued to ignore him, as if he hadn't spoken. He remembered pronouncing in his sternest voice, "I'm not going to tell you again, that the next person who speaks without being called upon is going to get a paddling."

As they'd looked into his determined blue eyes, they'd realized he meant what he was saying and quiet descended upon the room. As he worked with the younger grades, leaving the older ones to complete work he'd already given them, from the corner of his eye he'd seen a girl turn in her seat to face Burrel, and to his distress, Burrel had spoken to her.

This was a time when he had to be a teacher, not a father. If he ignored the fact that his son had disobeyed his order, he might as well give in to chaos. He'd lose the hard earned respect he'd gained from the older students.

As he related this story to his granddaughter, he could hear himself that day, twenty-five years ago, say, "Alright Burrel, I said no talking and I meant no talking. Come up here."

"But, sir," Burrel, who could never quite call his dad Mr. Ulysses, said, "She wanted to know what problems we were working on. I had to answer her."

Maybe if this had been any boy other than his son, he might have been able to accept the excuse, but glancing around the room at some of his more difficult students, they looked as if they were daring him to favor his son. He knew this wasn't the time to make an exception.

"I said, come up here, Burrel," he'd said, sounding much firmer than he'd felt. He remembered his son's reluctant steps as he obeyed his father and took that long trek to the front of the room. As if it were yesterday, he remembered how awful he felt when he brought the paddle down on his son's behind.

He knew Burrel's pride was hurt much more than his bottom, since this was winter and he, like all the students, was wearing several layers of clothing.

"I know Burrel always felt his punishment was unfair," he told June, "And, you know, I could have sworn that evening when I overheard him talking to Mace about it, I heard him call me Old U", he mused.

June had heard this story before, but from her dad's point of view. If he had been angry at his dad, time had softened it. He usually re-counted it as an example of how important it was to mind the teacher, something he expected from his children.

On the way back to the farmhouse, Grandpap pointed out long healed over holes and gashes in some of the trees. "This was the site of some fighting during the Civil War. Those holes were made by bullets," he told her. "Some of the bullets have been dug out, but I wouldn't be surprised if some are still in there."

Even though he hadn't taught school for several years he was still a teacher at heart and spent the rest of the ride talking to her about that war and how his father had fought in it, how he had been born four years after the war was over, and named after the hero General Ulysses S. Grant, who later became president. "I wonder if his troops ever called him Old U," he mused.

Having these days with her grandpap and knowing that she and Cecil were going to spend some time in Washington with their father and Tony and Pauline Eno, made it easier for June to go back to her aunt's. Besides her Grandpap had said he would talk to Burrel. Unrealistic as it was, since she knew her dad lived in one room in a boarding house, she still daydreamed that this talk would result in their dad telling them that they could come live with him after their visit in Washington. This didn't happen, but for June, something almost as good did.

~

The next time her dad came to see her, he told her that when school was out she was going to live with her Aunt Calcie. She could hardly believe her good fortune, getting to stay with Bonnie and Ruby, two of her favorite cousins.

As if that news wasn't enough in itself, she was going to get some new clothes. She'd had a growth spurt during the winter and all her skirts and dresses had become mini skirts, years before it was fashionable. While she was wearing the long stockings, her dad hadn't noticed how much she'd grown, but when he saw her at Easter with her long legs bare, her short skirt barely covering her hips, he knew something had to be done.

He, his sister, and June sat down with the Sears and Roebuck catalogue and ordered some dresses for the rest of the school year and a few playsuits to wear during the summer. "Haven't you noticed how much Cecil has grown?" his sister asked. "He's going to need some new things, too. Do you want to go ahead and order some pants and shirts for him?"

Feeling guilty that he hadn't noticed, Burrel nodded his head and turned to the boys wear section. He'd always left this sort of thing to Priscilla, but he knew he was going to have to get used to being both mother and father. For now, though, he was glad to have the help of his sisters.

Excited at the prospect of the trip and her escape from this house, time seemed to crawl for June, but finally the last day of school arrived.

Although she wasn't sorry to leave this school, it was sad for her to leave Miss Nina and Louise.

She and Louise hugged and said they'd write and see each other again, but even as she said it she knew this goodbye was going to be forever.

Cecil and Clyde graduated from the eighth grade at Germany Valley School. Cecil wasn't concerned about leaving his friends behind, since he'd be staying where he was and in the fall most of his friends would be riding the bus with him to the high school in Circleville.

~

On the trip to Washington, June and Cecil sat in the front seat with their dad, listening to him talk about his plans for them on this visit. "We'll drive into Washington and go by all the monuments before we go to Tony and Pauline's. Before I leave, I'll give you some money so you can go into the city every day if you want to. Tony and Pauline will be working, but there's a bus stop close to their house. Tony will tell you where to catch it and where you'll need to get off."

As their dad drove through all the traffic, past the Capital building, the White House, Washington Monument, and Lincoln Memorial, June and Cecil were in awe, feeling as if they'd stepped into the pages of their geography books. Even though, now they knew the pictures hadn't been able to portray the ambiance, or the way it made them feel at being part of history as they stopped in front of the White House and their dad commented, "This is where almost all our presidents have lived."

Both children craned their necks, hoping for a glimpse of the President or First Lady, but much to their disappointment no one was visible, not even the first dog, Fala, President Roosevelt's Scottish terrier.

The next couple weeks proved to be educational in more ways than one. The first day of their visit as they listened, Tony called in sick. "I'm not going to be able to come in today," he told the person at the other end of the line. "I've got the runs and can't get two feet away from the bathroom."

Then in response to a question, "Yes, I think I'll be able to be there tomorrow. This feels like one of those twenty-four hour things."

As he hung up, he turned a mischievous smile on his audience and said, "That's all taken care of, I can take you sightseeing and show you how to get around in the big city. Are you ready?"

"Sure!" they both said as they tried to hide their feeling of cultural shock, not only at hearing an adult tell a blatant lie, but seeming to be proud of himself for getting away with it. This went against everything they'd ever been taught.

By the time the day was over, they'd toured the Smithsonian Institute and the National Museum and gone up in the Washington Monument. They'd both listened and been observant and felt confident they could get around during the rest of their stay.

Knowing this was their first time in the city, Tony was surprised at their lack of fear at the prospect of being on their own. The next few days, like their pioneer ancestors, they set out on exploratory trips. One day they walked to Arlington Cemetery to The Tomb of The Unknown Soldier and watched the changing of the guard.

Other days, they rode the bus to the Lincoln Memorial, walked from there to the White House and the Capital Building, saw the Disney animated movie, the Reluctant Dragon, and never tired of browsing through the Smithsonian.

In the evening they found out, first hand, what it was like visiting in the home of a nudist. As he earlier had with Burrel, Tony explained his philosophy to them about the freedom one feels in being unencumbered by the constraints of clothing, and his feeling that everyone should have respect for the beauty of the human body.

Having said this, he practiced what he preached, although Pauline did not. Every evening when he came home from work, within the privacy of the house, he wore only his shoes, socks, and horn-rimmed glasses. At first, they were embarrassed, averting their eyes when he walked into the room, but Tony seemed so relaxed with what he was doing that, while they never quite felt comfortable with it, after awhile they were no longer shocked.

Their education continued. Tony and Pauline wheeled their bicycles out of the garage and proceeded to teach them how to ride them. It was to be decades before this English style bicycle became popular in this country. Never having seen any quite like them, June and Cecil thought they were truly magnificent and couldn't believe their good fortune at being allowed to ride them. It took a couple evenings before they were able to pedal without wobbling, but eventually they became aware their host or hostess was no longer holding onto the bicycle and that they were riding quite competently on their own.

They practiced every evening until they went home and became quite proficient at pedaling, steering, and using the hand brakes. They both thought they knew all they needed to know about biking. A few weeks later June was to discover otherwise.

As they had learned during the Eno's visit in West Virginia, that although he was an amateur, Tony was a very good photographer. After teaching them to ride the bikes, he took it upon himself to instruct them in the rudiments of photography, including developing pictures in his home darkroom. During those lessons he fueled an interest in the subject in both of them, one they never outgrew.

Before their dad took them back to West Virginia, Tony had the talk with them Priscilla had so long ago promised. At last, they were officially told the facts of life. Of course, by now, they'd heard most of it from their friends, but Tony was much more factual. Not being embarrassed, he no doubt, did a much more thorough job than their mother could ever have done.

Armed with their newfound knowledge, Cecil returned to stay with Aunt Gussie and June moved in with Aunt Calcie. Cecil never said whether he shared the facts of life with Clyde, but June didn't waste any time telling Bonnie and Ruby.

~

On one of his trips to Aunt Gussie's and Aunt Calcie's, Burrel brought a bicycle for Cecil and one for June. Although they were used, to them, they looked shiny and new.

June waited to try hers until her older cousins rode it around the country roads. They were all as excited about the bicycle as she was. June shared with all of them and within a few weeks Bonnie and Ruby had also learned to ride. That first day, after all the older boys had ridden, and she had wiped the dust from the fenders, she got on and started to ride down the hill in front of the house. As she rode, she found herself going faster and faster. She reached for the brakes on the handlebar to slow her descent, but they weren't there.

She remembered hearing that with American made bicycles, you had to use the pedals to make it stop. "How?" she thought as she went faster and faster, heading for a big curve, an open sided bridge, and the river.

No matter what she did with the pedal, it wasn't the right thing to do. She couldn't seem to stop. Everything she tried seemed to make it go faster and faster. Seeing the curve and a sure drop into the river looming ahead, she knew she had to find a way to bring an end to her downward descent.

To her right was the barn. It appeared she had two choices, and she didn't like either one of them. She could continue on her course to the river or stop herself by running into the barn. To the amazement of everyone watching, she steered toward the barn and with a loud thud crashed into the half open doors landing in a carpet of soft hay.

Fortunately, neither she nor the bicycle were hurt, but before letting her take off again, her cousins, Harman and Gerald, saw to it she had a few lessons on the intricacies of the brakes on an American made bicycle.

～

In Mansfield, Bill had joined Priscilla and Dickie, and they were becoming a family. Although they were happy, Priscilla wasn't yet ready to allow him to be Dickie's father. This was all right with Bill, as he wasn't quite prepared to have his new stepson take the place of the son he'd left behind. He hadn't gotten over missing little Bill.

The same age as Dickie, his picture, a constant reminder of the two boys' uncanny resemblance to each other, occupied a prominent place in the living room. Many times, in years to come, Priscilla was to observe a look of sadness and longing cross her husband's face as he sat staring at the picture.

Burrel had sued and received the divorce and was granted custody of all three children. This didn't mean Dickie would be living with them. Since Dickie and Priscilla were living outside the court's jurisdiction, the only way Burrel could get custody of his youngest son was to initiate action in the Mansfield court to have the order enforced. He was in no position, financially or otherwise, to do this.

He still had periods of depression when he thought of what he'd lost. In addition to his wife and youngest son, his house, car, and shares in Smoke Hole Cavern were gone.

He had been unable to think of any way to get out from under all his debts, other than to let the house revert back to the bank. His car had been repossessed and needing one to get to and from work and to come see June and Cecil, he'd sold the only thing he had left, his shares in the cavern.

Sometimes, waking in the middle of the night, he'd lie there remembering all they'd had during their years together and wonder if he'd been more sensitive to what Priscilla had been saying things might have been different. He knew all the wishing and praying and wondering wasn't going to change anything. He was going to have to start all over and try to pick up the pieces and go on with their lives.... His and June and Cecil's.

Although he appreciated his sisters helping him by taking them in, he was aware of June and Cecil's unhappiness at not having a home of their own. He knew things were better now for June than they had been, but he had been surprised to see a look of longing cross her face when she was watching a mother and daughter at the restaurant table next to theirs, talking and laughing as they drank their Pepsi.

He felt certain it wasn't much better for Cecil, but being older and a boy, he didn't let it show as much.

CHAPTER FORTY-NINE

THE SUMMER OF 1941

His first effort at dating since Priscilla left him was with a divorcee named May Knight. She was a single mother of two children. He had become friends with her employer, an older woman, who owned a roadside inn on the Washington Boulevard. She had introduced him to May, her assistant.

May was a couple years older than Burrel, of medium height, trim, neat, always fashionably dressed with her dark hair perfectly coifed. He'd never seen her with even one hair out of place. After a few dates they'd discovered they had a lot in common, not the least being each one's need for a parent to help raise the children.

May, anxious to meet June and Cecil, broached the subject one evening as they sat in the rustic dining room at the inn. "You've met Tommy and Bobby. When am I going to meet June and Cecil? The children are all about the same age. I think they'd like each other."

This wasn't the first time they'd talked about it, but it seemed to Burrel she was becoming more insistent. His resistance wasn't because he didn't want to get her and the children together. He just wasn't ready to take a woman home to meet his sisters or his father. It looked like too much of a commitment.

Noticing his reluctance, but not yet willing to give up, she came up with an alternative. "Why don't you bring the children for a visit. That way I'd get to meet them. You'd be able to spend some time with them, and they'd get to know Bobby and Tommy."

"I'd really like to do that, but how can I? You know I only have a sleeping room, and there aren't any vacant ones in the boarding house," was his response.

Undaunted, May replied, "I didn't mean for them to stay with you. They can stay here at the inn. We always have a couple empty rooms and I'm sure Mrs. Simpson would be happy to have them."

As Burrel mulled over her suggestion, she teasingly added, "You know how she mothers you. Haven't you ever noticed how much more food you get on your plate than anyone else? Do you think she's keeping the dining room open after hours just for me?"

Then before he could respond, she answered her own question, "No, it's for you. You bring out all her maternal instincts, and I'm sure June and Cecil would, too."

"Hmm, if she were twenty years younger, you'd have some competition," he replied, his mischievous smile reminding her of one of her boys.

"Well, what do you think?" she persisted.

"If it's alright with Mrs. Simpson, I'd really like to bring them here," he responded, then added, "Do you think I should ask her or do you want to?"

"Ask me what?" Mrs. Simpson asked as she quietly entered the room.

They both explained what they wanted to do and to no one's surprise, she welcomed the idea. Before Burrel left that evening, they had decided he'd bring June and Cecil back with him when he went to West Virginia the following weekend. It was agreed they'd stay a couple weeks.

～

There was little similarity between this trip and the previous one when they had stayed with Burrel's friends, Tony and Pauline. Here they were too far away from anything to go off on their own. The inn was a typical country one, miles from either Washington or Baltimore, quiet during the day, a little more active during the dinner hour. It would really come alive in the evening when the band would either play soft ballads or swing into a boisterous boogie-woogie.

June and Cecil were free to explore the inn during the day, but during the evening the bar and dance floor were off limits but hard to resist. The sound of the music and the laughter floating up the stairs into their rooms would act like a magnet, drawing them downstairs. There they found a potted palm in the lobby that provided the perfect cover where they could see and hear without being seen or heard. Most evenings found them in that spot. If anyone was aware of it, it was never mentioned.

Both being free on Sunday, Burrel and May got all four of the children together and went into Washington to the National Zoo. This being their first visit to a zoo, June and Cecil were enthusiastic and interested in seeing all the animals. On the other hand, Tommy and Bobby, wanting to appear more sophisticated, tried to act disinterested.

No matter how hard they tried, though, they didn't quite pull it off, and soon found themselves laughing along with their visitors at the antics of the monkeys.

Having been told by Tony of June's interest in photography, Burrel had bought her an inexpensive camera. She had snapped pictures of almost every animal so that when she got back she could share this wonderful experience with Bonnie and Ruby.

Although she, like the boys, liked the monkeys, her favorites were the polar and brown bears. She loved to watch as they scratched themselves against the rough walls of their pens or cooled themselves in the pools of water, shaking like large shaggy dogs when they got out.

The afternoon was capped off with a stop at a frozen custard stand where they all had chicken in a basket and cones of frozen custard, a forerunner of the current soft serve ice cream. The stand itself looked like a giant igloo with a wide opening in the front where Burrel placed their order.

The atmosphere was festive as they all sat around the outdoor table eating their dinner. Looking around at the four blonde, blue eyed children, Burrel thought that anyone seeing them would think they were a family. From the possessive way May had been looking at him, he was almost sure she would like to see that happen.

It would be good if he could have June and Cecil with him, but he just wasn't ready yet to share his life with another woman. Not yet able to picture himself married to anyone except Priscilla, he wondered if he ever would be.

As they piled into the car for the trip back to the inn, June started to take her usual seat next to him, only to have May tell her that she was going to sit there. June could sit on the other side of her.

Observing June's disappointed face as she slid into her assigned seat, he couldn't help think, "I'd better take this whole thing a little slower. The kids have to be happy with whatever I decide to do." No doubt about it, right now, from the look on her face, his daughter wasn't very happy.

The next evening, when he saw May at the inn she said, "Burrel, you simply have to do something about June's clothes."

"Her clothes!" Burrel exclaimed. "I just got her some clothes before school was out. Don't tell me she's already grown out of them!"

"Oh, they still fit her, but nothing goes together. Today she wore brown sandals with her blue dress. You just can't wear blue and brown together. When I told her to go back upstairs and put on her blue shoes, she said she didn't have any!" she continued. "When I looked over her wardrobe, I found out she doesn't have red shoes to go with her red dress or white shoes for her white play suit."

He raised his eyebrows as a puzzled look crossed his face. He couldn't imagine what she was talking about. He had always left this sort of thing to Priscilla, but he couldn't ever remember his wife or daughter having a different pair of shoes for every outfit. Before he could answer, May said, "I can take June into town tomorrow and help her pick out some. I think, if she gets three pairs, red, blue and white ones, she'll be all set. You don't want her to be out of style, do you? After all, things like that are important to girls."

Burrel couldn't keep the grin from his face as he wondered what May would have said if she'd seen June's short skirts at Easter time, or the unsightly stockings she'd worn all winter.

"Alright, if you think that's what she needs, I'll give you the money," Burrel agreed, although he couldn't imagine anything any more ridiculous than a child of eleven with coordinating shoes for every outfit. It was going to cost him at least six dollars, money he could ill afford, but he would rather spend it than disagree with May.

He'd had to add a couple more dollars to the shoe money so June could coordinate her hair ribbons and berets to her shoes and dress. As May had said, "It just wouldn't do for her to wear her one pair of tortoise shelled berets with everything. What would people think?"

This woman was making him feel that he didn't know anything about raising a girl.

He tried to keep his eyes and ears open to see how well his children and May's got along and how June and Cecil reacted to her. He observed, as May had said, the four children were close enough in age to get along well. Cecil seemed to like both boys, while June didn't pay much attention to Bobby. It was obvious she had a slight crush on Tommy, who, in turn, treated her like one of the boys. Burrel didn't know whether to be alarmed or amused.

Another thing he noticed was June and Cecil's extreme courtesy toward May. There didn't appear to be any warmth, either on their part or hers.

She seemed to compete with June for his attention, as evidenced by her continued refusal to let June sit between them. He'd even mentioned it to her, only to be told that maybe it would be better if June sat in the back seat and let one of the boys sit up front. She was sure none of them cared where they sat. "Maybe the boys don't care," he replied. "But June is going to stay up here with me."

May's face paled, but she didn't respond. She was intimidated by the way Burrel thrust his chin forward when he spoke to her, and by the protective look he bestowed upon his daughter. That was the last time she ever tried to relegate June to the back seat.

It was almost time for the visit to be over, so he decided not to make an issue of it. He did know though, that if they ever were to become a family, the time wasn't yet right.

The two weeks went by quickly and it was soon time for Burrel to take June and Cecil back to West Virginia. June had a great deal to tell Bonnie and Ruby, although not quite as scintillating as what she'd learned from Tony Eno.

~

The three girls spent the rest of the lazy days of summer playing, riding June's bicycle, or swimming in the river down the country road from the house. They all had bathing suits, but sometimes they'd go skinny dipping, hidden from sight by the bridge. One day, a teen-aged neighbor boy, one none of the girls could stand being around, came walking by. When he heard them laughing and splashing in the water, he called out to them, "Hey, who's under there?"

All three girls yelled, "Stay up there! Don't you dare come down here!"?

"Why not?" he asked as he started to scurry down the bank, laughing at the girls' screams of protest. Then while they tried to hide under the much too clear water, he stopped half way down the bank, plopped down on the ground, and sat waiting to see what they were going to do next.

The girls remained still, listening, knowing he hadn't left and expecting him to loom up in front of them any second. Instead he said, "Well, if you don't want me to come down, I'll just sit here and talk to you. I have all my chores done and don't have anything to do the rest of the afternoon. There's nothing wrong with that, is there?"

One quick glance had shown them that when they'd peeled off their suits, they'd carelessly thrown them on the ground in full view of anyone walking by. Quite obviously he'd seen them laying there and intended to give the girls a rough time.

One good thing, though, he didn't act as if he were coming down. He was just sitting there like a cat under a bird nest, waiting for them to come out.

"What are we going to do?" June whispered. "I don't think he's going to go away."

"I don't either," Bonnie said. "We can't stay here all day. I'm starting to get cold."

Now that she'd mentioned it, they all noticed the water was getting colder. Standing, shivering in water up to her shoulders, Ruby said, "I wonder what time it is."

"The way my tummy feels, it must be supper time," June answered.

The boy could hear them, but not well enough to understand what they were saying. "Aren't you girls getting tired of swimming? Why don't you get out? Don't tell me those bathing suits are yours," he said in a teasing manner. "I know what must have happened, you must all have fallen in with all your clothes on." Having said that, he started softly singing the words to a popular song, "Three Little Fishes In An Itsie Bitsy Brook."

When he stopped his infuriating singing, he said, tauntingly, "Girls, those three little fishes swam and swam all over the dam. I don't hear you swimming. Aren't you going to swim anymore?"

He stopped talking when he heard someone walking down the road calling the girls' names. "Bonnie! Ruby! June! Time for dinner."

It's Max!" Bonnie cried, referring to her older sister, Maxine.

"Max! Max! We're under the bridge!" she shouted. "Come help us!"

As Max scooted down the bank, she almost collided with the boy in his mad scramble to get out of there. When she realized the girls' predicament, she yelled after him. In his rush to put as much distance between himself and this newcomer, he didn't stop to listen or reply.

After she saw for herself that the girls were all right, she could see the humor in the situation, but the three shivering girls never did.

Even though they never went skinny dipping again, this wasn't to be their last encounter with this method of swimming. A few days later when they were playing on top of the hill above the river, they could hear laughter and splashing coming from the direction of the bridge. Looking toward the sound, they saw Harman and his friends diving off the bank into the river. Their bathing trunks were thrown on the ground, and they truly looked like disciples of Tony Eno.

Embarrassed and not wanting the boys to know they'd seen them, they turned and slipped back to the house. Although they blushed later that afternoon when Harman and his friends came walking up the road, carrying their dry bathing suits, they were as quiet about what they'd seen as they'd been about their own experience.

~

This household was in contrast to Uncle Luke's. There was sunshine and happiness in place of shadows and gloom. Around the dinner table there was laughter and conversation and a great deal of teasing from the older boys.

Aunt Calcie and Uncle Gordon were the parents of nine children. All except their oldest son Garth, twenty-three, and daughter Bea, twenty-five, were still living at home.

Maxine, nineteen, had just finished high school and was working in Franklin at the hotel while she finished her business course. She planned to move to Washington with her cousin, Avanelle, and June's guardian angel, Maggie.

Gerald, seventeen, and Harman not quite fifteen, were in high school and helped their father on the farm. Bonnie, though a few months older than June, would be in the seventh grade with her, while Ruby, two years younger would be in the fifth.

Virgil was seven and going into the second grade. Estel, the baby, who was only five, still had a year to go before he started to school.

The dining room was full when all ten of them gathered around the long harvest table. The young people sat at long benches on each side and Calcie and Gordon sat in cane-seated chairs at each end.

Sometimes, in the middle of the crowd, June would feel lonely, missing her parents, brothers, and the home they'd had.

The trips to Washington with Cecil and their visits with their father had made her more homesick for them. It made her realize she didn't belong anywhere, not with her dad or here with this happy family.

She would compare all those sitting around the table to ingredients in Aunt Calcie's special fruit salad. The cousins represented most of the ingredients; the apples, pears, cherries, plums, all home grown, native to the farm, belonging together, while she was like the orange or pineapple that Aunt Calcie sometimes added. It blended in, but anyone eating it knew it was a foreign ingredient.

Aunt Calcie and Uncle Gordon were good, kind people. As Priscilla had said years ago, they took their large brood in stride. They hadn't even appeared to blink an eye at having June join them. Although she was much happier here and truly loved her aunt and uncle and all the cousins, they still couldn't quite take the place of the family she'd lost.

Cecil, twenty-five miles away, was having the same thoughts and feelings, but like June, he wasn't sure May and her ready-made family were the answer. He and June were beginning to think they'd better get used to the idea a couple weeks after school started, when their dad brought May and her boys with him.

Gussie said later, she thought her eyes must have been deceiving her when she looked out the window and saw Burrel with a woman and two boys, walking toward the kitchen door. The woman, decked out in a blue and white silk dress, white turban and blue and white spectator shoes, certainly didn't look like someone visiting a farm. "Definitely a city woman," she thought when Burrel introduced them as his friend, May Knight, and her sons, Bobby and Tommy.

After Gussie had set out a bite and they'd all eaten, they left Bobby to stay with Cecil for a few days. Then Burrel, May and Tommy drove across the mountain to see June.

Calcie's reaction was similar to Gussie's when she saw May in her fancy hat and high-heeled shoes. She didn't say anything to her brother, but she couldn't help wonder if this woman was right for him. It was obvious she'd never been on a farm before.

Since they were staying a few days, Tommy boarded the school bus and went to classes with June and Bonnie. This big city boy impressed most of their classmates. The boys crowded around him to hear his tales about city life while most of the girls vied for invitations to come home with June and Bonnie. None were issued.

May, helping Calcie around the house, proved to be a good cook and an excellent housekeeper. She taught the girls how to make a bed with hospital corners and to roll the pillows and tuck them under the bedspread to provide a finished look, like something out of a home decorating magazine.

Burrel could have told his sister that May was a perfectionist, something that sometimes made him proud and other times irritated him.

His main reason, though, for inviting May to come to West Virginia was to give her and the children a chance to become better acquainted. He was hoping they would all warm up to each other, but when he returned the next weekend, it was obvious it hadn't happened.

Sounding Calcie out, he discovered that May had spent most of her time with the adults and very little with June. Calcie cautioned him not to rush into anything. He was inclined to agree with her.

June felt like a person on a seesaw, again in a larger school with single classes and a separate teacher for each grade. Miracles of miracles, as far as she was concerned, they only had to walk a few steps outside the front door to catch the bus and were deposited a few miles away at the front door of the Brandywine Elementary School.

Not being exposed to the weather, she could wear knee socks to school. The ugly long stockings were a thing of the past. In fact, when no one was looking, she threw them away.

One of the things June missed about no longer living in town was going to the movies. She hadn't been to one since they'd left Petersburg. With the farm located several miles from Franklin there was no question of going unless taken by an adult.

Bonnie and Ruby told her they'd probably only gone once a year. No one had to tell June that farm people weren't free to come and go as readily as those living in town. Before going away, even for a few hours, arrangements had to be made to feed the animals and milk the cows.

One Saturday the older boys volunteered to stay home and take care of the chores if the rest of the family wanted to go to a movie. In exchange, they bargained to borrow the car to go into town in the near future. The boys and their parents soon came to an agreement, and movie plans were made for the next weekend.

Anticipating the outing, the children were as excited as on the night before Christmas. The trip lived up to their expectations. The movie, The Philadelphia Story with Katherine Hepburn, Cary Grant, and Jimmy Stewart was all the girls could talk about for weeks.

In contrast to their enjoyment of the movie, the newsreel showing pictures of the war escalating in Europe disturbed them. In addition, now there was talk that Japan might become a threat to our country.

Their teacher had been telling them about the war rumors, but had assured them that there was no danger. "They're not a threat to us," he said. "After all, they live in paper houses. They couldn't possibly go to war with us."

CHAPTER FIFTY

THE NEW WOMAN IN THEIR LIFE

Burrel had heard the talk of war, too, and was aware of the increased activity at the shipyard, but like June's teacher, he didn't take it seriously.

He had other things on his mind, not the least being a young woman he'd met a few nights before. He'd been in a corner grocery store buying snacks for his lunch when he heard a decidedly southern female voice asking the clerk if she knew how to get to Boone Street.

While the clerk was saying she wasn't sure, Burrel had moved from his spot behind the cookie shelf to get a look at the young questioner.

He didn't know when he'd seen a woman with such pretty red hair. It was long and smooth with the top in a pompadour and the ends turned under in what he later learned was a pageboy.

In four long strides he was standing beside her, saying, "I know where it is. I have my car outside. I'll take you."

The woman gave him a long cold look, before haughtily replying, "Oh, no you won't! I'm not getting in a car with you."

He could see her point. "You're right not to get in a car with a stranger," he responded. "Come on, I'll walk you there. It's not very far."

As she took a second look at this tall blonde stranger, there was something about his smile and soft manner of speaking that made her decide to trust him, so she agreed. As they walked along, he had to slow his long stride to allow her short legs to keep up. She was short, maybe five foot two, with the top of her head barely coming to his shoulder.

She was wearing a white uniform, either that of a nurse or a waitress. Since she wasn't wearing the traditional nurse's white stockings, he assumed she was a waitress.

Looking up at him, she said, "I'm Polly Srite. I've just rented a room in a house on Boone Street, and this is the first time I've walked there from work. I can't believe I couldn't find it."

He introduced himself and assured her it was no problem. He was glad he'd been there and could help her. As they walked along together, the sights and sounds around them enchanted his senses. Each house they passed had the gleaming white steps characteristic of this section of Baltimore. Some people were sitting on their steps trying to catch a whisper of the late evening breeze. The sound of music and people's voices were coming from the open windows of most houses. He could hear a dog barking in the distance and the blare of a horn from a few blocks away. This was a nice family neighborhood, one he liked.

He asked questions, trying to find out more about her, but she wasn't giving out any personal information. Not wanting to frighten her by appearing to pry, for the rest of the way he switched to safe topics, like the weather.

When they got to her door she quickly said goodnight, thanked him for his help, dashed into the house, and firmly closed the door behind her.

He noted the house number before turning and walking back to his car. Even though she had given him no encouragement, he had decided he wanted to get to know this woman better.

∼

The next day, after getting off work, he rushed home, showered, shaved, and dressed in his good blue suit and drove to the house on Boone Street.

The door was opened by a dark, angular woman, slightly past middle age. At her look of inquiry, he smiled and said, "I'd like to see Polly Srite. Would you tell her Burrel Harman is here to see her?"

"I'm sorry. She's at work," she replied. Her voice sounded genuinely regretful. Polly hadn't been with her long, but during the time she had, there'd been only one male caller, one her landlady didn't like.

"I'm Mrs. Ratcliff," she said. "I can't imagine Polly forgetting she had to work tonight."

"I can't rightly say she forgot," he replied. "We didn't really have a date. She couldn't find the house last night and I walked her home."

"Why didn't you say so?" Mrs. Ratcliff exclaimed. "Come on in," she said as she threw the door open and led him into a bright yellow and white kitchen.

"Sit down. I'll get us both a cup of coffee, and you can tell me all about this date that's not really a date," she continued. After he added a couple spoons of sugar and ten times that much cream to his coffee, he took a big swallow and said, "This is really good coffee, Mrs. Ratcliff. Just the way I like it."

She laughed, "How can you tell? I'd say you like a little coffee with your cream and sugar."

"I guess so, but the coffee still has to be good to start with," he replied, "And as I said before, this is good!"

After refilling his cup, she sat across the table from him and said, "Alright, Polly told me someone had walked her home last night, but she didn't say anything about seeing him again."

"She didn't exactly encourage me. In fact, when we got here she just said thanks and ran up the steps and closed the door, before I even had the chance to ask if I could see her again," he explained.

Mrs. Ratcliff had been encouraging her young roomer to meet a nice young man, but since she'd known her she'd been involved with a hotheaded Argentinean, one she'd been trying unsuccessfully to break up with.

He'd been stalking her, hanging around the house and the restaurant where she worked. Mrs. Ratcliff had to admit that he was handsome, with his dark skin, black curly hair and big brown eyes. With his looks and charming accent, she could see how he could turn any young woman's head, but in her mind's eye, she saw him as a dangerous man.

In contrast, this blonde, blue-eyed, soft spoken man sitting across the table from her looked solid, respectable, the kind of man she'd like to see Polly dating. She knew she shouldn't become so involved in her roomer's life, but since Polly had confided in her she found herself starting to think of her almost as a second daughter.

She had been so deep in thought she'd only been half aware Burrel was speaking. "I'm sorry, what did you say?" she asked.

"I was just wondering if you thought Polly would go out with me.

What do you think?" he anxiously asked.

"Of course, I can't speak for Polly, but I certainly think you should give it a try. She works at a restaurant called Hashslingers. Have you heard of it?" she asked.

"I sure have. I've never been in there, but I have driven past it. Pretty nice place!" he responded, before asking, "How late does she work?"

"She doesn't get off tonight until they close at nine thirty. I'd say, if you left now you'd have a chance to get there in plenty of time to talk to her," she encouraged.

Leaving, he thanked her for the coffee and the information, got in his car and headed for Hashslingers.

~

A short time later, Polly was walking toward the kitchen to turn in an order for table five when another waitress came up to her and said, "Hey, Srite, some good looking guy in the bar is asking for you."

"Who is he?" she asked as she grabbed an order and headed for table seven.

"How do I know? Am I your secretary or something?" the other waitress responded as she picked up her own order and hurried away.

Polly waited until she had a break before checking out her visitor. She hadn't expected to see him again, but there he was, the man she'd met the night before. Her intention was to tell him to go away, but when he unfolded himself from the bar stool and stood up, as she told Mrs. Ratcliff later that night, "When I looked up, up, up into the bluest eyes I'd ever seen, the words stuck in my throat. There was no way I was going to let him get away. When he asked if he could wait and take me home, I said yes."

As Burrel waited in the bar for her to get off work, he wondered what had changed her mind. It was months later before she told him she couldn't resist his big blue eyes.

They stopped for a drink on the way home and talked for hours. He learned she had grown up in Mississippi and Louisiana, that her father, a telegraph operator for the railroad, owned a farm between Peelahatchie and Jackson, Mississippi.

She had studied to be a nurse at Charity Hospital in New Orleans, but couldn't stand all the suffering and bureaucracy she'd encountered.

Her sister Ruby, ten years her senior, had always encouraged her to be a nurse and had been deeply disappointed when, with only one semester to go until graduation, she'd quit.

"I couldn't stand to lose a patient. Every time one died, I'd cry for hours. The Sisters tried to help toughen me up, but it didn't work. I'd much rather work as a waitress anyway. The only way I've ever lost a customer is if he sits at another waitress's station."

He told her about his divorce and showed her pictures of Cecil, June, and Dickie. She could hear the pain in his voice when he said, "The two older ones are with my sisters in West Virginia, but the little one is with his mother in Ohio. I haven't seen him for months and don't know if I'll ever see him again."

"That must be really difficult for you and the children," she said. "How old are they?"

She was surprised to hear that the oldest was thirteen, the girl eleven, and the little one nine. She wouldn't be twenty-two until her birthday a few weeks away, in September. She wondered how old he was.

When he lit his cigarette, she asked, "Is that a Camel? If you have another one, you can light one for me."

He hadn't gotten used to women smoking or casually having a drink, after his years of living with Priscilla's opposition, but he found he really didn't mind.

When he parked in front of Mrs. Ratcliff's house a few minutes later, they'd made a date for him to pick her up after work the next night.

Looking in the rear view mirror as he drove away, he thought he saw a dark figure standing in the shadows at the side of the house. When he drove around the block for a second look, no one was there. "Must have been my imagination," he thought as he headed for home.

~

A few days later they celebrated Burrel's thirty-eighth birthday, then in a few weeks her twenty-second. They were both a little concerned about the difference in their ages, but not enough to stop seeing each other.

She had introduced him to her favorite Chinese restaurant and her favorite drink, a Tom Collins. They would often go there when she had a day off, trying various menu items and lingering over their drinks and cigarettes. One evening when they came out of the restaurant, they were confronted by a very angry young man.

Dashing from the shadows, he grabbed Polly by the arms, shaking her and yelling, his accent so thick Burrel had difficulty understanding what he was saying.

"What in the devil is going on here?" Burrel demanded as he moved to her side.

Letting go of her arm, the young man turned, glared at Burrel and shouted, "This is none of your business! I'm talking to my girlfriend! You stay out of it."

"I am not your girlfriend," Polly said. "I told you weeks ago that I wasn't going to see you anymore. Just go away and leave us alone."

"I'll never leave you alone," he declared. "You're never going to get away from me." Then looking Burrel in the eye, he continued in a quiet deadly voice, "She's mine and I'm telling you to stay away from her, or you'll be sorry."

Watching him stride away, Burrel asked, "What was that all about? Who was he?"

"His name is Tony Torintino. I met him when I first came to Baltimore. We had a pretty heavy romance going for a few months, but he was so jealous and possessive that I broke off with him. Since then, he's been following me around and making threats, like tonight," she said. "I don't like it, but I don't think he'd do anything to hurt me," she added.

"Don't think for a minute he might not mean what he's saying. It's just as likely he means it, as not," he said, and then told her about his experience with Ernest.

"Oh, my God," she said when he'd finished telling her. "Maybe I should be more careful. It looks like I've gotten you mixed up in it. I'm really sorry."

"Hush," he said, pronouncing it "hursh". "Don't worry about me, but we are going to have to be more careful. I'll pick you up every night after work, and I think you'd better ride the trolley when you go to work."

"I'll feel a lot safer with you around," she said. "I've never felt safe walking home anyway. Besides Tony, some other creep tried to pick me up. He drove up beside me and asked if I wanted a ride. Come to think of it, it was the night I met you. I didn't even look at him, just said 'Get lost' and kept walking. Not everyone in this town is a gentleman like you are."

As she talked, he could feel the blood drain from his face. He couldn't tell her, but he'd been the one she'd called a creep. Right before he'd met her in the grocery store he'd seen her walking alone. He'd been frightened for her safety and had stopped to offer her a ride, never thinking she'd look on him as a danger. For a moment he felt like a naive country boy loose in the big city, but he was smart enough to know this was one time he'd better keep his good intentions to himself.

True to his word, he was waiting every night for her when she came out of the restaurant. They thought they'd seen Tony a few times, standing in the shadows, watching as she got in the car, but nothing had happened.

Lulled into a false sense of security, they were beginning to think his bark was worse than his bite. They soon found out they were mistaken.

~

One evening, Burrel had been waiting in his usual place for several minutes, and though other employees had come out, Polly hadn't shown up. Worried, he opened his car door, ready to step out and go inside to check on her when he heard a sound from the alley in back of the restaurant.

Straining to hear, he thought he'd heard someone calling his name. If so, the voice was so faint he couldn't be sure. Getting back in the car, rolling up the windows and locking the door, he backed slowly into the alley. At first he couldn't see anything, then he was able to make out a white clad figure standing against the back wall. "Have I driven into a trap?" he wondered.

His answer wasn't long in coming, as the figure dashed from the shadows, grabbed the door handle, and tried to pull the door open. His foot was poised on the accelerator, ready to take off when he saw Polly's frantic face framed in his car window. "Open the door! For God's sake, open the door," she cried.

Reaching across the seat, he threw the door open and helped her scramble in. Not waiting for an explanation, he floored the gas pedal, and peeled out of the alley. He didn't slow down until they were several blocks away.

"It's alright," she said. "You can slow down now, but Tony was in the restaurant and he had a gun. He was at one of my tables, so I couldn't avoid him. When I was about ready to leave, he moved his napkin aside and showed me the gun. He said if I didn't go with him he was going to use it."

"Are you alright?" he asked. At her nod, he added, "How did you get away?"

"I acted like I was going to go with him, but right before we left, I told him I'd be with him in a minute, but first I had to go to the rest room. A couple other waitresses and some customers were standing close to us, so he let me go. When I got in the rest room, I locked the door and climbed out the window. It was a tight squeeze, but I made it. The hardest part was letting go and dropping to the ground," she said, rubbing her ankle.

"That was smart thinking," Burrel said, his voice full of concern. "Did you hurt yourself?"

"I'm okay. My ankle is a little sore, but nothing is broken or sprained," she replied.

Pulling over to the curb, turning to her he gathered her in his arms, and said, "Thank God, you're alright. I don't know what I'd do if something happened to you. One thing for sure, you can't go back to Mrs. Ratcliff's. That's the first place he'd look. Do you have any friends you could spend the night with?"

"I can call one of the other waitresses, but first I think I'd better phone and warn Mrs. Ratcliff. I'm going to tell her to lock the doors and to call the police if he shows up," she said.

He drove to a restaurant where they had coffee and made their phone calls. "I think we'd better call the police ourselves," he said, "Then we have to make plans to get you away from here until they can do something about him."

"I don't know where I could go," she said. "I don't know very many people other than Mrs. Ratcliff and the girls I work with. I wouldn't feel very safe with any of them."

"How about where you lived before you moved to Mrs. Ratcliff's? Could you go back there?" he asked.

She shook her head and replied, "That wouldn't work. That's where I lived when I was going with him. I left there, in the first place, to get away from him."

They sat, deep in thought, for several minutes before he spoke, "I'm going to take you to my sister Calcie's house in West Virginia. You'll be safe there and it will give you and June a chance to get to know each other."

For the first time since Tony had showed her the gun, she felt safe. "I'd love it," she said, and then as he watched in amazement, she burst into tears.

"If you'd love it, why are you crying?" he asked.

"I'm just so relieved and happy that you came up with that idea. I thought I was never going to get to meet your family," she replied.

Neither of them got much sleep that night. Most of it was spent on the phone, making arrangements and later in the police station answering questions.

Polly still had a picture of Tony she was able to give to the police, along with his address and the names of some of his friends. The police agreed it would be a good idea for her to go away for a few days. They assured her everything would be under control when she returned.

∿

Burrel couldn't have picked a more beautiful time of year to take her to West Virginia. It was mid October and the trees were aflame with red, yellow and orange foliage. As they continued through the mountains, Polly turned from one side to the other, looking out the windows, exclaiming, "Oh, look at that! Look at that! Look at that!"

Although Burrel laughed at her reaction, she continued to swivel her head from side to side, saying, "I don't want to miss any of it. I've never seen anything so beautiful in my life."

For the rest of the trip, he teasingly called her "Swivel Neck."

Aunt Calcie had told June her dad would be arriving that afternoon and that he was bringing a young woman with him. "You mean he's not bringing May?" she asked.

"No," Aunt Calcie said. "He just said he was bringing a young woman to stay with us for a few days. I'm sure if he was bringing May, he would have said so."

That afternoon, while June, Bonnie, and Ruby were playing on the hill above the house, they saw Burrel's car stop by the front gate and her dad and a young woman step out. "Dad," June yelled as she ran down the hill toward them.

Standing beside Burrel, Polly watched this long legged girl running with her long blonde hair flying in the wind and her arms outstretched ready to throw them around her father. As if it were the most natural thing to do, Polly found herself reaching out and enfolding her in her arms.

June was astounded at this stranger's action, and at how happy it made her feel. When she was finally released, she stood back, shyly looking at the young woman her dad had brought with him. She had the most beautiful hair she'd ever seen. It was a deep red, but the sun shining on it seemed to set it aflame, reminding her of the blaze of color in the trees around them.

It was long and smooth. The ends falling to her shoulders were turned under in a pageboy style, one she'd tried, unsuccessfully, with her own hair. The dark green wool dress she was wearing was fastened from the neckline to the hem with brown leather buttons. The smooth lines of the dress complimented her rounded figure. She wasn't very tall, not much taller than June, but no one would have mistaken her for a child.

Smiling at June, she linked her arm through hers as they walked to the house, all the time telling her how much she'd wanted to meet her and how pretty she thought she was. Polly didn't know it at the time, but those first few moments and the attention she'd shown this child, so starved for affection, had earned her a friend for life.

In the days that followed, June found herself the center of this newcomer's attention. When she got off the school bus at the end of the day, Polly was waiting at the gate with questions about June's day and stories about her own with Aunt Calcie. She taught the young people games and songs and told them stories about growing up in the Deep South.

Having an adult spend this much time with them was a new experience, not just for June but for her cousins as well. They were accustomed to the adults in their lives spending their free time with each other while the children played together. Only twenty-two years old, exactly twice June's age, this young redhead wasn't far enough removed from childhood to have forgotten how to play.

June had always hated her straight blonde hair, yearning instead for the curls that were then in style. At night while Polly ran the brush through June's hair for the mandatory one hundred strokes, she would sit, almost mesmerized as Polly spoke in her soft southern accent, complimenting her on its color and shine, trying to help her see that it wasn't necessary to be like everyone else. This was the first time she had heard it was all right to be different.

That week in that farmhouse marked the beginning of many things. The seeds had been planted that would lead to a renewal of June's feeling of self worth. She and Polly had developed a strong bond, and for the first time since she'd learned her mother wasn't coming back, she'd felt a mother's love.

She knew this was irrational, as neither her dad nor Polly had mentioned marriage, but whether or not Burrel had chosen this woman for his wife, June, without a doubt, had chosen her for a mother.

Her determination was further strengthened that weekend when Burrel returned and took the two of them to see Cecil and Grandpap. As they were getting into the car, June started to climb into the back seat only to have Polly say, "Where do you think you're going, Missy? Come up here and sit next to your daddy."

Beaming, she settled herself between the two of them as they rode across the mountain. There was singing and laughter and Burrel teasing Polly and calling her "Swivel Neck" as she exclaimed about the beauty of the surrounding foliage.

The visit at Grandpap's was over too quickly. Gussie had set out a bite and afterwards they sat around the table and talked. June didn't move from her seat next to her newfound friend, even when Hilda coaxed her to come play with her paper dolls.

In this pre-Barbie doll era, paper dolls gave girls an inexpensive way to play with pretty dolls and their fabulous wardrobes. All the girl cousins had big collections and never missed the chance to play with them. But June knew her dad and Polly would be on their way to Baltimore soon and she didn't know when she'd see them again. She wasn't going to let them out of her sight for a minute.

Cecil thought Polly was nice. He liked listening to her talk about life in the city, but to him, at this point, she was just a nice woman his dad had brought to visit. He and Clyde had more important things to do than sit at the table and listen to adults talk. No sooner had they cleaned their plates than they were out the door, pursuing their own interests.

The next day as June stood by the gate watching her dad load his and Polly's bags into the car, Polly, as she had done when she first arrived, threw her arms around her. Hugging her she said, "I'll be back, and I'm going to talk to your dad about having you and Cecil visit over the holidays."

After June watched the car disappear from view, she slowly walked back to the house, the sound of her footsteps on the wooden walkway seemed to echo Polly's words in her mind, "I'll be back. I'll be back." Oblivious of her aunt, uncle, and cousins watching her, she smiled and thought, "I know you will. You'll be back."

～

In the car on the way back to Baltimore, Burrel told Polly no one had seen or heard anything from Tony Torintino since she left. He'd checked with some of the waitresses at Hashslinger's, and they said they hadn't seen him. Mrs. Ratcliff said she'd followed their advice and kept the doors locked, and watched for anyone hiding in the shadows. She was sure he hadn't been around.

Apparently the police had gone to his apartment and talked to him, warning him he'd be in danger of being deported if he came near Polly again. The officer said Tony seemed to be frightened at the prospect of having to leave the country. "He doesn't think you'll have any more trouble with him. Just to be on the safe side, I'm going to continue to pick you up after work. I still don't want you wandering around by yourself," he concluded.

"I won't," she promised. "After seeing him with that gun, I'm not going to feel safe until I know he's out of the picture."

"The police say they'll have someone drive by the restaurant around closing time to make sure he's not hanging around," he said, smiling reassuringly.

Moving closer, sounding pensive, she said, "I don't want to talk about Tony anymore. I want to talk about June. Do you know, she's a lonely little girl?"

"Lonely!" Burrel exclaimed. "How could she be lonely with all those people around?"

"Maybe lonely isn't the right word, but she doesn't really feel she belongs. Even though Calcie and Gordon are as good to her as they are to their own kids, she misses her own family," she responded.

"I know that, but our family no longer exists. I feel guilty that I can't have them with me, but I wouldn't feel they were safe in the city while I'm at work. They need their mother," he replied.

"I agree. They do need a mother," she responded.

The fact that she had changed what he'd said from "their mother" to "a mother" wasn't lost on Burrel. He drove along in silence for a few seconds, thinking about her and what she'd said. Polly might be young, but she had a good head on her shoulders. Besides that she was fun to be with and a very attractive woman. There was the age difference, but she seemed so mature he didn't think it would really matter.

She interrupted his thoughts to point out something along the road, but he didn't forget their conversation or the feelings it had roused in him.

Over the next few weeks, he spent all his free time with her. He was always at the restaurant to take her home after work. First because he wasn't sure the danger from her former boyfriend was over. Then when it was obvious Tony Torintino was no longer a threat, he admitted to himself he was there because he loved her and wanted to be with her. It was soon obvious she felt the same.

~

His workload had increased at the shipyards with more and more ships being built for the war effort. Although we were not yet in the war, Congress had enacted the Lend Lease Act that year of nineteen forty-one, to allow the United States to provide materials and supplies to Great Britain and their allies in the fight against Hitler and the Nazis.

All this overtime was affecting his private life, interfering not only with the time he could spend with Polly, but also the weekends he could go to West Virginia to see June and Cecil.

On one of these weekends, he brought June a small green tabletop Motorola radio. He explained that it wasn't new. That was obvious because of the crack on the outside casing. The crack started at the top, and then ran all the way across and down one side. June was too happy with the gift to mind the flaw in its appearance, especially since it played well. To her, that was all that really mattered.

This radio reminded her of one she'd seen in May's room when she had visited last summer. She could remember May humming along with the soft strains of the music coming from a radio suspiciously like this one.

It wasn't until later she learned this was the same radio and how it had become damaged. Burrel had felt, even though there had been no commitment on either side, it would be the gentlemanly thing to do to tell May, in person, that he had met another woman, one he planned to marry.

He hadn't known how he expected her to react, certainly not with such fury. He found himself, first, defending himself against the words of anger that poured from her mouth, then ducking as the radio came flying across the room, narrowly missing his head.

As it crashed against the wall behind him, she screamed, "You can take your damn radio. I never want to see it, or you, as long as I live!"

It had been a gift, and he had no intention of taking it until he saw her reach for it. The fire in her eyes signaled her intention to again use it as a weapon. He quickly scooped up the radio and hastily made his escape. "Whew!" he thought on his way home. "That was like a replay of the nightmare, years earlier, when I told Della about the new woman in my life." Over the years, this story became a classic as Polly retold it, laughing and teasing him about his narrow escape from the flying radio.

~

With the beginning of December, the talk of the danger of war with Japan escalated. Radio commentators had been discussing it, but June's teacher continued to reassure them that this was something that would never happen. In fact, he told them, emissaries representing the Japanese government were in Washington, at that very moment, meeting with President Roosevelt and his cabinet. This certainly demonstrated Japan's peaceful intentions. Didn't it?

Sunday, December seventh, nineteen hundred forty-one was an unseasonably warm day. Taking advantage of the sunshine, June, Bonnie, and Ruby had gone for a long walk on the country roads. Since this was the first time they'd been able to get outside for several days, they took their time, not returning until close to dinnertime.

On their way back they'd taken a detour through the woods and gathered some pinecones to use for Christmas decorations. "Look what we found," Ruby called out as they walked into the kitchen, dumping the pinecones on the center of the table.

Instead of the expected expressions of interest or appreciation, her remark had been met with stony silence. All three girls became aware something was wrong. Aunt Calcie and Uncle Gordon were usually encouraging of their children's efforts, but today, it was as if they weren't aware of the girls' presence.

"What's the matter?" Bonnie asked. "What's wrong?"

June didn't think she'd ever seen her aunt so somber as when she turned her gaze on them and said, "There was a special announcement on the radio this afternoon that the Japanese had attacked Pearl Harbor. This means we're going to be at war with Japan."

No one in this household, and most others in the country, had ever heard of Pearl Harbor, but they knew what had happened on that day thousands of miles away would affect them, their sons, their neighbors, and their neighbors' sons.

Garth was old enough to be drafted, and Gerald soon would be old enough. They sat in stunned silence, wondering how this could have happened? Hadn't the President assured the American people their sons would never go to war?

The next day in school the children were told that Pearl Harbor was located near Honolulu, on South Oahu, in Hawaii. The Japanese had launched a sneak attack on the large United States naval base located there. At dawn while most of the people were sleeping, Japanese planes had dropped bombs on the ships in the harbor and the planes at the airfield. Hundreds of sailors had gone down with the USS Arizona, and other ships and airplanes were crippled or destroyed. There were a large number of casualties. This attack had apparently been planned for weeks and possibly months. It appeared that the Japanese emissaries, meeting with government officials in Washington, had been sent as a smoke screen to lull the government into a feeling of false security.

That day, Congress declared war on Japan, and President Roosevelt's address to the American people was broadcast over the school's public address system. While the children sat, white faced and solemn, they heard the President announce the declaration of war. The beginning of that speech was to go down in history. No one old enough to understand the words would ever forget hearing his voice, full of sadness, say, "Yesterday, December seventh, nineteen hundred and forty-one, a date that will live in infamy, the United States was attacked by naval and air forces from Japan...." He went on to say that we had suffered great losses.

June sat silently at her desk, overwhelmed with the knowledge that this country was now at war. Since she had been eight years old, she had worried about and prayed for children in war torn countries. Now as she looked around at her classmates she wondered what was going to happen here.

Turning her gaze on the teacher, sitting quietly behind his desk, she thought about his reassurance that there was no danger from Japan. She was certain that she wasn't the only student thinking, "A lot you knew." As if reading their thoughts, he looked first at them, then down at the blotter on his desk. For the first time since June had been in his class, he had nothing to say. Then four days later Germany declared war on the United States, throwing the ill prepared country into war on two fronts.

Every evening, all over the country, the American people pulled their chairs closer to the radio to hear Lowell Thomas talk about events taking place in far away places with names they'd never before heard. The news of the war and the country's continued losses in the South Pacific overshadowed everything else happening in the world.

Aunt Calcie and Uncle Gordon at the farm, Burrel and Polly in Baltimore, and Priscilla and Bill in Mansfield, along with millions of other Americans, heard the news and wondered how this was going to affect them and the people they loved. As they sat by their radios and listened, they all knew that their lives would never be the same.

It was hard, that year, for everyone except the very young, to get into the usual spirit of Christmas. Ministers looked out on full pews as people flocked to Christmas Eve and Christmas Day services. They were there to pray for the young fighting men and for an early peace.

CHAPTER FIFTY-ONE

A NEW LIFE

June's spirits had soared when she heard about a belated Christmas gift she and Cecil were getting from their dad and Polly. During their school break between Christmas and New Years, she was going to receive, what she wanted more than anything else in the world, her own home and family.

She, Cecil, her dad and Polly were going to become a family. Her dad and Polly had already moved to Zanesville, a small town in Ohio, about twenty-five miles from Newark. Her dad was working in a nearby town on the construction of an electrical power plant. They had rented a house and had scoured stores for its sparse furnishings. Now they were coming for June and Cecil.

This time, it wasn't difficult for June to say goodbye to her classmates. The only close friends she had were Bonnie and Ruby, and she knew she would be seeing them often.

Packed and ready to leave at dawn, June waited impatiently, running to the window every time she heard a car go by. "I declare, Child," Aunt Calcie said, "You're going to wear the rug out if you don't quit that pacing. They'll be here when they get here. Looking out that window isn't going to make them come any sooner. Come on out in the kitchen and eat your oatmeal. They won't be here for awhile."

On reluctant feet, June followed her. Sitting around the table with her cousins, she only half listened to their teasing. "If we didn't know better, we'd think you didn't like us," Gerald said.

"Oh, no it's not that," June said. "It's just that..."

"Don't pay any attention to him," Bonnie said. "He's just teasing you."

Since she'd been living here that had been their favorite pastime. She'd never quite gotten used to it. "Oh, well," she thought. "Now I won't have to!"

Her thoughts were interrupted by the sound of the front door opening. She felt like shouting, "They're here!" Instead she ran to the door to meet them.

Laughter followed her two-word greeting, "Let's go!"

They talked her into letting them stay long enough to have a cup of coffee and give Calcie their new address before loading June's things into the car and heading for Grandpap's house to pick up Cecil.

The first time Polly had seen Cecil, he'd been sitting on the wooden walkway outside the kitchen door. He'd looked up and smiled at her, his blue eyes, so much like Burrel's had been solemn. But today, as she and Burrel walked into the warmth of Gussie's kitchen, his eyes were sparkling.

"We're going to our new home," Polly said. "Do you want to go with us?"

She never forgot his response, "Sure, Mom. Let's go!"

Total happiness flooded through her at his words. She'd always known how June felt about her, but Cecil was, like his dad, a man of few words. "With words like that," she thought, "he doesn't need a lot of them."

∼

This was a bittersweet journey, full of happiness, but tinged with sadness. Always before, when they had traveled the sharp curves of Route 50 between West Virginia and Ohio, they had been a family of five on their way to visit the relatives in Ohio.

While the memories of their other family mingled with thoughts of the present, they made their way over the mountains. As they traveled the narrow, steep, winding road, with no guardrail, June felt fearful of what was to come. Then as she looked at her father who was carefully maneuvering the car, she calmed down.

Beside her, Cecil teased, "You always hate these mountain roads, don't you, June?" as he quickly poked her in the side.

Though she disliked his teasing, she was glad he was beside her again.

As the road widened, and they began down the slope of the mountain, June felt excitement as the car gained speed. She felt happiness at the thought of having been unexpectedly plunged into this extraordinary family.

Then as she heard Polly's contagious laugh from the front seat, she poked Cecil in the side and remarked, "Actually, I think this is a pretty exciting ride."

Just then a bump in the road gave them a jar and Cecil yelled out, "It's like a roller coaster!"

As Burrel shouted back, "Are you ready for the next hill?" June, Polly, and Cecil all chanted in unison, "Yes!"

Not knowing what was beyond, but excited about the fresh prospects, this new family of four headed for a new home and a new life.

Bumpy? Maybe, but undoubtedly thrilling!

THE VAGABOND YEARS

The Vagabond Years is a heartwarming story of life on the home-front during the World War II years. It is filled with humor and pathos as the family adjusts to the changing world around them and their life as vagabonds. Upon being reunited with his children, he'd vowed not to be separated from them again. This led to some interesting adventures as, with family in tow, he followed the war jobs.

CHAPTER ONE

ON THE ROAD

They waited in anticipation for the sound of familiar steps on the wide front porch. When they finally arrived and the front door opened, they were ready to yell, "Surprise!" Before the words could escape their lips, though, Burrel beat them to it when he called out, "I have a surprise for you!"

Delighted, Polly said, "We didn't think you would remember." Then wrapping her arms around his neck, she murmured, "Happy Anniversary, Honey."

Burrel let her words roll around in his mind as he frantically tried to remember what anniversary he had apparently forgotten. Polly and the children, in their Sunday best, the party decorations, and the glowing candles on the table made him aware he had forgotten an occasion important to his family. For the life of him, though, he couldn't remember what it could be.

Especially attuned to her father's feelings since they had been re-united, 12 year old June was the first to realize Burrel's predicament. She quickly filled in the gaps for him when she announced, "It is hard to believe that we have been a family for three months today, isn't it, Dad?"

He rewarded her with a quick smile before he echoed Polly's words, "Happy Anniversary." As they sat around the dining room table and he listened to the happy chatter around him, not for the first time, he counted his blessings. It was difficult to believe that only three months earlier, this family had been separated by miles. Now thanks to the twenty-two year old red-headed woman sitting across from him, they were a family again.

While people they'd met since they moved to Zanesville, Ohio were surprised at the youth of the mother, no one suspected that they hadn't always been a family. The fact that June and Cecil had called her Mom from the first moment helped.

During a loll in the conversation, Polly remembered Burrel's pro-nouncement that he had something for them. Not seeing a gaily wrapped gift, curiosity got the better of her, and she asked what his surprise was. Stunned silence greeted him when he announced, "I got a new job just outside of Washington, D.C. I have to be there in a week."

While the rest of the family absorbed his words, tears spilled down June's checks. This was too reminiscent of what had happened before when their original family circle had been forever shattered. She didn't think she could bear the thought of again being separated from her father. Was it possible that this family, like her other one, was being broken before it had a chance to begin?

Becoming aware of his daughter's unhappiness, Burrel tousled her blonde hair and reassured her that this time, they were all going togeth-er. "With the war just started, there will be a lot of defense construction going on. At first, I will be working on the building of a new army base. This time, there won't be any house hunting. We are going as a family." After a short pause, he added, "And we are taking our house with us!"

That was the beginning of their vagabond years.

Printed in the United States
90119LV00004B/220/A

9 781425 988548